Tainted Kitten
The Insatiable Series (Book Two)
Sarah JD

ISBN-13: 978-0-9756312-4-9

2024 Cover by DAZED Designs
Many thanks to my Beta Readers: Alana, Anoesjka, & Melissa and my proofreader, Jen.

For my PA and friend, Bibi.
Your honesty, above and beyond support, and
friendship mean so much.
Thank you for keeping me sane when things get
tough.
And thank you for loving Kitten as much as I do!

SARAH JD'S BOOKS

Sarah JD's Books

https://sarahjaneduncan.com/book-links/
https://sarahjaneduncan.com/my-books/

Tainted Warning

It's your Kitten speaking! Welcome back to my dark and depraved world.

Once again, I'm here to give you a heads up!

What you are about to read contains extreme smut. Like filthy, descriptive, no holding back sex scenes.

It also contains some other things that could be triggering to some readers:

- Non-consensual sex acts.

- Taboo – Age gap with a minor.

- Reverse Harem – meaning I'm worshipped by multiple partners in a sharing relationship that includes group sex.

- Humiliation.

- Fetishes such as food play, feet, blood play, and golden showers.

- Addiction.

- Blackmail.

- Suicidal thoughts.

- Bullying.

- The backstory includes references to child grooming, and molestation.

Like the first instalment of my story, it will likely make you cry, laugh, get angry, and of course, I'll continue to edge you until you need to take a cold shower. I am
Rhys George, after all!

So sit back, re-charge your Big Jim's, Little Jim's, and Peter Rabbit's, and prepare for another Kitten rollercoaster!

CHAPTER ONE
CASANOVA

The Feast is packed. I'm relatively new to Vixen's Lodge Feast nights, but I'm pretty sure it's not common for there to be so many people in attendance. The scene before me looks more like an overflowing nightclub breaking their capacity limits. There's barely enough room to weave through the patrons, which is kinda weird with everyone being naked and all. Flesh on flesh everywhere you look. For the first time since coming to this secret sex club, it doesn't seem all that appealing.

Where's my girl?

Rhys George owns my balls, my dick, and my fucking heart. It started out as fun, and to my shock, I was struck down with more than lust for this chick. These Feast nights are set up to be anonymous. I'm not meant to know who I slide Thor inside. My only task is to enjoy the ride, but fuck, all I'm interested in doing is finding Kitten and getting lost with her. I'm even happy to include Skipper in the scenario, if I must. Being with her, no matter how that looks, is all I'm interested in.

It still blows my fucking mind that Rhys' sponsor here at Vixen's Lodge is Tyler Foster, otherwise known to me as Mr Foster, my fucking PE teacher at Fox Pines Catholic. When I think about it, I know how fucked up it sounds, yet when I see them together, all concerns fall away because that motherfucker cares about Kitten, much the same way I do.

Fucked up? Hell yes!

But it is what it is.

After doing three laps of all the rooms available to Feasters in the lodge, worry trickles its way in because I can't find Kitten anywhere. I know she arrives late sometimes, but Tyler is usually here fucking whoever he can from the get-go. Weirdly though, I can't find Skipper either.

Rhys told me she was coming to the Feast tonight. She said she'd probably have to grovel for what she did on Sunday night when she turned up uninvited with no mask, and in an agitated state. I assumed her grovelling would most likely involve Madam Vik, but she's right here in the middle of the room setting up some chain thing from the ceiling over the podium, and Rhys is nowhere in sight.

My eyes focus on Madam Vik as a waiter walks up to her and murmurs quietly in her ear. She nods enthusiastically and turns around, an excited expression lighting her face. Madam Vik and Master Hill are the only people who don't wear masks to hide their identities. Since we are in *their* home, I guess they can do whatever the fuck they want, while the rest of us Feasters have strict rules to follow.

"What's going on?" Moxie comes to stand next to me, and I shake my head, not wanting to take my eyes off Madam Vik. There is something going on. I just haven't figured out what it is yet.

"No idea." I shrug and glance at Moxie. She's gotta be in her twenties. I could be wrong since it's hard to tell with the floral mask she's wearing, but her skin is firm and youthful, so I'm only going by assumptions. What the fuck do I know? "Have you seen Kitten or Skipper?"

"No." She shakes her head. "Maybe they aren't coming tonight. They weren't here Sunday night either."

I wanna tell her that Rhys said she was coming tonight, but that will give away that Kitten and I know each other personally.

The sound of a bell draws my attention again, and I glance back over to Madam Vik, who is now holding up the offending noisemaker.

"Darlings. Hello. And welcome to a special evening of the Feast. Tonight, we need to address an unfortunate incident which resulted in the rules being broken." Madam Vik smiles like it's a good thing while murmurs spread through the naked audience.

Ice slithers into my veins as I replay her words.

> *"We need to address an unfortunate incident which resulted in the rules being broken."*

Is she talking about Kitten?

"As you know, rule-breaking can have serious consequences for us all. The rules are in place to protect everyone who walks through our door and to ensure we can continue operating for *your* pleasure." Madam Vik sweeps her eyes over her minions as they hang onto her every word. "Unfortunately, one of our most treasured Feasters broke two stringent rules. Therefore, we must administer punishment here before you all this evening so that she and everyone else here remembers the seriousness of breaching the rules."

"Kitten," I whisper, and Moxie darts her head to me.

"What?" She whispers back, and I nod.

"What's the punishment for breaking the rules?"

Moxie's mouth drops open, and her eyes widen in panic. "Humiliation."

"What?" I blurt a little too loudly, but no one pays me any attention. They are too wrapped up in Madam Vik.

"Let's not put this off any longer. Please bring in our *adored* Kitten." Madam Vik raises her arms in the air like she's announcing a fucking game show.

The Feasters cheer like they are in the audience of a fucking game show, and the crowd parts, making a path for Master Hill. As usual, he's in a black suit—the only person fully clothed under this roof—and he swaggers in like he's a fucking king. Trailing behind him, Brock, the bouncer, is carrying Kitten over his fucking shoulder, her dark loose hair falling past his calves. That's when I realise she is bound and gagged.

No!

I step forward, but Moxie stops me, her hand wrapping around my wrist.

"You can't intervene."

"Why the fuck not?" I hiss.

"Because they will drag it out longer for her if you do. Any interference will only be worse for her."

"What the actual fuck!" I hiss, glaring at Moxie like she's the one who made up the sick rules. I know she didn't, but fuck, this is bad.

"It's the only fucked up thing about this place. Something like this hasn't happened in a long time." Moxie mumbles, and I glare at her. Is she being fucking serious right now? How isn't she freaking the fuck out?

"You've seen this happen before?"

"Once. About four years ago." Her lips contort into a grimace.

"What did they do to that person?"

"You don't want to know."

Fuck. This is bad. Where the fuck is Skipper?

My silent question gets answered the next moment when commotion draws all eyes as four shirtless waiters drag Skipper in, bound to some sort of metal bars and silenced with a similar ball gag to Rhys.

What the actual hell is this fuckery?

I need to do something. But what if Moxie is right? What if my interference makes things worse for Kitten?

Fuck! FUCK!

I don't like this. Not one bit. Something doesn't feel right.

Leaning forward, Brock tips Kitten off his shoulder and sits her on the podium, her eyes wide with fear as he attaches the chains Madam Vik had been rigging up from the ceiling to the wrist and ankle cuffs my girl is wearing.

My poor Kitten. She's shaking her head frantically, her lips trying to move past the ball gag with words she can't speak. It's clear that she's saying *no*. Anyone who has half a brain can see the fear in her eyes. Why are they doing this? She clearly hasn't consented.

"Good evening, everyone." Master Hill turns to face the mostly naked crowd, his black suit pristine as he stands before his guests. "Now, I can tell by some of your expressions you're clearly upset to see that tonight's punishment is to be dealt to our beloved Kitten. I understand, *really*, I do. We all love and worship her, so it's hard to accept. However, just remember that *she* put *you* all in jeopardy. Your identities could have been exposed had her infraction gained the attention of the authorities."

What? Authorities? What the fuck is he talking about?

Gasps sweep through the room as most of the Feasters' masked clad faces turn from concern to anger. Is he filling their heads with lies to rile them up and turn against Kitten?

"Since Kitten has a sponsor, he too will be punished." Master Hill gestures to the back wall where Skipper is being secured by more fucking chains. "His punishment will be to watch."

The air in the room changes as some of the bystanders get excited by the prospect. This is fucked. So fucked in so many ways!

Master Hill holds up both of his hands. In one hand, he has some sort of egg-shaped object, and in the other is what looks like a remote device.

"For those of you who are worried about our Kitten, fear not. I will ensure she receives some pleasure as well. I'm not a total bastard."

The Feasters clap as Master Hill chuckles like he's a fucking good guy. Fucking hell. This is all sorts of screwed up.

Master Hill turns to Kitten and nods to a waiter who pulls a lever on the wall. The chains attached to Kitten go taut, spreading her arms and legs wide. Electricity zaps through the air as the Feasters get riled up, and Brock, the fucking cunt, steps forward with a pair of scissors and cuts the red lace panties off Kitten before doing the same to her red bra.

Fury like I've never felt before travels from my head to my toes as I ball my fists, trying to ignore the cheering Feasters. Kitten's eyes dart around the room frantically, searching for someone to help her. She's trying to yell, but even if she didn't have a ball gag in, her voice wouldn't be heard over the crowd and the music.

Master Hill ignores Kitten's pleading, and he holds up the egg thing between two fingers so that Skipper and the rest of the crowd can see it before he steps in between Kitten's spread legs. Skipper goes ape shit, growling and trying to thrash, but his restraints don't allow him much movement. When I notice Skipper's eyes widen, I dart my attention back to Kitten to see her head shaking frantically as Master Hill lowers his hand, the egg directed towards her entrance.

"Stop!" I yell. I can't fucking help myself. I know she doesn't like Master Hill. She hasn't told me why, but the arsehole freaks her the fuck out, and right now, she's clearly terrified of him touching her.

"Hey! Shut the fuck up or get out!" Brock hisses from beside Skipper, shooting his finger out aggressively towards me.

"No! She's clearly not consenting to this!" I yell again, and Brock steps away from the wall, puffing his chest out to glare at me.

"Give it up, kid." A weird fucker wearing a tiger outfit turns to me. "Everyone signs that consent form when we join. It gives Madam and Master power to inflict punishment even if consent isn't given at the time. No one gets in without agreeing to that clause." The weird guy turns back to Kitten, his eyes wild with excitement as his hand strokes his hard cock.

"This can't be legal," I say in disbelief.

"Master Hill is a Lawyer, Cass." Moxie leans into me. "He would have covered his arse somehow in those membership contracts."

She's right. She's fucking right!

Rhys throws her head to the side as Master Hill pushes the egg inside her, his fingers disappearing and lingering way too fucking long before he slips them free and proceeds to lick them clean.

Turning to face us with a satisfied smirk, Master Hill holds up the remote.

"No one touches her. No one goes near her until I give the ok. For now, let's enjoy the show."

Madam Vik pulls up a couple of chairs for her and her sick husband, and they sit together as if they are about to watch the fucking opera, linking their arms together before Master Hill presses something on the remote.

Kitten stiffens and throws her head back, her eyes rolling back before her hips start to gyrate slowly. As Feaster's watch, moans fill the room as onlookers touch themselves or the person next to them, their excitement building as my poor Kitten unwillingly gives them a show. Her bare body trembles and vibrates with building pleasure as the egg works inside her.

My heart starts to slow as I calm down. This is ok, I guess. Kitten's getting pleasure. She loves being watched, and she loves to come, so yeah, this is ok.

Scaring her wasn't ok, though. Neither was that sick pervert putting his fingers inside her. But this? Yeah, this is ok.

It only takes a few minutes for her orgasm to hit. It's intense, causing her to scream loud past the ball gag as she throws her head back. Her climax is long, and I kinda feel a bit shit that *I* can't make her come for that long.

I'm a fucking idiot, though. Dumb as dog shit because it takes me a minute to realise that something isn't right, especially when Skipper starts screaming again, going crazy. My eyes dart back to Master Hill, and I realise he hasn't stopped the remote.

Kitten's pleasured cries turn almost painful as he draws out her orgasm with that fucking thing inside her, but a moment later, she falls silent. Her body slack as she pants, her chest heaving as she tries to catch her breath. Good. That's good. The egg thing has stopped. It's over.

Master Hill stands from his seat, turning to his writhing crowd and, with a smug grin, yells over the noise.

"More?"

"More!" The Feasters cheer, the celebration causing Kitten to go rigid again as Master Hill holds up the remote for all to see before he presses the button again.

"Fuck." Moxie shuffles nervously next to me, and I glance at her.

"What?"

She turns her eyes to me. "Too much pleasure can be a form of torture."

My eyes widen. "What!" I shoot my eyes back to my girl and watch her body convulse as another orgasm hits her quickly. The waves of it going on and on as Master Hill doesn't let up on the remote.

Feral roars rip from Skipper's chest as he loses his shit, the muscles in his shoulders straining, his arms bunching as he fights against the restraints. I wouldn't be surprised if he breaks through the chains soon. I hope he does because his reaction tells me someone needs to put a stop to this.

Shit, *I* need to put a stop to this. But how?

"I have to stop this." I turn back to Moxie, trying to tune out the increasing moans of the people getting off around us. "How do I do that?"

"You can't. Even if you try, you'll make it worse for her. They won't stop until they're ready. Until they are satisfied with her punishment. She has to see it through."

"No. Fuck that. This isn't right!"

Kitten's screams fill the room again as she comes, orgasm on top of orgasm on top of orgasm. Moxie was right. This isn't pleasure. This is torture. Fucking hell. This is pure torture. She doesn't deserve this. Fuck, no one deserves this!

When Kitten finally falls limp again, I know it's because Master Hill has stopped the remote, giving her a moment to recover. Feasters watching on find their own releases, revelling in the show before them. I can't deal with them, though. All I can focus on is the quiet sound of sobbing as the music fades between songs.

Kitten.

It's her. She's crying. My Kitten is crying.

I move then, unable to stand by any longer, and I push through the crowd until I can see my girl's face. Tears are streaming from her eyes, washing away some of the face paint to mask her identity, her beautiful creamy skin shining through the trail left by the salty tears.

Then her body stiffens like she is being electrocuted, going rigid as the remote is activated again.

"Stop!" I scream, pushing past the last of the people, dashing towards her. I need to stop this.

Rough hands grab my shoulders, reefing me back before tackling me to the ground. My face slams into the side of the podium, splitting pain searing through my cheek before I'm tugged up and held in place by two of the waiters.

"Stop! This isn't right!" I scream, and a moment later, my girl screams again. There's no pleasure in her screams. It's pure pain. Pure torture. Her body trembling so badly it almost looks as if she's seizing. Then she falls limp again, and this time she's not crying. This time her eyes are closed, and she's not making a sound.

Shit! Has she passed out?

Master Hill stands. "Time for you to leave, boy! I'll let Kitten know the extra half an hour of punishment is because of you."

"What? No!" I thrash against the fuckers who have me by each arm as they drag me away from my girl through the crowd. My eyes dart around the room frantically before locking with Moxie's. "Help her, Moxie! Help her please!"

Moxie's worried eyes shoot over to Skipper, who has the same fear swimming in his eyes, but before anything else can transpire, I'm dragged from the room.

"Let me go, you fucking cunts!" I hiss, but the fuckers just chuckle as I thrash in their hold, trying to fight my way free.

As we enter the foyer, another waiter darts in front of us, opening the front door wide before the arseholes push me with force out into the chilly night air, where I land hard on my bare arse.

Fuck! Fuck! Fuck!

I jump up from the cold ground, ignoring the small pebbles sticking into my arse cheek, and try to open the door, but it's locked.

"Shit!" I yell, trying to break the fucking knob.

Turning from the door, I dash along the veranda, testing each window I pass to see if one is unlocked. It's no use. They are all fucking locked.

Fuck! Fuck! Fuck!

I shove my hands through my hair, gripping tightly as I think.

I need to get Rhys free. I don't fucking care if I die trying.

Since I am already familiar with this property, I know there's a glass door around the back of the house. With a new plan in mind, I bolt around the back, my ears picking up the faint sounds from inside. I can hear my girl screaming again. I can hear the Feasters cheering. They are fucking sick. Cheering over her torture. I'm going to kill every one of them.

Coming to the back door I typically use for wine deliveries each Feast night, I try the handle, but it's locked, too. I thought it would be. I was just hoping it wasn't to save me having to smash the glass. But fuck it, I can hear my girl inside. I'm getting in there one way or another.

When a guttural scream meets my ears, I lose my shit, and without thinking twice, I elbow the glass, smashing it enough to slip my hand in and flip the lock. Once it clicks open, I leap over the broken glass and charge inside.

As I come around the corner to the main floor, no one notices me along the side. Darting my head around, I peer through the cracks in the crowd before I see that creepy fucker in the tiger suit. He's standing next to the podium, his fingers on my girl's clit, rubbing it like crazy while the egg vibrates inside her.

Watery fluid spouts from Kitten as she screams again, and tiger guy doesn't let up on her sensitive spot as everyone goes crazy. It's like the Feasters have turned into wild animals. Crazed with lust, they get off on whoever or whatever is closest to them. Fuck. One chick is grinding on the arm of the fucking couch. It's like porn chaos in here!

"Time for the last stage of Kitten's punishment." Master Hill's announcement gains the attention of the Feasters, and they quieten a little as they wait for more details. "Time for the humiliation finale. I give you all permission to mark her with your fluids. Make sure to give her everything, so she understands never to break the rules again."

As Kitten falls limp, barely conscious, male Feasters walk up and surround her.

No! I can't let this happen. No fucking way!

I start pushing through the crowd, not caring if I get caught again because fuck that, I need to get to her and kill every fucker that has bad intentions against her. My attempt to reach her is futile. The crowd is too thick, and as if they know my plan, they seem to cram closer together and won't let me through.

Fuck it!

I start swinging punches.

No motherfucker is keeping me from getting to my girl, so I try to keep my eyes on her as I throw my fists, connecting with whatever gets in my way. I clock a guy across the back of his head, and when he drops from the shock, I push my way through, ripping some chick back by her hair.

As I claw and punch my way through, I see the first group of men surrounding Kitten pumping their dicks and showering her with their grotesque spoof. The white cream spurts between her legs, on her tits, on her face. Then some fucker starts pissing on her chest, and I lose it.

Fucking motherfuckers! She hates piss!

No! No! NO!

I pull another bitch by her hair and elbow some lanky pin dick guy in the nose before I break free of the crowd and reach the fuckers humiliating Kitten. Skipper is roaring, his guttural war cries coming from the edge of the room where he's still restrained. I don't look at him, though. My focus is on my girl as I start tearing through the arseholes looming over her. My fists fly, punching one guy in the face and another in the dick before the room suddenly falls into darkness.

Everyone falls silent for a moment as the shock of the blackout sinks in. Then, a female voice that sounds a hell of a lot like Moxie yells, "the cops are here!"

As her words register with the Feasters, chaos breaks out, and people start running blindly in the dark while screaming with panic.

Master Hill's vile voice calls over the chaos, yelling at everyone to calm down, but no one listens.

"Cass." Moxie's voice next to me is a surprise, and I feel dainty hands on my shoulder. "Help me get her down."

I feel her move away from me, and as my eyes adjust in the darkness, I can see her silhouette at Rhys' ankle, undoing the cuff.

I don't hesitate a moment longer.

Springing into action, I leap towards Kitten, finding her foot and set to work to release her ankle from the other cuff. The sound of glass and porcelain crashes to the floor around us as chaos fills the room. I don't bother looking at what's happening behind me. Fuck that! I need to get my girl out of here!

Once I have the ankle cuff off, I hesitate as I feel her foot fall lifelessly to the podium, and my lungs seize up.

Shit.

Kitten.

I want to check on her, but that will have to wait. I need to get her out of here. Away from these sick fuckers. Once she is safe, I can focus on waking her up.

Moving to her wrist, I fumble in the dark with the cuff, my fingers feeling like fucking fat useless sausages right now.

Work you stupid things!

Finally, the cuff slips free, and I slide my hand to her shoulder just as Moxie gets her other wrist free.

"Rhys?" I don't care if anyone hears her name. These fuckers are monsters. "Baby, can you hear me?" I cup her face with my free hand, ignoring the vile bodily fluids under my touch as I feel her shift.

"Shaun?" Her sweet voice is like music to my ears.

"We have to go." Moxie urges, right as light illuminates the room.

Some Feasters stop in their tracks, looking around with squinting eyes, while others realise they are heading in the wrong direction and start rushing towards the door. My eyes lock with the death glare of Master Hill as he watches from the den entry.

"We are so fucked." Moxie mutters, yet doesn't stop trying to help Rhys up.

I look down over my girl now. Her lids are heavy, and her eyes look distant. It's the kind of distant that has nothing to do with the exhaustion she is feeling. As my eyes glance down over her marred body, they pool with tears and my stomach rolls. Her skin is damp. She smells of piss, and there are slimy trails of cum all over her. Even her beautiful silky hair has been tainted.

I clench my jaw tight, so tight that my teeth feel like they will shatter into a million pieces at any second, boiling heat flaring inside my chest as rage threatens to engulf me.

"Kitten. Can you walk?" Moxie's voice gains my attention again, shaking me out of my head.

Get a hold of yourself, arsehole!

I can lose my shit later. Right now, I need to focus.

At the gruff tone of Skipper's voice, I look up to see a guy wearing nothing but chaps and a cowboy hat with a sheriff's badge and another guy in only a tradie's tool belt and hard hat, helping Skipper free of his restraints.

Rhys mumbles something incoherent, and I know the quickest way to get her out of here is by carrying her. Bending down, I ignore the gore coating her skin and lift my girl in my arms. She curls into me, a whimper escaping her even as she loses consciousness again.

With my girl in my arms, I rush to Skipper as he struggles to get the last restraint off.

"Hurry up!" I hiss.

"I'm fucking trying, arsehole!" Skipper hisses back as the cowboy and construction worker guys help him. When the last chains fall free from his ankles, his eyes fall to Rhys, hanging limp in my arms. Emotion I didn't expect to see glasses Skipper's eyes as they travel over her, his mouth working as he tries to hold in his reaction.

"We have to take her somewhere. I'm guessing she can't go home like this?" Moxie gains Skipper's attention.

"No, she can't go home. Let's get out of here." Skipper points to the door, and we all move quickly as the last of the Feasters push through to escape.

I follow behind Moxie, with Rhys in my arms and Skipper at my back, and we head down the hall towards the foyer.

"Moxie, can we use your place?" Skipper calls over my head, and Moxie looks over her shoulder in concern.

"My place? Uh... Can't she go to your place?" Moxie asks as she dashes into the cloakroom and grabs her stuff. I hover in the doorway but get shoved a little as Skipper barges past me, searching for his things.

"No." Skipper grits out in response to Moxie before darting his eyes to me. "Where's your stuff, Fuckboy?"

Gesturing my head towards my bag on the floor, I watch Skipper move quickly to gather up my things, too.

"Where's Kitten's stuff?" Moxie asks, darting her head around.

"Out in the Barn. I'll grab it as soon as we get her in your car." Skipper hitches my backpack on his shoulder and picks up another bag before bee-lining for the exit.

We follow behind quickly, the cool night air refreshing after being in the stuffy over-packed Lodge, and Moxie moves ahead, leading us to her car.

"I can look after her. Just lay her in the back seat. I'll make sure she's ok." Moxie instructs as she unlocks a little red car.

"I'm not leaving her," I growl, and Moxie's eyes widen behind her mask.

"You can't come to my house with her then." She looks to Skipper. "I can follow you and drive them to your place. You came on a motorbike, right?"

Skipper nods, but then shakes his head.

"They can't come to my house. I'm sorry."

"Why? It's clear the three of you know each other." Moxie accuses, and I cringe. We aren't meant to know identities, but what the fuck does it matter now? There's no way we are going back to the Feast nights ever again.

"We do, you're right. I'll explain later, but right now, we need to get her somewhere safe, and my house isn't it." Skipper looks down at Rhys in my arms and strokes a thumb over her cheek.

"Fine. Throw those bags in here and follow behind." Moxie opens the back door and gestures for me to climb in, but before I do, Skipper leans down and whispers something in Rhys' ear. She whimpers in response, and then not wanting to be on this property a second longer, I slide into the back seat, holding her close, knowing I'm never going to let her go.

Ever.

CHAPTER TWO

SKIPPER

I failed her. I didn't do the one thing I was meant to do. Protect her. Why didn't I see this coming? I should have. Or at least I wish I did, but how could I? In the six years I've been attending the Feast nights, never have they done something so vile. There was a guy a few years back that received a punishment. Pure humiliation. He was whipped, made to drink Vik's piss, and cum on by over twenty fucking sick cunts, but the thing is, he liked to be whipped, he liked to drink piss, and he loved other men's cum. The only thing he didn't like was being the centre of attention. He hated people watching him. So really, that was his only humiliation.

My Kitten, though, she hates Master Hill, and he knows it. That's why he was the one to insert that fucking vibrator inside her. He knows she's avoided his touch for the two years she's been attending the Feasts. He knows she will never give him consent to touch her like that, so he used this opportunity while she was bound and gagged and unable to express herself and tell him no. Even though she fucking did. She shook her head, damn it! That was a clear fucking NO!

Master Hill knows she doesn't like golden showers either. She told me she put it on her hard limits, and yeah, she would have fucking hated all those motherfuckers sprogging on her. She's picky with who she plays with, and I know for a fact that she has steered clear of most of those arseholes. Not to mention that fucking Tiger son of a bitch. To touch her that way.

FUCK!

"You're growling again." Shaun holds the front door open of Moxie's apartment as I carry my girl in my arms. As soon as we pulled up, I opened Moxie's car door and scooped Rhys out of Shaun's arms. And yeah, I may be growling like a fucking psycho, but I can't help it. What happened tonight should never have happened. I should have fucking protected her!

"Shower." I snap as we enter a living area, and Moxie points behind me. I haven't seen her without her mask before, but I realise she looks familiar. Does she know who I am? That I'm Kitten's fucking teacher?

"There's a guest room and bathroom back there."

I spin on my heel and head through the door she pointed to while Shaun offers her a thanks. As I make my way through the guest bedroom, Shaun flicks the light on, and I find the bathroom, using my elbow to flick the light on.

"Fuckboy! Get in here and turn the shower on. Not too hot." I demand, and Shaun's reflection appears in the mirror as he stands behind me, rolling his fucking eyes. I ignore him and look down at Kitten. "Baby, we need to clean you up. I'm gonna give you a shower, ok?"

"O… k." Rhys rasps. Her lids still closed, her body still heavily lifeless in my arms.

The shower turns on, and Shaun adjusts the temperature. His eyes dart to Rhys in my arms every few moments, his worry for her matching mine.

"She's gonna be ok, right?"

I glance up at him, and my lips thin.

"Physically, she will be. In a few days."

Testing the water with his hand, Shaun nods to himself and steps out of the shower's entry.

"But not mentally?" His question is more of a statement.

I shake my head.

"No. This is gonna take a while for her to get over."

Emotions I'm not used to feeling twist my gut in knots just thinking about what happened tonight. What my poor Kitten would have been thinking while it happened. How helpless she would have felt.

Vik and her deranged husband will pay for this. Somehow, I will make them fucking pay.

With Rhys still firmly in my arms, I step into the shower and let the warm water rush over us. Rhys' lids flutter open as the water cascades over her, and those normally bright with life chocolate eyes peer up at me like the light has been switched off behind them.

"Ty." She whimpers, and my fucking heart breaks.

"It's ok, baby. You're safe. It's over."

"I'm sorry." She murmurs, her face twisting in pain as tears pop free.

"Why? You have nothing to be sorry for." I brush the water over her stomach, feeling the vile slime of other men's cum as I try to clean it off.

"B-roke the rules."

"No, baby. What they did tonight was wrong. So wrong."

What they did tonight went too far. That fucker and his wife have something against Kitten. I don't know how I know that, but I can sense something more. Something I don't understand. What they did to her tonight was more than a punishment. What they did tonight was torture.

"I didn't think he was going to stop." Rhys' bottom lip quivers as she whispers the words.

Fuck! I've never seen her so distressed. Rhys wears sex as armour. It's her façade. Her currency. Now, though, it's been used against her. Now, she's broken.

"I'm sorry I couldn't get to you." I choke on the words as I try to get them past the lump the size of a fucking cricket ball in my throat.

A sob escapes her then, and she curls into my chest as she lets go of her last bit of control. Her cries are agonizing, and it rips my chest wide open. My knees buckle, and I collapse to the cold tiled floor of the shower, water raining down over our heads.

The glass door opens, and Shaun steps in even though there's hardly any room, and I'm thankful he's wearing jocks now, so I don't have to get an eyeful of his dick. He does something over our heads, and then the falling water shifts, so it's aimed at our huddled bodies.

When Shaun squats down, he has a weird pink fluffy looking thing in his hand, and he glides it over Rhys' body. Soap-suds bubble over Kitten's creamy skin, washing away the filth as it flows from her skin and down the drain.

Even though Kitten is still curled into my chest, she lets Shaun take her arms, and he gently scrubs them clean. Then he moves to her breasts, tummy, and down her legs. When he parts her legs a little, knowing he has to wash her there, he curses.

"Shit."

My eyes snap to his. "What?"

"Uh- the… thing is still inside her." He cringes, and I dart my eyes down, peering between her parted thighs. A blue rubbery thing dangles free of my girl's pussy, and my stomach drops.

Shit! Fuck! Shit shit shit!

"You want me to handle that?" Moxie's voice gains our attention, but Rhys doesn't hear her. She's not really hearing anything as she cries into my chest.

"Uh…" I glance back down at the blue thing, but Shaun answers for me.

"No. Thanks for the offer, Moxie, but I'll do it."

"Agatha."

"What?" Shaun asks, and I look up again.

"At the Feast, I'm Moxie, but outside, I'm Agatha."

Shaun offers her a slight smile. "Oh, right. Agatha." He holds his hand out to her. "I'm Shaun."

Agatha smiles warmly, taking his hand before turning her eyes to me. Fuck. It's bad enough that she can see my face now that my mask is off, but now I have to tell her my fucking name? It's the least I can do, I suppose, since she is exposing herself and taking such a risk by letting strangers into her house.

"I'm Tyler. And this is Rhys."

Agatha nods. "Yes, I know Rhys. She's spent the night here a few times."

"Oh. Then why didn't you want us to come here?" Shaun asks, and she shrugs.

"I know *her*, but I don't know the two of you, despite how many times we've fucked."

Shaun nods. "Right. Sorry."

"It is what it is, I guess." Agatha shrugs again, and Shaun nods before looking back down at Rhys in my arms. Then he sucks in a breath before squatting down to us.

"Rhys?" He strokes her hair, "Rhys, baby." She shifts her head a little, cracking one eye open to peer up at Shaun. "That vibrator thing is still inside you. I need to take it out. Ok?"

She stiffens, her slack body going rigid. Needing to comfort her, I tighten my hold and place a kiss on the top of her head.

"Kitten, it's ok. It's not switched on, and it won't come on, but we need to take it out. Will you let Shaun do that?"

"No. No." She shakes her head and starts wriggling in my hold.

"Shhh, it's ok." I stroke her head, hoping it will remind her that I'm here and that she's safe. "Shaun will remove it quickly. Then it will be over."

"No. It hurts. No."

Shaun shifts to his knees then, bending over to speak closer to Rhys' ear, and I try to ignore the fact that one of my male students is nearly naked in a fucking shower with me.

"Rhys, can you hear me? It's Shaun. Can you hear me?"

When Rhys nods against my chest, Shaun continues.

"I swear I will be gentle. I'm so fucking sorry that we even need to do this, but we have to take it out. Will you *please* let me do it? *Please*?"

Rhys shifts her head again and looks at Shaun through the wet, tangled mess of her hair.

"Please. Let me help you." Shaun pleads with her, and after a few moments, she nods her head. "Ok." Shaun nods. "Ok."

I think he's trying to talk himself into it. Shit, maybe I should do it.

"Right, uh- I'm just gonna move your legs a bit wider. Alright?"

Rhys nods against my chest again as she re-buries her face, and Shaun rubs his hands together like he's trying to warm them up. I don't think that's why he does it, though. He's mentally preparing himself.

Maybe I should do it. I'm the adult here, after all. But fuck, isn't that a sick and twisted problem? I'm the adult, and they are fucking teenagers.

Shaun reaches out and hooks his hand under Rhys' knee. "I'm moving your leg now." Slowly, he lifts her leg and moves it to the side, parting her legs wide to open her up.

This is fucked. This is *so* fucked.

Shaun lowers her leg and sucks in a deep breath as his eyes widen at the sight between her legs. He takes a moment to clear his throat, his Adam's apple bobbing as he tries to gain control.

"Ok, baby. Now I'm going to remove it. Ok?"

Even though she whimpers, Rhys nods again, keeping her head buried in my chest.

Shaun's eyes snap to mine. I can see he needs reassurance, so I give him a firm nod, and after a moment, he drops his eyes back between her legs.

My eyes follow, watching his shaking hand as he reaches for the blue rubber, gripping it, and slowly starts to pull.

Instantly, Rhys cries out, her body stiffening, but just like the tough girl she is, she doesn't close her legs.

"Just do it fast. Like ripping a bandaid off." Agatha demands from over Shaun's shoulder, and Shaun nods, tugging it quickly and pulling the blue egg free.

Rhys gasps, a slight scream ripping from her as the blue thing pops out, and with it, some blood.

"Shit!" Shaun's eyes go wide with panic, and he looks at me for reassurance again, but I can't give it because I have no idea what the blood means.

"It's ok, guys. Don't panic. It's only a little blood. Nothing too serious." Agatha is the one to reassure us as Rhys trembles in my arms. "Finish cleaning her up and get her into bed. I'll get her some paracetamol and a drink."

Thank fuck Moxie, or Agatha, or whatever the hell her name is, is here. I don't know about girly stuff like this. Nodding up at her, I hold Rhys tight as Shaun washes her gently between her legs before we work together to turn her around and clean the other side of her body. When we take too long, Agatha returns to the bathroom and shoo's Shaun out of the way, moving in to wash Rhys' hair while I keep my girl upright on my lap. Then she washes off what's left of the paint on Kitten's face, and the three of us work together to get Rhys out, dried and into bed in a clean pair of panties and an oversized band t-shirt that was in her bag.

Agatha manages to get her coherent enough to swallow down the pain meds before Shaun tucks her in, and for a moment, the three of us just stand around the bed, looking down at her. At my girl.

Fuck! How did this happen?

How did I let this happen?

"Stay with her." I point to Shaun first and then down to Rhys. "I'm gonna take a quick shower."

He nods, and I turn, shutting myself in the small bathroom to clean the invisible filth of Vixen's Lodge off my skin. I make quick work of my shower, needing to get the mundane task done so I can get back to Rhys. Every time I close my eyes under the stream of water, my mind flashes to the sight of her strung up by the chains on the podium, while shockwaves rippled through her in the most painful way.

Fuck!

I pry my eyes open, not wanting to ever see Kitten like that again. I don't know how she's ever going to get through this. I've fucked up so badly by letting her blackmail me. I should have called her bluff or gone to her parents. If I had stopped her from joining the Feast, this would never have happened.

She already carries dark secrets. Of that, I'm sure. Add this to it, and her already spiralling behaviour lately, and my girl is likely to break. I'll be there for her, but will that be enough?

One thing is for sure. Terrence fucking Hill, the Master of the Feast nights, hasn't seen the end of me yet. We have only just fucking begun!

When I return to the room in my t-shirt and jeans, Shaun swaps places with me, heading into the bathroom to clean himself up. Agatha is gone, but the door is open, and I can hear her clanging around in the kitchen, so I leave it open and pull back the covers on the bed.

I hesitate.

I shouldn't hop in this bed with Rhys.

She's my student.

You fucking cock head! You've fucked her, eaten her, made her come, and now you're fucking worried about her being your student?

Fuuuck! This is so bad. I should leave. I know I should. I should put distance between us and restore the boundary, so there's no blurred lines. I should return to being nothing but her teacher.

The thought sends a sharp stab through my chest. I know I should do all of those things, but I don't want to. I *want* to be here with her, for her. I need to protect her and make sure no one harms her again.

The mouse-like whimper that comes from Rhys kicks my arse, and I slip in under the covers, gently cuddling up behind her. When she whimpers again, I stroke her long dark hair back off her face and bring it over her shoulder so I can see her better.

"It's ok, baby. I'm here."

"Ty?" Her voice sounds so small, and I hate to say, very much like the young person she is.

"Yes. I'm here. Is it alright if I cuddle up to you?"

She nods on the pillow, her eyes still closed. "Please."

That's all the confirmation I need.

Snuggling right up against her back, my body moulds to hers like we were always meant to fit together, and I inhale the fresh scent of strawberry shampoo as I slide my hand over her waist and hold her tight.

Then she starts to cry.

"I'm so sorry," I whisper as pain lashes the centre of my chest.

She shakes her head, unable to speak as the tears flow almost silently.

The bathroom door opens behind me, and Shaun steps out with steam billowing around him, his face twisted in grief as he takes in our fragile girl. He's dressed in grey sweatpants and a black t-shirt, moving quietly around the other side of the bed to glance down at Rhys. Again, his face contorts in agony as he chews the inside of his cheek, struggling with his own emotions.

"So, since I'm putting my identity on the line here and I'm giving you both access to my house, do you wanna tell me how the three of you know each other?" Agatha is leaning against the door frame, her arms crossed over her chest and her golden-brown hair no longer in the slick ponytail thing she had it in earlier. Her hair is long. Not as long as Rhys', but long all the same. She has to be in her late twenties if I had to guess, but what the fuck do I know?

Shaun darts his eyes to me, clearly unsure of what to say.

"These two know each other from school," I answer and glance back at Agatha.

"Ok. So how do you know the two of them?" One of her brows hitch accusingly as she waits for my response.

Yeah, I'm fucked either way. Clearly, I'm an older guy, and they are both underage, but Agatha said Rhys has stayed here a few times before, which means they have hooked up outside the Feast, even with *their* age difference... so hopefully, it won't be a big deal?

"I ahhh... teach them."

Agatha's eyes widen. "You're a teacher?"

I'm about to plead my case, but Shaun jumps in before I can.

"Hey, don't judge. Age means nothing to Rhys. You, of all people, should know that since she's spent time here."

"But I'm not her fucking teacher!" Agatha hisses, and Shaun growls like a fucking bear or something.

"Stop!" Rhys rasps out in a strained tone, her eyes fluttering open as she shifts her head to look at Agatha. "They are mine. Both of them. Age and job title don't mean shit…" She sucks in a deep breath as more tears fall. "They are mine."

Her eyes flutter closed as her emotions take over, and Agatha's face softens. "Damn."

"Do we have to worry about you telling anyone?" Shaun asks Agatha, and her eyes drag from Rhys to him as she shakes her head.

"No. You don't have to worry about me. I'll keep your secret. But you fuckers better keep my identity a secret, too, or we will have a problem."

We both nod, and Agatha takes one more look over us before clasping the door handle and pulling it shut.

Shaun sits down on the edge of the bed, propping one knee up so he can face Rhys and me.

"Can we trust her?"

I nod. "I think so. At least I hope so."

How in the fuck did things get so out of hand? With Fuckboy of all people helping me? My life is seriously weird as fuck.

Rhys lifts a heavy hand out towards Shaun, and he takes it as she pulls it back towards her, silently telling him to climb into the bed next to her. His eyes dart to mine in question, and I shrug.

"Get in if you wanna, but don't fucking touch me."

Shaun smirks before leaning over to flick off the lamp.

"Homophobe." The faint light filtering in through the cracked bathroom door illuminates his face enough that I can see the stupid smirk he's wearing.

"Not a homophobe. Just a student-ophobe." I mutter, and feel Rhys shake under my hold.

"Are you laughing at me, Kitten?"

"Yes." She rasps out as Shaun lays down in front of her, shifting close to our girl.

Fuck! Our girl? Really?

"I'm here," Shaun whispers, and Rhys' eyes flutter open.

"Thank you." She whispers back, squeezing my hand before falling asleep.

CHAPTER THREE

RHYS

The bed shifts behind me, and the warmth of the Tyler and Shaun sandwich quickly disappears. Forcing my eyes open, Shaun's sleeping face comes into view. He has a reddish bruise on his left cheek. I can only imagine how he got it. I hate that he has been dragged into my shit show. Seeing him here with me makes me want to cry. I'm a fucking mess, and I don't know how to pull myself out of this spiral into reckless darkness that I've visited so many times before. The difference is that this time, I have these guys in my life. They've cast some sort of spell on me, making me want things I've never let myself think about before. I don't want to lose my guys, but I just don't know if they are enough to keep my head above water right now.

Last night was… too much.

"Go back to sleep, beautiful." Tyler's voice is raspy, probably from the screaming he did at the Feast, trying to get someone to help me. Trying to get them to stop.

Despite the tears popping free from my raw eyes, I roll my aching body over to face my man.

"Don't go." I plead quietly, and I'm met with his concerned blue gaze.

Reaching out, his large hand cups my face, wiping away my tears before more fall.

"I have to go. I'm sorry. I hate that I can't be here for you all the time."

I shake my head. "It's ok. I understand." Even though I do understand, I don't have to like it.

"You should stay home from school today. Get some rest and let yourself heal."

I know Tyler means well, but being home alone is the last thing I need. Explaining why I'm not at school to my mum is also something I'd rather avoid.

"I think I'm better off being around my friends today," I admit, and for a moment, Tyler is quiet as his piercing eyes study me. Then he nods.

"Take it easy, ok? I'll touch base with you later?"

I nod. "Yep. Ok."

Tyler doesn't move. It's like he can't bring himself to leave me, and I kinda wish he wouldn't. I don't really understand my attachment to these guys. Multiple guys. But I just know I need them, even though I've trained myself into thinking I don't need anyone.

Sucking in a shuddering breath, I can see Tyler is fighting emotions of his own as he leans down and presses his warm lips to my forehead. "I'm so sorry."

Before I get a chance to tell him to stop apologising, that last night wasn't his fault, he bolts out of the room like someone has lit a fire under his arse. I listen to his footsteps retreat, and then I hear his deep voice as he talks quietly with Agatha before leaving.

My heart feels emptier without Tyler here. Loneliness seeping in, even though Shaun is still here next to me. I snuggle in closer to him, inhaling his scent and listening to his slow breathing as he sleeps. I do this until my heart can't take it anymore and then spend the next hour crying silently, my tears soaking the pillow under me.

At 7am, Agatha comes in to get us up, and thirty minutes later, she drops us at the end of Shaun's long sandy driveway. The sun is already warming the air as it rises higher in the sky, and for the first time, I soak in the natural beauty of Shaun's family's property.

Grapevines line both sides of the driveway. The right side filled with larger plants than the left side, so I guess they were planted earlier. I don't really know. I know nothing about a vineyard, but one thing is for certain. It's beautiful.

"What are you thinking about?" Shaun's voice gains my attention as we walk up his drive, and I drag my gaze from the landscape to my Spanish Casanova.

"Just how beautiful it is here. I've never really looked at plants and nature and been so drawn to it like I am with this." I gesture to the grapevines. "Your family has a beautiful property."

"Really?" Shaun frowns, looking around at our surroundings. "I've never really thought of it as beautiful. It's just hard work to me."

"That's really sad." I glance back at the rows of vines and let the peace soak in. "I'm going to come here to die. I want my last moments to be here, amongst these vines when it's my time." I spin with my arms open wide, gesturing to our surroundings. I try to ignore the biting pain between my legs and the way my whole body aches. "I want to lie down in the middle of them and look up at the sky, surrounded by this beauty."

Shaun chuckles, "I'll be sure to install a track accessible to a wheelchair or walking frame for when you are old and grey, then."

I turn back to Shaun, grinning. "You are so thoughtful."

"I know, right?" Shaun grins like the most adorably sexy dork ever. I don't know how it's possible, but he pulls it off.

When I glance up as we reach the top of the small incline, my eyes land on the roofline of Vixen's Lodge in the distance. Like a bolt of lightning, memories swarm me as the reality of what happened last night sinks in.

Last night, my right to choose was taken away from me.

Last night, I was forced into a situation I didn't want.

I was restrained, so I couldn't fight.

I was gagged to keep me silent.

Last night, I was tortured and humiliated by using the one thing I love against me.

Sex.

"Hey, Rhys?" Shaun steps in front of me, his warm hands gripping my shoulders, as his eyes dart frantically over my expression. "What just happened? What's wrong?"

I can't speak. Tremors work their way up my body as my vision blurs, so I slowly point at the colonial-style building that houses two of the vilest people I've ever come across. Fuck, they are just as bad as Brian and Julie. I bet if they ever crossed paths, they'd be the best of friends.

Shaun glances over his shoulder to see where I'm pointing and then he curses quietly before pulling me to his chest.

"I'm so fucking sorry, Kitten." He stiffens, "Shit, sorry. I probably shouldn't call you that."

"No, don't stop calling me that." I mutter into the crook of his neck, "I like it when you and Ty call me Kitten."

"Ok. If you're sure?" The poor guy sounds so uncertain, so I nod into his neck, wrapping my arms tighter around him, seeking more of his comfort.

We stand wrapped together on his sandy driveway for a few minutes until I loosen my grip on him, letting him know I've pulled my shit together. Then, in silence, Shaun links our hands and walks me to his picturesque farmhouse.

His mum and dad are nowhere in sight, and it's only after we stumble out of the bathroom together, steam flowing out with us from our shower, that we run into his brother Derek. He doesn't bat an eyelid at my presence, just gives me a warm smile and a *hi* before telling us both to be ready to leave in thirty minutes. Then, Shaun and I go up to his loft to get ready for school.

There's a big part of me that can't fathom going to school and putting up with teachers and bitchy girls and grabby guys, but it's the thought of the still loneliness of being home by myself that urges me on to go to school. Unfortunately, by the time we arrive, my mood has flattened tenfold, and I struggle to even put on a fake smile.

Big bad moody Garrett spends way too long studying my face when he sees me walk into school, making me feel all sorts of self-conscious. Simon throws an accusing glare Shaun's way for my clearly visible mood, and Lexi asks me what's wrong each time we cross paths, but I just tell her I'm not feeling well today. Even Bell, who's been annoyed at me for spending so much time with my new friends, looks concerned when she sees me.

My first class is Food Tech, and Simon works in overdrive, trying to tease me with the food we are cooking. I love this part about him. His playfulness. His love for food play. They are things I love too… well; I *did* love them, but now, suddenly, his sexual innuendo's make me uncomfortable. They make me feel dirty, which is crazy, right? I already know I'm the dirtiest bitch around Fox Pines Catholic. So why does it make my skin crawl?

My second class is Viscom with Simon again, and this time, he tries to coax me out of class to see if the photo lab is free. That room is my domain. My lair. So why does the thought of walking into that room and locking the door make my heart race for the wrong reason? What the fuck is wrong with me? I should be on my knees blowing Simon, yet the only blowing I'm doing is blowing off his advances and pretending like I actually want to revise for my exam.

I leave Simon looking like a hurt puppy as soon as recess starts, and I avoid everyone, opting to go to the back of the school to my old hangout. I sit on the steps, my knee jumping up and down like it's having a seizure, and I squeeze my eyes shut, trying to will away this rising panic.

"Rhys?"

My eyes snap open at Tillie's voice and the moment I see her and Bell looking at me with concerned curiosity, I break. I fucking cry. Like what the actual fuck. I don't, and haven't cried in front of them. Ever. Yet here I am, silently letting the floodgates open.

"Shit. What's happened?" Tillie climbs the few steps, coming to sit next to me, wrapping an arm around my shoulder. I want to answer her, but I can't fucking speak right now.

"Here." Bell lights up a joint, and after sucking in a drag, she offers it to me. "Some Mary Jane will help."

There's a reason Bell, Tillie and I are friends. We aren't like the other kids at FP Catholic. We never grew up in loving homes. We were never offered the luxury of security until our last few years. And we each carry a dark past that we don't speak of but know each of us has it hanging over our heads, just waiting to engulf us.

Should we use substances as a coping mechanism? No, yet we do. My biggest indiscretion when it comes to this is some good quality marijuana and a shit load of alcohol. Tillie is much the same as me, but Bell, well, she's a different kettle of fish. That Wednesday Addams look-a-like dabbles in some hard shit that I'm too chicken to even glance at.

I accept the joint and bring it to my lips, closing my eyes as I suck back, the smoke sweeping deep into my lungs. I hold it there. I don't want to let it go. I need the THC to do its thing and work quickly so I can pull myself together. Then, when I can't hold it in any longer, I slowly release the smoke, exhaling it like a savoured dessert. I repeat this a couple more times, knowing full well that I am going to be baked, but it's better than walking around like a crying headcase.

"Rhys, you wanna tell us what this is all about?" Tillie asks, her head tilting towards me in a way that makes her look even more pixie-like.

"I fucked up at the Feast on Sunday night. Broke the rules, so last night… I was punished."

Tillie's auburn brows shoot up. "What does that mean, exactly?"

I go to answer her, but the words won't come out, so I take another deep drag of the joint before handing the last little bit back to Bell. These girls know a little about Vixen's Lodge and the Feast nights. It was part of my deal with them when they agreed to be my cover while I go to the Feasts. They lie to my rents for me if they call and have a bed available for me to crash in after the Feasts if I don't end up falling into someone else's bed. In exchange, I tell them about my experiences. Of late, they haven't really cared to know unless something weird or different happens, but I haven't been around them much to divulge, even though I've still used them as my cover.

"I was bound and gagged even though I didn't give consent for them to do that part exactly. Then, the Master basically tortured me with one of those remote vibrators." A shiver runs down my spine as my mind's eye goes back to the look on Master Hill's face as he inserted that thing inside me. "He didn't let up."

"Shit," Tillie mutters as Bell's mouth drops open.

"It was so intense. At first, I thought that maybe I'd be ok. But I hadn't counted on him turning up the vibrations in the middle of my orgasm. I didn't count on him not switching it off." A sob escapes me, but I swallow it, sucking in deep breaths, "It fucking hurt. Bad. I can't even explain it."

"That motherfucker!" Bell hisses. "I'm going to tie him to a chair, chop his dick off, make him watch as I put it through a blender, then make him drink it!"

"Fucking hell, Bell. That's…" Tillie gets cut off by Bell.

"Fitting?"

Tillie shrugs, "Actually, I think it is."

I don't laugh like most people might from Bell's comment. They'd think she's joking. Idiots! Bell Bishop isn't a joker. Most of the words that pass her black lips are factual. I'm well aware that one of my best friends is most likely going to be a serial killer one day, and I'm ok with that.

"After that, the Master had one of the creepoids that he knows I avoid, add to the sensations by using his hand to rub over me, which hurt even worse, even though I kept fucking coming. I thought I was going to die. Like, can that happen? Death by orgasm?"

"I read an article once that a submissive had a brain aneurism from orgasm torture, and she died." Bell comes to sit on the other side of me.

"Bell, I don't think that article was real. I can't see that happening." Tillie counters, but Bell just shrugs like she doesn't care either way. Then Tillie turns her blue eyes back to me. "What happened after that?"

"I think I might have passed out. I don't know, but it scared the living shit out of me. When I woke, there were men surrounding me, coming on me. I've had a cum shower before, so I kind of thought maybe I could get through it, but then..." I shudder, shaking my head and squeezing my eyes shut briefly. "The shower turned yellow. Someone started pissing on me."

"Oh my god! That's disgusting!" Tillie cries, her pixie face morphing into horror.

"Piss doesn't taste that bad, actually. Especially if the giver is well hydrated. It's a bit salty. Sometimes bitter, but it won't kill you."

Tillie and I gape at Bell as she talks about drinking piss like it's nothing.

"What the fuck, Bell. Whose piss have you tasted?" Tillie asks, and I'm almost too scared to find out. This conversation has taken a turn.

"I don't drink someone's piss and tell," Bell shrugs, "but let me just advise you away from Aaron Miller. His piss is rank!"

After a beat of silence, Tillie and I burst out laughing.

"Oh my god, Bell! You are utterly disgusting!" Tillie blurts past her laughter, and I just shake my head.

"Yes, I know. But without me, how would you know not to drink Aaron's piss?"

"Umm, by not wanting to drink anyone's piss!" I state, and she shrugs again. Nothing bothers this chick.

"Did anything else happen?" Tillie brings the conversation back to me, and my heart sinks.

"I kept passing out, so things got a little fuzzy, but Skipper was trying to get to me, and then the lights went out, and everything went chaotic. Skipper and Moxie got me out of there, and I spent the night at her place, trying to recover." I keep Shaun's involvement out of it. They don't know that Casanova attends the Feasts now.

"Fuck Rhys. This is serious. You should report them." Tillie stands, taking me by the arm and urging me up. I realise then that the bell has gone.

"I can't. Exposing them will put *me* in the spotlight and also expose Skipper and Moxie. They've been good to me. I don't want them to suffer because of my mistake."

"Mistake or not, what those uptight rich fuckers did was fucking wrong." Bell links her arm on my other side, and we stroll toward the side of the school hall.

"I know," I whisper, not feeling like crying anymore, thanks to the MJ in my system. I feel nearly boneless I'm so relaxed, which will probably work against me since it will be noticeable to my teachers, yet right now, I can't find it in me to care.

And that is also the MJ at work.

Tillie walks me to my Maths class and gets Allister to take the reins of leading me to my seat, sitting next to me so he can do damage control. Simon is in this class too, but I don't see him through the haze of my lazy high. Marcus is usually in this class. I miss him. Like a lot. I want to talk to him. Feel his arms around me. Get lost in his earthmoving kisses. Even though I can't have him, it doesn't stop me from pulling out my phone and sending him a text… because I'm weak.

Rhys George
I miss you.

I'm a little surprised when he messages back straight away. But then again, he's probably sitting at home serving his suspension, bored out of his brain.

Marcus Grady
You do?

Rhys George
Yes.

Marcus Grady
What's happened?

Rhys George
Why would you think something has happened?

Marcus Grady
*You've never said something like that to me before.
It worries me.*

Rhys George
I'll be ok.

Marcus Grady
What's happened?

Rhys George
I got what was coming to me, I guess.

A faint pang reaches my heart when I read back over my response to Marcus, but the chemicals running through my veins do their magic and usher that pain away.

Marcus Grady
What does that mean?

Rhys George
Did you know that Mr Thompson has an aura around him?

Mr Thompson is at the front of the class, explaining an equation on the board. I can't hear him. Should I be worried about that? Am I deaf?

Marcus Grady
Rhys, I don't care about Mr T!
I care about you!
Now tell me, what's happened?

Rhys George
I care about you too.

Marcus Grady
Are you high right now?

Rhys George
Hehe. I'm a little baked.

Marcus Grady
A little? I'm thinking you are a lot baked!

Rhys George
Did you know that pee tastes salty?

Marcus Grady
What?

Rhys George
Bell told me.
FYI don't drink Aaron Miller's piss!
She said it was rank!
vomit emoji

Marcus Grady
Jesus, I didn't need to know that, Rhee!

Rhys George
I love it when you call me Rhee.

Marcus Grady
You do?

Rhys George
Yes.

Marcus Grady
Rhee?

Rhys George
Yeah?

Marcus Grady
I'm worried about you.

Rhys George
Don't worry about me, Marcus!
I'm a warrior!!!

Marcus Grady
Even warriors get hurt.

And there's that little pang again.

Rhys George
Yeah… They do.

Before I realise it, Allister is urging me up off my seat and leading me out of the classroom. I still can't really hear anything, but I can see other students moving around, so I figure class is over, and we are heading to Pastoral Care.

The warmth of another body presses up against my right side, and my eyes flicker over to see Simon has taken my other arm. We really do have a lot of classes together. I could have been playing with him for longer if our genitals had accidentally fallen together sooner.

Bell meets us outside the classroom for Pastoral Care and says something to Allister and Simon. I try to read her lips, but that shit is hard. How do people do that? Just when I think we are about to enter the classroom, the boys, with Bell leading the way, walk me away from the door.

"Where are we going?"

Bell spins around, frowning, her finger coming up in front of her mouth, shooshing me. I am definitely deaf. I didn't hear my voice when I spoke just now. Did I? Maybe I should tell someone?

Bell picks up the pace, and we end up in the library. I'm not sure why we are here, but I don't really care. The library is cool. It has books and shit. I stumble a little as I look around, but Simon and Allister grip my arms tighter, holding me up as we move to the back corner, away from prying eyes.

I can see them talk to me at one stage or another, but I can't answer them or talk back since I can't bloody hear them, so I just grin and rest my head on Simon's shoulder as we share a bean bag.

The loud ringing of a bell makes me jump awake with a gasp. My eyes dart around as I try to figure out what the fuck is going on, and my eyes land on Shaun and Garrett as warm arms squeeze me from behind. Turning, I see Simon's goofy grin as he reaches up and brushes a stray hair back into my bun.

"What's going on?"

"She talks!" Simon chuckles, and I frown.

"The end of lunch bell just rang," Garrett explains, and I frown.

"What? Isn't it still period four?"

"Nope. You slept right through period four and lunch, Kitten." Shaun explains, his lips only offering me the slightest of smiles.

"Oh."

"You were pretty baked. I can't believe the teachers didn't notice." Simon adds, and my hazy memory kicks in.

"Marcus messaged us as well. Said he was worried." Garrett adds, his icy-blue eyes roaming over my face. He's worried, too. I can see it. Does he know about last night?

My eyes dart to Shaun, but his neutral expression doesn't tell me shit.

"Is Marcus talking to you guys again?" Hope fills me as I wait for someone to answer.

"Not exactly. I guess his concern for you outweighs his need to distance himself." Garrett offers, and I frown.

We really betrayed Marcus. He didn't deserve that. He didn't deserve me coming into his life and ruining it.

"Where's Allister and Bell?" I look over Garrett and Shaun's shoulders, but I can't see any sign of them.

"They left at the start of lunch. Bell is fucking scary. I totally believed her when she said she'll peel the skin from our dicks if we don't look after you, Kitten." Shaun grimaces, and a slight grin tugs at my lips. I wonder if I should tell him he should be scared.

"We should get to class," Simon mumbles next to my ear and the guys nod, standing from the fraying grey carpet in the library.

Shaun offers me a hand, and when I take it, he hauls me up from the beanbag before I hear Simon grunting as he tries to lift himself up.

My last class is Health, and for the first time ever, I don't want to see Tyler. It's not that I don't care about him. It's more that I'm likely to start crying again now that the joint I smoked earlier has mostly worn off.

"Actually, I think I'm going to head home." I brush my hands over my skirt, trying to straighten it out as the guys' eyes land back on me.

"You are?" Shaun asks, his neutral face now twisting with concern.

"Yeah. I'm gonna nap before I need to get ready for the Halloween party tonight."

"We don't have to go to that, you know. We can all hang out at Simon's, or even my place. We have a man shed we can kick back in." Shaun smiles hopefully at me, but I shake my head.

"There's no way I'm missing a Halloween party!"

"But Kitten… Last night…" Shaun steps in front of me, stopping my path to escape, so I rise up on my tiptoes and peck his cheek. The one that isn't marked red from whatever happened to him last night.

"Last night was last night. Tonight is Halloween, and we are going to party."

I dart around Shaun, ignoring his protest as I speed walk to my locker.

"I really don't think it's a good idea, Kitten." Shaun catches up with me, with Simon and Garrett on his heels.

"Why isn't it a good idea?" Simon asks, having no idea what happened last night.

Reaching my locker, I hastily load up my bag with my books, not considering what I need to take home.

"What's going on?" Garrett demands with a hiss, and I shut my locker, turning back to the guys.

"Nothing is going on. I'm just having an off day. But a nap and a bath will get me back on track. I will see you guys later tonight." I kiss the air and push through them, ignoring Shaun's curse.

The bus is pulling up across the road from the school when I walk out the gates, so I run across quickly, climbing on and taking a seat. Pulling my phone out from my blazer, I open it to message my mum to let her know I've gone home, but instead, it starts ringing with the name *Fuck You Julie* flashing across the screen.

I hold my breath, wondering if I should answer it or not. It's not going to be a nice call, but I should probably speak with her and ask her to back off.

I hit accept.

"What?" I snap, and I'm met with laughter.

"Your foster parents pay for you to go to that uppity school, and that's how you've learnt to answer the phone?"

"I know how to answer a phone, Julie, and I'd be polite if you deserved it. But you don't."

"You've finally grown some balls, Patrice. Go you!"

"What the fuck do you want?" I snap again, glaring out the window of the bus, watching Fox Pines pass by.

"Well, Patty, I wanted to ask you why you're not taking me seriously? I told you to return to the prison by Wednesday, and guess what day it is today? It's fucking Thursday!" Julie screams the last part into the phone, and I move it back from my ear for a moment as the speaker crackles.

"I'm aware of the day, Julie. I didn't go to see him because I have no fucking interest in seeing him again. Feel free to pass the message on."

"Oh, he already understands from your deliberate no show, but you forget about the warning I gave you. I said there will be consequences if you don't go, and since you didn't go, you're going to have to pay." Julie's voice is calm again. No sign of her little outburst a few moments ago.

"What are you going to do? Stand over me and scream in my face like you did when I was little? I'm probably taller than you now." I laugh, but there's no joy in it. "Just fuck off, Julie. I've got better things to do than listen to your pathetic voice."

I hit end on the call before Julie can get another word in, and I look down at my trembling hand as I clutch my phone. Hot tears prick the back of my eyes, and I suck in a shuddering breath right before a new text message pops up on my screen.

Fuck You Julie
Your mistake is thinking that I won't follow through.
Well, Patty. We'll soon see if I can change your mind about that.

CHAPTER FOUR

GARRETT

The guys are probably gonna kick my arse once they find out it was me that went to Lexi for help. They can try, but it won't change the fact that Rhys needs our help, and none of us can do that properly with all the secrets and this rift between Marcus, Shaun and Simon.

"Why exactly are we here again, Lex?" Simon hasn't been able to sit still since we entered Ayden's loft a few minutes ago. He's freaking out that Marcus will see him and mess his face up the same way he did to Bossi.

"I want to talk about Halloween costumes." Lexi lies. Badly. She turns her back on us to hide the flush that heats her cheeks as she chews nervously on the corner of her fingernail.

"You're a terrible liar," Jared smirks at Lexi as he leans against the wall by the door. His eyes remain on her, even when she shoots daggers his way. It makes him smile wider. Fucking hell, this guy really isn't easing off on his obvious affection for Lexi, even though she's helplessly in love with Ayden.

"I smell a rat!" Bossi hisses. "What's going on, Lex?"

"Nothing." She lies badly again, starting to pace as she twirls some of her blonde wavy hair in her fingers.

It's then that voices flow up from the stairwell, and a moment later, the door opens, and Ayden steps in with Marcus behind him. It takes Marcus a second to realise that we are all there, and as his smile falls, his eyes turn to pits of raging lava. Ayden pre-empts

Marcus' need to turn and storm from the room, and he quickly shuts the door, blocking his path.

"What the fuck?" Marcus hisses as Bossi and Hastings shift nervously. Jared and I don't move. We already expected this since we both know the real reason why we are here. "Fucking move Ayden or I'll make your face match that traitor's over there!" He glares over his shoulder briefly at Shaun, his hands balled in fists at his sides.

"Don't be a dick," Ayden mumbles, not at all scared by the threat his cousin just delivered.

"You touch him, and I'll fuck you up, Grady!" Lexi raises her voice, her firecracker temper showing.

Ayden smirks but keeps his eyes on his cousin. "Give us five minutes. Then you can run off and sulk."

"You're a prick!" Marcus hisses through clenched teeth, but Ayden just shrugs.

Sweeping my eyes across the room, I see Hastings slowly inch further and further away, hoping to get more distance between him and Grady. Meanwhile, Bossi eases back in the corner of the couch, not looking at all bothered. In fact, as I look closer at his expression, I'd almost say he looks relieved.

"Marcus, I'm sorry to trap you like this," Lexi turns from Marcus back to us, "all of you, but we need to talk about Rhys. Not just about the relationship stuff…" Lexi hesitates, her brows meeting in the middle as her concern for her friend shows on her face, "Something is going on with Rhys. I think she's in some sort of trouble or something. I'm not sure, but I do know she's been different since returning to school, and I know from experience how hard it is to go through something on your own." Lexi sighs as Marcus slowly turns to face her and the rest of the room, giving his cousin his back. "She needs my pack, guys. She needs friends looking out for her, ready to catch her. She needs you guys to be there for her like you were with me."

"Lexi is right. I know stuff has gotten… messy within our group, but maybe some things need to be put on the back burner for a bit so we can help Rhys." I say before I glance at Marcus. "Even today, despite how pissed off you are at Bossi and Hastings, you still reached out to our group after she sent you those messages. You knew she was acting out of character, and you knew helping her is more important than the other shit that's going on."

Marcus bites the inside of his cheek as he struggles to hold in his anger. I get it. His mates betrayed him in the worst way. Fuck, even I kind of have, which just makes me feel like a fucking prick even more. Rhys George is hard to refuse. But there's just something inside me that won't let me step over that line. I guess, in a way, I look at these guys as my family. And I don't want to lose my family. They are everything to me.

"Fine. We can talk about helping her, but I'm not talking about that other shit." Marcus grumbles, his shoulders dropping a little as he begins to relax.

"What if sorting out that other shit will help her?" Bossi's words seem to surprise everyone. He's not shying away from the hard truth here. I can respect that. "She has a lot going on, and in a way, it's all linked."

Lexi nods knowingly. What does she know that we don't? "Shaun's right. Maybe sorting out this," she waves her hands between the guys, "will help Rhys."

"How am I meant to sort out this shit?" Marcus yells, glaring at Lexi. "They fucking betrayed me!" He points a finger toward Shaun and Simon before turning his glare to them. "You fucking betrayed me! You knew how much I fucking cared about her, yet you still fucking went there with her!" His nostrils flare as his rage takes control, and instead of shying away, Lexi steps in front of him, peering up at her childhood friend.

"It's fucked." She nods. "What they did was wrong. It really was. You understand now why Rhys is the way she is, but they don't suffer from the same condition…" she turns to look at Shaun, "well, maybe

Casanova over there might." She turns back to Marcus, "So yeah. They are total douches for doing that to you, but maybe you can hear them out. Maybe it will help you understand where they are coming from."

"Shit, Lexi. You're like a therapist or something." Simon's tone is nothing but serious, and Lexi smiles over her shoulder at him.

"Hopefully, one day, I will be."

The room falls quiet as we each take in the words spoken.

"What condition does Rhys have?" Simon's voice breaks the silence, and all eyes turn to him. "You said before that we don't suffer from the same condition that Rhys does. Is she sick?" Simon frowns. Poor Guy. His head is probably leaping to a hundred different scenarios.

"Ahhh, well. Not exactly. Well… maybe, kinda. I'm not sure how to class it." Lexi stumbles over her words, shaking her head.

"She's a sex addict." I offer, trying to save Lexi.

All eyes swing to me in shock. I guess they really didn't know that about her.

"How the fuck do you know that?" Marcus hisses. "I was under the impression that she didn't share that information with anyone."

"She didn't really share it with me. I guessed." I shrug. "I could see the signs of addiction and put two and two together, and when I called her out on it, she didn't deny it."

"Cherry is a sex addict?" Hastings asks, and Marcus growls.

"Who the fuck is Cherry?"

"Rhys is Cherry." Simon shakes his head, shooting Marcus a duh look.

Fucking hell. This is going to get worse before it gets better.

"Why the fuck do you call her Cherry?" Marcus grits between his teeth.

"Well, there was the Cherry pie, and–."

"We are getting sidetracked." Lexi chimes in, talking over Simon. "Rhys told me about her addiction the other day," she glances back at Marcus.

"So all of you fuckers knew about it?" Marcus shoots us an accusing glare, and I hate that I'm included in it. "I was the only one that didn't know until the other night?"

"Hey, don't yell at me. I thought I just established I didn't know." Hastings holds up his hands in surrender, and Marcus turns his glare to Bossi.

"I had my suspicions, but Kitten never told me."

"Kitten! Are you fucking serious right now?" Marcus bellows, and Simon steps forward, nodding.

"Oh yeah. It's like a pet name he has for her. Just like Cherry-."

"I don't want to fucking hear this!" Marcus screams, fisting his hands in his dark hair, his face turning red like he's about to explode. "What about you?" He turns to Jared. "What the fuck do you call her?"

"Uh… Rhys, obviously, man. I don't have a fucking pet name for her. Don't put me in the same category as these fuckers." Jared points his finger our way. "I have no interest in fucking your girl, dude."

"Not his girl." Bossi must have grown some big motherfucking gonads because he stands from the couch. "She's *our* girl."

"Like fuck she is!" Marcus steps forward, but Lexi steps in the way, causing Marcus to pull up.

"You said she told you about her addiction, so why haven't you figured it out yet?" Shaun hisses as he steps forward. "She cares about you, man. Like really fucking cares, but she can't commit to *just* you. It's fucked up, I know, but it is what it is, and the only way to be with her is by sharing her. At least if we can get her to commit to *us*," Shaun circles his finger in the air, "then she can have some sort of meaningful relationship. I know it isn't normal, but nothing about Rhys is normal. She's… everything, man. All I want is for her to be happy."

I hold my fucking breath, waiting to see how Marcus will respond.

"You think, if we share her, that she'll stop looking for sex elsewhere?" It's a genuine question, Marcus' face softening as he speaks.

Shaun shrugs. "It's worth a try. If it's the only way to be with her, then isn't it worth a shot? If it doesn't work, it doesn't work, but don't you owe it to yourself to try? Would it really be so bad to share her with us?" He gestures to Simon and then to me.

I stiffen, my eyes going wide as Marcus turns his eyes to me, his brows shooting up.

"You fucking too?"

I sigh. "I haven't done anything with her, man."

"But you like her?" His brows lower and tug in close.

"I'm drawn to her, but I'll never betray you, Grady," I admit truthfully, feeling uncomfortable with everyone looking at me.

"So, if I didn't have a problem with it, you'd wanna fuck her too?"

"Jesus fucking christ. There is more to a relationship than fucking! That's the problem with Rhys. She doesn't know that. She thinks everything is about sex. She's never known a relationship that is about sharing your secrets. Your wishes and dreams. About cuddling, holding hands, and spending time together laughing. All she fucking knows is sex, and if you arseholes only want her so you can get your dicks wet, then we are going to have a fucking problem!" By the time I'm finished yelling, my chest is rising and falling rapidly as I struggle with the anger raging inside me. This is something Rhys and I have in common. We both struggle to control our urges. Hers is to have sex. Mine is to punch the fuck out of the nearest object.

"Wow. You fuckers really have done your nuts over this chick." Jared chuckles, and just like that, Marcus grins.

"Fucking looks like it." He admits.

The tension that filled the room only moments ago slowly seeps away, and our shoulders visibly relax.

"Now, doesn't that feel better to have the truth out?" Lexi beams at us as Ayden leaves his post by the door and wraps his arms around her from behind.

We all grin, nodding because she's right. It does feel better to have the truth out.

"In the spirit of being honest and shit," Marcus mutters quietly, his eyes dancing between us. "I'm not sure if I can share Rhys. I don't know if I have it in me to sit back and watch you guys with her... but I'll think about it."

"Good." Lexi smiles. "You shouldn't rule it out, Marcus. Not if you care about her as much as you do. It's worth fighting for."

"Such a romantic," Ayden mutters against Lexi's temple before he presses his lips to the side of her head.

"Can I go now since I have no interest in sleeping with Rhys?" Jared asks, and Lexi glares at him.

"No! Rhys is our friend, and she needs our help. You stay."

Jared rolls his eyes but doesn't move to leave.

"So, does anyone know what's going on with Rhys?" Lexi asks, and I glance over at Shaun. He and Rhys have that sex club thing, and I get the feeling something might have happened last night when they went to that place, but I also know she's got shit happening with her old foster parents.

"Her old foster mum has been harassing her," I say, gaining everyone's attention. "This Julie chick has been calling her and sending her messages, blackmailing Rhys into going to see her old foster dad in prison. She went to see him once. Rhys didn't really divulge what happened, but she seemed pretty on edge about it. Then this lady said there would be consequences if Rhys didn't go back to see her foster dad by Wednesday night. Last night."

"Oh. So maybe she went? Maybe that's why she was so out of sorts today." Lexi frowns, trying to put the pieces together.

"She didn't go to see her foster dad last night." Shaun declares, gaining a murderous glare from Marcus. "She was with me last night."

Marcus snarls and spins away, still struggling to wrap his head around the fact that his mates are seeing the girl he loves.

"Did something happen last night?" Lexi frowns at Shaun, and he shakes his head and shrugs.

He just fucking lied. I don't know how I know, but I do.

"Did her foster mum say what the consequences will be?" Lexi asks, looking back at me, and I shake my head.

"Nope."

"Hmmm." Lexi thinks over everything, looking at the floor.

"I guess all we can do is be there for her, right?" Hastings asks, and we all nod in agreement.

"Yeah. We all need to be there for her, despite our relationship status. Her happiness and safety outweigh how we feel about her or each other." Shaun shoots Marcus a pointed look, and he nods.

It takes a strong man to put aside your differences, especially matters of the heart. Marcus Grady is a better man than the rest of us, and at the end of the day, if Rhys is happy to pick only one guy, Grady is the only one deserving of her heart.

Chapter Five

Rhys

B onnie Mayer's Halloween party is lit! Aussies aren't big at celebrating Halloween like Americans do. Some Aussies recognise it on October 31st, but it's nothing in comparison. Bonnie Mayer and her family are from the United States, so they really know how to throw a frightful party. Their whole house has been transformed from the outside in, and while many in the community drive-by, getting out of their cars to take a photo with the coffin and skeleton on their front lawn, the FP Catholic kids are inside ripping it up.

Bonnie's theme for the night is gore, so anyone who turns up in just a regular costume that doesn't look like it's walked through the set of the Walking Dead gets fake blood thrown at them. Not viciously, but Bonnie is on a mission to ensure everyone is as gory as hell.

I'm feeling a good buzz from the shots Lexi and I had while we were getting ready at her house. She looks freaking amazing! She makes the best Harley Quinn, and with Ayden dressed as the Joker by her side with blood spattered all over them, they look like a deliciously frightful couple.

Tonight, I'm Cleopatra. I'd chosen the look because her sexuality resonates with me. Well, it did before last night. Now, I think I'd feel more comfortable dressed as a nun. I do look pretty hot, though. At least that's what I keep telling myself as I plaster on a fake smile and pretend to own the black fitted, barely covering my arse dress.

It's strapless and has a princess neckline, with a shiny gold belt and some sort of Egyptian looking triangle thing hanging down the front of the skirt. Around my neck is an intricate beaded something or other—I don't know since I'm not an Egyptian—and I have gold wrist cuffs and gold strappy heels. Of course, it's not a Rhys outfit without my black lips. I considered wearing my hair down, but as usual, I didn't want everyone to see it, so I wore the black bob wig that came with the costume. Something I'm regretting with every passing minute, as it's itching the hell out of my scalp.

"Oh, Cleopatra. I do believe your servant men have arrived." Lexi grins at something behind me where we stand in the cobweb riddled living room, so I turn around. My eyes widen when I take in not three but four guys that make my heart do a little flip in my chest.

Shaun, Garrett, Simon, and *Marcus* are here… together, and they are standing before me dressed as pharaoh men. Even Marcus. They are Cleopatra's pharaohs. With bare chests and some ridiculous gold thing that covers their shoulders, and the only real article of clothing they have on is white baggy pants. Oh, and they are all slathered in blood. Obviously, Bonnie's doing.

"Wow. You guys look ridiculous, but in a hot way." I grin, and my eyes dart to Marcus. Is he going to get annoyed that I called them all hot?

"What about me, George? You into Gangsters?" Jared asks, standing next to the others, looking like a gangster that lost the gunfight. I laugh.

"Not really. And I'm pretty sure you're not into Egyptian women either, Crowley." I tease, and he nods, grinning. The poor guy is still hooked on Lexi, even though she's taken. I feel sorry for him. He's such a nice guy.

"Jump in the middle of your pharaoh men, Rhys. I'll take a picture." Lexi nudges my back, urging me forward.

Poking my tongue out at her over my shoulder, I approach the guys, noticing Jared sneaking off into the crowd, obviously feeling out of place.

"Hey, Kitten. You look ravishing." Shaun grins down at me with mischief in his eyes, and I sink into him as he pulls me to his chest before taking my lips in his. It's a quick kiss but hot as hell, and for the first time since last night, I feel Kitty stir.

"You make ridiculous look hot, Bossi." I tease, and he grins.

"Are you ok?" He asks, and I nod before pulling back. I don't want to talk about last night. Like, ever.

Once again, my eyes dart to Marcus. He just witnessed the exchange between Shaun and me, and the tension is noticeable as he tries to avoid my eyes.

Please just share me, Marcus.

"Ravishing is an understatement." Simon's grin is from ear to ear as he nudges Shaun aside and wraps his arms around me. Then he dips me and slaps his lips against mine. For the second time, Kitty stirs, but only a little. Even though it's only the slightest of sensations, I'm fucking thankful because the way I was feeling earlier today scared the shit out of me. I thought my pussy was broken!

When Simon releases me from his onslaught, I lick over my lips, my eyes darting to Marcus again. This time, his eyes are on me, but his breathing is heavy, like he's struggling to control his anger. I don't want to make him angry. I just want him to join us.

"My queen Cleopatra." Garrett takes my hand from Simon's grip and pulls me towards him. He doesn't do the same as Shaun and Simon did, though. Instead, he gets down on one knee and bows his head.

I fucking blush.

What the fuck. Did I really just blush because he held my hand and bowed? His icy-blues dart up to me, looking mischievous, and I realise the smart-arse enjoys tormenting me.

Fucking sexy tease!

"Shall I refer to you as my loyal servant?" I ask Garrett, and a grin tugs at his lips.

"You can refer to me however you like." He's still on his knee, looking through the brown curls that have fallen over his eyes.

Fucking hell, his smouldering looks should be illegal.

I think I just got pregnant!

"How about my *sex* servant?" I tease, knowing I'm pushing his boundaries. So far, he's refused my advances, claiming he'll never do anything to hurt Marcus. Yet, here he is blatantly showing his affection in front of Marcus, even though it could be misconstrued as nothing but playful banter.

"Sexless servant is more suitable." He teases back, grinning broadly.

Fucker.

As he rises off the floor, my eyes dart back to Marcus. This time, he looks a little calmer.

"Come on, you guys! I wanna take a photo." Lexi whines.

Shit. I completely forgot about that.

We move in close together. Garrett and Shaun go down on their knees in front of me while Simon and Marcus stand next to me on either side. As I smile for the picture, warm fingers brush mine. Once, twice. The third time, Marcus' fingers link with mine, and as Lexi wraps up her photography skills, Marcus leans close to my ear.

"I really miss you."

My heart flips. Then races. Then stops.

Fuck, am I about to die? I can't tell if it's a good sensation or not, but I'm helpless not to turn my head, so we're nose to nose, our chests rising and falling in unison as our control falters.

"Marcus." I breathe out in a loud whisper, not able to say anything else because I fucking miss him, too. So much it hurts.

There's a large screen TV hanging on the wall with a compilation of horror movie scenes playing on a loop, but it goes off, and a gory-looking Bonnie comes onto the screen, capturing everyone's attention. It barely captures mine, though. I can't even bring myself to step back from Marcus, and he seems to be having the same problem.

"I don't know what happened to make you so upset today, but I do know that I don't want to be shut off from you, Rhee. Tell me what I have to do to win you back?" Marcus' voice cracks a little as he speaks, so only I can hear. Even though we're surrounded by people trying to cram into the living room to see the TV, it feels like it's just him and me.

"You know what you have to do, Marcus." We get nudged closer together by the growing crowd, and I have to put my hand on his bare chest to steady myself. It's torture, in a good way.

"I need you to say it, Rhee. Tell me what I have to do."

Shit! I've struggled with admitting certain parts of myself to Marcus for some reason. Now, though, he's asking me to say it out loud, and if I don't, we will likely never move forward. Or back. It depends on how he reacts. I have to say it though, and knowing that causes me to shake a little as I prepare to say the words.

"Share me."

There I did it. I said it. And even though I know he was expecting me to say it. I didn't miss the way he flinched a little.

Cheers ring out around the room, and I'm nudged away from Marcus as two drunk idiots jump up and down. It's only then that I pay attention to what is happening. Bonnie is giving out prizes for people's costumes. A drink appears in front of me then, and I look to the side to see Lexi smiling with her hand outstretched. I smile back, taking the Vodka Cruiser from her, and tip it back as I take a drink.

Things go a little crazy after that, and I know my brief chat with Marcus will have to wait until later when we aren't surrounded by hordes of drunk teenagers. After the week I've had, I decide to clear my mind of all the bullshit, including the phone call from Julie earlier, and I dance with Lexi and the guys for a couple of hours.

We have fun. All of us together. No one tries to claim me as theirs. No one tries to steal kisses off me or lure me away for sex. We all just party as friends, enjoying each other's company and sharing laughs.

When my bladder reminds me of its existence, I excuse myself and go in search of a toilet. Everyone is messy as hell. I doubt there will be many year 11 students at school tomorrow. Couples are coming together left, right and centre, and I do a double-take when I see our bloodied gangster, Jared, with his hand up a girl's skirt.

I grin.

Dirty dog.

After finding a toilet and emptying my bladder, I make my way back through the crowd to see everyone watching the large TV screen again. Bonnie must be doing another round of prizes. At least that's what I think until I hear people gasping and Bonnie's dad yelling for someone to switch the TV off.

There, on the large screen, is a man on a bed, stark naked, his pole at full mast, while a girl... a little girl, uses her hands ...

What?

She is naked too. Her skin is creamy. Her dark hair is long and straight...

No.

Moans fill the room, coming from the speakers.

"That's a good girl Patty. Make me feel better."

Patty?

No. It can't be.

Captions pop up on the screen then, and gasps fill the room as partiers read the bold font.

HELLO FOX PINES CATHOLIC STUDENTS.
CAN ANYONE GUESS WHICH OF YOU USED TO BE THIS
LITTLE GIRL?
LOOK CLOSELY.
SHE'S A LITTLE KITTEN AMONGST YOU!

My head swims as I look past the words. The camera pans out, and the man's face comes into view—Brian's face.

Air fails to fill my lungs, and I glance away from the screen momentarily to see Shaun and Garrett swing their gazes to me, where I stand at the back of the room.

This can't be happening. This can't be real.

> *Your mistake is thinking that I won't follow through.*
> *Well, Patty. We'll soon see if I can change your mind*
> *about that.*

No! I clutch at the itchy wig on my head as I start backing away, remembering the phone conversation and text message I got from Julie earlier.

No!

The chime of message alerts ring through the room, and like everyone else, I take my phone out to see what the message is, even though I know it won't be good.

From an unknown number, everyone has received a copy of the video, and in addition is an email address and a screenshot with the words:

> *Who is this good little FP Catholic girl?*
> *$1000 reward to the first person to email through the*
> *correct name.*

Tears fill my eyes as I turn and hightail it out of the party, but not before I take a good look at the picture of the naked little girl with long, dark hair and brown eyes.

My brown eyes.

Chapter Six

Shaun

I hardly believe it, yet I can. I knew my girl had a dark past, and for the life of me, I would never have conjured up this scenario. But as crazy as the whole situation seems, I know without a doubt that the little girl in that video is my girl. *My* Kitten.

"It's her," Garrett mumbles as his eyes watch the back of the room where Rhys bolted from a moment ago.

"Nah, man. We don't know that." I say, even though I fucking know it's her.

Garrett turns his fierce blue eyes to me, his top lip lifting in a snarl. "I fucking know it's her, Bossi."

I shake my head, not caring about anything but getting to Rhys.

"I'm going to find her. Get the others or don't. I don't fucking care." I storm away before I even finish talking, pushing through the crowd as they all look at their phones, replaying the video. The video containing illegal acts against a child. Don't those idiots know they can get charged just by having that sort of video on their phones? Dickheads.

I race out to the front yard, where passers-by are still pulling up to take photos with the ridiculous Halloween display on the front lawn, and I look around frantically, trying to find Rhys.

Where are you, Kitten?

I tug my phone back out and call her number, holding it to my ear while I shuffle anxiously. A moment later, I hear the Paramore song,

Ignorance, start playing nearby, and I dart my head in that direction. That's Kitten's ring tone!

I bolt towards the music, rounding a car parked on the nature strip, only to find that she's not there. Her phone is, but there's no sign of Rhys.

"Rhys!" I bellow into the night, hoping to get an answer, but it never comes. Picking up her phone, I key in her passcode that I memorised yesterday when we were in class, and I check her call log to see if she called anyone before bolting.

Nothing. She didn't make a call.

Fuck!

"Any luck?" Garrett's anxious voice sounds next to me, and I look around to see Simon and Marcus coming up behind him as I shake my head in response.

"What's going on?" Simon asks, no sign of his usual playful tone.

"We need to find Rhys." I hiss, and Simon frowns.

"Where'd she go?" Simon asks, and I hiss again.

"How the fuck do I know?"

"Wanna tell us what the urgency is?" Marcus steps closer, and I dart my head around to see too many ears in our vicinity.

"We need to go somewhere to have a quick chat." Garrett declares, but I stomp my foot like a fucking two-year-old.

"We don't have time for this. We need to find her. Now!" My face feels flushed with panicked anger, and I wish they would stop asking questions and just find her already.

"Hey man, I get that this isn't a good situation, but maybe she just needs to cool down a bit. We will find her soon enough." Garrett tries to reason with me, but I freak the fuck out, bellowing up into the night sky as I fist my hair.

Not able to stay there a moment longer, I storm off down the road, needing distance from the party, ignoring my mates when they call out to me. They don't fucking understand what's going on, and I can't expect them to. They have no idea what happened last night to Kitten, and now *this*. It's all too much.

Something on the ground up ahead under a streetlight gains my attention, and I dash forward, needing to see what it is. There on the road is a black wig. Rhys' black wig.

Feet skid to a stop next to me, and Garrett curses as he bends down to pick up Kitten's Cleopatra hair.

"Is that hers?" Marcus asks, and I nod, unlocking Kitten's phone and searching her contacts for Skipper's number.

It rings twice before his deep voice comes over the line.

"Kitten?"

"Nope. It's Fuckboy. We have a problem." I glance up to see Garrett, Simon and Marcus standing before me, wearing frowns as they listen to me talk on the phone.

"What's happened?" Tyler's menacing tone sends a chill up my spine.

"I'm going to send you something. A video. Once you watch it, you'll need to remove it from your phone, but you need to see it to know what's happened."

"Uh… ok." Tyler mutters, and I pull the phone away from my ear and send the video from Rhys' phone. Then I listen again, waiting quietly until I hear the video playing and then listen for his reaction.

"Fucking hell! What the fuck! Who the fuck sent this? How do you have it? I'm going to kill whoever is responsible for this!" He's a madman.

"So, I guess you know who you're looking at, right? The little girl?" I ask, watching the curious gazes of my mates as they try to put the pieces together. Garrett knows it's Kitten in the video, but the other two haven't caught on yet.

"Yes, I would fucking know those eyes anywhere!" Tyler booms, and I know my mates can hear his words crackle through the speaker.

"That video got sent to all the kids at the Halloween party tonight. I'm pretty sure it has something to do with her old foster parents. The mum has been calling and messaging Rhys, threatening her. She demanded Rhys go to visit her old foster dad in prison, and she went. I don't know what happened when she went there, but I have a feeling she did something she didn't want to do, and this Julie chick won't get off her case. She told her that if she doesn't go back to see the man in prison, that Rhys will regret it. I think this video is the repercussions of her not going back."

I watch Garrett's face turn red as his anger bubbles to the surface, and Simon and Marcus look at each other as if they both realise at the same time that the video was of Rhys. A little girl version of her, anyway.

"Where is Kitten?" Tyler demands, and I flinch as regret fills me. I should never have let Rhys come to this party. Not after what happened at the Feast last night.

"I don't know. She ran off. She dropped her phone and the wig she was wearing. Do you have any idea of where she would go? I'm worried about her after last night."

"What the fuck happened last night?" Garrett booms.

"Am I on speaker?" Tyler hisses.

"No, you're not on speaker," I tell Tyler and then address Garrett in a hushed tone. "I'll fill you in soon."

"Fuck. This is bad. I have no idea where Kitten would go." Tyler sounds distraught. "I'll jump in my car and drive around. Keep her phone with you." Tyler demands, and I agree before hanging up.

"Start fucking talking, Bossi! What happened last night?" The menacing tone is from Marcus this time, and I know I'm about to reveal a big fucking secret, but Kitten needs our help, and I need them to understand the seriousness of what's going on.

"Right, well, let me put this in the simplest way I can." I give Marcus and Simon pointed looks because they are the ones who know nothing about what I'm about to reveal. "Rhys has been going to a sex club for a while now, and I started going, which is how we hooked up." I give Marcus an apologetic look, but his eyes narrow as his anger rises. "Anyway, Kitten... I mean Rhys. Kitten is her name at the sex club. Anyway, she did something that was against the rules, and last night she was punished for it." I cringe before I can even get the words out. "She was basically humiliated in front of everyone at the sex club and tortured through pleasure."

"What? Tortured through pleasure? I don't understand." Marcus asks, and Simon asks his own question.

"You both go to a sex club?"

"Yes, Hastings. Focus. Rhys was punished at the sex club. And to answer your question, Grady, extreme pleasure stimulation is a form of torture. She was in a bad way by the time I got to her, and got her out of there. It was non-consensual, so even though her body will heal, she was effectively assaulted last night." I suck in a breath and shake my head, looking down at my feet for a moment as I try to form more words. "They fucking pissed on her!"

An explosion of pain pelts my face, causing me to stumble backwards, and I fall on my arse. The harsh asphalt of the road isn't kind at catching my fall, and my palms graze while the white pants of this ridiculous costume audibly rips.

"You fucking prick! You should have stopped that from happening! How could you stand by and watch that be done to my girl!" Marcus screams, his fists flying towards me again, but they don't make contact this time. Garrett's thick arms wrap around his waist, holding him at bay.

"I did try to stop it! They fucking kicked me out for interfering, but I broke back in. I fucking tried!" I scream back, ignoring the porch lights that flick on at the houses surrounding us. "This isn't helping, man! We need to find her. Don't you understand? After what happened last night and what happened tonight, I'm scared that she'll do something stupid."

"That little girl was her in the video?" Simon asks quietly, still trying to comprehend what happened, and we all fall still as I nod.

"She told me she was eleven years old when she lost her virginity." Garrett rasps, not able to hide his emotions, "She said she didn't even know what virginity was when it happened."

"Eleven?" Simon asks, and Garrett nods.

"She's going to hurt herself," Marcus whispers.

That's what I'm scared of. I can't say those words out loud, though. I'm not willing to admit that my Kitten has been pushed that far, but I know she has. She's been hurting for a while now, and this is fucking as close to rock bottom as you can get, so I need to find her before it's too late.

"Who were you talking to on the phone just now?" Marcus asks, and I feel like shit for revealing all of this stuff that he has no idea about.

"It was the other guy Rhys has a thing with. His name is Tyler, and that's all I can tell you." I stand up off the road and dust off my arse.

"Why?" Simon asks, and I shrug.

"He's an older guy, and she's only seventeen. That's why."

"Shit," Marcus mutters, a look of defeat flitting across his face.

"We need to figure out where Rhys would go. Does she have a special place she likes to go to be alone?" Garrett asks, and both Marcus and I shake our heads. "Think damn it! Where would she want to go if she wanted to end things?" Garrett hisses, and we all flinch at his words.

It takes me a moment, but a thought crosses my mind, and my eyes widen.

"My place!" I blurt. "She told me this morning that she wants to die looking up at the sky in my grapevines when it's her time." I move to take my phone out, but before I can even make a call, it starts ringing, and Derek's name flashes across the screen.

"Is she there?" I ask, not even saying hello when I answer the call.

"Yeah, your girl is here. Well, when I say here, I mean she is laying out in the grove. What the fuck is she doing?"

"Thank fuck! Derek, man, you gotta go sit with her until I can get there." I plead.

"Why?" He sounds like I just asked him to pry his own eyes out.

"She's had a bad day. Like one of those days that might lead her to make a bad decision that can't be reversed. Do you understand what I'm saying?"

"Shit. Yeah, I get it. I'll go out there but hurry up. I'm no good at that talking stuff." Derek complains, and I nod, even though I know he can't see me.

"Thanks. We'll be there soon."

CHAPTER SEVEN

RHYS

I wonder if aliens have feelings like us weak humans do? I wonder if they commit depraved acts on each other and reap pleasure from it? I wonder if they ever get so sick of living the alien life that they just want to quit their existence? They probably don't have feelings. Otherwise, they'd be all depresso about their shitty green skin. Surely.

The night sky is crisp and clear, with not a cloud in sight. The stars are bright, teasing me with their twinkling and the possibility of alien life somewhere out there beyond this shitty world I live in. When you think about it, we are all just tiny organisms in a gigantic universe. Does my existence even matter? If I were never born, the world would still be the same place. I guess the only difference is that all the crap I have endured at the hands of other people would have happened to someone else.

That doesn't seem very fair. No one deserves this shit. Well, except for those who dish out the bad stuff. I hope they all suffer an anaesthetic free castration. It's a pity I won't be around to witness that joyful event. I'm sure I'd get great satisfaction from watching it.

"Did you know stars don't actually twinkle?"

I pop my head up off the dewy grass to see Derek cast in shadows as he looks up at the sky. How'd he know I was here?

"They don't?" I ask, confused. "They sure look like they do." I lay my head back down on the grass and gaze back up at the stars.

"Nah. It's the earth's atmosphere that makes them appear to twinkle. Kinda doesn't seem as magical when you know that." Derek looks down at me, and I frown.

"Well, now that you put it that way."

He chuckles. "Sorry. We can pretend they twinkle if you like?"

I nod. "Yes, I think I'd like that."

"Can I sit?" He asks, and I shrug even though he probably can't see the action in the dark.

"It's your property. You can do what you want."

"Huh! I wish." He grumbles, and I pop my head back up to look at him again as he sits down near my feet.

"You wish you could frolic in these fields with another guy and not disappoint your dad?" Poor Derek is a closet gay. Apparently, his dad is a homophobe.

"Yeah, something like that." He responds, sounding as down as I feel.

"I'm sorry. I really hope you can be *you* one day without worrying."

"You're good people, Rhys. My little brother is lucky." At Derek's words, I let my head flop back on the grass again.

"More like *I'm* lucky. He's the good people. I'm just… trash."

"Nah, you don't smell like trash, so you can't be trash." Derek chuckles, and a small smile tugs at my lips.

"Shaun knows I'm here, doesn't he?"

"Yep. He's on his way." Derek's words induce my eyes to start leaking.

"He's too good to me," I whisper as a sob escapes.

"I'm pretty sure he's in love with you."

"I'm pretty sure I'm in love with him, too. That's what makes this so hard." I admit.

"What's so hard?" Derek asks.

"Making the decision whether to stay or go." I sob again.

"Stay Kitten. Always." Shaun's words cut through the silence of the night, and another sob escapes as the stars blur before my eyes.

"Cass," I whisper, and the next moment a warm body lays next to me, an arm slips under my back, and I'm drawn tight against Shaun's bare chest.

An emotional storm erupts from me as my pained sobs float up into the night sky. Another warm body moves behind me, and more arms wrap around me, even as someone starts stroking my flyaways off my forehead and someone else starts rubbing my feet. The dam wall is broken, the river is flowing, and with it, my pain. It's raw, unkempt and devastating.

I'm nothing more than a damaged soul fighting to find a path back to a place of happiness and contentment. It's overwhelming and feels like an impossible feat as memories swarm in of a little girl named Patrice who just wanted someone to love her, care for her, and want her. She just wanted to belong. To feel normal, but instead, she got the opposite. No love. No care. No want unless there was an exchange or transaction. There were conditions to all aspects of her life, and she would never be or feel normal. She would never belong.

New memories flood in then, batting away the sick and twisted past of a little girl that didn't know any better, and in their place is something she didn't realise she had until this very moment.

Love.

Cynthia and Will love me. It's unconditional. It has to be. Otherwise, why would they keep me around all this time after the shit I've put them through? Charlotte loves me in her aggravated way. I know the twins, Connor and Archie, adore me. They *are* my family. We have a nice home together. It's always warm. There's always food on the table. My clothes are always clean. Hell, my mum even lets me have my promiscuous freedom, which is unheard of for most seventeen-year-olds.

I belong to *them*. With *them*. No matter what… right?

Then there are these guys, here with me now, offering me support, even after I've kept them in the dark about so many things. They feel like home to me, which I know is strange because it's not normal to care about more than one guy. But I'll never be normal in the typical way. I can be Rhys George normal, though. And Rhys George is a fighter. She's a carefree, fun-loving, live each moment like it's your last kind of person.

She's just a little off-kilter at the moment. That's all.

She can get through this.

I can get through this.

"Kitten. You've gone quiet." Shaun's voice is low. "It's unnerving."

A grin tugs at my lips as I try to blink away the remnants of my tears.

"Don't interrupt my thought process while I'm the filling in a man sandwich."

A round of chuckles meets my ears, and my grin broadens. My guys are here with me.

"My bad. Please continue." Shaun's tone tells me he's smirking, and I wish it weren't so dark out here. I love seeing him smile.

"Who's here?" I ask, not wanting to move and interrupt the connection I'm wrapped in.

"Well, obviously, I am." Shaun chuckles.

"I'm here too." Garrett's voice comes from above my head, and I feel his fingers stroke over my forehead.

"I'm here, Cherry." Simon declares down by my feet, using the name he's been calling me after our cherry pie sexcapades.

"And I'm here, Rhee," Marcus whispers in my ear from behind me.

Another sob escapes when I realise he is the one holding me tight from behind. I've fucking missed being in his arms.

"Don't cry. We've got you. Nothing else matters." Marcus says louder, and Simon chuckles.

"So close, no matter how far." Simon sings.

"Couldn't be much more from the heart." Garrett chimes in.

"Forever trusting who we are," Marcus adds.

"What are you dickheads singing?" Shaun huffs, and I giggle.

"Come on, Cass. What's the next line?" I peer up at his confused expression.

"How the fuck do I know?"

All the guys laugh then while I sing.

"Nothing else matters."

"What song is that?" Shaun asks, and Marcus answers.

"Nothing Else Matters by Metallica."

"As if I would know that. I don't listen to that heavy shit." Shaun protests. He prefers pop music.

The sound of my phone ringing quietens us, and Shaun pulls my phone from the band in his white pants, looking at the screen before offering it to me.

"It's for you, Kitten. It's Skipper."

My brows shoot up, and I hesitate for a moment before I hit accept.

"Hello."

"Kitten! Thank fuck! Are you ok? Where are you?"

"Hey, Ty. I'm ok now. I had a freak out there for a bit, but I'm ok."

"Fucking hell, I was so worried. Shit!" Tyler sounds distraught, and I feel guilty for worrying him so much. I didn't mean to. "I'm so sorry about what happened tonight. I wish you had told me what has been going on. It all makes so much sense now."

"Sorry. I guess I'm not used to people caring." I'm not sure what he means by *what has been going on*, but I guess Shaun may have filled him in.

Arms squeeze me tighter from behind and in front, and I relax into their hold, needing the support.

"I fucking care, Kitten." Tyler rasps. "A hell of a lot. You mean so much. Please don't ever forget that."

A tear pops free again, and I let it roll down over my nose, not wanting to break the hold the guys have on me.

"I'll try not to, but you'll probably need to remind me. Daily. With your tongue." Even as I say the words, it feels kind of wrong, but I push the thought away and ignore the round of groans from the guys as they listen to my conversation.

Tyler chuckles. "It's a deal. I'm coming to see you soon, beautiful. Put Fuckboy on the phone for me?"

"Ah, yeah. Ok."

I hand Shaun the phone, and he presses it to his ear, talking quietly and then telling Tyler his address. There's a bit more talking, mainly from Tyler, so I can't hear what he's saying, but then Shaun ends the call and smiles at me.

"He's got it bad for you, Kitten."

I can't hide my satisfied grin. I think I've got it bad for my teacher too.

We lay in our huddle for a little while longer before we unravel ourselves and walk up to the shed. It looks old and rusty on the outside, but on the inside, it's decked out as a man-shed with a table tennis table, a small bar, a wide-screen TV on the wall, and some mismatching couches. Shaun disappears for a few minutes but returns with clothes for everyone, and I end up in one of his Element t-shirts, thrown over my Cleopatra costume.

Now that we are no longer in the dark of the night, I'm finding it hard to look the guys in the eye. Shame is seeping in, ruling me at my show of vulnerability. I feel raw and exposed, knowing the guys have figured out the little girl in the video was me. How can they still care for me after knowing I was the star of that disgusting show? That little girl didn't look like she was scared or that she was being forced. She looked like she loved it, and the sick thing is that she did. She thought that's what daddies and daughters did together. She thought that's how love was shown, and you want to know what the real fucked up part is? I still think it's the only way you show someone you love them.

I sneak a glance at Garrett, my big brooder and the one who is determined to leave sex out of the equation. He wants to show me how things can be without getting naked, like as a friend. I want to believe there's a possibility of a friendship like that, but the thing is, I see him as more than a friend, and I know he feels the same way.

My eyes lock on his, and I realise he's been watching me this whole time, his icy-blue gaze filled with pain and pity. I hate to see both there. I like it when he gives me glimpses of his smile and the lighter side of him. He doesn't offer those sides to many people, so knowing he sometimes shows it to me makes me feel special.

Dumb right?

As Simon and Marcus dust off the table tennis table, Garrett approaches me, where I linger by the door. With each step closer, my heart rate picks up. It's bizarre to me that these guys affect me so much. I'm normally the over-confident life of the party chick, yet right now, I feel like a timid fucking mouse.

I need my mojo back.

I crane my neck back as the towering height of Garrett dwarfs me, and my breath seizes for a moment as he reaches up and cups my face with one of his large palms.

"You scared me." His deep voice is low and raspy, filled with emotion I wasn't expecting.

"Why?" I lean into his palm and close my eyes for a beat, enjoying the sear of his skin against mine.

"I thought you might take *you* away from me... for good."

I understand what he is getting at. I wish I could lie and tell him there wasn't a chance that I even considered it, but he deserves my honesty.

"I thought about it," I admit past the lump forming in my throat, which just gets bigger when I see Garrett's eyes glass over.

"Rhys." His nostrils flare as his other hand cups the other side of my face, trapping me in his hold in a loving way. A way I'm sure friends don't do. "Don't fucking leave me here in a world without you in it."

Fuck. My heart slices open, and with it, tears begin to fall. I can't remember ever crying this much.

"I... don't want... to leave... you." I sob, not able to contain my girly emotions.

"Promise me you will stay. Always." He demands low, his chest rising and falling like he's struggling to keep himself in check.

"I promise." I give him the words he wants, knowing too well that promises are often broken. Even so, I mean them in this moment.

"I want you to remember this phrase, Rhys." His eyes pierce mine like he's looking into my soul. "This too shall pass."

My breath hitches as I let his words sink in.

"Good or bad. Nothing lasts. You have to make the most of the good moments before they pass by. And you can be assured that the bad will pass by too. You just have to keep fighting. Promise you will always keep fighting."

I nod as he leans forward, pressing his forehead against mine, looking at me past the fan of his dark lashes.

"Repeat the phrase to me." His gaze burns into mine. "This too shall pass."

"This... too shall... pass." My breathing shudders as raw emotion grips me.

"Again. This too shall pass." He demands, so I suck in some air, hoping my lungs will work properly.

"This too shall pass." It's a loud whisper, but this time, it's confident as I repeat the words to him.

Garrett sighs, his shoulders relaxing as he lifts his head away from mine. We are so close. Close enough to kiss, yet he doesn't even try. I guess the current situation doesn't really scream romantic or sensual, but even so, the scent of Garrett mingled with Shaun's hoodie he's wearing wraps around me, and my mind instantly wishes I was naked and in a Shaun and Garrett sandwich right now.

Of course, as a big Fuck You, Kitty starts to rouse, but pain shoots through my core and images of Master Hill's face, smug with satisfaction as he looms over me, sends ice through my veins.

"What's wrong?" Garrett frowns, noticing me stiffen.

"I-I..." Shit. I can't tell him. I shake my head and try to pull away as my heart races for the wrong reason.

"Kitten?" Shaun asks, stepping up beside us and my frantic eyes dart to him for help, even though he has no idea what's going on in my head. "Talk to us."

I shake my head again, opening my mouth to answer, but snap it shut again.

"Are you in pain or something?" Shaun asks as Garrett drops his hands from my face and frowns as I take a step back.

I shake my head, but then nod, but then shake it again and squeeze my eyes tight.

"What did you do to her?" Marcus hisses.

"He looked like he was going to kiss her," Simon adds unhelpfully. "I didn't realise Bossi had extended his sharing invitation to you too, Cole."

"Shut up, dickhead! Can't you see our girl is in pain?" Shaun hisses, and that's when I notice a new bruise on the side of his face.

"What happened to your face?"

Shaun snaps his attention back to me, and when he realises I'm talking to him, his fingers reach up and touch the bruise.

"Bossi fell into Grady's fist again." Simon offers, earning himself glares from the other three guys.

"You're really starting to piss me off." Garrett hisses at Simon, who just shrugs, not really caring.

I glance between Marcus and Shaun. "You hit him again?" I ask Marcus, and he nods.

"The arsehole deserved it." Marcus doesn't sound the least bit sorry.

"Why?" I frown, and he shoots an angry glare at Shaun.

"He told us what happened last night at that fucking sex club thing you go to. He got reacquainted with my fist because he didn't protect you!"

"What!" I dart my panicked eyes to Shaun. "You told them? How could you do that?"

"Hey." He frowns, stepping forward. "They needed to know Kitten. They didn't understand why I was so frantic to find you. They needed to know what those sick fuckers did to you last night, and they needed to know that it was you in the video tonight."

I can't breathe. My lungs have officially failed me. I'm going to fucking die!

I fall to my knees and try to gasp for air, but it won't come. I can't hear anything but the rush of blood, and as I blink, my vision blurs and darkens.

I'm going to die!

Isn't that what you wanted earlier, Rhys?

To leave this shitty world?

I can feel my body being moved, but I can't make any sense of anything. Then I feel something on my neck. Then ear. Then arm. Then lips. Like a freight train slamming into a snowbank, my lungs kick in, and I gasp, sucking in the much-needed oxygen.

"That's it, Kitten. Just breathe." Shaun's voice sounds distant. Like he's talking to me through a thick pane of glass.

"You're ok, Rhee. You'll be ok." Marcus' voice registers next.

"Come back to me, beautiful." Garrett's voice is next to penetrate my barrier, sounding louder than the others.

"Simon says, breathe."

A giggle bubbles up my throat as I hear Simon's words, and my vision begins to clear, the rustic surrounds of the man-cave coming back into focus, and with it, four of the guys that have stolen my heart.

"Dude! Did you just play Simon Says while our girl was having a panic attack?" Shaun asks, and Simon nods proudly.

A giggle bursts free again, and I slap my hand over my mouth as I peer up at the guys who are on their knees on the dirty concrete floor with me.

"You are one weird motherfucker." Garrett shakes his head at Simon.

"Maybe, but our girl likes my kind of weird. Don't you, Cherry?"

"I really do." I smile, and Simon beams.

"Kitten." Shaun's voice turns serious again, and I sigh, dropping my chin to my chest in defeat. "Please understand that I had to tell them. They care about you, too. They want to keep you safe as much as I do."

"I didn't want anyone to know any of it," I whisper, but it's loud enough for them to hear.

"Why?" Garrett shifts closer to me and takes my hand in his. I'm helpless not to look up into those blue eyes of his. It hasn't escaped me that he called me beautiful before.

"I'm vile. Disgusting. If you guys found out the whole truth, then you wouldn't be interested in me anymore."

"Why would you say that? We are *here*, Kitten. We aren't going anywhere." Shaun takes my other hand, and my eyes dart to Marcus, who is looking perplexed.

"You realise what you saw on that video, right?" I nearly choke as I ask that question.

"Yeah, a paedophile!" Simon growls, and I flinch. They didn't notice the little girl enjoying herself. That's ok. Maybe it's better if they don't know that part?

"You know what? I don't want to talk about it. Any of it. It's all in the past." I tug my hands free from Garrett and Shaun and stand up, dusting myself off. "Do you have any weed, Bossi?"

"Ah-. No." He darts a confused expression to his mates before standing, and they follow suit.

"Booze?" I lean to the side, looking across the room at the small bar, hoping to spot something that can dull my turmoil.

"Beer. That's about it." Shaun offers, and I screw my face up.

"I guess beer will have to do, then. Hit me with a beer, please." I smile and flutter my lashes at Shaun, ignoring the confused expressions of the other three.

Yeah, I get it. I was falling apart only minutes ago, and now I want to pretend shit didn't happen. It's a coping mechanism. Probably not a healthy one, but it's all I have right now.

"Ah-. Sure." Shaun frowns before turning to the others. "You guys want one too?"

They all nod, and Shaun wanders off towards the rustic bar made of old corrugated iron.

"Wanna play?" Simon asks me, holding up a table tennis bat, and I shake my head, moving to sit on a rickety barstool close by.

The guys settle in to have a few rounds of table tennis, trying to lighten the mood, their eyes darting to me every few minutes to check that I haven't disappeared. I usually enjoy being watched, but I prefer to be naked and riding someone or something when I have eyes on me. I feel too exposed right now. Not so much so that I want to leave. The thought of not being around these guys seems terrifying right now, but they know so much more about me than I ever anticipated anyone knowing. I'm just waiting for the moment they realise they don't want a bar of the Rhys George mint anymore.

Surprisingly, I relax into the atmosphere the guys create, and even though my entire world has been turned upside down, the fun banter we all have is comforting. I'm on my second beer when I notice Shaun speaking quietly with the others before approaching me and taking my hand, leading me out of the shed.

"What are we doing?" I'm nervous all of a sudden. Is he leading me away for some sexy time? And if he is, why the fuck does that thought make me nervous? Rhys George doesn't get nervous about sex. Ever.

"I'm walking you up to the front gate. There's someone here to see you."

"There is?" I'm confused, but I turn my gaze up ahead when Shaun gestures that way, and I see a shadowed figure in the distance.

"Tyler wanted to see you in person to make sure you were ok."

I remember now. He said he was going to come and see me, but I didn't know how he was going to do that since the other guys are here too, and they don't know who he really is. Nervously, I look back over my shoulder in the dark, checking to see if Garrett, Marcus or Simon are anywhere to be seen.

"Don't worry, Kitten. The guys know they have to stay in the shed. You run along and see your man." Shaun pats my arse, and I grin before lunging at him and kissing him hard.

He kisses me back fiercely and then chuckles as he peels himself back, breaking our connection. I miss his lips instantly. Why was I nervous about having sex with him?

"Thank you, Cass," I whisper, doing an excited jump before running into the dark towards the large, towering shadow.

As I get closer, Tyler strides toward me, and a few moments later, I leap into his arms, wrapping my legs around his waist as our lips collide. Our kiss is fevered and mingled with more pesky tears as they escape my treacherous eyes. The few times Tyler and I have kissed has never been like *this*. There's so much feeling and emotion in the kiss. It's utterly intoxicating.

"Kitten." Tyler rasps as he breaks our lips apart, pulling back to see what little he can in the dark night.

"Ty," I whisper, seeing the shadow of a grin spread across his face.

"I like it when you call me Ty." He rasps again.

"You do?" I smile and bite my lip, a little embarrassed for some reason.

"Fuck yes. Say it again."

"Ty." I breathe out, and he moans.

"I want to turn around with you in my arms, throw you in my car and take you to my bed for the rest of eternity."

"Fuck. I want that too." I admit, and he growls, biting at my lower lip before kissing me hard. But do I want that? To be in his bed where he can do anything to me?

What the fuck is wrong with me? Of course, I do. It's Tyler. Skipper. Daddy! He would *never* hurt me.

Our kiss is long and heated and speaks more than words ever can. It's a reminder to me that Ty and I are more than fuck buddies. Much like Shaun and me. Hell, to be honest, it's much like Simon, too. I just hope I can include Marcus and Garrett in that one day.

"I should go, Kitten."

"Noooo," I whine, and he chuckles.

"I have to. I can't risk getting caught. I'd die if I were forced to stay away from you."

"I'd die too," I admit and nip at his lips.

"A lot has happened. I want you to seriously consider speaking with your mum about the video. She loves you, Kitten. She will help."

I can't bear the thought of revealing the video to Cynthia. I know I probably should because it's clear that Julie wasn't bluffing. She could do worse, like reveal to everyone that *I'm* the little girl in the video if I don't bend to her will.

"I'll think about it."

Tyler smiles and takes my lips again, and I melt, tugging him close even though there's no room left between our bodies.

"Kitten." He draws back. "Stay safe, please. If things get too much, reach out to me. Don't go running off on your own."

I nod, and he kisses me once again. It's like he can't get enough of my lips, and I'll admit, I can't seem to get enough of his. Then he releases me, and my legs drop to the ground.

The loss of his body is instantly felt—the need to jump back into his arms almost overpowering. I know I'm being greedy, wanting him and the other guys too, but I refuse to fight it anymore.

I am Rhys George, and I'm determined to have my reverse harem!

Chapter Eight

Rhys

It's been two hours, and staring at Big Jim, Little Jim, and Peter Rabbit hasn't made Kitty stir once. I pick up Big Jim since he's my favourite, and I glide my tongue up the long shaft and circle it around the wide head. Still, my vag stays asleep.

Fuck!

My coochie is broken!

It's Friday, and I've taken a sick day, which is fucking warranted since I can't get my Kitty to play. I woke up realising that it had been over twenty-four hours since I came, which is fucking unheard of in Rhystown, so I figured I should do the deed… yet I can't get my lady boner.

I've tried soft porn, hard porn, lesbian porn, gay porn, animal porn—hey, don't judge—I even jumped on a live cam, and still, there's nothing going on down south. I'm officially damaged goods.

My phone starts ringing, and I see it's a SnapChat video call from Shaun. I answer it quickly and wait until his smiling face comes onto my screen before I speak.

"Bossi, my vagina won't work."

Instantly his eyes go wide, and his smile drops as he darts his head, looking around him before whispering something to someone next to him. There's some sort of commotion, and when he focuses on me again, a stupid grin is tugging at those full lips of his.

"Well, hello to you too, Kitten. Perhaps wait to make sure there are no eavesdroppers around before saying something like that out loud."

Chuckles come through the phone, and I realise Shaun isn't alone.

"Who's with you?"

"Now that we have cleared the gym out, it's just me, Gaz, and Simon."

I lean closer to my phone as if that will help me see who's with him, and Garrett and Simon's heads squeeze in close to Shaun's. My smile is instant, loving the sight of them as they look back at me.

"Hey, guys. Miss me?"

"You know we do, Cherry." Simon grins.

"Why is your vagina broken?" Shaun asks, and Simon cringes.

"Do we have to call it that?"

"It is the technical term for it, Hastings." Garrett rolls his eyes, but Simon shrugs.

"There are so many prettier names for it, though."

"Like what? Flower?" Shaun teases, and I screw my nose up.

"Let's get one thing straight! My pussy is no fucking flower. She's a fucking Queen. You can refer to her as Queen, or Kitty, like I do." I smile sweetly, and they all grin back at me.

"Queen Kitty, more like it." Simon wags his brows. "Don't you think, guys?"

"Fuck yes." Shaun nods.

"I wouldn't know." Garrett shrugs. And wait... Is that disappointment I see cross his face? Hmmm. It seems like my big guy is finding it harder to fight his attraction to me. Something I'll definitely need to take advantage of next time we are alone together.

"That sounds like a *you* problem. Maybe take your head out of your arse, and you might finally find happiness." Shaun rolls his eyes at his friend.

"Gee, I'm sorry for not wanting to betray my mate." Garrett hisses back in anger, looking like he's almost ready to headbutt Shaun.

"You could talk to Marcus about it. He seems to be dealing with me and Bossi better now." Simon suggests, and Garrett growls. Like actually growls like he's a fucking bear or something.

"You know what? What George and I do is none of your business, and not everything is about sex, you know. Ever heard of being friends with someone?" Garrett's anger is rising, and Shaun shifts uncomfortably in between them.

"Guys!" I call and smile when I regain their attention. "Can we focus on my Kitty, please? She's broken, and I don't know how to fix her."

Shaun's face morphs into a soft smirk. "Explain why you think Kitty is broken?"

"Well, I haven't wanted to fuck… anything."

"Anything?" Shaun frowns, and I nod.

"Anything." I reach down and grab Big Jim, holding him up so they can see him. "Big Jim hasn't even caused a spark."

"Fucking hell, Kitten. That thing is monstrous." Shaun's eyes practically bulge out of his head, and Simon's mouth drops open to form an O.

"Cherry, how are we meant to compete with that?"

"Speak for yourself, Hastings. There's no competition for me."

"Garrett Cole!" My mouth drops open this time as Shaun chuckles. "Are you telling me your dick can match Big Jim?"

"Baby, my cock outdoes Big Jim."

Kitty stirs.

"Oh my god!" I quickly glance down at my panty-clad lap.

"What?" Simon asks in concern.

I glance back up to the screen, honing in on Garrett. "Cole. Tell me more about your giant dick."

"It's not giant!" Simon protests.

"It's fucking giant enough!" Shaun disagrees, and Simon glares at Garrett.

"I mean, you're hung like a horse, man, but does it *really* turn into a giant dick when you're hard? I don't think so." Simon's face reddens as he gets more frustrated with hearing about Garrett's dick.

Kitty starts to purr.

"I've fucking seen it hard, and it's worthy of being called giant." Shaun nods slowly in an exaggerated way. Meanwhile, Garrett is watching me, looking fucking smug. How dare he be a smug prick and dangle this treat in front of me, knowing he has no intention of giving me a taste.

Fucker!

"When have you seen his dick hard?" Simon hisses, and I raise my brows as Kitty starts circling.

"Yeah, Bossi. When have you seen Garrett's dick hard? Tell me *all* about it."

Shaun smirks. "I walked in on him when he was showering at your place one time, Hastings. He was stroking that monster *real* good. Had both hands wrapped around it, his eyes watching his hands work while he thrust like a fucking animal."

I moan, and all eyes fall on me.

"You ok there, Kitten?" Shaun asks, and I nod, my lips parting as I move my hand between my legs.

"Yes." I pant.

"Fuck." Garrett hisses. "Kitty's not so broken now, is she?"

I shake my head. "No. Keep talking. Tell me more."

"Fuck, my dick just got hard," Simon admits, and Shaun glares at him.

"Keep your dick away from me."

"Oh, come on, Cass. I bet you would like to slip a dick between your lips." I breathe out as I circle over my panties, right where it feels oh so good.

"Fuck Kitten, you don't play fair." Shaun licks his lips like he's picturing a big hard dick ready to slide in past his lips.

I close my eyes briefly, and an image fills my head of Simon, easing his cock into Shaun's mouth while Garrett strokes his monster cock with both of his hands. I moan again as Kitty begins to gush.

"Fuck." Garrett hisses. "I'm outta here." He stands and walks off, and I have to be honest, I'm extremely fucking disappointed about that.

Garrett Cole. You can run, but you can't hide from me forever!

"You do realise that if we don't come in our jocks like fucking twelve-year-old's, we are gonna need to rub one out in the bathroom before lunch finishes?" Shaun mutters, and I nod.

"Just jack each other off. It will be more enjoyable." I plead, rubbing over the fabric with fast friction.

"Fuck, that's it. I'm finishing this call in the toilets." Shaun starts moving, and Simon protests behind him as he rushes off. Everything goes blurry as Shaun walks or runs. I'd say the latter, given the way the camera jerks around.

"Hurry!" I beg. "I'm nearly there."

I hear the telltale sound of the bathroom door squeaking open, followed by murmurs and shuffling feet before Shaun growls a protest.

"Hey, get your own fucking stall!"

"There are only two, and this one's the biggest. Plus, you have the phone. I want to see Cherry when I come." Simon ignores Shaun and takes the phone, sitting it on a ledge to face the inside of the oversized stall.

"This is so hot," I say before biting down on my lower lip.

"You're so hot, Kitten. Look what you do to us." Shaun's straining cock comes into view, and I almost come.

"Show me yours, Simon," I ask, and a moment later, his hard dick comes into view next to Shaun's.

"How much can I pay you to take Simon's dick in your mouth, Cass?" I giggle, knowing Shaun's refusal is coming.

"You don't have enough money, Kitten." Shaun moans then, probably thinking about giving in to my request. Fuck, that would be so hot to witness.

I see their hands moving up and down their shafts, so I take a moment and prop my phone up in front of me, and then wriggle around to slide my panties free then I sit in place, spread my legs wide in front of my phone, and revel in their moans as they get a close-up view of my bare pussy.

I slide my fingers down over my needy clit, happy she has reawakened, and start circling just the way I like. As I work her, I hear the almost slapping sound of cocks being wanked, and it sends a rush of moisture between my legs.

"Cass, look at Simon's cock. Do you like watching him?"

"Fuck Kitten. I'm not fucking gay." His voice is strained as he pumps his dick.

"You don't have to be gay to enjoy some dick, Bossi. Just like I'm not into girls, yet I love to eat a good pussy."

"Fuck, I'm going to come!" Simon hisses, and a moment later, I see the white ropes pulsing from his dick. The moment I see one of those ropes land on Shaun's cock, I explode, an intense orgasm hitting me hard and long, while Bossi explodes, too.

My O is intense. So intense that it turns painful. I stiffen, feeling the familiar pain deep inside. It's the same pain I felt the other night at the Feast when I was taught a lesson.

"Shit. There's cum on my phone." Shaun whines, and Simon chuckles.

"Whose cum is it?" I ask, trying to hide my pain as I speak.

"That's the problem. I don't fucking know." Shaun complains as he tucks his cock back into his pants.

"Gee Cherry. Kitty looks pretty happy now."

From where I have my phone sitting, I can see Simon's face come into view, moving up close to the screen to get a good look between my legs, so I slide my fingers through my folds to show him how wet I am, even though Kitty is hurting inside.

"Fuck, I want to taste that." Simon moans right before Shaun nudges him out of the way.

"Get in line. That pussy is mine."

"Hurry up, idiots." Garrett's voice comes from somewhere beyond their cubicle, and the next moment, Simon pulls the door open and grabs Garrett, tugging him inside with them.

Before Garrett gets a look at my happy Kitty, I pick the phone up, so only my face is showing again. I don't know why I do that. I normally wouldn't care, but with Garrett, things are different. I know he's fighting his attraction to me. And weirdly enough, I don't want to shove my Kitty down his throat. He hasn't seen my most vulnerable flesh. Strangely, I'd like to keep it that way. For a little while, at least. When he does see it, I want it to be because he's truly happy to share that intimacy with me.

"You two are really gay. You know that?" Garrett teases, but surprisingly, Shaun and Simon don't seem to care.

"Says the guy that creeped in to listen to us."

As Simon retorts, the squeak of the bathroom door sounds again, and the guys go still, right before a knock taps at the stall door. The three guys look around at each other with wide eyes before Simon moves to unlatch the door again.

"Oh-Uh-Hi, Sir." He says and steps back as someone on the other side of the stall door eases it open. Shaun's phone is still sitting on the ledge, so I feel like I'm in the stall with them when familiar blue eyes take in the scene.

"You boys wanna tell me what's going on in here?"

They all stay silent, so I bite back a laugh and speak for them because, why the fuck not?

"Hi, Mr Foster. We were just having a group… discussion."

I bite my lower lip for good measure, and even through this shitty video connection, I see Tyler's eyes darken.

"Whose phone is that?" Mr Foster asks, brows raised.

"Mine," Shaun admits, not sounding too much like he cares about getting sprung for obvious reasons that Garrett and Simon don't know about.

"Of course it is." Tyler nods knowingly. "Right then, you two get out of here. I need to speak to Mr Bossier alone about phone use and privacy." As Garrett and Simon shuffle past Mr Foster and leave the bathroom, Tyler adds, "Leave the call on Mr Bossier. Let's head to my office for a chat."

As Shaun follows his PE teacher, he holds the phone up to pull faces at me every now and then, and my chest feels warm, and my heart feels full.

Once inside Tyler's office, he locks the door and snatches the phone off Shaun, bringing it up so he can see me and I can see him.

"Kitten, what did I just walk in on?"

"We were just talking." Shaun butts in, winning a glare from Tyler.

"If I wanted you to answer, I would have asked *you* the question, Fuckboy."

"I'll answer you once you apologise to Shaun for calling him Fuckboy." I demand, raising a single, dark brow.

Tyler rolls his eyes. "Sorry, Fuckboy."

"You need to work on your apology skills," I smirk, and Tyler shrugs.

"Whatever. Tell me what I want to know."

"Everything?" I ask innocently, and Tyler nods. "Ok, well, I thought my coochie was broken because I hadn't come since... well, you know... the other night at the Feast, and I hadn't really wanted to, which is weird as fuck because my Kitty is a horny bitch and needs to come on the regular. But Big Jim, which is my magnificent vibrator, or any other of my toys, just didn't wake Kitty up. So then I turned to porn, and none of the regulars worked, so I watched some pretty fucked up twisted shit because let's be honest, I'm always pushing boundaries with Kitty, but none of that worked either. Then when Shaun rang, and the guys were with him, I told him about my dilemma, and before we knew it, we were talking about Garrett's monster cock, which I haven't had the pleasure of yet, but Shaun has seen it in action, and he described what he saw and HELLO, Kitty started to wake up. So, you know, it kinda went from conversation to needing to come, and the guys went to the toilets, and fuck Ty! Shaun and Simon went in the same stall together and jacked off in front of the camera, and, oh my god, I really wanted Shaun to touch Simon's dick. Meanwhile, Garrett was pretending like he didn't want to join in, yet he still snuck in the bathroom all stalkerish and listened to the whole thing, which, to be honest, is a pretty big turn on. Oh, and now Kitty is waking up again, but I'm just so happy that she isn't broken because I really thought she was after what happened the other night at the Feast."

"Fucking hell, Kitten." Tyler looks shocked. His face pale as he stares at the screen.

"Think of it as therapy." My statement sounds more like a question, and I hear Shaun chuckling in the background.

"Are those other two like me and Fuckboy to you?" Tyler shifts uncomfortably, and I realise I've never considered having this conversation with him. In my defence, all of this with these guys has happened pretty quickly.

"Is that a problem?" Nerves creep in while I wait for Tyler to answer.

"No, Kitten, but there needs to be a limit. If you are finding happiness with multiple people, then that's good. That's what you need, as long as they all know that they are sharing you with others. I just worry because, in order for that to happen, they should know about each other. Know who each person in the relationship is. But... I can't do that. I'm sorry, Kitten. It's already too much that Fuckboy knows about us."

My heart sinks, and tears well in my eyes.

"I'll fucking kick your arse if you're about to break up with her!" Shaun growls from somewhere.

I try to speak, but I can't. My bottom lip starts having a fucking seizure. Shit, I'm a real pussy lately.

"What? I'm not fucking letting her go!" Tyler snaps. "I'm just saying that Kitten needs to understand that the others can't ever know about me."

"Ever?" I ask quietly, gaining Tyler's attention again.

"Well, I mean, maybe one day, if you keep me around when you're older and legal, maybe we can discuss it."

I nod. "We will be having that discussion, Ty. The day after I graduate from Fox Pines, you can be sure as shit that we will be discussing it."

Tyler grins at that. "Ok, Kitten. I look forward to that conversation."

I smile, the brat in me poking her head up.

"Now that we have that sorted out, I'm ready for round two."

"Is that so?" Ty asks while Shaun's eyes peer over Tyler's shoulder to look at me.

"Yes, Daddy." I flutter my lashes. "I want you to slide your dick in Casanova's mouth."

The call ends, but not before I hear Ty's voice.

"Fucking hell!"

CHAPTER NINE

RHYS

W hen Lexi sets her mind to something, she is a force to be reckoned with! After I spent my Friday at home trying to teach Kitty how to work again, my guys were at school getting talked into a camping trip this weekend with Lexi and Ayden. By the time I got dragged into the conversation, it had turned into a big trip that involved all of Lexi's pack, plus my friends, Tillie, Bell, Allister and Dale.

My mum thought it was a great idea to go on a camping trip, and we bonded over packing bug spray, torches and batteries, and sunscreen. I've never been much of a camper, but I'm never one to pass up an opportunity to have fun. Especially adult free fun.

Ebony Falls is about forty minutes drive northeast of Fox Pines. Still in Timber Valley, it's nestled below the towering cliffs that line the edge of the small mill town, Woodall Ridge. The falls are a popular spot to hang out on hot days and swim in the clear rock pools that lay at the base, which is the backdrop for our campsite. Since we have a long weekend off school because of the Melbourne Cup coming up on Tuesday, it's the perfect time to get away and enjoy a break before we start exams.

While Lexi drives to the falls with Ayden in his car because he's a lucky bastard that's already eighteen, Cynthia and Will drive me up, twins in tow and the others get rides with their parents or share rides. Marcus jumps in with Jared, and Simon and Shaun get Derek to take them. Meanwhile, Dale gets his mum to drive him, Allister,

Bell and Tillie in their people mover, and Garrett arrives with his mum and sisters.

While we set up our tents, the rents gather together, setting up a cooking area and barbeque snags for lunch. Archie and Connor have been trying to help me put my tent up, but the three of us make nothing but a mess of it until my dad comes along to save the day.

"Thanks for the help, dad." As much as it feels weird for me to call someone my dad, it also feels right. Will *is* my dad.

"That's ok. I'm kind of jealous that you get to spend the weekend here. It's been such a long time since Cin and I did anything like this."

"You guys should book a trip or something soon. Char and I can look after the boys for a few nights. I'm sure we can refrain from burning the house down."

Dad laughs. "I'm sure you and Charlotte won't burn the house down. I'm not so sure about the twins."

"Hey!" Archie complains, freezing with a frisbee mid-swing.

"Honestly, those two are probably more responsible than Char and me. Maybe you should leave them at home to look after us instead of the other way round?" I grin and hear Connor hoot.

"Yeah, Dad. Rhysie is right. We are more responsible."

Dad chuckles.

"Need any help over here?" Garrett's voice makes me stiffen, and for some stupid reason, I panic at the thought of him talking to my dad.

"Oh, hey. Garrett, isn't it?" Will asks, holding his hand out.

I turn in time to see Garrett smile and nod, taking my dad's hand in a shake.

Oh, would you look at that smile? It instantly makes me relax. I have no fucking idea what I was panicking about. It's not like Garrett will tell my dad about the video chat yesterday, and it's not like my dad will tell Garrett about finding me in a spit roast when I went on a sex bender last month. Right?

You're trash.

Shut the fuck up!

Ugh! I'm still not feeling like my normal, chirpy self. The Feast really fucked me over the other night. I guess Julie did, too, by sending that video. Not that anyone but my guys know it's me, but for me to see that video, see the evidence of that willing little girl, is just too much. I've worked so hard to repress those memories.

"I think we're all good for help. Thanks anyway." Dad says to Garrett, who smiles politely and nods before two girls run up and barrel into his side.

"Garrett, Polly wants to play frisbee with those little boys, but she's a scaredy-cat and doesn't want to ask them." The little girl, who must be his little sister Britney, dobs as his other little sister glares at her and pokes her tongue out.

"You can play frisbee with the boys." I offer and turn to the twins, who are too busy jumping around like they have ants in their pants to concentrate on tossing the disc. "Arch! Con! Can the girls play frisbee too?"

The boys stop goofing around and smile, both pushing their glasses back in place in unison. It's a creepy twin thing.

"Yeah, sure!" Archie calls, waving them over, and both the girls smile at me before running off to join the twins.

"You're gonna be their favourite person after sorting that out for them." Garrett chuckles, and my dad joins him.

"Kids love me." I beam, flashing my teeth.

Garrett is staring at me a little too long, and I can tell my dad notices. I know why he's staring at me. Today, my lips aren't black, they are natural, and even though there is black liner on my eyes, it's simpler. Not as thick. I decided to forgo the goth girl look for the camping trip. I might scare the fucking animals away or something. My hair, however, is still in the two side buns. I didn't want to shock everyone by looking like a completely different person.

Dad finishes up doing something to my tent and then stands back to assess his work, nodding his head in pride that he managed to get the job done.

Guys can be so weird.

"Right, well, remember that there's no phone reception up here, but the boy, Jared, has a satellite phone. Just use that if you need to contact us. We also have the number, just in case we need to reach you." I nod as my dad approaches me and notice Garrett still watching in my peripheral. When dad reaches me, his smile drops, and he sighs. "Are you ok?"

Shit. Can he tell I'm all sorts of fucked up right now?

I clear my throat, "Yeah. Sure, I'm all g Daddio."

He smiles again and shakes his head. "Just… be safe. Ok?"

Biting the inside of my cheek to try and fend off the overwhelming emotions that his simple request has ignited, I nod quickly and smile, not able to talk. Then he steps closer, holding his hands out a little.

"Any chance of a hug?"

I swallow the lump in my throat, reminding myself that Will is not Brian. Will cares about me unconditionally. Will is my dad.

I step forward and hug him. My dad.

By the time he pulls back, I have tears falling down my cheeks, and he offers me a sympathetic smile.

"Rhys, I really want you to try to have fun this weekend. Just enjoy this beautiful place." He gestures around him. "Enjoy some laughs with your friends. Enjoy and accept how much everyone cares about you. And have a think about talking to us about whatever has you so rattled when you get back home. We only want to help. We only want you to be happy."

Well, fuck. More tears spring free, and I nod before Lexi comes up to my side and throws her arm around my shoulder. Then my dad leans forward and kisses my forehead before moving away to join the kids in their frisbee game.

Lexi shifts her hold and pulls me into her, wrapping her arms around me, and I bury my face in her neck.

"I don't know what's wrong with me," I whisper, and she strokes over my head, avoiding my buns.

"My guess is you have a lot going on, and you've been keeping it all in. In my experience, it's better when it comes out. Don't worry, though. We all have your back, no matter what. We are here for you whenever you need us."

"Thank you," I whisper again, and Lexi gives me a little squeeze.

"I think Garrett wants to speak to you." Lexi whispers, and a smile tugs at my lips.

I nod into her neck and stay that way for another minute before pulling back and sucking in a deep breath.

"You good?" Lexi asks, her blue eyes roaming over my face in concern.

I nod, "Yeah. I'll be ok. How's my face? Did I ruin my makeup?"

Lexi grins, "The waterproof stuff you wear never budges. You still look perfect. Oh, and I'm really digging the look you have going today." Her smile is wide, and man, she's lucky all the parents are still here, or I'd slap a kiss on those perfect lips of hers.

Lexi nudges my shoulder before walking off, and I turn to see Garrett still watching me from the other side of my tent.

"Come for a walk?" He asks, and I nod, which sends his lips into a quirk.

I scoop up my camera, looping the strap over my neck, and we walk across the clearing to where the river weaves through the reddish rocks along the bank. I follow Garrett's lead, taking a seat next to him on a boulder. He's quiet, just looking out over the water, so I use his silence to take a few snaps of the falls. I'm not sure if I should be talking or not, but eventually, Garrett beats me to it.

"I want you to know that I want you to be my girl."

My brows shoot up, and I lower my camera, darting my eyes from the water to look at Garrett as he maintains his stare over the river.

"The thing is, I'm not going to make it a thing until Marcus is ok with it. We all had a talk yesterday after school, and while he's still royally pissed about everything that's happened, I get the feeling he wants to try and make things work." He turns those piercing blue eyes to me then, "So until he's ok with me being with you, then we need to remain just friends."

I stay silent for a moment, processing what he's just said. Is it greedy of me to want him to be right about Marcus wanting to make things work? If it's true, then I really could have Marcus and Garrett as part of this group thing I have going. They already feel like they are part of it in a way, but to have it all with them, the intimacy and the friendship, would be something I've never believed I could have.

"Say something." Garrett urges, and a small smile tugs at my lips.

"So, what you're saying is that if Marcus is cool with it, you will share me, too?"

Grinning, he nods. "Yes. Weirdly, I'm ok with it as long as it's just within our group."

"Dude, I'm not inviting Jared." I joke, and he chuckles.

"I know you're not. I was referring to me, Bossi, Hastings and Grady."

"You really think Marcus will want that?"

"Maybe. I get the feeling he's trying to talk himself into it, but he's struggling. He might just need time to wrap his head around it." Garrett shrugs and looks back out at the water as I think over what he said.

"You know there's another guy, right?"

"Yep. And I'm not sure I'm happy about that." He admits.

"Why?"

Garrett's fierce eyes return to mine, swimming with a brewing storm. "I don't know this other guy. I don't like that you and Bossi know and won't tell us. What's the big deal? I get that he's older, but if he's a decent guy, then I don't see the problem with us all knowing each other."

This is what Ty was talking about yesterday. It all comes down to secrets. They are toxic. I already know that. But I can't reveal Ty's identity.

"I can't say who he is. Not yet anyway. Maybe in a year or two, but it's too risky right now. I can't say any more than that, Garrett. I'm sorry."

His Adam's apple bobs as he swallows, and he turns his glare out to the water again.

"Tell me some things about him, then. I need to know he's a good person."

"Ok." I smile, happy that this isn't a deal-breaker. "He's pretty tall and built like a gym junkie. I'm pretty sure he is, actually."

"You don't know if he's a gym junkie or not?"

"No." I shake my head. "We became acquainted at Vixen's Lodge, so most of my interactions with him have been there."

"So, you don't really know him? Only through sex?"

"I'm trying not to get defensive here, Big Guy. I want to answer your question as best I can, but don't fucking judge me, or whatever you and I have going is going to be over before it begins."

That earns me a smirk. "I fucking love that mouth of yours." He shakes his head and sighs. "I'm sorry. I'm not trying to be judgy. I'm just trying to understand."

"Well, buddy, understand this. Everyone in our little group met Kitty before they met *me*. All except for you. I'm all about sex. You know that. You know why. So why would my interactions with Ty be any different?"

"I don't know. I guess the fact that he's older worries me a little. If you have to hide it, then maybe it's wrong." Garrett shrugs, and I sigh.

"You need to trust me on this. Ty is a good person. He cares about me."

Garrett's blue eyes dart between mine, studying me for a moment before his face softens and he nods.

"Ok. But there should be some rules."

"Like what?"

"I don't know. Maybe that everyone needs to wear protection. We don't know who else this Ty guy fucks."

Garrett has a point. Aside from the Feast nights, I have no idea who Tyler sleeps with. Fuck, that thought feels like a knife is twisting in my gut. I recognise it for what it is. Jealousy. But how can I feel that way? How can I say to him and the others that they can't fuck anyone but me, but I can fuck all of them?

"Ok. I'll tell him to always wear protection." I frown, remembering the barn and how he said that when we are together outside of the Feast that he would fuck me bare.

"Where does he work?" Garrett asks, and my eyes widen.

Shaking my head, I shoot him a duh look. "I can't tell you that."

"But you know where he works?"

"Yes." I nod. "It's a respectable job."

Garrett nods this time, but our conversation ends abruptly as something like a banshee call pierces the silence, screaming out that lunch is ready. There's only one person I know that can scream that loud, and it's my flamboyant friend, Dale Martin.

We get up slowly from our peaceful boulder and make our way back towards the camp, my mind swirling with more and more worry as each moment passes.

"I'm sorry." Garrett rasps, obviously seeing the frown creasing my brow. "I didn't intend for that conversation to get so intense given the crap you are dealing with at the moment. I just really want to be upfront and honest about things, so there's no confusion, and you don't take my rejection personally."

I smile up at Garrett as we walk, feeling a little better at his words, and I playfully nudge his shoulder.

"So basically, what you're saying is, Marcus is the one cock blocking us?"

Garrett chuckles. "Yes, George. You can blame Marcus for keeping my gigantic cock from meeting your Kitty."

His tone is playful, and I throw my head back, laughing before bringing my camera up and snapping a picture of the rare smile Garrett offers the world.

"You and Bossi are talking it up a fair bit. I hope I'm not going to be disappointed when you finally introduce me to your mammoth shlong."

"Oh, don't worry. You won't be disappointed. Once you have it, you'll be hooked."

Well shit. Kitty is wide awake now. I can't do anything to sate her since we are surrounded by parents and siblings.

Ugh! FML!

About an hour after we eat, all the parents finally leave us to our fun. We plunge into a drinking session while playing Cards Against Humanity. My guys are keeping their distance, not touching me, but still sitting on either side of me, making sure to get me a drink when I'm empty or to feed me food when they think it's been too long since I've eaten. It takes a couple of hours for me to relax into my usual self, all but the sexual innuendos I typically throw around.

I can't bring myself to talk about sex in a playful way unless it's directly to one of my guys. Even then, it's nearly non-existent. I may have had video sex yesterday and talked of Garrett's mammoth dick earlier, but my connection with sex is waning.

Am I no longer a sex addict?

Was I ever one?

What the fuck is wrong with me?

"I'm over this game. Can we play something else?" Dale whinges and tosses his cards on the small camp table in front of him.

"Wanna play strip poker?" Bell asks, "Hastings loves to get naked."

"She's right. I do love to get my gear off." Simon grins goofily, Bieber flicking his blonde hair back.

"That's why you lose poker all the time, isn't it, Simon?" Bell stands and tosses her cards on the table too. "So you can show me your dick?"

"He won't be showing you his dick anymore, Bell!" I hiss, the words escaping me before I even realise what's happening.

"Rarrr! Got your claws out for one of your fuck buddies, hey Rhys? Are they *all* off-limits?"

I bolt up from my camp chair. "What the fuck is your problem, Bell?"

"I guess I don't like greedy bitches. Maybe some of the other girls want a good fuck. Doesn't seem fair that you take all the meat."

Furious, I storm around the unlit fire pit, getting in Bell's face, as the sound of people moving behind me reminds me we have an audience.

"What makes you think they'd be interested in your cunt?"

Bell smirks, her black lips still painted on for this camping trip. "Oh, they *are* interested."

"Bell, shut the fuck up already! You know George will kick your arse. Your mouth is running off white powder courage right now." Dale walks up behind Bell and drags her away from me. That's when I notice her eyes. She's under the influence of something potent.

"What are you high on right now?" I grit out between clenched teeth, but Bell just raises a lazy, dark brow at me.

"You brought drugs into the camp?" Lexi hisses, coming to stand next to me.

"What?" Bell curls her lip, looking Lexi up and down. "Little miss princess, too good for the hard stuff?"

"Lex, come on. Let's go for a walk." Ayden comes up behind Lexi and takes her hand, gaining her attention. She hesitates a moment, looking between Bell and Ayden before her face softens, and she chooses to walk away.

I don't, though. I wait until Lexi and Ayden are out of earshot before I lunge forward and wrap my hand around Bell's throat.

"You stupid bitch! Ayden is a recovering addict. How could you bring that shit here?"

Bell laughs. "You know, grabbing me by the throat only turns me on. Wanna give the boys a little show?"

I growl in her face before pushing her away, the move making her stumble backwards, nearly falling over. "Get the fuck away from me. And stay away from my guys!"

"Which ones are yours again?" Tilting her head to the side, Bell eggs me on.

I could kill this bitch right now. Who the fuck does she think she is? I want to teach her a fucking lesson, but common sense peeks up and says hello, so I ignore her and give her my back.

"I'm her guy." Garrett declares loud enough to gain everyone's attention. Even Lexi and Ayden's attention, who are halfway across the clearing, hear his loud declaration, causing them to stop and glance back over their shoulders. I'm shocked because isn't he waiting until Marcus is alright with the situation?

"I'm her guy too," Shaun speaks up next, standing tall and puffing out his chest.

"Me too. I'm definitely her guy." Simon nods with a shit-eating, playful grin.

I smile at them as they look at me and not Bell.

"I'm hers too." Marcus' declaration is quieter than the others and doesn't hold as much confidence, but he said the words, and that's all that matters.

"Come on, Cherry, let's go for a walk." Simon holds out his hand, and I fucking blush. Their satisfied grins at each other tell me my guys notice my flushed skin.

I don't spare Bell another glance as I step up to my guys.

I don't need toxic in my life right now. I need love.

CHAPTER TEN

MARCUS

I did it. I admitted I wanted to be a part of this weird group relationship Rhee has going with my mates. I didn't plan on admitting it out loud. I've been reluctant to concede, because it's a fucking lot to wrap my head around being ok with other guys touching her. I want her for myself, but I understand *now* why that can't happen. Even though sharing her goes against everything I've ever thought a relationship should be, I realise I'd do anything to have her back. Even share her. It's an absurd thought. Who the fuck shares their girl with other guys?

A fucking wimp, that's who.

But fuck, I guess I'm a wimp then, because here I am declaring that I'm hers.

I wish I could say I know what the fuck I'm doing, but I don't.

When I first found out that my girl and Bossi had been hooking up, I absolutely lost it. I saw motherfucking red and nothing else. I still feel shit about the beating I gave Shaun until I remember his betrayal, and I feel like pummelling him all over again.

Rhys was never really mine, though. She'd said as much when we first started flirting. She told me she doesn't do boyfriends—only sex. I didn't care at the time. I was only interested in getting my dick wet, but each time we came together, it was less about burying myself inside her and more about getting lost with her. I don't know when it happened exactly, but she fucking claimed my heart, even if she had no interest in it.

So yeah, knowing one of my best mates had sunken his cock inside her tipped me over the edge. I thought there was some kind of unspoken Bro Code. Shouldn't she have been off-limits? Shouldn't my mates have stayed away from her? I was wrong to think they would because not only had Bossi dipped his wick, but fucking Hastings had, too. And now, Cole had his sights set on her, even though I know he won't actually be intimate with her until he thinks I'm ok with it. That's the sort of guy he is. The problem is, he doesn't realise he's already stepping over the line because what he's already doing is having an emotional relationship with her. I haven't called him out on it, though, because honestly, it's more what Rhys needs right now than just another dick to fuck.

That day at school, when I'd seen the matching hickeys on Rhys and Shaun's necks, I'd wanted to call her a slut. A whore. I'd wanted to spew vile words at her and make her feel like shit, yet I couldn't go through with it because, despite the betrayal I'd felt at the time, I fucking loved her. And I still fucking do.

The day she admitted she was a sex addict, I didn't know what to think. Sure, I knew she liked sex. We couldn't keep our genitals from clashing when we were together. But a sex addict? It was hard for me to comprehend. She is only seventeen. How can a seventeen-year-old have an addiction to sex? If only I knew *then* what I know *now*. Now, things are starting to make more sense... kind of.

She told me about the sex parties, which I know is what Bossi was referring to the night of Halloween, when he said they hooked up at a sex club. She also admitted to having feelings for me, but she also has them for Shaun as well. Apparently, Bossi said he'd share her, and she seems to be happy with that arrangement.

I've struggled to wrap my head around that, if I'm being honest. I'm struggling to understand how my girl has changed so much from the Rhys George I first hooked up with. Then again, did I ever really know her?

Sure, I know her body. I know exactly how to milk an orgasm from her, but when we were hooking up, I had no idea she was a regular visitor at a sex club. No idea she's a sex addict. No idea about this older guy she's been seeing. Me not knowing all these things about Rhys is just as much on me as it is on her. She told me how it was from the beginning, but I was too dick-blind to get to the bottom of why she didn't want a relationship. Sure, I tried to ask, but I didn't try hard enough. I just thought I could sex her up good, and she'd be as into my body as I was into hers.

Now, these secrets have come out about her. Secrets I could never have imagined were possible in a million years. It fucking breaks my heart to know she lost her virginity when she was only eleven.

How the fuck does Garrett know that about her? She must have told him, yet she never told me any of her secrets. He hasn't even fucked her, and she divulged that information to him. Maybe that's it, though. Maybe she trusts him because he hasn't gone to that place with her. He's working a different angle, and it pisses me off that I'm not the one she's confiding in.

Was that how old she was in that video? Eleven? She was so fucking young. Too fucking young to be doing the things we witnessed. There's something about that disgusting video that's not sitting well with me. I'm not talking about how wrong it is for a full-grown arse adult male to be doing those things with a child, either. That shit is fucked and sick, and he should have his dick cut the fuck off for doing that shit!

What I'm referring to is the little girl. She didn't seem unwilling. The little girl version of Rhys looked like she was enjoying herself, and I can't fucking get that thought out of my head. I don't understand it. Maybe she was drugged or something? Surely, she knew what she was doing was wrong?

Fuck! I don't know! I just don't fucking know!

This has all gotten too much, yet here I fucking am, declaring that I'm one of her guys without really knowing if I want to be *one* of her guys.

It's just so fucked up.

"Dude, you're growling," Simon whispers in my ear, and I flinch back, looking around to see if anyone else heard.

We're walking along a hiking track that runs along side the Timber River. Bossi and Rhys are up ahead, looking around and pointing to birds or lizards as they walk, chatting away about nothing important while Rhys uses her camera to capture things she likes the look of. Garrett is behind them, watching Rhys like he owns her, while Hastings is walking with me at the back.

I don't know what the fuck we are doing out here in the bush. There's nothing exciting out here, yet we keep walking deeper. We will probably get fucking lost and die, and we'll be remembered as those teenagers that thought they knew how to fucking camp.

"Wanna talk about it?" Simon nudges my shoulder, and I shoot him a glare.

"Not really."

"Come on, man. It might make you feel better." Simon smiles. I appreciate that he's trying to help, but it's just pissing me off more.

"You don't wanna know where my head is at." I hiss, and his brows lift as he raises his hands to show he is backing off.

"Hey, look! A cave!" Rhys yells from up ahead, gaining my attention, and I'm about to call out to her to stay on the track, but it's too late. She's already run off into the forest.

"Fucking hell. Going off track isn't a good idea." I grumble, and Garrett looks back at me, his lips thinning.

"Oh, come on, Grady. Where's your sense of adventure?" Simon shoulders me before taking off in a sprint to catch up with Rhys and Bossi.

Garrett chuckles. "You should just give in and let down your guard, Grady. Who knows, you might have fun."

I roll my eyes at him and drop my shoulders, knowing he's probably right. This shit with Rhys will never get better unless I try to go along with it. What's the worst that can happen? I realise I *can't* share her and spend the rest of my days watching her in some sort of group relationship with my mates? Is there even a name for this sort of relationship?

Fucked if I know!

I take in my surroundings as I walk, making a mental note of anything that can easily be identified just in case we *do* find ourselves lost, and I follow behind Garrett, off the track and through the scrub that lines a cliff face.

Rhys is right. There's a cave here. The entrance is a wide cavern, tall enough to stand five Garretts tall in, and the deeper it goes into the cliff face, the smaller the cavern becomes until all you can see is darkness.

"This place is sick." Bossi turns in a circle, looking up to examine the space.

He's right. It is pretty sick. It's big enough to provide shelter from the weather, and the ashy pile of burnt branches shows we aren't the first campers to find this place. Someone has been here before and had a campfire.

I watch Rhys from the corner of my eye as she grins up at the vast space, the shutter of her camera clicking before she sits down on a boulder off to the side. The cavern is cool, a nice reprieve from the afternoon sun, and I watch Rhys sit her camera on the boulder, take the cap off her water bottle and pour some of the liquid over the back of her neck.

"Hot Kitten?" Bossi asks, and I feel like punching the fucker. Every time I hear him call her Kitten, my blood boils. And surprisingly, every time I see how she responds to that name, my madness eases a little. She likes being called Kitten. She told me she likes it when I call her Rhee as well. I like that she likes that, and fuck, I think I like that she likes Kitten as well.

My head is seriously screwed up right now.

"You're growling again," Simon whispers next to my ear, and I flinch.

Jesus! Fuck!

I drop my eyes from Rhys as Bossi approaches her, knowing too well he's probably about to kiss her. Part of me wants to kill him for laying his lips on her, but the other part of me, which I don't fucking understand yet, likes to watch how she responds. My dick gets hard to see her get turned on by someone else, and isn't that just fucked up?

See! I have no fucking idea what to make of any of this.

"Why'd you declare that you're one of her guys if you can't even watch one of her other guys show her attention?" Garrett's voice is low, so only Hastings and I can hear, and I snap my eyes up to his, letting him see my anger.

"I don't fucking know."

Garrett frowns, tilting his head to the side while he studies me. "Hmmm, I think you do know, but you're struggling to accept it."

"What the fuck does that mean?" I hiss a little too loudly, and Bossi pulls away from his lip-lock with my girl to look over his shoulder at me.

My eyes glance past Shaun, noticing a flicker of nervousness across Rhys' face. She shifts back from Bossi a little, her brows tugging in as she glances down at the space she put between them.

"You really should talk to us, man. That shit helps." Simon pipes up, and I shoot him a dagger.

"Oh really? *I* should talk about *my* feelings? What about *you*, Hastings? You haven't spoken about what's going on with your parents. Why don't you give the talking thing a go?"

I'm an arsehole. I know. I never used to be, but I fucking am now.

"Fine." Simon shrugs. "They're getting divorced, and they haven't made a decision on me yet. My old man wants to live in London, and my mum wants to move back to Perth to be close to her sister. They haven't once asked me what I fucking want." Simon glares, his playful nature nowhere in sight. "Does that make you happy, Grady?"

"No, it doesn't. Sorry, man." I feel like shit. And I should too. I'm a fucking prick, and I'm going to lose my mates if I don't pull my fucking head in.

Rhys and Shaun have made their way over to us now, and Rhys steps in front of Simon, cupping his face and pulling him to her in a heartfelt hug. His breathing is deep and quick, his revelation upsetting him. Rhys' arms help him, though. The moment she has her arms locked around him, he relaxes into her hold and buries his head in the crook of her neck.

Fuck. Maybe she is good for all of us?

Maybe we can do this sharing thing?

"Sorry," I say again, but this time I look at my three mates, wanting them to see that the apology is for each of them. They give me a nod, all while Rhys stays wrapped around Simon like a vice. It's only a moment later when she pulls back a little and speaks to Simon quietly before kissing him.

It feels wrong to watch this, yet I can't fucking help myself. Maybe I like killing myself on the inside, torturing myself. All I know is that I want her to kiss me like that again.

"Should we… talk?" Shaun asks, and Rhys darts back from Simon, shaking her head.

"Nope." She skips back over to the boulder she was sitting on before and climbs back up to retake her seat.

"Come on, Kitten. You know the five of us should probably clear the air a little and maybe set some boundaries." Shaun approaches her, but as he gets near, she draws her legs up to her chest and wraps her arms around them, effectively closing herself off from him.

What's going on there? It's not a very Rhys-like move.

"I don't do rules, Bossi. Rules are suffocating."

"Ok, I get that, but we just declared that we are all your guys, so we should discuss a few things. Don't you think?"

She shakes her head at Shaun, and Garrett chuckles.

"Dude, haven't you learnt anything about her yet? She won't talk about the hard stuff willingly." Garrett sits on a rock opposite Rhys, and he shoots her a wink, but she just rolls her eyes.

"Oh right. I remember. We have to swap answers for pleasure." Shaun grins at Rhys, and she blushes but looks nervously down at her feet.

"Nope. Not playing that game." She declares, and Bossi pouts.

"Hey, I like the sound of that game. We can do, Simon Says again, Cherry. You enjoyed playing that last time." Simon nods enthusiastically, but Rhys shakes her head, looking even more nervous. I consider that perhaps I'm just imagining it, but when Simon starts towards Rhys, her eyes dart frantically to the entrance of the cavern.

She looks like she wants to run.

"Stop!" I shout, the echo bouncing off the rock walls, causing everyone to flinch. It does the trick, though. Simon stops in his tracks, skidding on the dirt gravel.

"What the fuck, man?" Garrett hisses, glaring at me, but I ignore him, instead, keeping my gaze trained on my girl.

Slowly, I walk towards her, and I watch as she shifts back a little, her nerves more obvious.

"Why are you scared, Rhee?" I ask, and her eyes widen briefly before she tries to force her expression neutral. It doesn't work.

"What?" She huffs out a laugh, trying to appear unaffected. "I'm not scared."

I close the distance, coming to stand at the base of the boulder, looking up at her.

"Rhee, what's wrong?" I keep my voice low and calm as I reach up to peel one of her hands off the death grip she has on her legs. She's wearing little black shorts today. I've never seen her in shorts, but it's not the only thing that's different about her today. She also isn't wearing as much makeup. Her eyes aren't as harsh, and her lips are natural and beautiful. Not a smear of black lipstick in sight.

When I feel the underside of her hand against mine, I know for sure that something is wrong. Her palm is clammy, and there's a slight tremble to her hand. Peering up at her deep chocolate eyes, I see the emotion swimming within them.

"Talk to me, Rhee. What has you so nervous?"

Her eyes dart behind me to the other guys before returning to mine. She shakes her head and swallows deeply, like she's trying to clear a lump in her throat.

"I don't… I can't…"

"You can't what?" I beg with my eyes, hoping she will let down her walls and talk to me.

"I can't do this." She whispers, but it's loud enough that the other guys hear too because I hear Bossi suck in a harsh breath.

"What can't you do?" I ask, and she shakes her head again, not willing to say more. "You can't do the group relationship? Is that what you are trying to say?"

Why am I scared to hear her admit she can't do the group thing?

She shakes her head, and the relieved sighs of the other three are audible behind me.

"Then what is it you can't do?" I rub my thumb over the back of her hand, hoping she feels my reassurance that I care. We care.

Tears pop free from her eyes then, and she sucks in a breath, trying to calm herself.

"S-s-sex."

I frown. Sex? Did she just say sex?

"Kitten. No one is asking you to have sex." Bossi comes to stand beside me, and he takes her other hand.

"B-but y-you will w-want it. A-and I j-just can't." My girl sobs and drops her forehead to her knees, trying to hide her face.

"I don't expect it, Kitten. None of us do." Shaun presses a kiss to the back of her hand, and she peers over her knees at us.

"Yes, you do. We were kissing just before." She shoots Shaun a duh look, and when Shaun goes to speak, Garrett cuts him off.

"Rhys, remember what I've been trying to show you? That you can have a relationship without sex being involved?" When Rhys nods, Garrett continues. "The four of us aren't here with you, so we can fuck you, Rhys. We are here because we care about you. Sure, we would love to share the intimacy of sex with you, but we don't *need* it. Not until you're ready. We know you've been through a lot. We don't expect anything but your time and, hopefully, your honesty."

"Fuck, man. You should be a therapist with Lexi." Simon mutters in all seriousness, and Rhys smiles.

"I've thought the same thing a time or two."

Garrett chuckles. "Whatever. I'm not wrong, though, and you know it. So be honest with us. If you don't want us touching you in any way, we won't. If you don't want us kissing you, we won't. And we sure as hell won't fuck you if you don't want to. But you have to tell us."

"I…" She shakes her head and hides behind her knees again. "I don't want Kitty touched." Rhys keeps her head buried behind her knees as she whispers the words, and I glance at Bossi next to me, who looks pained at hearing her say that. I know it's not because he disagrees with her words. It's because he's hurting over what was done to her the other night at that fucked up sex club.

"Can I kiss you still, Kitten?" Bossi asks, and I see now how much he really does care for my girl. He fucking loves her.

Rhys pops her tear-filled eyes up from behind her knees and nods right before Shaun launches himself up on the boulder and gently claims her lips.

As I watch them settle into the kiss and start clutching at each other, desperate to show how they feel by the kiss alone, I'm not as jealous as I thought I'd be. Mostly, I'm happy that my girl is working through her fears. I really just want her to be happy. She deserves that.

Chapter Eleven

Rhys

My mojo is long fucking gone. I need to get a grip and find it again instead of being scared that my guys are going to try and get me in a gang bang that I can't get out of. And fuck, I wouldn't normally want to get out of a gang bang. I'm all for the ganging and banging… usually.

Ugh! Stupid Kitty. Always controlling me. Always ruling my fucking emotions.

After the whole cave confessions, we head back to camp because Simon is hungry. Of course, he was hungry. That guy loves food more than anyone I know.

We stumble into the camp, me on Simon's back as he pretends to be a horse, with the other three guys trailing behind. The sound of my camera clicking over and over while we walk told me that Garrett was taking pictures behind us since he's the one I left in charge of looking after it. He's probably been snapping pics of my arse.

I could also hear them murmuring to each other as we followed the path back, but my ears couldn't pick up what they were saying. In a way, I'm glad I couldn't hear. There's been too much serious shit happening. Too many serious deep and meaningfuls, and I just want a break from it. I hate serious. I'm the least serious person I know.

Thankfully, Bell was riding her high on the other side of the clearing with Dale and Allister keeping her company. I don't normally clash with Bell so much, but she's been a right bitch lately.

Tillie, on the other hand, seems ok, and I find her with Lexi, Ayden and Jared as they work together wrapping potatoes in foil.

"Food! Yes!" Simon whoops and lowers me down off his back before he bounds up to the table and swipes a handful of potato chips.

We all laugh, but mine is cut off by a salty chip as Simon tries to feed it to me.

"Eat Cherry. Let me feed you."

"Ew. Don't be gross." Tillie whines as the others laugh again.

And that's how our night goes. Food and laughter, a lot of laughter. Exactly what my soul was searching for. We all cook together, eat together, and wind down around the campfire with some strong drinks. Bell returns to us but stays quiet, and wanders off to bed before eleven, while the rest of us listen to Simon tell scary camping stories. As with most things Simon, his stories are mostly funny and less scary.

Eventually, Lexi and Ayden sneak off, probably to fuck in their tent, and Tillie joins Bell while Jared disappears into his swag, leaving me by the campfire with my guys.

"Do you think you're going to be alright sleeping alone in your tent, Kitten? Simon's stories didn't scare you, did they?" Shaun smirks, and my nerves flutter as I think about sleeping alone.

I sleep alone at home, so what's the big problem?

I'll tell you what the big problem is. Have you ever heard the noise wombats make in the dead of night? Or the thump of a huge kangaroo as it bounces somewhere nearby in the dark, or the creepy fucking hissing noise they make? Let's not forget the terrifying growl of a koala mating call! Fuck that! These creatures are terrifying!

"Because we were talking earlier," Shaun continues after seeing my expression, "and thought that if you need a tent sharing buddy, maybe Garrett would make you feel more comfortable."

I shoot my gaze to Garrett, and he holds up his hands. "Just tent sharing, not bed-sharing. No touching involved." His eyes and words are sincere, like I knew they would be, so I nod.

"Okie Dokie Gazza. Let's share a tent."

The guys chuckle at the extra bogan I put into my voice, and Garrett rolls his eyes even though he's laughing at me.

They're all sweet. They chose Garrett because we haven't had sex or any physical contact other than hand-holding. Unfortunately, just like my brain normally does, it thinks about being alone with Garrett and his so-called monster cock. Kitty is confusing me. Or maybe I'm confusing Kitty. How did I get off yesterday on the video call, but then today get terrified of the thought of having sex?

When I notice the guys stand from their camp chairs, I do the same and realise that I need to pee, bad. Simon bounds up to me, skidding to a stop and grinning as he takes my hands.

"My Cherry. Simon says, have a good sleep filled with peaceful dreams... that involve me."

I giggle, shaking my head at my adorable dork. "I can't imagine any dreams of you being peaceful. You have too much energy."

He shrugs before his eyes drop to my lips. "Can I kiss you goodnight?"

I bite my lip and nod, catching his excited hazel eyes with mine. Then he palms my nape and pulls me gently to him. His lips are warm and soft, and taste of the sweet marshmallows he's been cooking over the campfire. I melt into his kiss, loving the feeling of calm he brings.

"Come on, Hastings. Don't hog our girl." Shaun whines, and Simon pulls back from our kiss, flipping the other guys off over his shoulder while keeping his eyes on me.

"Goodnight, Cherry. See you in the morning." He lifts my hand and presses his lips to it, and I fucking feel myself blush.

Jesus, I'm turning into a sap!

As Simon walks off, grinning from ear to ear, Marcus steps forward before hesitating. We haven't really talked about his decision yet, and I can tell he's unsure what he should do right now.

I reach my hand out to him, and without any further hesitation, he steps forward and takes it, bringing my hand up to cup the side of his jaw.

"I…" He's lost for words. My poor Marcus is still hurting. He's still coming to terms with whatever this is, and I fucking hate myself for it. He deserves more than what I can give him, but I'm a greedy bitch, just as Bell said, and I want him. I want all of them.

"Marcus." I whisper as his dark eyes stare into mine. "I really have missed you. So much."

Leaning forward, Marcus presses his forehead to mine, maintaining eye contact as he struggles with his emotions.

"I've missed you too, Rhee. I feel like there's so much I need to say, but at the same time, I have no idea what that is."

I nod, understanding completely. "I know. Me too."

He sighs, "Can I kiss you goodnight too?"

I nod, licking my lips, my heart racing with longing to feel his pressed to mine once again. It's been too long since I've tasted them, and thankfully, Marcus doesn't waste another second. He cups either side of my jaw and crashes his lips into mine. The familiar taste of Marcus mixed with beer engulfs me, and I wind my arms tight around him as a whimper escapes me. The kiss is strong and deep and filled with so much emotion that I don't realise I'm crying again until we pull back.

Marcus' face softens as he sees my tears, and he swipes them away with his thumbs, his voice soothing when he speaks.

"Don't cry, beautiful. We'll work this out, and all the hurt will be behind us soon enough."

"I don't deserve you," I whisper, and he shakes his head.

"Don't say that. You deserve the world, Rhee, and I'm gonna spend my whole life making sure you have it."

Shit! I forgot how raw Marcus can be. He wears his heart on his sleeve, and he loves profusely. How am I lucky enough to have his attention?

"Sweet dreams. I'll see you when the sun comes up." Marcus offers me one of his warm smiles, and my insides melt again. I really have missed him.

I can see his reluctance to let me go, but he does, stepping away slowly and heading towards the guys' tent. When he's far enough away, I turn my eyes to Shaun. My Spanish Casanova has a devilish grin on his face as he waits for me to acknowledge that it's his turn. I can't hide my stupid grin in return.

"Cass, I need to pee. Come with? I'm scared of getting mauled by a horny wombat."

Shaun throws his head back, laughing while Garrett chuckles beside him.

"I'll grab my sleeping bag. Meet you at your tent?" Garrett asks, and I nod.

"Come on, Kitten. I'll race you over to the toilet block." Shaun nudges my shoulder and then takes off, running across the clearing towards the toilet block.

With a squeal, I run after him, pushing my legs hard to catch the fast bugger. He beats me there and turns around to catch me in his arms when I try to keep running past him, the momentum sending us crashing to the dewy grass in a tangle of arms and legs. Our laughter floats up into the crisp night sky, and I find myself hovering over my Casanova. My laughter eases off as he brushes my flyaways back.

"Kitten, why don't you ever wear your hair down like you do at the Feast?"

Shaun's question catches me off guard, and I debate whether or not to lie. The lie would be so easy, but the guys have asked for my honesty, and they deserve it.

"Uh… well, it kinda has something to do with the video that was leaked," I admit, and Shaun's brows furrow. He moves to sit up, and I follow his lead until we are sitting face to face on the grass. Reaching forward, he tugs me closer by my hips until I'm sitting cross-legged in between his legs.

"What do you mean?"

"Brian used to like my hair out like that. He used to spend a lot of time brushing my hair. He said he liked the way it felt on his skin." I fight back a gag and take a deep breath, momentarily closing my eyes. When the storm subsides a little, I open my lids to find Shaun looking at me with so much care that I almost cry again. Almost. "Then, when I turned up at my first Feast night. Master Hill came to the barn to show me where everything was, and he sat in the corner and watched me get ready. Once I had my painted mask on, he beckoned me over to him, and he asked me to take my buns out, so I did. Then he sat me down and brushed my hair, just like Brian used to. Master Hill liked what he saw and told me that Feasters will like the way it looks and feels, so I must always wear it down." I shrug, "So I kind of associate my hair down with the Feast and with Master Hill and my old foster dad. I guess it makes me feel wrong when I wear it down anywhere else. Kinda like wearing underwear on the outside of your clothes."

"I'm sorry you feel that way, Kitten. It really is beautiful hair, and I wish you could enjoy it. Maybe you should consider cutting it shorter? Do you think it will feel different then?"

I shrug again. "Maybe."

Shaun offers me a sympathetic smile, and I can't help myself. I lean forward and press my lips to his. Shaun Bossier is an amazing kisser. The type that would have my leg cocking to wrap around him if we were standing up. As our tongues dance and he tastes and nibbles my lips like they're a delicate dessert, he holds me tight against his chest, letting me drown in him. We kiss for the longest time. I don't recall ever kissing anyone for as long as that before, and even though Kitty stirs, I don't do anything about it. I ignore her and just let myself feel the passion behind this lip claiming.

Eventually, we pull back from each other, knowing we have to end this day so we can start a new one tomorrow, and Shaun waits outside the girl's toilet door while I go in and do my business.

By the time we make it back to my tent, Garrett has made himself at home, setting up his sleeping bag next to mine, leaving a small gap big enough to walk between, and Shaun pecks my lips before zipping the tent closed. The first thing I notice as I move forward is that Garrett's chest is bare under that sleeping bag, leading my mind to wonder if he's wearing something on the bottom—not that it matters, I'm not going to find out—and the muscles of his arms bunch and flex as he lays with his hands behind his head, his icy-blues studying my face the whole time as if he's assessing my reaction.

"You look comfy." I smile down at him and then glance around, wondering how I'm meant to get changed with him in here.

"I'm very comfy." He grins.

"Sooo… I need to get changed," I state, feeling nerves I'm not used to feeling. Normally I'd whip my clothes off, but Garrett and I are dancing around each other, and I'm not ready to cross the line yet. I never fucking thought I'd consider that scenario, so I hope it's worth the wait.

"I can close my eyes if you like?"

A laugh bursts free, and my eyes widen. "You really think I'll fall for that?"

He grins broadens. "Rhys, I'm no perve."

"I know you're not. But you *are* a guy."

"A guy who hasn't made a move on you." His eyes narrow pointedly at me.

"True. Are you gay, Cole? I'm pretty sure I can convince Shaun to suck your dick if you like?"

The deep rumble of Garrett's laugh fills me with warmth before he shakes his head. "No way am I letting any guy near my dick."

"Nawww, not even for me?" I flutter my lashes. "Not even if I beg because it will turn me on soooo bad?"

"Nope. Not even then. Besides," Garrett shifts and rolls onto his stomach, resting his head down in the crook of his arms, "Once you see my cock, you won't want to share it with anyone."

"Ha!" I clutch my chest and laugh. "Touché, Big Guy."

Making use of Garrett's back to me, I quickly search my bag for my Flyleaf t-shirt and get changed before slipping into my sleeping bag.

"You can look now," I say quietly, and Garrett rolls on his side, bunching his pillow under his head as he gets comfy and looks at me.

"Aren't you going to let your hair down?" He asks, and I frown.

"What is it with you guys and wanting my hair down?"

He frowns this time. "Who wants your hair down?"

"Oh, you know," I shrug, "Brian, Master Hill, the Feasters… Shaun and Tyler."

Garrett pushes himself up, his sleeping bag pooling around his naked waist, and all I can do is look at the sculpted God before me. I can just imagine what it would be like to run my fingers over the ridges of his abs. Much the same as Ty's, I'd guess.

"Fuck, Cole. Do you have anything on under there?"

He grins, "I have jocks on. Don't worry. My mammoth snake can't get to you."

"Stop calling it mammoth. You're making my mouth water." I bite my lip as images of a dick so big that it drags on the ground flash through my mind.

Ouch!

"I thought you weren't interested in sex?"

My brows shoot up. "I'm a sex addict. Every second thing I think about is sex-related, but yes, I'm on a sex-free cleanse right now, so don't talk about mammoth, or gigantic, or hung like a horse around me. It will only confuse me. I'm trying to be good."

Garrett smiles. "Don't worry. I'll make sure you behave."

Oh really? *He* will make sure I behave? Fucking hell. Doesn't he know what that statement does to my insides? It fucking wakes Kitty up. That's what it does!

Down Kitty!

"Garrett Cole, you do realise I have a thing for different kinks, right?"

"What? Did I say something wrong?" Confusion creases Garrett's brow. It's kinda cute with the way his full lips pout a little. It's almost playful, which is something I've never seen on him.

"The words, *I'll make sure you behave*, are totally a daddy kink line. Fuck Cole, you're killing me."

He chuckles. "Daddy kink, hey? Are you gonna start calling me daddy?"

"Nope. I already have me a daddy, and he likes to punish his brat."

Garrett's brows disappear under his curls.

"Who?"

"Ty." I grin.

"Oh. The older dude?" He frowns, almost disappointed that he can't be my daddy.

"Yeah. He pretends he doesn't like being called daddy, but I know it turns him on. It also pisses him off, which just means more punishment for me."

Garrett goes quiet as he thinks about that, and I get the feeling he's trying to figure out how he's going to fit in with Ty and the other guys if he ever takes us further.

"You seem to have a thing with dishing out orders, Cole. The way you instructed me in the girl's toilets the other day was very commanding. I'd submit to you if you want to be my master?"

A low growl sounds at the back of Garrett's throat, and my eyes widen.

"You like the sound of that?" I ask, and he nods. "Good." I beam.

"Since I'm your master, I have a request."

I still. Maybe this conversation could have waited until tomorrow when there were other people around, so I couldn't do something rash like jump on his dick when he commands me?

"What sort of request?" I ask, and fuck, my voice sounds shaky.

Come back to me, pussy mojo!!

"It's not sexual. Don't worry. You're safe with me." Garrett's eyes are full of honesty when he says that, so I nod. "Take your hair out and show me it down."

I still, keeping quiet for a few beats as I stare into his eyes. I can tell he's just curious, nothing more. He wants to know what the big deal is about my hair.

"We need a safe word first," I interject, and his brows rise before he nods.

"Of course. Sorry. What would you like that to be?" Garrett licks his lips nervously, and it instantly makes me feel better. I'm glad I'm not the only one who is struggling with nerves today.

"Ummmm." I grip my chin, over-exaggerating my thinking stance. "Uhhhh. What about… Cactus?"

"Cactus?"

I nod. "Cactus. It's the safe word at the Feasts, so I won't forget it or get confused."

"So, cactus means stop?" Garrett confirms, and I nod.

"Yes, if I say cactus, then you must stop. No questions asked."

He nods this time. "Ok, cactus it is." He smirks. "Are you about to say cactus to my request?"

"No," I grin, shaking my head. "I'll concede and take my hair out for you. *Master*."

He grins back as I start working on my hair, searching for the bobby pins holding the twists together.

The light in the tent is dim, the small torch lying on the floor of the tent only giving off a weak warm glow, creating a serene ambience.

Bobby pin after bobby pin, I tug free, putting them in a pile, until all that's left is two hair ties which secure the piggy tails. Once I've pulled the hair ties free, I go to run my fingers through each side to comb out any lumps, but Garrett reaches out to stop me.

"Let me do that."

My heart rate picks up again as I slowly drop my hands to my lap, reminding myself that I'm safe. This isn't Brian. This isn't Master Hill. This is Garrett Cole, and he would never do anything to hurt me.

My lids flutter closed the moment Garrett's fingers brush through my tendrils. A shiver runs its way up my spine like sparks of electricity. It feels nice. Really nice. I'll never admit this out loud, but

I've missed this feeling. Having a man's strong fingers stroke gently through my hair. Each brush of his nails against my scalp fills me with a sense of peace. A feeling of home.

"You're stunning."

Garrett's whispered words draw my eyes open, and I'm met with his piercing icy-blue gaze.

"Thank you for sharing this with me." His hand moves to cup my face, his thumb brushing over my top lip. "Now, be a good submissive and go to sleep."

Fucking hell, it's going to be a long night. Because Kitty just purred, and my mojo just jumped back under my skin.

Chapter Twelve

Rhys

E verything I look at or think about turns into something sexual, so it's safe to say that Kitty has reunited with my mojo in tow, and she's ready to play. Eating the breakfast sausage turned into thinking about the smooth silk of a cock sliding between my lips. Wiping up sauce with my finger turned into thinking about licking it off Simon's chest. Bending over to pick up a stick turned into thinking about bending over in front of a mirror for Ty to spank me. Watching Shaun eat cantaloupe with only his fingers and mouth turned into thinking about him eating me. Even the way Marcus slipped his fingers inside a cup as he washed it had me thinking about his fingers sinking deep inside my Kitty.

Needless to say, by the time breakfast is over and the boys move off to have a hit of cricket in the clearing, I'm a hot mess. My skin is flushed with need, and the friction of walking is doing all sorts of teasing to Kitty, so when Lexi announces that she's going swimming, I decide to join her.

Now I'm not tooting my own horn or anything, but something has to be said for a girl's confidence when I step out of my tent in my little red bikini and manage to stop the cricket game mid bowl. Simon's fastball ends up smacking Jared in the shoulder, causing him to cry out in pain. Meanwhile, my guys pay him no attention, their heated stares following me as I make my way to Lexi, who has on her own cute floral two-piece.

"Damn, girl. You have them all drooling." Lexi grins, her eyes flitting to Ayden, who only has eyes for her. So does Jared. Even though he's clearly in pain, his eyes stay trained on Lex, a deep longing adding to the pained expression he wears.

"You can talk." I fan myself. "I think I just turned full lesbo! You look hot, Lexi!"

Lexi throws her head back, laughing. "Stop it! You like pretty cocks too much. Remember?"

She has a point.

"I do love me a pretty cock." I lick my lips as we ignore the drooling guys and make our way toward the bank of Ebony Falls. We aren't the only campers up here this weekend. There's a family of four who are currently paddling knee-high in the cool water, two young children squealing with joy as their dad splashes them, and another group of about eight, mostly guys with a couple of girls who look like they are in their mid-twenties. They've set themselves up on the far bank, which means they must have waded all their chairs and their eski across the water.

"Looks like you're making *all* the guys drool today, Rhys." Lexi giggles as the mid-twenties group of guys direct their attention to us, and the dad does a double-take.

"Girl, they are drooling over both of us. Wanna make out and give them a show?"

Another giggle bursts from Lexi's lips, right as warm arms snake around my waist.

"I'd watch that show." Shaun's warm breath feathers over my ear before his lips kiss a trail down my neck. Just like a feline would, I automatically stretch my neck to the side and arch my back, pressing my arse back to feel Shaun's solid length nudging forward.

"Don't be gross, Bossi." Lexi whines, turning in time to see Ayden charging for her. With a squeal, she drops her towel and sunscreen, trying to dart out of the way. She's not fast enough to escape Ayden Mitchell, though, because a moment later, he has her lifted over his shoulder like a sack of potatoes, while Lexi tries to use her hands to shield her arse as it's barely contained in her swimmers.

"Ayden! No! Put me down!" Her screech echoes off the rocky cliffs surrounding the falls, and Ayden gives her arse a little smack before agreeing.

"Ok beautiful. Your wish is my command."

Lexi's scream is deafening as Ayden launches her into the water, where he is already waist deep. As her body hits the water, cheers ring out as the rest of our group comes to join us, and Shaun chuckles against my skin, his lips not halting in their onslaught of peppering kisses over my bare shoulder.

"You're so hot, Kitten." His teeth nip at the curve of my neck. "You're making me hungry. I want to eat you."

My moan is audible, catching everyone's attention, except for Lexi and Ayden, who are having a splash off in the water.

"Rhys, that sound burns my ears!" Dale whines, and Alister chuckles, nodding.

"You'd better find somewhere else to play then." Simon declares, and Dale rolls his eyes dramatically.

"Perhaps your little groupie gang can save our eyes and ears by taking your sexcapades somewhere else? I'm sure little Jack and Jill over there aren't ready to learn about the birds and the bees." Dale flits his hands around with flamboyance, his face looking disgusted with the concept of a public sex claiming with me and my guys.

"He has a point. I love you, Rhys, but some of us aren't into voyeurism." Tillie adds, and Bell frowns, looking at Tillie like she's in total disagreement.

"Don't be like that, Til. Voyeurism is your middle name." I laugh, and she grins, poking her tongue out at me.

"What's voyeurism?" Simon asks, his head darting back and forth between where I stand in Shaun's embrace, to where Tillie stands with Bell, Dale and Allister by the water's edge.

I grin, loving how Simon is never afraid to ask questions. He doesn't care if it makes him look silly or not. He just wants to know.

"Voyeurism is when you get pleasure from watching." I offer, "Is that you, Simon? Does it turn you on to watch me? Would you like to watch Bossi make me come?"

"Aaaand, on that note, I am going to insert firecrackers in my ears and set them alight." Dale huffs, turning and storming off down the bank in the opposite direction.

"Yes." Simon blurts, ignoring Dale and the others as they walk away. "I wanna watch that."

Kitty flutters.

"Are you feeling a little more interested in sex today, Kitten?" Shaun purrs next to my ear. "Because I was watching you during breaky, and you've been wearing your horny face all morning."

"What?" My brows shoot up, and I twist in Shaun's arms to face him. "What do you mean?"

"Back off, Bossi." The deep rumble of Garrett comes from over my shoulder as his strong hand settles on my hip, letting me know that he's here for me.

"Hey! I'm not trying to convince her, bro! I'm simply stating what I noticed." Shaun defends, looking over my head at the towering hulk behind me.

"I noticed it too." Simon's voice comes from my left as he sidles up next to us.

"What about you, Grady? Did you notice how our girl was biting her lip as she watched you wash the dishes this morning?" Shaun asks, and I turn in time to see Marcus glare at Shaun.

"Fuck it. I think I'd rather hang out with the gay boys." Jared hisses, storming off

"Leave me out of your group sex talks." Marcus snaps before throwing his towel down on the sandy bank and wading out into the water.

"Someone got out of bed on the wrong side this morning." Simon rolls his eyes like Marcus is being melodramatic, but all I feel is my heart sink.

"Hey." Shaun gently grips my chin and steers my gaze back to his. "He didn't mean anything by that. I'll go have a talk with him."

"No." I shake my head. "I will." I stand up on my tiptoes and press my lips against Shaun's in a quick peck before pulling out of his hold. I instantly feel the loss of his combined touch with Garrett. There's just something about having them touch me at the same time.

I feel the heated eyes of Shaun, Garrett and Simon as I slowly step into the water, its chill doing nothing to calm the building heat inside me. As horny as I am, I'm still feeling a little out of sorts, but maybe all I need is a good fuck to wipe the memory of Wednesday night's Feast. Maybe a tangle of limbs, pounding flesh, and breathy moans will fix me right up.

My heart races at the thought of that. Am I cured of my broken vagina? Am I ready to go ham on a pretty dick? I glance back over my shoulder to see my guys still watching on, and heat pools between my legs when I take in their gazes. Fuck yes, I think today's the day I get some action.

Grinning, I turn back to focus on the current problem, which is Marcus. He seemed to come around to the concept of sharing me yesterday, but today, something has changed. I could leave him to brood his way through this alone, but lack of honest communication is what blew things up between us, and I'm desperate to have him back.

The tanned, toned arms of Marcus propel him through the water as he swims out into the deepest part of Ebony Falls, and I rush into the water, swimming out to catch him. The water here looks darker and kind of scary. What if there's some creepy river monster living at the bottom of the falls? What if there are dead bodies down there? The bones of the monsters' meals. I get a sudden fear of not knowing what the fuck is down under the water. Shit, do I have Thalassophobia? I'm learning so much about myself lately. I'm not a fan of Australia's cute and cuddlies in the dead of night, and I'm scared of fucking water. Ok, maybe not just water, but deep water. Shit, are there crocs in here?

"Marcus!" I call, panic setting in as I swim in desperation towards him.

He stops swimming, treading water as he turns back to see me, his face contorting with confusion before his eyes widen, and he starts back towards me.

"Marcus! I don't like this!" I'm practically splashing about like a fucking beetle on its back, probably scaring away any creatures lurking below. Or maybe I'm waking them up. Disturbing their peace. Aggravating them. "Marcus!" I squeal irrationally.

"Hey, it's ok, Rhee. I got you." Marcus' soothing tone wraps around me as his hands find my waist under the water and pulls me close. I hope he's a good swimmer because I'm not letting go. "It's ok. I have her!" Marcus calls over my shoulder, and I turn back to see the concerned faces of Shaun, Garrett and Simon waist-deep in the water.

Were they coming to rescue me?

"Marcus," I whisper, and his eyes return to mine, his body still moving with the motion of keeping us afloat.

"What are you doing out here, Rhee?" He asks, his dark eyes soft and concerned.

"Coming after you. Duh!" I roll my eyes, and he grins.

"Coming after me, huh? Without your entourage of lovers?"

I roll my eyes again. "You're part of my entourage... aren't you?"

Marcus' face falls, and my heart sinks.

"We should talk, I guess." He rasps.

He's changed his mind.

"Famous last words. They never mean anything good." I pout, and he grins briefly.

"Let's find somewhere to sit before we both drown." He doesn't disagree with my comment, which must mean one thing. He's already done with me.

"I don't know. I think drowning sounds like a good idea right now." For once, I let him see the fear in my eyes. I let him see the sadness building. This is the guy I told over and over that I didn't want and couldn't have a relationship, but now, it's all I want. And now, it's too late.

"Don't say that. Come on, let's swim to the bank."

"I think I'll take my chances with the wildebeest." I start pulling away from Marcus, but he grips me tighter, not letting me escape.

"The wilde-what? Isn't that an antelope or something?" Marcus chuckles.

"I don't know, but there's probably some sort of human eating creature lurking below us right now."

"All the more reason for you to come with me." Marcus grins. "Come on, let's go check out the waterfall."

Before I can protest, Marcus is swimming us towards the towering falls. The closer we get, the wetter we get as the mist coats us. I'm about to suggest we turn back when Marcus glances to the edge of the falls and moves in that direction. The pelt of the cascading water is less brutal here, and as we get closer, we can see a break in the screen of water, revealing a small rocky cavern behind it.

I don't get a chance to think any more of it before Marcus darts us under the falls, past the shower of h2o, and into the cavern. Weirdly, it's quite bright in here, the white rush of water letting through some of the daylight beyond. I'm surprised when Marcus suddenly stands up, showing me we are now on a shallow ledge that runs the length of the falls. It's like a little hideaway.

"How sick is this?" Marcus grins, turning to check the place out.

"It is pretty sick." I agree, letting its natural beauty fascinate me. Damn, I wish I had my camera. The way the light flickers over the rock wall would make a great shot.

Marcus turns back to me, smiling for a moment before it falters, and his shoulders drop as he sighs.

"You've changed your mind," I state, and his eyes drop to the water filling the mere feet between us.

"I thought I could do it. I thought I could share you. Even yesterday, I didn't feel the need to kill my mates just for touching or kissing you. Well, not as severely as before." He shakes his head.

"But?" I urge, because we may as well get this heart-breaking shit over with. I can't stand not knowing. I can't stand the sense of dread filling me.

"But the thought of them being inside you has me all sorts of fucked up." With jerky movements, Marcus rakes his hands through his dark, wet hair. "It's weird because that whole voyeurism shit you guys were talking about... I thought that was me. I thought I was someone that liked to watch. Especially after the whole Lexi and Ayden thing on my couch last month."

"Excuse me? What?" My eyes widen, and Marcus' panicked eyes dart up to meet mine.

"Shit. I said that out loud, didn't I?"

"Uh-yeah, and you'd better start talking, Mr! What Lexi and Ayden thing on your couch?"

Marcus releases a nervous laugh and sweeps through the water to lean back against the boulders at the rear of the cavern.

"Yeah, so... this thing happened. I was like asleep in the armchair, and when I woke up, I saw Ayden... uh."

"Marcus, come on. It's *me* you're talking to. No need to get sex shy now." I remind him, and he smirks.

"Basically, Ayden was going to town with his head between Lexi's legs, but it was over the top of her clothes. She wasn't naked or anything. I knew when I woke to find them that I should just get up and leave, but then I remembered they were in *my* house on *my* couch, and I decided to stay and watch."

"Holy shit! Why didn't anyone tell me about this? This is gold!" I laugh. "Wait. Did Lexi and Ayden know you were watching?"

"Uh... well, Lexi kinda realised and panicked, but then Ayden pushed her back down even though he saw me there, and he finished the job."

"And Lexi didn't protest?" My eyes are wide with excitement. I can't wait to give her shit about this.

"Not until afterwards. She kind of forgot I was there, I guess, and when I agreed with Ayden about how beautiful it was to watch her come undone, shit kinda got real. She got mad and stormed out, and Ayden ran out after her with his fucking boner pointing at Lexi like a compass." Marcus chuckles as he remembers, bringing a familiar joy to his face that I miss seeing.

"Did you rub one out after that?" I tease, and he ducks his head as embarrassment washes over him.

"Uh-yeah. I don't think I've had such a quick wank since I was thirteen."

My laughter echoes around the small space, and Marcus joins me, his eyes bright and carefree.

If only it would last.

"It was easy to watch Lexi and Ayden because Lexi isn't mine." He glances away, not able to look at me any longer. "You're mine, Rhee." His voice is quiet. "I don't think I can watch someone else bring you pleasure."

Heat pricks my eyes at his admission. Even though I already expected as much, it still fucking hurts.

"I hate being me," I admit as a sob escapes.

"What?" His head darts in my direction again before he pushes off the boulder and wades closer to me.

"I hate it, Marcus. I hate being this freak! This sex-crazed animal that needs abnormal things. I'm vile. The things I've done are vile. You and the guys have no idea of the things I've done just to get my fix. It's sick, Marcus. Really sick, and I can't fucking fix it. I've tried. So hard. So much therapy. So many self-help books and videos. Fucking rehab and retreats, and still I crave the need to get high on sex, uncaring of the consequences." I shake my head and back up as he moves toward me again. "I was stupid enough to listen to some advice that made me think I could have a relationship, in a Rhys George kind of way. Find someone willing to share you, they said. Find someone who will let you explore your sexual desires, they said. Well, you know what, Marcus? Maybe such a thing doesn't exist. Maybe those books about reverse harems are a load of bullshit. Maybe polyamorous relationships are a lie."

"What are you talking about? You already have a group of guys willing to share you." Marcus reaches for me, grabbing my hands so I can't back up any further.

"But I don't have *you*."

There it is. The truth I was too scared to admit when I was seeing him last term. The truth I was too scared to admit to anyone, even myself. I wanted Marcus to be mine, and I still do.

"Shit, Rhee." His eyes glaze over as his emotions take control. "I just don't know if I can do it. I don't know if I can share you, but it doesn't mean I don't want you. I fucking ache for you."

I have no control over how I react. I fling myself at him and crash my mouth into his. Our teeth clatter as he accepts my onslaught, and we grapple each other in desperation. His hands find my arse, and he tugs me against his straining cock, my legs lifting to wrap around him, bringing him tight against my core.

I'm crying, I realise. Hot tears are rushing over my cheeks, falling onto his, and every now and then, a sob escapes my throat instead of the moan I mean to set free. The cold, rough surface of the cavern wall presses against my back right before Marcus releases my mouth and trails kisses down my neck. I arch back, giving him better access and feel his fingers hook under my bikini top to lower the fabric and let my aching pebbled nipple free. The cool air turns it rock hard, and a moment later, the molten heat of his lips close over the pink flesh as his tongue does a familiar dance.

My sob sounds more like a moan this time, pleasure coursing through me as well as something else. The need I feel is more than lust. More than horniness. It's raw and aching and desperate. I'm terrified of this perfect moment ending. I don't want to let Marcus go. Ever.

The grind of Marcus' cock has me forgetting my fears and remembering how good he dicks me.

"Fuck me, Marcus. Please."

"I can't." He pants over my nipple. "No condom."

"Fuck it. I don't care. I need you so bad. I feel like I'll die if you don't bury yourself inside me."

"Fuck. Rhee." Marcus pulls back to look at me, his eyes lust drunk yet filled with concern. "Are you sure?"

"Yes. Please!" I beg, but he shakes his head.

"Fuck!" He growls and then turns his head over his shoulder. "Bossi!" The boom of his voice echos off the rocky cavern, and I freeze.

"What are you doing?" I feel like I'm fighting an electrical current that's filling my head with haze.

"Bossi, bring me a rubber!" Marcus bellows, his voice thundering around in the small space and hopefully reaching Shaun's ears across the water.

"Marcus. It's fine. Don't worry. We can stop." I pant, internally fighting against all my inhibitions.

"No! I'm not stopping unless you beg me to, Rhee." Marcus nips my bottom lip as his hand trails down the goose-bumped flesh of my stomach between our pressing bodies, to find my aching mound. The moment he puts pressure over my red bikini bottom, I forget my fucking name.

I gasp and moan, tilting my hips forward, seeking more. So much more.

"You want my fingers, baby?"

"I want all of you," I admit, and he chuckles against my lips before slipping his hand down the front of the thin fabric to circle those skilled fingers over my clit.

"You're so wet. It's so good to feel that again, Rhee. So fucking good." He runs his fingers teasingly through my folds. "Does it feel good for you?" Marcus doesn't let me answer straight away, his desperate tongue diving deep in my mouth, reminding me of its magical ability to spear into my cunt, nice and deep.

"Yes." I cry out when he releases my mouth.

"Uh… someone call for a condom?" Shaun's voice breaks through my daze, and my eyes jerk to where the silhouette of my Casanova stands, blocking some of the light filtering through the curtain of water.

"Yes!" Marcus darts his head around and reaches out his free hand while the fingers on his other hand still rub over my nub.

Shaun chuckles, wading forward until I can see his eyes, which are trained on us, taking in the scene.

"Any chance you want me to join in?" Shaun asks, and Marcus growls, snatching the condom from Shaun's fingers.

"No. Get the fuck out!"

Shaun chuckles, not fazed by Marcus' arsehole attitude. "Ok then. You kids have fun."

As Shaun turns and disappears through the veil of rushing water, part of me longs to call out to him to come back and join us. A fantasy that's plagued me for some time now, for Marcus to share me, at the same time with one of the other guys. The other part of me knows that this time with Marcus, with just the two of us, is necessary. It will make *us* or break *us*, and my heart is begging for the *making us*.

Turning his eyes back to me, the heat behind Marcus' gaze is searing. With his fingers still rubbing my clit, he slips them lower and eases three digits inside. My lips part and my head tilts back as my moan escapes, my body nothing but a slave to him.

"Rhee." He growls, curling his fingers up, "The whole not caring about a condom thing is a deal-breaker. If I'm going to share you, then every other motherfucker better tarp the fuck up as well. We don't know where else they stick their dicks."

"Oh-oh-ok." I pant, willing to agree to about anything right now.

"How does that work, anyway? Do they see other chicks too? Is that how this arrangement works? Just one big fucking sharing game?" He keeps moving his fingers while he talks, making it hard for me to concentrate. "Because I'm telling you right now, I'm yours and *only* yours. I'm not fucking anyone else but you."

"It's hard to… concentrate when you're finger fucking m-me, Marcus." I pant my way through the sentence, struggling hard to focus on anything but the feel of his fingers buried deep inside me.

"I can stop for a minute. We need to be clear about this." Marcus moves to draw his fingers out, but I grab his wrist between my legs, holding him in place.

"I know it's not fair for me to ask you guys to not sleep around with other chicks when I'm asking that you all share me, and I get the five of you, but that's what I'm asking. For you all to commit to just me, and I will belong to the five of you."

Marcus growls, "Five. I don't understand how that works if we don't get to meet this other arsehole who's sticking his dick in my girl. How do we know he's treating you right? How do we know he's not seeing other women?"

"I will speak to him about the commitment part. But you can't know who he is, Marcus. I'm sorry."

"Ever?" He frowns, anger in his tone.

"I mean, maybe one day. Just not in the next couple of years. If you guys have put up with me for that long and have still stuck around, then you will eventually get to meet each other." Using my hand, I start moving Marcus' between my legs, urging him to give me what I need.

"Rhee?"

"Yeah?" I pant as his fingers curl again.

"I'm not leaving you. Regardless of what the other dicks do. I'll be right by your side, no matter what."

Marcus sinks his fingers in deep, giving me the most delicious stretch, rendering me speechless. At first, it's pure pleasure that I feel, but then an intense shooting pain causes me to tense.

"Do you understand me?" His eyes are fierce as he pushes close, not realising that I'm in pain. "They are *my* terms. *Everyone* wears protection *every time*. No slip-ups. It's too dangerous for you. I will share you with the other four guys…" He huffs. "I'll figure out how to deal with sharing you with the other four guys. But no one else, Rhee. No new additions. If those other fuckers bow out, then it's their loss, but I'm never leaving you." He takes that moment to tear the condom wrapper open with his teeth, spitting the foil into the water at our knees as he pinches the tip of the latex. "I'm not saying that I'm not going to get pissed off about you and the others. I need more time to accept that shit, but I can tell you right fucking now. When you and I are together, it will just be the two of us. I can't even wrap my head around the possibility of group action yet."

Marcus shifts back, and my greedy eyes follow his hand as he lowers it to tug down his shorts and release his straining cock. Just the sight of it makes me gush, all pain forgotten, and I start writhing on his hand, his fingers picking up the pace.

"Yet?" I pant.

"What?" Marcus frowns, his eyes still trained on his dick as he rolls the protection down his shaft.

"You said *yet*. That means you might consider group action some time down the track?"

Those deep pools of darkness glance back up at me, his brows furrowing as he leans closer. Then Marcus surprises me when he rasps. "Maybe."

I moan at the thought, and he drags his fingers out, shoving them in his mouth, briefly savouring my taste as I grip his cock and guide it to my entrance.

"Fuck me hard, Marcus. Just the way I like it."

The devilish grin he shoots me is a reminder of my *old* Marcus, the one I let myself get lost in not too long ago. I'm glad that version of him is mostly back. I'm yearning for him desperately.

Marcus wastes no more time. In one swift move, he impales me, and any pleasure I felt vanishes as deep stabbing pain shoots through my core. The squeal I release is anything but good, and Marcus automatically freezes, feeling my whole body tense up around him.

"Shit, Rhee. What's wrong?" He draws back, his dark eyes filled with concern.

I shake my head, not able to speak, as tears stream from my eyes.

"Fuck." He curses again and slowly eases out. The moment he is nearly free, the pain lessens to a dull ache. "Talk to me. What just happened? Was I too rough?" The torment lacing Marcus' voice is what brings me back to him.

"N-no. It's me. I mean… I think it's from what happened the other night at the Feast. It really hurts. Like deep inside."

His brown gaze flits across my face, emotion filling the dark pools as he takes in my words. Then he tries to pull away from me.

"No. Don't stop," I beg, and he frowns, shaking his head in confusion.

"Are you kidding? I'm not going to hurt you. We don't have to do this."

"Yes, we do." I snap. "We need to seal the deal. Let me suck you off or something." I reach for his still straining erection, but he slaps my hand away.

"Rhys, no." He snaps back, but as he takes in my panicked state, his expression softens. "Before I shoved my dick in, it felt good, right? My fingers didn't hurt?"

I shake my head. "No, it mostly didn't hurt."

"Mostly? So it did hurt?"

"Only when you went deep," I admit, reaching for his cock again and loving the feel of the latex covering under my touch. I start to slowly pump his dick, needing to feel his arousal more than I need to feel my own. I need to remind him of how good I can make him feel.

"So, it felt good when I did this?" He reaches forward again and glides his fingers over my needy nub.

"Yes." I breathe, giving his dick a little squeeze as I slowly pump it.

"What about when I do this?" Slipping two fingers just inside, Marcus curls his fingers up, hitting that magical spot. My moan speaks for itself. "You like that, Rhee?"

I nod, leaning in, and he meets me in the middle, taking my lips in his as he wraps his free arm around my waist. I spread my legs wider, giving him full access, the move making Marcus moan deep as I work my hand up and down his shaft. It's primal, the way he grunts with desire each time he thrusts into my hand, building his pleasure as his fingers work fast over the sweet spot just inside Kitty while his thumb pays attention to my needy clit.

Marcus' pretty cock is blessed with girth. It's a stretching mouthful designed to give a girl lockjaw, so maybe that's why it was too much for me to take after the Feast a few nights ago. Who knows, but right now, as my fingers squeeze a little, not able to meet, wrapped around him, I imagine him deep inside me, the way he has been so many times before. I remember what it's like to be stuffed full with him, and as his scent wraps around me, my memories swarm, his fingers knead me, and his cock pistons in my grip. Everything suddenly feels overwhelming.

I don't understand what's happening as I hang on to his broad shoulder with my free hand and ride this high with him. Hot tears scorch my cheeks as my heart swells inside my chest, and a warm, full feeling washes over me and settles around my beating organ that gives me life.

I'm not going to say what I think it is. No analysing is necessary when you have Marcus Grady's balls slapping your wrist every so often. Even though we have fucked so many times before, and although we aren't technically fucking right now, this is the first time that I feel like he is claiming me.

He owns my heart and my Kitty, and as I scream and come, gushing over his fingers in a rippling explosion, I'm fairly certain he owns my soul as well.

Chapter Thirteen

GARRETT

My dick is as hard as stone. It was a mistake swimming out here with Bossi and Hastings after we heard Grady call out for a condom. It was also a mistake to float around and listen to our girl come apart on our friend's cock behind the wall of water. What the fuck was I thinking, putting up boundaries and telling Rhys she *can* have a relationship without sex? Fucking hell, my balls are so blue they are almost black.

"Fuck." Simon hisses, "On a scale of one to ten, how dead do you think Grady will make me if I join in without his permission?" Simon's face normally resembles a playful puppy, but right now, he's nothing but serious.

"If ten is dead as a fucking doornail, then I'm going with fifty." Shaun grins, and Hastings pouts before a surprised smile crosses his face.

"On a good note, it seems like our girl isn't feeling opposed to sex anymore."

"Yeah. You're right." Shaun grins before eyeing me. "Did you have something to do with that, Cole? Did you end up showing her your mammoth cock last night?"

I roll my eyes. "Dude, if I did, she wouldn't have come out of the tent today. She'd be so hooked on riding me that she'd never climb off."

Shaun scoffs, "whatever."

I chuckle as he ponders while Simon ignores us, swimming closer to the waterfall.

It's gone quiet behind the falls where Marcus and Rhys just reunited. I guess they're done extracting orgasms from each other.

Lucky fuckers.

"Oi! Are you two done? The Hastinator wants to play too!" Simon hollers, and Shaun snickers as I roll my eyes. Simon isn't going to give up.

Suddenly, a hulking mass erupts from behind the waterfall as Marcus launches himself at Simon. They go straight under in a splash, only to come up seconds later laughing.

"Fuck, for a second there, I thought it was Simon's turn to meet Marcus' right hook," Shaun admits, and I nod.

"I guess he's feeling better after his *chat* with our girl." Ignoring Shaun's response, I propel myself forward, swimming for the falls until its heavy weight hammers over me. When I resurface a moment later, I find myself in the small rocky cavern behind the falls.

"If you're here to intervene before I spread my legs, it's too late." Rhys' voice is playful, and as I wipe the residual water from my eyes, she comes into view as she rights her bikini top. Damn, if only I had been thirty seconds earlier, I might've got a look at those plump mounds on her chest.

"Yeah-Nah, I figured I was too late when I heard you screaming."

She giggles. "Whoops. I guess I was a little vocal."

"A little is an understatement. The couple with the two kids fled."

"They did not?" Her eyes widen as she waits for me to confirm.

"They did, baby girl. Sorry." I can't hide my smirk as I take in her expression. It went from mortified to satisfied, like she did a good job.

Little minx.

"I bet the parents fled because I turned them on. Ten bucks says the wife blows her husband on the drive home when the kids fall asleep."

I throw my head back, laughing. This chick. She's hilarious, and fun, and beautiful, and playful, and fuck, she gets my dick harder than any other chick ever has.

"Ah-ha, and how are we going to know if she does that?"

"It's a given. The hubby will subtly rub her pussy first, maybe even before the kids fall asleep. She'll try her hardest to keep quiet, and she's going to come quick and hard. By that time, she'll be an animal, so those kids better fucking fall asleep, or they are going to be scarred for life when they watch mummy deep throat daddy."

"Stop." I chuckle and approach her. Unfortunately, her little red bikini is covering all the parts I yearn to taste. I'm so tempted to reach out and rip the thin layer of fabric from her creamy skin. I refrain, though.

Not only am I waiting for Grady to give me the ok—if that ever happens—I also want to hold off and show Rhys that there's more than sex in a relationship. My dick is protesting my life choices right now, but I will keep my word.

"Are you alright?" I ask seriously, running my eyes over her face as I study her reaction. Then her cheeky grin drops.

"Yes." She nods, her eyes darting down to the water lapping at her thighs.

It's rare to see Rhys George lose her confidence. I'm glad she feels comfortable around me to show me her vulnerability, but what I really want is for her to feel happy and content again.

When I step up to her and will my body not to be a prick and point my dick at her like she's a beacon, Rhys drags her eyes from the water, craning her head back to look up at me. I focus on her beautiful face and notice she is wearing less makeup than yesterday. Reaching up, I stroke my thumb over her cheek, where there are small red blotches covering the skin.

"Have you been crying?"

Those chocolate eyes dart from mine to my lips as she shrugs. "Maybe."

"Did Marcus hurt you?" I growl. I can't fucking help it. The thought of him hurting her turns me into a beast.

"No." She answers quickly, shaking her head, her eyes finding mine again. "I mean, not intentionally. It was a little too painful to have him inside me. I guess the thing at the Feast hurt me more than I realised. But we improvised." She shoots me a slight grin that doesn't reach her eyes. "I'm feeling a little overwhelmed, I guess. I've missed him. It was nice to be with him again, even if it wasn't the way I wanted."

I nod. "Good. That's good, baby. Not the part about you hurting. That's not good. But the you and Marcus thing is good."

She smiles and nods back. "It is, isn't it?"

"Sure is." I grin. Fuck, she's beautiful. "And he's happy to share you?"

Her face morphs into a seductress. "He's working on it, but he did admit that some group action isn't out of the question."

"Really?" My brows shoot so high that I get an instant headache. "And you'd be into that as well?" I don't know why I asked her that. She goes to sex clubs and has orgies, for fuck's sake. Of course, she'd be into it. I never thought I'd be into it, but my nearly bursting through my skin dick contradicts that.

"Actually, the thought makes me horny, but it also makes me nervous. Sure, I've done the group thing before, but I didn't know those people. I couldn't even see their faces. The thought of sharing that with you guys…" She trails off, not able to finish, but that's ok. I get what she's saying.

"You don't have to do anything you don't want to do."

"I know." She whispers.

"Do you, Rhys? I worry you think you have to be sexual in order to keep the guys interested."

She frowns. "Isn't that what a relationship is for, though? Having easy access to fuck whenever you want?"

"Fuck no." I cup her face, so she has no choice but to look at me. "The sex part is just a bonus. It's a way to share how much you care for each other, but it's just a small part of a relationship. The rest is made up of sharing feelings, hopes and dreams, worries, and milestones. It's like having a best friend—a soul mate. You share your lives. They intertwine, and when things get tough, it's ok because you don't have to face it alone. You have someone by your side willing to fight for you and with you."

"Have you been in a relationship before?" Her voice is so small, almost like she's scared to know the answer.

"No. I read a lot of romance books, though. I'd like to think I know a thing or two."

A laugh bubbles up from Rhys' throat.

"You read romance books?"

"Yes." I frown. "What's wrong with that?"

"Uh… you're a dude!"

"Are you stereotyping romance readers?" I drop my hands from her face. "Can't a guy read romance? Is there some unspoken law I don't know about?"

She beams, "Actually, no, there's no law. In fact, more guys *should* read romance books. They would learn a helluva lot."

"And you? Do you read romance books?" Her skin is cool under my touch, and I glide my hands down her neck, to her shoulders and down her arms.

She shrugs, "I've read a few reverse harem books, but mostly I read erotica, but only when I can't watch porn freely."

Shaking my head, I grin and look back towards the wall of water separating us from the others. I can hear Simon and Marcus still splashing around like annoying kids. It's nice to hear.

"Are you ready to go back out there?" I point over my shoulder when I turn back to Rhys. Her blotchy cheeks have lightened now.

"Yeah, I could use some sun." Rhys wades through the water to go past me, but I gently grip her upper arm, stopping her by my side.

"I know you and Marcus re-united, but I want you to know that it doesn't mean you have to have sex or anything like that with anyone else yet. You've had a tough week. It's ok if you need to take a step back and just be a girl hanging out with some mates."

Her face softens, and she sucks in her lower lip as her eyes study mine.

"Thank you. For once, I could really use some mates instead of fuck buddies."

Rhys rises on her toes, leaning towards me, so instinctively, I lean down and offer her my cheek, like a friend would do. Her lips are warm as they press gently against my skin, and as she pulls back, she whispers in my ear.

"I appreciate your kindness, but if I don't get away from you, I'm going to slip my hand down your shorts and pull out your hard dick, and once I have that beast in my hands, Cole, there's no turning back."

I release her arm when she lowers herself back down, giggling to herself as she leaves the cavern. Thank fuck she walked away. If she had done what she said, I don't think I'd be strong enough to hold myself back. Ugh! I tip my head back, glaring at the rocks above me before I re-adjust my dick in my shorts. The fucking thing is nearly poking out the top. I want Rhys so bad. I crave sinking into her wet heat. It's getting harder to be around her and not act like a horny fucker.

I'm determined, though. I need to show her that there's more to it than just sex. I can see she feels it, but her addiction clouds her judgement. It's like there's a barrier around her heart, stopping her from truly understanding what it feels like to love someone and have them love her back. I don't know if me and the guys are good for her. I have no idea if we can pull off a shared relationship, but hopefully, Rhys can finally experience something more meaningful that will help her through her life, even if we aren't in it.

Chapter Fourteen

Rhys

Today has been the best. We spent the whole day in the water. If we weren't swimming or trying to drown each other, we were having races in the two blow-up dinghies that Jared brought. When we got sick of that, we sat in the water in our camp chairs, drinking. Aside from Lexi and Ayden, who are glued at the hip but in the best way, everyone mingles, and we are all just mates hanging out. Even Bell makes an effort in her drug-free state, giving us a glimpse of her smile more than a handful of times, which is a rare occasion. Much like my Big Guy, Garrett.

As the sun starts to go down, the air grows chilly, and I join the girls for a quick hot shower while the guys light the campfire and get started on dinner. There are only two showers in the public bathroom, so Tillie and I go first and then Bell and Lexi barge in after us covered in goosebumps.

As they shower, I comb through my wet hair, studying my completely makeup-free face in the mirror. I'd intended on re-painting my liner and lashes, but for the first time ever, I don't want to. Tyler and Shaun are the only ones who have seen me completely natural, and they told me I'm stunning and beautiful that way. Were they being serious?

Leaning closer to the mirror, I rest the comb on the bench and examine my face again, turning from side to side.

"You ok?" Tillie asks, gaining my attention. She's standing next to me, brushing her pixie hair as she looks at my reflection.

"Do I look weird without makeup?"

Her brows shoot up at my question, and she turns to me, her eyes no longer watching me in the mirror.

"Are you kidding? You're fucking beautiful, Rhys. Why would you think you look weird?"

I shrug and face her. "I don't know. Maybe because everyone is used to seeing me in my war paint."

She shakes her head. "You don't look weird without makeup. You just look different, and not in a bad way. You look like a fucking model, Rhys."

I turn back to my reflection, taking in my dark brown eyes and naturally thick dark lashes. My eyes look bigger without the frame of black liner on them. They also look softer. Sweeter. I'm not sure if that's the correct representation of who I am. I'm not sweet.

"What if they don't like me this way?" I turn back to Tillie. "What if they prefer the sexed-up look?"

Tillie offers me a sympathetic smile. "I've seen the way they look at you when you're not aware. It's more than lust, Rhys. They care about you, and if you show them the real you," Tillie reaches out and takes a lock of my dark, damp hair and lets it slide through her fingers, "They are going to care about you even more."

"What do you mean?"

"That group of boys are rare for our age. They want more from you than your coochie, Rhys. They want you to open up to them, to trust them. The war paint is a mask. Why not show them who Rhys George really is?"

I frown. "Can't I do that and keep my war paint on?"

She smiles, "I think you'll find you'll be more yourself when you let yourself trust them completely. Showing them this version is showing them you trust them with your vulnerability."

"You sound like a therapist." I pout, and she giggles.

"I'm pretty sure my therapist has said something similar to me before. Turns out she's worth the money."

I grin and turn back to the mirror, staring into my own eyes.

Can you do this, Rhys? Can you show them the parts you hide?

My thoughts are cut off by Lexi and Bell joining us at the bench, and I take in Lexi's natural beauty. She doesn't hide behind a metaphorical mask anymore. She let down her walls, especially to Ayden, and now she has someone by her side. He's willing to fight for her. Hell, he *did* fight for her against her own dad. He'd do anything for her, and she'd do anything for him. I think I'm starting to get it. If she hadn't let him in, then they wouldn't have the secure relationship they have now.

But can *I* do it? Can I really let them in completely? Does that mean I have to tell them everything? I've never told anyone everything. And what if I tell them, and they run for their lives in the opposite direction?

Fuck, when did I become such a pussy?

"Stop overthinking it." Tillie's voice is quiet next to my ear, and I glance at her reflection in the mirror. She offers me a small smile, and I nod, thankful for her distraction.

I decide to do it. I leave my makeup in the bag and put away my hair ties. I won't be needing them tonight. I'm going to show my friends, all of them, not just my guys, who Rhys George really is under the bold makeup and fun hair buns.

I feel confident about my decision until we approach the campsite, and all eyes fall on me, lingering. Normally I like that. I thrive on it. Not now, though. Now I feel exposed. Like I'm being judged. As the girls veer off towards their tents to put their things away, I'm left to face eight males as their eyes study me.

My heart rate skyrockets and panic creeps in. Fuck. I shouldn't have done this. I shouldn't have shown them what I really look like. What the fuck was I thinking?

"Hey, Kitten." Shaun smiles warmly, approaching me and kissing my cheek like I didn't just flash them all my bare face. "Let me help you with these."

I look away from the staring eyes to where Shaun pries my fingers open to take my bag, and then he links his fingers with mine, tugging me towards my tent. As we pass by Garrett, he stops for a moment to mutter something quietly that I can't make out, and a moment later, we are slipping inside my tent.

I stand like a fucking mute while Shaun puts my bag down in the corner and turns back to me.

"What's wrong, Kitten?"

"I... uh... Need to put my makeup on. I forgot."

I move toward my bag, only making it a few steps before Shaun's strong arms wrap around my waist and pull me back against him.

"Stop. Leaving it off is a good call."

"Why?" I whisper, kind of scared of his answer.

"Well, aside from the fact that you are the most stunning creature on this earth, I think it will mean a lot to the guys that you are sharing this with them. It's important that you be yourself with us."

I spin in his arms and peer up into his steel-grey eyes. "What if myself is all that heavy makeup?"

Reaching up, Shaun brushes my hair back off the side of my face, letting his fingers glide all the way down its long length before he settles his hand on my lower back.

"The makeup *is* part of you, Kitten. But so is this," he brushes the pads of his fingers down my cheek, "and it will show them you trust them. That's big, Kitten."

"But... they just stared at me. Like I was weird or something."

Shaun chuckles and tugs me closer. "They were stunned by your beauty. There's nothing weird about you."

"But even Dale and Allister were staring."

"Just because they are gay doesn't mean they don't admire beauty, Kitten. Shit, they're probably questioning if they are gay or straight right now."

A laugh rips from my chest, and I smack Shaun playfully on his shoulder.

"Stop. That's just weird."

Shaun shrugs. "It's probably true, though." He leans down and presses his forehead to mine. "I miss you."

My brows shoot up at his confession.

"Why? I'm right here."

He shrugs. "It's hard sharing you. Part of me wants the others to spend time with you, but I can't help but want you all to myself. I fucking ache to fall asleep with you in my arms again."

"Ache as in Thor? Does he ache to be inside me?"

Shaun frowns, "No, not Thor. My heart aches to hold you close, to have you near. All the fucking time."

"It does?" My voice is quiet and lacking any real confidence.

"Yes, it does. I think I'm addicted to you, Kitten."

Well shit. "I think I'm addicted to you too, Cass. Is it strange that I miss the Feast? I know what happened wasn't good, but I miss it. It would normally be on tonight. I'd be getting ready now, painting my face in the barn and slipping into whatever outfit Master Hill chose for me. Do you think after what happened on Wednesday night that it's still running tonight?"

"I get it, Kitten. We have a lot of fun at the Feast nights, so yeah, I miss that. I'm pretty sure it's still happening. I got the message yesterday morning, even though I assumed I'd been taken off the guest list. Maybe they wanted me there to punish *me* this time for trying to help you."

I frown, "Those motherfuckers better not touch you, or I'll chop their dicks off!"

Shaun throws his head back, laughing, "I'd pay to see that, Kitten."

Grinning, I lay my head on Shaun's chest and squeeze my arms, needing to feel him as close as possible. "I miss you too."

Even though I whisper it, I can tell Shaun hears by the way his arms tighten around me. Glancing back up, I watch as he licks his lips before leaning down, and I meet him halfway, pressing mine against his. As we kiss, our tongues brush, and I melt into his hold, giving myself over to this moment. It's slow, long and torturously good, and I realise it's one of those special kisses that isn't happening for sex. It's happening because we care. It's a carnal display of, dare I say it… love.

Even though I can feel how hard Shaun is, Thor straining between our bodies, and even though my Kitty is purring with need, we don't act on it. We let the kiss linger and then slowly pull apart, our eyes wild with something other than lust as we fight to peer into each other's souls.

"I heard you the other night when Derek told you he thought I loved you, and you said you were pretty sure you loved me, too." Shaun takes a deep breath. "Did you mean it?"

Be honest, Rhys. That's the only way this will work.

"I meant it, but I'm not sure that I understand it yet. I'm so messed up." I shake my head and try to look down, but Shaun's fingers come to rest under my chin, keeping me in place.

"I need you to know that Derek was right, Kitten. I know it hasn't been long, and I know we are still getting to know each other, but I also know that I can't live without you. You consume my every thought, and I have this obsessive need to know everything there is to know about you. I've never loved anyone before, but I'm pretty sure what I'm feeling is it. I'm in love with you, Kitten."

I'm lost for words. I open and close my mouth but can't form a single word. My hands are trembling, and my chest feels full and, dare I say, happy. Since I can't speak, I use another language I'm good with, and I lean up, taking his lips in mine again.

Our kiss is hot and fevered this time, and I feel like I'm going to swallow him whole if I don't get a grip. I understand what he means by obsessive and consuming. It's how I feel about him too, and I show him with each stroke of my tongue and each nibble of my lips, all while fisting my hands into his dark curls and holding him tight.

Eventually, breaking our kiss, Shaun pulls back, smirking. "Uh, we should probably get back out there."

I want to disagree, but I know he's right. I need to go out there and show the guys who I am under the mask I've worn for years, so I nod, feeling flushed and thoroughly kissed.

After Shaun steps back from me, I stand awkwardly, not really sure if I'm prepared to face the guys again, but Shaun doesn't let me think too much about it. He takes my hand in his and leads me from the safety of my tent.

The night air is cool, and it feels refreshing on my flushed cheeks as we walk over to the fire, the smell of sizzling barbequed meat wafting around us. Everyone is in some sort of conversation while the faint sound of music plays in the background. It sounds like Lexi's music. One of the Archer 9 songs she loves so much. They're a legit sick band. I'm kinda jelly that she got to meet them. She told me all about it today while we were lying in the sun. I hadn't put two and two together until she mentioned that Archer 9 created the Archer Network, an organisation that finds homes for children in the foster care system who have had it tough. Connor and Archie found their way to Cynthia and Will through the Archer Network. It was lucky they were still young enough that their past didn't change them too much. The Archer Network do great work, and now that I know Archer 9 are behind it, I'm even more intrigued.

I feel eyes on me as I sit on a camp chair by the fire while Shaun leaves me to grab us some drinks. Every time I look up to see whose eyes are lingering, I'm met with turned heads or cast down eyes.

Am I being paranoid?

Just as Shaun takes a seat next to me and hands me a can of Gordans Pink Gin, Garrett squats down in front of me, catching my eyes with his.

"What would you like to eat? We have rissoles, marinated chicken kebabs, or sausages."

Opening the can of Gin, I grin wickedly at Garrett.

"I'm quite fond of sausage. Are they thick sausages or long and thin?"

"Stop it." He smirks.

"Mmmm, or are they long *and* thick? I do like a thick girthy sausage."

A low growl sounds from Garrett's chest as he glares at me with heat behind his eyes.

"Behave."

"When I eat a thick girthy sausage, I like to see how much I can fit in my mouth before I gag."

"You aren't playing fair, George. I thought you appreciated the boundaries I put up." Garrett's voice is deep and husky, and it makes Kitty purr. She's very awake. Very needy and very ready for some action. Too bad for her. I'm all talk and no action at the moment. After finding out that things are still painful down below, I'm not too keen on revisiting that agony. Still, I can't stop my mouth from playing dirty.

"What I appreciate, Big Guy, is a good deep throating."

Garrett growls, and Shaun leans over from his chair, speaking close to my ear.

"Kitten, I have a raging boner now. If you want a good deep throating, I can help you out."

Turning to Shaun, I grin and lick my lips before I guzzle down some Gin.

"Back off, Bossi. She was referring to my sausage, not yours," Garrett growls, and Shaun raises his brows.

"Dude, you don't have a fucking sausage. You have a fucking meatloaf."

With all my control lost, I spit my drink out, spraying Shaun and Garrett with Pink Gin as a laugh rips from me uncontrollably.

Garrett leaps up, and Shaun nearly falls off his chair as they try to escape the sweet drink, but they aren't quick enough.

"Jesus, woman! Now my white shirt is pink." Shaun whines, stretching out his t-shirt to examine it while Garrett chuckles.

"You're pansy enough to wear pink, Bossi." Garrett teases right as Simon bounds up to us.

"Here, Cherry, I have some food for you." He nudges Garrett out of the way and falls to his knees in front of me, holding up a large plate with basically everything on it.

"Hastings, I'm not *that* hungry," I complain, and he rolls his eyes.

"It's for me too. Duh." Simon grins, placing the plate on the log next to my chair and proceeds to feed me. "Here, taste the chicken. It's delicious."

I have no choice but to open my mouth and take a bite of the chicken when Simon presses it to my lips. He's right. It is delicious. But even more tempting than the food in my mouth is the way Simon watches me as he feeds me. His eyes are wild with arousal. His lips part as I open my mouth, and he licks his lips as I take a bite. He watches my mouth like it's a delectable dessert that he's desperate to taste, and fuck it's a turn on. Kitty is raring to go, but my brain is telling me to stop.

I fucking love sex. I fucking need it like I need to breathe, so why am I letting a little pain control me?

As Simon slowly slips another tender piece of chicken between my lips, I focus on his face and let myself relax a little more.

Enjoy this, Rhys. Just go with it.

This time, when Simon feeds me more chicken, he slips his finger into my mouth. Like a bolt of lightning, Kitty pulses with so much arousal that I have to fight the urge to slip my fingers between my legs. Unfortunately, I'm helpless to stop my moan.

"Fucking hell. How come feeding her is so hot?" Shaun rasps next to me, and I hear the agreeable grunts of Marcus and Garrett.

"It's called food play, boys. Watch and learn." Simon's proud grin would be adorable if I wasn't filled with so much aching need.

"Uh-yeah, I'm out." Jared's voice comes from behind me.

"Hey, where are you going?" Tillie calls out to Jared, who grunts something about going for a long walk.

"Hastings, maybe you should take this inside our tent." Garrett points out, but Simon ignores him and keeps feeding me, each time slipping his digit into my mouth.

"The tent will block the visual, but it won't stop us from hearing it." Tillie points out, and I want to turn to her and laugh or something, but all I can do is watch Simon as he keeps his eyes trained on me.

"Simon says, go for a walk."

Simon's tone is deep and commanding, causing me to moan and watch as he directs the hottest fucking glare toward Tillie and the others.

"Come on, Lex. I've got something to show you," Ayden says quietly from behind me and Lexi giggles.

"We all know what you want to show her, Ayden." Finally, I find my voice and Ayden chuckles, not denying anything, as he grabs a blanket from the back of his car and walks off with Lexi in the dark.

"Ok, I'm just saying. You are all gross!" Dale whines, picking up his plate and storming off towards the riverbank. A moment later, Tillie, Allister and Bell run off, following him, leaving me alone with my guys.

"That's one way to get rid of everyone." Shaun chuckles before he guzzles his drink.

"Cherry. Are you still hungry?" Simon's deep voice hits all the right places.

"I am… but…"

"But?" Simon asks, and I shrug, suddenly feeling self-conscious. Where the fuck has my mojo gone? One minute it's back, and the next, it's nowhere to be found.

"What's wrong, Kitten?" Shaun leans closer, lifting my hand and linking our fingers.

"I…" I shake my head and look down at my lap. I've turned fucking fridget, haven't I? WTF!

"We can just hang out, Rhys. Wanna play cards or something?" Garrett, my Big Guy, is still looking out for my non-existent virtue.

Will the guys be happy with that? And do I wanna play cards?

Nope. I don't want to play cards. I want my mojo to learn to stay put, and I want to know that I can get railed without it hurting.

"Yeah, we can play cards or go for a night hike or something Cherry." Simon is still kneeling before me. If I part my legs, I know he'd move forward and settle between them.

"I don't want to play cards or go on a hike. I want to do something else, but I'm having a little trouble."

Shaun strokes his thumb over the back of my hand. "Kitten, it's understandable after what happened at the Feast. No one expects you to do anything. We are here for whatever you need."

"The thing is, I want more. I'm horny as fuck, and Kitty is dripping. That's no lie. It's just… things aren't quite healed, I guess."

Crickets. It's all I hear for a beat while the guys interpret my words, and right as Marcus takes a step towards me, an unknown voice bursts our bubble.

"You fellas wanna join our party?"

In unison, we turn toward the voice to see four of the guys that were on the other side of the river earlier today.

"Uh, Nah, man. Thanks, anyway. We're all good." Shaun answers, and I notice a short, stocky guy holding up a bag of something that definitely isn't legal. Shit, I hope Bell or Ayden don't come over and see what he has.

"Oh, come on. We'll share our sugar if you share yours." A taller guy with arms covered in tatts gestures his head to me.

Shit.

My heart seizes for a moment as I realise the danger I could be in.

"Like I said," Shaun practically growls, "we are all good. This is a private party. Sorry fellas."

"Ok, fair enough." The stocky guy asks as he pockets his drug baggy. "So where are you from? Are you locals?"

"Yeah. Close by." Garrett grunts, standing tall with his arms crossed over his chest and a deadly glare on his face.

"Cool. Same. We're from Redfield. I haven't seen you there, though. Are you from Fox Pines or Woodall Ridge?" The stocky guy keeps his focus on Garrett while the others in his group dart their eyes between the rest of us.

"Nah, they ain't from Woodall Ridge." The lanky guy at the back of their group offers, "They're too clean." The four guys laugh.

"You're right. They must be from Fox Pines." The tatted arm guy drags his gaze over me before glancing back at my guys, and a sickening chill runs up my spine.

"They look too preppy to be anything but Catholic students." The stocky guy eyes each of us. "You from FP Catholic?"

"What of it?" Simon snaps. I can imagine he's glaring right now. I don't know for sure since I refuse to take my eyes off these intruders for a second.

"Hey, chill, man. We're just making conversation." Tatt guy tuts at us as the stocky guy gets his phone out before holding it up.

"You see this? A friend of a friend sent it to me. It's a fucking ripper."

My breath hitches as I see myself as a child on his screen. I feel like I'm in one of those movie scenes where everything zooms in, and all you can see is the video playing and nothing else. I want to react and tell the arsehole to stop, but my words seize in my throat.

"Hey! Turn that off!" Shaun launches forward for the guy's phone but doesn't make it far before Garrett wraps his arms around Shaun, holding him back. "You sick fuck! That's a child!"

"Ooohhh, someone's a bit touchy. What's wrong? This your little sister or something?" The stocky guy laughs, and Marcus leaps forward this time, launching his fist into the side of the guy's face.

Chaos erupts as all the guys lunge at each other while I stay rooted in place for a few very long seconds before my brain catches up. Then, feeling a little more like the old me, the one that is bitch arse crazy, I leap on the stocky guy's back as he pushes Marcus to the ground.

A banshee scream rips from my chest as I hook my arms and legs around the guy's back and bare my teeth right before sinking them into his ear. An odd-sounding wail comes from the stocky guy as he tries to throw me off his back by spinning around over and over. My teeth stay clamped onto him, even when I taste blood, and I dig my fingernails into his shoulders, hoping to inflict more pain.

More yelling echoes around me. I can't see what's going on since the guy keeps spinning this way and that in jerky movements. It's when I hear other female screams that I know cavalry has arrived, and a few spins later and the stocky guy falls forward to his knees.

The ground moves fast towards me, so I squeeze my eyes shut, bracing for impact, yet it doesn't come. Strong arms wrap around me, pulling me free before I hit the ground, and the next thing I know, I'm being carried away from the melee.

"Calm down, Rhee." Marcus hisses in my ear as I flail, eager to get back and tear the guy's ear from his head. "Stop, will you!"

His tone sounds more annoyed than anything, so I stop trying to attack thin air and let my limbs drop as I give in to defeat. My feet meet the ground, and I try to look toward the others, but Marcus takes my face in his hands.

"Please tell me that's his blood and not yours."

I nod before bringing my arm up and wiping the blood from my lips and chin with the sleeve of my hoodie. Marcus grins.

"You're crazy. You know that?"

"Yep." I nod. "You just figuring that out, Grady?"

He shakes his head, not able to hide his smirk. "Nah, I've known all along. It's part of why I love you."

Did he just say he loves me? Is it really possible that two guys have told me in one night?

"She ok?" Jared asks, jogging up to us before leaning forward to brace his hands on his knees. He's puffing like he just ran a marathon.

Glancing over his shoulder, I realise that our unwelcome visitors have disappeared.

"She's fine. Apparently, she's hungry, though." Marcus chuckles.

"Cherry, I didn't know you liked to eat ears." Simon grins, bounding up to us, all hyped up on adrenalin.

"It's not exactly the type of flesh I prefer to put in my mouth." I grin, and Jared rolls his eyes.

"On that note, I'm outta here… again."

CHAPTER FIFTEEN

SIMON

On instinct, I reach out for my girls' feet. I fell asleep cuddling one of them last night after she passed out in Bossi's arms. That fucker is getting more Cherry time than me, and it's starting to piss me off. So is Grady. When I went to lie down on Cherry's other side last night, he fucking pushed me away and glared at me like I had no business trying to lie next to her.

Motherfuckers! She's my girl too!

When my hand only finds a blanket and nothing else, I crack my lids, and my eyes slowly adjust to the orange-tinted daylight seeping through the tent walls. My girl isn't there. I sit up and look around the tent, confused. Shaun, Marcus and Garrett are still in the same spots, but Rhys is nowhere to be seen. Maybe she went to the toilet.

I stretch, releasing a big yawn and feeling the sore spots on my body from last night. We had a fucking punch on with some fucking tossers from Redfield. I can't believe we came out as well as we did. After all, those pricks were a few years older than us.

After everyone calmed down, Rhys went unusually quiet. She didn't seem happy. Didn't seem sad. She was just quiet. When Tillie asked questions about how those arseholes had gotten a hold of the video, Cherry didn't flinch. She didn't look angry, didn't even look like she cared, although I know she did. The other guys noticed her mood as well, and when Shaun mentioned we should go to bed, she just gave him a nod and stood up, walking silently next to him to our tent.

I even tried Simon Says on her, but it was no use. She still wouldn't speak. Instead, she just laid down, cuddled into Bossi, and closed her eyes. I saw something, though, right before she closed those chocolate eyes of hers. A flicker of something across her expression. Shame? Guilt? She had dark secrets behind her eyes, and I want more than anything for her to just open up to me. To us. It's hard to know how to help her when we don't know everything. I have no idea what's going through her head. What it must have been like to see that video of herself with that sick fucking prick of a foster dad.

It must be unbearable.

Why are her old foster parents doing this to her? Is it payback because they got caught in the first place? We should probably talk Rhys into going to the cops. The video is bad enough, but what if they are dangerous? What if they try to hurt my girl?

I'll fucking kill them if they lay a hand on her!

It's my overfull bladder that makes me get up and slip out of the tent. I notice the zipper has been left undone, and as I uncurl myself in the crisp morning air, the glare of the rising sun is almost blinding. I shield my eyes, gazing around the campsite. There's no sign of Cherry, so I glance over to the toilet block across the clearing. She must be over there. I don't know why she would go alone after those fuckwits were hanging around last night, but maybe she's with Lexi or something.

I find the closest tree and take a leak, closing my eyes as the satisfaction of releasing all the fluid takes over.

"Where's Rhys?"

"Fuck!" I jump at the sound of Garrett's voice behind me, nearly pissing on my feet.

"How about a little warning before you creep up on a man taking a piss?"

"I would, but I can't see any men around here." Garrett comes to stand beside me, pulling out his fucking boa constrictor and starts to piss.

"Oh, ha fucking ha!" I glare at him and try not to feel intimidated by the sheer size of his dick.

"So, where's our girl?"

"Toilets, I guess." I shrug, shaking my snake and tucking him back into my shorts.

"You guess? How long have you been up?" Garrett glares at me, ignoring the fire hose he's holding, watering the tree in front of us.

"Maybe 10 minutes. I was gonna go see where Lexi is. She might know where Cherry is."

Frowning, Garrett cuts his piss short and tucks himself in as he walks over to Rhys' tent like a man on a mission. I follow, hovering behind him as he bends down and looks inside.

"Shit." Garrett hisses.

"What?" My heart rate picks up as a bad feeling creeps in.

"Her toiletries are still here. I don't think she's over at the toilets." Garrett stands back up to his full height just as Jared unzips his swag over the other side of our camp, and he rolls out.

"Dude, have you seen Rhys?" I ask as I make my way toward him. He stands and stretches, yawning before focusing on me.

"What?"

"Have you seen Rhys?" I snap, and he glares.

"No. Why would I?"

"Shit. I'll go see if Lexi is in her tent." Garrett mutters, walking by us.

"I heard someone walk past my swag earlier. Thought one of you fuckers was going for a hike or something."

My eyes widen, and I turn to see Garrett's concerned gaze as he looks back at us. Then he practically runs over to Lexi and Ayden's tent.

"Lex, you in there?"

"Yeah." Her soft voice murmurs from inside, and the zip opens before Ayden pops his head out.

"What's going on?"

"We can't find Rhys. Can Lexi go check the toilets for us?" Garrett asks, but before he's even finished talking, Ayden gets nudged out of the way, and a blonde mess of wavy hair climbs out of the tent.

"Yep. I'm on it." Lexi offers a half-smile before jogging across the clearing towards the toilets.

She's worried. I can tell.

Shit.

Where are you, Cherry?

Ayden climbs out of the tent and talks quietly with Garrett, so I pace, not able to stand still as I watch Lexi disappear into the girl's toilets. A moment later, she flies out the door, looking panicked.

"She's not here!" Lexi yells across the clearing, and my gut drops.

"Get up!" I yell and turn to the campsite. "Get the fuck up now!" I start toward Tillie's tent. Maybe she's in there. "Rhys!"

I fall to my knees in the pebbled dirt outside Tillie and Bell's tent and tear the zip open. "Rhys!"

"Hey fuck face. She's not in here!" Bell hisses as Tillie sits up, startled, her pixie hair all over the place.

"Simon man, calm down." Jared lays his hand on my shoulder, but I shrug him off.

"Rhys! Where are you?"

My yelling causes everyone to come out of their tents, all with confused gazes.

She's not here. SHE'S NOT HERE!

"RHYS!!!"

"Garrett!" Lexi calls, and I spin to see her climbing out from Rhys' tent. "Her phone is gone."

On instinct, everyone rushes for their phones in panic, only to remember after we try that there's no phone service here. I tear my hands through my hair, frantic. I need to find her. Where is she? Did those fuckers from last night take her? Did her old foster mum take her? Did she run away? Does she feel like everything is hopeless again?

The distant sound of Paramore drags me out of my panic, and I turn to see Jared holding the satellite phone up to his ear.

"It's ringing, but she's not answering," Jared informs us, and we all look around, trying to figure out which direction Rhys' ringtone is coming from.

"Rhys!" I call out again, this time with my hands cupped around my mouth.

Lexi, Shaun and Marcus join me, calling out over and over, hoping to get a response.

"Hey, is that someone up at the top of the falls?" Dale asks, his eyes trained high.

We all follow his line of sight, and that's when we see familiar black boots dangling over the ledge of the cliff—Cherry's boots.

In unison, we call out to her again, but she either can't hear us or is ignoring us. Either way, the situation isn't good. She's sitting on the edge of a fucking cliff.

Fuck! Fuck! Fuck!

This feels the same as Halloween night when we couldn't find her. She ran off then, and she's done it again now. Last time she had dark thoughts. Thoughts that if she followed through with, we would be attending her funeral this week.

Is that what's happening now? Is she back at that place of helplessness?

Chapter Sixteen

Tyler

The shrill of my phone wakes me a little after sunrise. Fucking annoying thing. I don't know why I bring the stupid thing into my bedroom at night. Wait. I do know why, but I'm gonna pretend it isn't in case a certain seventeen-year-old girl calls me.

My sleepy fingers fumble to pick the damn thing up off the nightstand, but the moment I see the word *Kitten* flashing across the screen, I wake the fuck up and answer it quickly.

"Kitten, you ok?"

"No. I don't think I am." Shit, her voice sounds so deflated.

"What's happened?" I sit up in my bed, kicking off the thin sheet and swing my legs over to plant my feet on the floor.

"I liked it."

What? What is she talking about?

"Liked what? Where are you?"

"In the video of me when I was little. I liked what Brian and I did together."

Fuck. She's not good. Something has happened.

"Tell me where you are, Kitten?"

"Oh, I'm just sitting at the top of Ebony Falls. It's so beautiful up here. I saw the last part of the sunrise. Have you ever done that? Watched the sunrise. It reminds you that there's a whole big world, and you are just one small insignificant part."

"Kitten, why are you at the top of the falls? Who's with you?"

"I needed to find phone reception, so I could call you. Turns out there's a really good signal up here."

"Who's with you, Kitten?" I growl. I don't want to be a prick, but I need her to focus so I can help her.

"No one. Just me and the birds. Noisey little fuckers, they are."

Jesus!

"Where's Fuckboy?"

"He's down at the camp with everyone else. Did you hear what I said before? I liked it, Ty. The things me and Brian did together never felt wrong when we did them. He made me feel good, and he made me feel safe. When I was taken away from him, I didn't understand why the therapists and social workers kept trying to make me believe it was wrong. He never hurt me. It felt unbelievably good… that's not normal, though, Ty. Me, what I did, what I felt… it wasn't normal. I'm still not normal. Even though I understand now that it was inappropriate and Brian is a paedophile, sometimes I wonder if his grooming stuck."

"What do you mean?" I stand and start pacing at the foot of my bed. I can't sit still when I know she's literally standing on a ledge.

"Sometimes I feel like *I'm* the predator. I'm this sex crazed girl who has barely any boundaries and has done some pretty disturbing things just to get a fix. And I say a fix because I'm an addict. Of sex, for fuck's sake. Although maybe I'm not. If I was an addict, I would have still let Marcus fuck me even though it really hurt yesterday, right? So maybe I'm not an addict. Maybe I'm just a sick human being."

Fuck, she's all over the place.

"Kitten. Slow down and take a breath. Can you do that for me?"

I start taking deep breaths, in and out, as if that will fucking help her.

"Ok. I guess."

I can hear the inhale and exhale Kitten makes through the phone, and I put her on speaker and open up my messages, pulling up the contact I need.

Skipper
Get your skinny arse up to the top of Ebony Falls NOW!

Fuckboy
Already on my way. I'm nearly there, but it's gonna take a minute!!

"That's it, beautiful. Nice slow deep breaths."
I can hear her doing as I instruct.

Skipper
I'm on the phone with Kitten.
She sounds unstable as fuck!
What the fuck happened?

Fuckboy
She was doing ok until some Redfield fuckers rocked up last night.
They had a copy of the video!

Fuck.

"Do you think I'm sick, Ty?" Her voice sounds so small. Almost distant. Is she crying?

This is heartbreaking. I just want to wrap my arms around her and protect her from everything.

"No, Kitten. Never. We all have baggage. Yours should never have happened, but it did, and for that, I'm sorry. You deserve more. You deserve a life filled with unconditional love and happiness." I hope she can hear the sincerity in my voice.

"How can I have that, though? I'm not normal. I've always been different."

"Different doesn't mean bad, Kitten. Why are you concerned about that now? You've always embraced your individuality. No one messes with Rhys George. She's a strong woman. A queen. Where has she gone?"

"I don't know. She fled when Julie started contacting me, I guess."

"She's still in there, beautiful. Things have been tough lately, but that brave warrior is still there. She just has to fight harder at the moment. It's ok for her to get tired and need to take a moment to reflect or scream or cry. In fact, that's probably the healthiest thing for her. For you."

"It hurts."

Fuck. There is so much pain in those two words. Her voice cracks as she speaks like she is fighting against her tears.

"I know. Sharing your hurt with me and your boy band will help, Kitten. Let us take some of your pain, too."

"I'm not sure how to do that."

"You already are. By talking to me, and to them. Opening up. Letting us in. Sharing your fears and secrets." I lay my phone on my tallboy and look at my reflection in the small mirror sitting on top. I have dark circles under my eyes. Fucking hell, I feel like I'm aging five years a day right now, yet somehow, I also feel like I'm only a couple of years older than the girl on the other end of the phone.

"Information is power, Ty. Aren't I just opening myself up to more potential hurt if I share my baggage? What if things don't work out? Won't my darkest secrets be used against me?"

"Some people would do that, but I have to admit, those boy-band-wannabes seem pretty into you. I think they would rather cut their own peewees off than hurt you."

That scores me a slight giggle through the phone. It's not much, but I can just imagine her dark eyes crinkling at the corners and those full lips quirking up at one side.

"They have names, you know. And let me assure you, there are no peewees in sight. They are all man, thank you very much."

"Not as man as me." The caveman in me wants to beat on my chest as if it would prove my point.

"I miss you. I know I shouldn't say that, but it's true."

Again, she's flitting from one subject to the next. I can tell she's torn between the things that make her feel good and the things that make her feel bad.

"Why shouldn't you say that?" I ask, and she hums.

"I don't know. It's not like you're my boyfriend or anything. I miss our time together, though. And the Feast. I miss having the freedom of no shame and the anything-goes atmosphere. I'm bummed that we won't be able to do that again."

"I miss you too, Kitten. And I get it. The Feast was unique, but even if we don't have that, it doesn't mean we can't have our own thing. Maybe we can find a new club to join."

"Do you think so? I think I'd like that." Her tone tells me she would. There's a hint of excitement, and right now, Kitten needs something to look forward to.

"Yeah, beautiful, I'll see what I can do."

"Kitten?" Relief washes over me as I hear another voice in the background through the phone speaker. I never thought I'd be so happy to hear Fuckboy's voice. Yet here we are.

Chapter Seventeen

Rhys

The surprise of hearing Shaun's voice has me jerking so much that I almost slip off the rocky ledge.

"Whoa, Kitten. Be careful." Darting forward, Shaun grabs me by the shoulders and tugs me back, sitting down to pull me back further between his legs. The moment his arms wrap around me, I slump in relief. "What are you doing up here?"

"I needed phone service to call Ty." It wasn't a lie. I did. But it's not the only reason I came up here. I needed to see something truly beautiful. I needed to remind myself that there's so much beauty in this world that it outweighs the ugliness. Unfortunately, it just made me feel small and insignificant.

"You should have woken one of us. We would have come with you." At the sound of Marcus' voice, I glance up to see his concerned brown eyes trained on me as he sits on the rocky ledge next to Shaun and me.

"I kinda needed some privacy," I admit, taking in the worry in Marcus' brown eyes.

"We could have given you some space to make your call." Garrett's voice comes from my other side, and I crane my head up and watch his towering body lower onto the ledge. "It's too dangerous to go off on your own like that."

"What do you need to say to this Ty fucker that you can't say in front of us?" Marcus grumbles, and I swing my head back to glare at him.

"Grady man, ease up." Shaun hisses, squeezing me tighter to his chest.

"What? If we are gonna be in this fucking group thing, then there shouldn't be secrets." Marcus hisses back.

"What's wrong, Grady? You think she's gonna love him more than you?" Simon's voice joins the conversation, and I turn in time to see him standing on the ledge next to where Garrett sits.

"Shut the fuck up, Hastings!" Marcus growls, shooting his mate a dagger.

I hate that I'm causing this conflict between them. If only I could learn not to be so selfish, then these guys wouldn't be at each other's throats.

"Why don't you both shut the fuck up? You're not helping." Garrett snaps before he lifts my hand in his and presses his lips to it.

"Jared called you from the satellite phone. We heard your phone ringing, Kitten. Why didn't you answer?" Shaun asks, and guilt grips my insides.

"I... just needed to talk to Ty."

"Kitten! Put Fuckboy on the phone!"

Tyler's voice comes through my phone speaker, and I jump, remembering that I'm still on the phone.

"Oh shit. Yeah, sorry, Ty." I hand Shaun the phone over my shoulder, and a moment later, he stands up and takes a few steps away to chat.

"I'm sorry. I know I'm being a selfish prick here, but how the fuck is it fair that Bossi knows who this Ty guy is, and we don't? How are we meant to make this work if there are different rules for different people?"

Ugh, I hate it when Marcus is all rational and shit.

"He has a point. Maybe it's something we need to talk more about *later*?" Garrett agrees, shooting Marcus a pointed look, and I nod, even though I know I can't give them anything else. I can't reveal Ty's identity.

"Here, Kitten." Shaun hands my phone back, and I place it to my ear.

"Kitten, I want you to do something for me." Tyler's voice is all business. It's a real turn-on.

"Uh… ok."

"I want you to promise me you won't go off on your own again. Can you do that?" Tyler asks, and I shrug, even though he can't see me.

"Yeah, I guess."

"No guessing, Kitten. Promise me. I need to know you're safe."

"If I disobey you, will you spank me again?" I tease, letting my grin show.

A round of groans sound from the guys, which tugs up my grin.

"No. This isn't one of those times to be a brat. You be safe. Promise me. No going off on your own. Stay with one of the guys at all times." Ty's tone is stern. It's a little like his teacher voice, yet not quite the same.

"Ok. I promise." I mean it too.

"Good. When you get back, I'll spank you for not taking my request seriously, ok?"

My grin broadens at his comment. "Ok, Daddy."

Ty growls before he sighs. "Kitten?" Ty's voice is quieter now. Still serious, but not demanding.

"Yeah?"

"I'm more than a boyfriend. I know I shouldn't be encouraging this thing between us, but just so you know, you're the only one for me."

It's funny. I didn't realise until this moment how much I needed to hear Tyler say that.

"I want you," I whisper, wishing only he could hear.

"All in good time, Kitten. Now go have fun. Stop thinking about the bad stuff, but if you can't stop thinking about it, try talking about it with that possessive fucker who smashed up the office. Or any of them will do. It will help, even though it's confronting. It really will help."

"Ok. I'll try." I smile.

"See ya in a couple of days, Kitten."

"See ya."

As soon as I hang up, Shaun pulls me up off the ground and drags me against his chest. Our bodies slap together from the force, and he buries his head in the crook of my neck.

"Don't fucking leave me, Kitten." There's so much pain laced in his tone, and I hate that I put it there. I need to stop thinking about myself all the time and remember that my actions will affect him. They will affect all of them.

I wrap my arms around Shaun, giving him a squeeze, needing to be closer yet feeling like I can't get close enough. It must be the clothes we are wearing.

"Sorry for scaring you. I needed to re-group. I needed Ty, but I need you, too. And the others."

Shaun pulls back, his steel-grey eyes capturing mine as he leans in to take my lips with his. As our lips part and clash in a long, deep kiss, someone moves up behind me, pressing their chest to my back.

"You scared me. I was losing my shit, Cherry." Simon's voice wobbles a little as if he's on the verge of tears. I break my kiss with Shaun and reach an arm back, tugging Simon closer and turning my head to find his lips waiting to take mine. As we kiss from this awkward angle, Simon cups my face, brushing his thumbs over my cheek. It's a nice feeling to have Shaun pressed against my front and Simon at my back while they show me how much they care with their lips and tongues. It's an even better feeling when someone takes my left hand, and I instantly know by its large size that it's not Shaun or Simon. I break my kiss with Simon to see Garrett lifting my hand to his lips again.

"We were all pretty frantic to find you." He admits, and I instantly feel like shit again for causing so much drama.

"I'm sorry," I whisper, and Garrett leans forward.

At first, I think he's going to kiss me. His eyes fall to my lips with hunger I haven't seen before, but before I can get my hopes up,

Garrett's eyes dart up to mine again, and he presses his forehead against mine.

I sigh. I'm a little disappointed he didn't kiss me. I'm starving for him. However, I'm also glad he didn't. It's not time yet. This thing between us isn't ready. Not to mention that Marcus might not be ready to give his mate the go-ahead just yet.

It's one thing to be the filling in a Shaun and Simon sandwich, but it's another to be the filling in a Shaun, Simon and Garrett wrap. Even without our lips meeting, I can feel how much Garrett cares.

Eventually, the guys break apart from me, and Marcus comes into view. He's standing about twelve feet away, his hands balled into fists by his sides as he glares. Is he angry again at the guys for touching me? I thought he was handling things better last night, but maybe I was wrong.

Right now, Marcus is akin to a charging bull. His face is red, and if this were a cartoon, he'd have steam shooting from his nostrils. Then he charges, storming up to me, bending down, and he throws me over his shoulder like a sack of fucking potatoes.

"Hey!" I squeal, which earns me a sharp slap on the arse. It's a firm slap, and I don't hate it.

"Grady! What the fuck are you doing?" Simon calls, and I try to find him in my upside-down state, but I can't get my bearings as Marcus walks us somewhere.

"Fuck off!" Marcus hisses over his other shoulder, not missing a step to wherever the hell he is taking me.

A minute later, after watching the earthy, gravelly path pass by, I find myself the right way up, being pushed against the smooth trunk of a gum tree.

"Don't do that again, Rhee." Marcus cages me in, his hands on either side of my head as he leans in close. "Don't go off alone when you're feeling low and vulnerable. Trust *us* to take care of you. *Please*."

His dark brown eyes swim with so much emotion as he pins me in place, so I nod in agreement.

"Why couldn't you say that in front of the others, Marc?"

His eyes widen, and he shifts back a little, but he's not letting me go.

"I'm not ready to share what we have with them. You gotta give me time."

I nod again, understanding that this is hard for him to wrap his head around.

"Say it again." He demands quietly, and my brows draw together in confusion.

"Say what?"

"Marc. You've never called me that before. No one ever calls me that. Say it again."

A smile tugs at my lips. "Marc."

His eyes flutter shut, and he moans. "I like that, Rhee. I really like it."

When his eyes flutter open again, I lean forward and press my lips to his.

"Marc." I nip at his lips, extracting another moan. "Marc."

He presses into me, leaving no space between us, and he deepens our kiss. Desperation takes over, and I claw my fingers into his thick dark hair, tugging not so gently, and in return, he does the same to me. Minutes pass as we grapple at each other, and then he pulls back panting, his lips puffy from our kiss.

"I wanna fuck you against this tree."

"Yes, Marc. Fuck me right here."

"No." He shakes his head, his expression confused as he takes a step back. "Not yet. You need more time to heal."

"I'll be fine." I reach out and grip his t-shirt, attempting to tug him back against me. It's no use, though. He stands strong, his expression torn.

"No, Rhee. Let's give it a bit more time. When I sink inside you again, I want no distraction. No time limit. Just you and me."

I nod. "Ok. We can do that."

"So, maybe we can have a date night or something?" Marcus' face turns red as he asks. OMG, is he blushing?

"Sure. We can have a date night. But you know, if I give you a date night, I have to give the others a date night, too."

"I figured as much." His smile falls, and he drops his chin to his chest, grumbling his words.

"Are you sure you can do this?" I step up to him and cup his face, needing to be closer.

"I think so. Like I said before, I just need time."

I nod and kiss him softly. When we were together last term, we rarely had moments like this where we would kiss for the sake of showing care. Everything involved getting each other naked. It was fun and so very Rhys George. But I don't feel like Rhys George these days. Or at least the old Rhys George. I feel different. I'm still trying to figure out if it's a good thing or not.

After some heavy petting, a very impatient Simon bursts our bubble, and we all make our way back down to the campsite. If my guys thought they were going to spend the morning with me, then they were delusional because the moment Lexi flings herself at me, nearly crying from worry, with Tillie doing the same, and a very neutral "I'm glad you're ok," from Bell, the girls don't leave my side.

It's probably a good thing, for Jared at least. He gets the morning with the guys, and they play more cricket in the clearing while the temperature is still cool. It's nice watching them muck around together while us girls toast marshmallows on the remaining coals in the fire.

"So, are you going to tell us what's going on? I don't know about anyone else, Rhys, but I'm worried about you." Tillie's blue eyes are really standing out today with the way the sun picks up the red in her auburn hair. It's hard to miss those eyes and the way they swim with concern as she directs her gaze to me.

"Everything is a mess. I'm a mess. Can we leave it at that?"

"Nope," Bell states and turns her dark gaze to me, ignoring the oozing sticky sweet about to fall from her stick. "Your mess is too serious to ignore, especially when you're running off and taking risks."

"I take risks all the time. Every time I fuck someone new, I'm taking a risk." I shoot her a glare, but she shakes her head.

"Not the same. Your self-destructive behaviour isn't what happened here today. You're usually an annoying optimist. Live for the moment. Make the best of every situation. Ride or die." Bell finally notices her marshmallow has fallen into a blob in the dirt near her feet, so she shoves another one on the end and sticks it over the coals. "Up on that ledge this morning. There was no riding Rhys. That could have ended badly."

"I needed to call Ty."

"Who is this Ty guy, anyway?" Lexi asks, and I shoot her a blank look, so she turns to Tillie and Bell. "Do you two know who he is?"

"No." Tillie shakes her head. "We only know he is her sponsor at the sex club she goes to. He's an older guy. It's all very hush-hush."

"It's going to stay that way, as well," I mutter, dropping my stick to the ground, no longer interested in food.

"How do we know he's good for you? For all we know, he's making things harder or worse." Lexi ignores her stick now, too, her focus solely on me.

"Ty is a good person. A *really* good person. Hell, he told me to talk about things with the guys or whoever I need to. He said it would help. Isn't that what we are doing now?"

Bell scoffs. "Hardly. We are asking questions, and you're giving us fresh air."

"Could you at least give us a run down? If you don't want to talk about anything in particular, can you maybe just catch us up on everything that's happened so we can understand your situation better?" Tillie's concern is what makes me cave. She's always been good to me and good for me. Just like I've done with everyone else lately, I've shut her out and kept her at arm's length. It just felt easier that way, but maybe I was wrong. So, I open up and tell the girls about the first voicemail from Julie while I was away with my family. I tell them how I ran off and went on a sex bender. I tell them about the retreat and returning back to school riddled with the need to fuck all the time. I tell them about Vixen's Lodge and how I came into contact with Shaun there. Well, my Kitty came in contact with his mouth, but it still counts. I tell them about Master Hill not being happy about me being absent. About my punishment and the options he gave me. And I reveal my first time with Tyler and how we both stepped over the thick line we had drawn to avoid each other.

I went on and on about everything that happened, leaving out who Tyler is, and I left out the part of what I did in front of Brian at the Allansdale Prison. I told them about the prison, though, and how I ended up at the Feast, which led me to the second punishment last week—the public humiliation. Then, I revealed that it was Julie who sent out the video of me when I was eleven or twelve years old.

When the girls fall silent, their heads probably swimming with a thousand thoughts, I admit to them, and also to myself, that the only thing that makes sense to me right now are my guys. Just thinking about them and how, in this short time, they have all fought for me in my daily battle to find a slither of sanity. I'd never be able to choose between them. They each bring me something different, both in the bedroom and in my life. I'm feeling less and less addicted to sex, and more and more addicted to them. Hopefully, they are a healthier substitute.

Exhausted after a morning of talking about feelings with the girls and a group hug that included tears by everyone but Bell, we made lunch and then moved our chairs under the shade of some trees for some quiet drinks as a group.

"Let's play Truth or Dare." Tillie announces, and my groan matches the guys.

"Do we have to?"

"Rhys. You love truth or dare! Aren't you the one that loves to extract juicy truths or push people's boundaries with dares?" Tillie frowns as I shrug.

"Yep. She is. So, we are playing." Bell declares.

"Can we just watch?" Dale asks, and Bell shakes her head.

"Nope. We are *all* playing."

"I'll play. I love games." Simon bounces in his seat, showing his excitement, and we all chuckle.

"I love the games *we* play, Sy." I shoot him a cheeky wink, and he beams.

"Guys. She called me Sy!" Slapping his hand over his heart a little too dramatically, Simon flops back in his chair, looking love-struck.

Goof.

"Girl, we don't wanna hear about your sex games." Dale tuts at me while Allister nods next to him in agreement.

"Ok. I'm going first!" Simon calls, and again, everyone chuckles. "Tillie, truth or dare?"

"What? Me? Why do I have to go first?"

"Oh, stop being a baby." Bell rolls her eyes at Tillie, who shoots her a dagger.

"Come on Till. What will it be?" I ask, trying to move the game along.

"Fine. Truth." Tillie mutters.

"Boo. Boring!" Bell calls, but Tillie ignores her, keeping her focus on Simon.

"Ok. Tillie, have you ever hooked up with Rhys?"

A round of whoops and hoots sound from everyone as I throw my head back, laughing. Tillie's face is priceless. She wasn't expecting Simon to come out with the big guns straight away.

Tillie glances at me, and as everyone quietens down, I shrug, letting her know I don't care if she reveals anything.

"Fine. Yes. Rhys and I have taken care of each other, on occasion. Well, that was before all this dick came along." She circles her hand in the air at the guys, and more whoops and cheers echo around the campsite.

"Cherry! You naughty girl!" Simon smirks, his eyes heated as I'm sure he imagines me and Tillie naked together.

"My turn." Tillie sings, and she turns to Jared. "Jared. Truth or Dare?"

"Fuck. Do I really have to? Isn't this a game for kids?" Jared whines, slouching lower in his chair.

"No way, dude. This game is definitely not for kids." Simon advises, and Jared rolls his eyes.

"Truth, I guess."

Tillie giggles. "Ok. At the Halloween party, I saw you kissing Gina Long, and then you disappeared. Did you guys hook up?"

"I'm changing to dare."

Everyone laughs at Jared as he shifts uncomfortably in his chair.

"Alright. Coward!" Tillie grins, thinking for a moment, "Jared, you need to stand by that tree, turn and face us all, drop your shorts and take a leak."

"Woo-hoo! Tills, you're good at this game!" Simon laughs as we all join him.

"Fine. But if you want to see my cock, Tillie, all you have to do is ask." Jared smirks smugly as he places his beer on the ground and stands, making his way over to the tree.

"I prefer tacos to hot dogs, Jared." Tillie giggles, watching Jared as he pretends to be cool, calm and collected.

"Liar Till. You love hot dogs just as much as tacos." I giggle, and she pokes her tongue out at me.

When Jared is at the tree, he turns and eyes everyone before he zeros in on Lexi. I glance over at her sitting next to Ayden, and she squirms uncomfortably, but she doesn't look away. She juts her chin up in a silent challenge, and Jared grins, dropping his shorts.

Hoots echo again, and my brows shoot up at the sight of Jared's pretty cock. Well, well, well. He's packing more than adequately between his legs. This is normally where I lock in my prey. I see a pretty cock, and I want it in my mouth. And while I'm definitely building more saliva in my mouth right now with Kitty waking up for a little purr, it's not Jared's cock I want. It's Marcus', Shaun's, and

Simon's. And I desperately want Garrett's since I haven't even seen it yet. And let's not forget Tyler's.

As Jared starts to take a public piss in front of us, he keeps his eyes locked on Lexi, even though Ayden is sitting right next to her.

"He's playing with fire." I lean over and whisper to Shaun, who is sitting on my right side.

"Yep. He sure fucking is." Shaun agrees, not taking his eyes off Ayden's face.

"You fucking done, Crowley?" Ayden hisses, moving to stand, but stays put when Lexi reaches her hand out to stop him.

Jared gives his dick a shake and nods. "Yep. It was a very satisfying piss."

As Jared leans down to pull up his shorts, Ayden leaps up and runs for him. Marcus and Garrett fly out of their chairs and intercept Ayden before he makes it to Jared, holding him back as Marcus talks quietly in his cousin's ear to calm him down.

"Smug much?" I mumble to Jared as he passes by to take his seat. He just grins and shoots me a wink.

"It's my turn now, isn't it?" Jared asks, and the guys re-take their seats. Lexi ignores Jared now, trying to calm Ayden down by sitting on his knee.

"Yep," I say, again trying to move the game along. Better that we not think too much about Jared's dick-measuring contest just now.

"Bell. Truth or dare?" Jared asks, and she shrugs.

"You pick. I'll do whatever." Bell looks like she doesn't care either way.

"Ok. Have you ever hooked up with Rhys?" Jared asks, and I frown.

"Hey! What is this? We all know I've fucked most of the people here. No need to bring up all my conquests!" I complain, and my guys chuckle.

"Ew. Leave me out of this disgusting conversation!" Dale's baby face morphs into a sour expression, and Allister's matches him.

"I watched her and Tillie once. Does that count?" Bell admits, and Tillie's mouth drops open.

"So much for keeping that a fucking secret, Bell!"

"What? It's not called Truth or Dare for shits and giggles." Bell states matter-of-factly, and Tillie huffs.

"We want details!" Simon sits forward in his seat, rubbing his hands together.

"I'm with Hastings. Deets, please." Shaun grins, looking eager.

"If you bitches start talking about scissor action, I'm outta here!" Dale cries, and we all erupt in laughter.

"No one is giving details!" Tillie yells over the laughter, while Bell actually smiles. She's going to have sore cheeks if she keeps this up.

"It's my turn. Truth or dare, Rhys?" Bell stands to gain everyone's attention, and they quieten down.

"Let's go with the truth." I smile at Bell, knowing it will piss her off. She rolls her eyes.

"Tell us who this Tyler guy is?"

At Bell's words, I fly out of my chair.

"Fuck you, Bell!"

"What?" She puts on an innocent face, and I immediately regret telling her all that stuff this morning. Yeah, I admitted to them that the guys are annoyed that they don't know who he is. Why the fuck is she throwing fuel on the fire? This is what I was talking to Tyler about. Information is power. Once someone knows something about you, they can use it against you. I just didn't think one of my closest friends would be the one to do that, though. More fucking fool me!

"It's a truth I want to know. And I think I speak for the majority here as well."

"I'm changing to dare!" I hiss, and Bell smirks, quirking a dark brow.

"Ok. Dare it is." She looks around the group and then turns back to me. "I dare you to kiss Jared."

There are a few quiet chuckles from Dale, Tillie and even Ayden. But my guys stay quiet.

"Choose another dare," I say, and Bell shakes her head.

"Nope. It doesn't work like that. What's the big deal, anyway? It's just a harmless kiss. I didn't tell you to fuck him. Just give him a quick kiss. Or," She fucking smiles again, but this time it's nothing but sinister, "you could always revert back to truth and answer my question instead."

I could just grab Bell's Wednesday Addams' braids and rip them off her head.

"It's ok, Kitten. It's just a game." Shaun says quietly to me, taking my hand and giving it a squeeze.

Just a game? Is he really alright with me kissing another guy?

What am I thinking? Of course he is. I kiss four other guys besides him. So why should he care? The thing is, I feel like he should be protesting. He should be angry and possessive and demand that I don't go through with it.

Glancing down to his steel-greys, I'm pretty sure all I see is sincerity. Why does it hurt to see that? Why aren't I happy about him being ok with this?

I'm too scared to look at Simon, Garrett and especially Marcus, so I avoid their gazes and walk across the circle to where Jared is sitting. He sits forward as I approach, looking smug again. He's an attractive guy. Tall, blonde, blue eyes, tanned skin and athletically muscular. He also has a pretty cock. These are all things that have the Rhys George seal of approval. Yet as I lean down, my face mere inches from his, I look him in the eye and speak the truth.

"I'm sorry. Nothing personal, but I can't kiss you, Jared. I will never betray my guys." Then I stand back up.

Four very audible sighs of relief sound behind me, which I'm relieved to hear. Their responses aren't as shocking as mine.

"I will never betray my guys."

Am I cured of my inability to commit to a relationship? Yeah, sure, I'm with four or five guys, but my commitment to them as a whole is something I've never felt before.

The words Marcus hissed at me when I returned to school flit through my mind.

"Everyone's welcome."

It no longer applies, I realise. Not everyone *is* welcome to the Rhys George experience. Only they are—no one else.

"I guess you have to answer my question, then." Bell tuts, and I shoot her a glare.

"Ask another. You fucking know I can't answer that one." I hiss, pointing my finger down at her in anger.

"Oh, fine. You're so boring these days." Bell rolls her eyes and then points behind me. "Have you had group sex with these four yet?"

"No," I answer truthfully and return to my seat, a mix of emotions rolling through me. I'm pissed at Bell. She's a fucking trouble maker. I'm happy that my guys didn't want me to kiss Jared. I'm scared about how hard I'm falling for the guys. It's new to me to feel this way. It feels almost impossible to feel stronger about them, yet as each day passes, I feel so much more for each of them than the day before. The scary part about it is knowing I could get seriously hurt if things don't work out. It's a pain I'm not sure I'd survive.

We play Truth or Dare some more. Shaun dares Simon to do a nudie run across the clearing to the toilets and back, which, of course, Simon does. Marcus dares Lexi to tell everyone their secret, to which she chooses dare, and he dares her to skull a beer which she hates and gags her way through. Garrett even dares Allister to kiss Dale, which he follows through with, making Dale blush, and they go awkwardly quiet afterwards.

"Bell. Truth or Dare?" Jared asks, and she gives him a blank stare.

"Dare, of course. Truth is so boring." Of course, the truth is boring to Bell. She loves the drama too much.

Jared smirks. "Bell, I dare you to make out with Garrett for at least thirty seconds."

All the air whooshes from my lungs, and everything moves in slow motion as I see Bell shoot Jared one of her rare smiles before she stands, making her way across the circle to Garrett.

My Garrett.

Before I can stop myself, I leap from my chair and skid to a stop in front of Bell.

"You touch him, and I'll end you!"

"Oooohhh," Jared says unhelpfully.

Bell smirks as I feel a large, warm hand settle on my hip from behind.

"I wasn't going to let her kiss me." Garrett's deep voice breaks through my anger, and I instantly sink back into his warmth, my eyes fluttering closed for a moment as I let myself relax.

It's ok, Rhys. He doesn't want to kiss anyone else.

"Shit Rhys. I think you're in love. With like multiple guys. Go you!" Bell offers me a big toothy smile when my eyes flutter open. "Don't be mad. I wouldn't have done it, anyway. I only kiss people who want me to."

"I was about to throw down with you." I glare at her, and she shrugs.

"I might stir shit and speak my mind, Rhys, but don't forget, I'll never betray you. Sure, I'm a fuckup, but you can be sure I'll never do *that*."

I know Bell is speaking the truth, and I also know this game has taught us all something I wasn't expecting.

This thing between the guys and me is serious, and I know I'll never be able to give them up.

Chapter Eighteen

Rhys

"**S**imon says, let's go skinny dipping."

I'm on a night hike with my guys, and we've come across another water hole, this one with a small waterfall and stream that runs into the main river. The moon's glow is bright, shining down on the small body of water like an overhead light, illuminating the reddened rocks and fern-like scrub surroundings.

"Yes. Let's do that." I sing-song, approaching the water's edge and dipping my toe in. "The water is perfect."

Without looking back at the guys, I lift my black swim dress over my head, revealing my red bikini underneath. Then, reaching back, I untie my bikini top, letting it fall to the ground before stepping out of my bottoms. The balmy night air has a slight breeze, sending a nice chill over my sweaty skin, and I stretch my neck from side to side, enjoying the feel as I turn around to face my guys.

They are all shoulder to shoulder about ten feet away, eyes wide as they take me in. My eyes linger on Garrett. This is the first time he is seeing me naked. I know he hasn't moved things forward with us, waiting for some sort of signal of approval from Marcus, but he's been open about his feelings. Not just to me, but in front of everyone else. It doesn't matter, though. This is just skinny dipping, right? It's not like I'm making him sink that big dick of his inside me.

Fuck! Don't think about dick! Don't think about dick!

Just the thought has Kitty purring and my nipples pebbling.

"Simon says, come here." That demanding tone Simon rarely uses sends a sensual shiver up my spine, and I grin, closing the distance between us, coming to stop in front of him. "Simon says, undress me."

I lick my lower lip and then bite it as my heart rate picks up, taking in Simon's heated hazel eyes. Reaching forward, I take the hem of his shirt and lift it over his abs. He raises his arms to help me tug it off, and then I hook my fingers into the band of his shorts, dragging them down, hooking onto his jocks on the way. I have to do a little manoeuvring over his hard cock, but it's not long before it bounces free and bobs in front of my face as I bend down to peel his bottoms off his feet.

"Your Simon Says game has always annoyed me... until now," Shaun admits, and I grin as I stand back up facing Simon.

"You should never underestimate the power of what Simon says, Bossi," Simon smirks, keeping his eyes on me. "Simon says, kiss me, Cherry."

I grin back at him and step into his space, his hard dick pushing up against my tummy as I reach up on my toes and do what he asked. As soon as our lips touch, my hands come to rest on his chest, but as he kisses me, he takes my hands in his, pulling them away from his body and holds them at our sides. Once the kiss breaks, he leans down to whisper in my ear.

"We are just gonna go skinny dipping. Nothing else. Ok?"

I nod, even though part of me wants to protest. How easy would it be to fall to my knees and tempt him into my mouth right now? It would be so easy, which is why I don't do it. Refraining is harder. The fact that he's willing to hold off means a lot. He understands things aren't the best for me right now, but I hope he also knows that once I've healed, there won't be anything holding me back from fucking him until we both forget our names.

Pulling back, Simon grins. "Simon says, undress Bossi."

I grin back and turn to look at Shaun standing on the end beside Marcus. I approach him slowly, loving the way four sets of eyes roam over my naked flesh. Then I repeat what I did with Simon and remove Shaun's clothes. When he's completely naked and sporting his own hard-on, he gives me a smirk and a wink before Simon speaks again.

"Simon says, kiss Bossi."

"I fucking love this game." Shaun beams, his eyes locking onto my lips in anticipation. I don't keep him waiting. I lean in and kiss him deeply, once again my hands coming to rest on his bare chest.

"Simon says, hands off."

Shaun and I groan into each other's mouths, but just like Simon did, Shaun takes my hands in his, bringing them to our sides.

"Simon says, stop kissing."

Reluctantly, I pull back and giggle when Shaun shoots Simon a glare. Simon isn't fazed by his mate's reaction, turning his eyes to Marcus.

"Simon says, undress Marcus."

My heart flips. This could go one of two ways. He'll either let me do it and join the fun, or he'll bail, not ready to get naked with the group. I'm nervous as I step over to him. I don't want him to bail. I desperately want him to stay and have some fun with me. With us.

Standing before Marcus, I take in his dark eyes, hoping to pick up on his mood and how this is going to pan out. Then he offers me the briefest of grins.

"Are you ok with this?" I look at him hopefully, holding my breath for his answer.

"It's just swimming. Right?"

I nod and shrug at the same time. "Right."

In response, his dark eyes dip and travel down my body, his tongue darting out to wet his lips as he studies my bare flesh. Then he glances back to my face, wearing the same grin again, and gives me a nod.

Yes. He's staying!

I'm so excited that Marcus is joining in that I practically tear his clothes off like they are on fire. He wears a smug smile once I'm done, and as his manhood bobs in front of my face, he gives his hips a little jerk forward, teasing me.

It's a fucking internal battle not to grab his dick and sink it into my mouth. A real fucking battle, but I giggle and stand and take slow breaths, waiting for my next instruction.

"Simon says, kiss Marcus without putting your hands on him."

I can't help it. I shoot Simon a glare, and he quirks a brow, grinning at me.

"Come on, Rhee. Kiss me." Marcus mutters, and I turn back to him and smile. Leaning up, I press my lips to his, feeling his dick nudge my belly as he, too, takes my hands in his so I can't touch him.

"Simon says, stop kissing."

When I go to stop, Marcus drops my hands and grips the back of my head, tugging me firmly against him, taking more. I moan, almost melting at the contact of our naked fronts, and I press my hips forward in search of more.

"Hey! Break it up! Simon says, stop!"

Hands roughly pry us apart as Simon glares at me like it was my fault.

"He did it. Not me." I point at Marcus, but Marcus just shrugs, flashing a shit-eating grin at Simon.

"Simon says, Grady and Bossi, go get in the water."

My brows shoot up, and I spin around, my eyes following Marcus and Shaun as they obey their friend, and Simon backs away towards the water as well.

"What are you doing?" I'm confused, and all Simon does is ignore my question, gesturing his head towards Garrett.

"Simon says, undress Gaz."

I turn back to Garrett, who still has his eyes on me, and I feel the dreaded self-conscious part of me rear its head. For some reason, I'm even more nervous than I was with Marcus. Garrett has been very steadfast in the line he has drawn between us. Yeah, it's gotten blurry a few times, but I don't want him to do something he's not into or ready for. It's a strange thought for me to have, but I kind of like the boundaries he's set. It reminds me of Tyler and me. We would never have crossed that line if we weren't forced to. I don't want to force Garrett.

"Should I do this? Should I undress you?"

"Yes," Simon calls from behind me, "you should! Simon said!"

I ignore him.

"Do *you* want to undress me?" Garrett asks, and I nod without even having to think about it.

Of course, I do. I've seen that chest. It's insanely lickable. And I've dreamed about his dick. I just kind of thought the first time I got to see it would be just the two of us, alone in the throes of passion.

"Is this ok, though? You seeing me like this? Me undressing you?"

"Are you going to try to fuck me, baby?" He asks, smirking, his icy-blue eyes looking almost white in the moonlight.

"Only if you ask me to," I admit, and he grins wider.

"I'll refrain for tonight."

Ugh! I really want him to give in.

"Hurry up, Cherry. Simon says, undress him." Simon's impatience is evident in his tone, so I give up trying to give Garrett an out, and I ease his shirt off. I try really hard not to touch his rippling abs as I pull the fabric up and over his head. It's almost too overwhelming to hold back.

Stay strong, Rhys. You can control yourself.

Once the shirt is free, I bite my lower lip as my eyes travel over the ridges of muscle before I see that always tempting V. My eyes dart back up to his, and I see the heat in his icy-blues through the fan of my lashes. Does he want me to touch him as much as I want to? Lowering my eyes again, I reach forward and hook my fingers in the band of his shorts. It's very apparent to me as I start sliding his shorts down that I'm going to get them stuck on his elephant dick.

"Uh-how do I do this without touching your cock?" I ask quietly, peering up again.

"I'll help," Garrett smirks, sliding one hand into his shorts, gripping his dick. "Try pulling them down now."

With his hand covering his large swell, the shorts come down easier, and I slide them and his jocks all the way off. In my bent compromising position, this is the same moment I came face to face with Simon, Shaun and Marcus' dicks. This time, there is no hard cock bobbing before me since Garrett has two hands covering the area.

"Simon says, drop your hands, Garrett."

Garrett doesn't look at Simon, but he listens to him. "You might want to back up a bit, baby."

My brows shoot up, and as I go to stand, I stumble over my own feet, falling backwards onto my arse. The guys chuckle behind me as I brace my hands in the dirt, so my head doesn't fall back, and as I look up to Garrett's towering height, I watch as his eyes widen. I'm now splayed out in front of him, naked and legs spread apart, giving him a very intimate view between my legs. A rumble sounds in his chest before he drops his hands to his sides, releasing his dick.

Sweet fucking lord, would you have a look at the size of his cock? No. It's not a cock. It's a fucking work of art. There is girth. So much girth. And length. Oh, so very long. And thank you, baby Jesus, my Garrett has a pretty head, no extra skin in sight.

Kitty is not purring. Kitty is not circling. Kitty is not sticking her tail up. No, Kitty has gone feral. So much need slams into me that I think I might actually die if I'm not filled to my capacity very soon.

"Baby, stop looking at me like that." Garrett hisses, and I dart my eyes up to his, which are just as stormy as I assume mine are.

"I can't help it. I need that beautiful beast inside me." I admit, and Garrett growls, his eyes looking more animal than human right now.

"No, baby. It's not time yet." Garrett takes a step back, causing a whimper to slip past my lips. I know it's not time yet, but I want what I want.

"Simon says, kiss Garrett."

My eyes widen at Simon's words, and I watch as Garrett's eyes dart to the guys behind me. Probably to Marcus, checking to see if he's on board with this. Garrett's face reveals nothing as I watch him, so I roll my head right back, looking at Simon upside down.

"Uhh, Sy. Cole and I haven't done that yet."

Simon shrugs and turns his head to Marcus, who is standing next to him, waist-deep in the water.

"What?" Marcus snaps at Simon, and again, Simon shrugs.

"I think Gaz is waiting for your permission."

Marcus frowns, looking from Simon back over to Garrett. "You're waiting for my permission? I thought you and Rhee…" He trails off in confusion.

"Just because I like her doesn't mean I can have her, man. I swore I'd never do that to you. Not unless you're ok with it."

Marcus' brows hitch high. "So, you're saying if I tell you I'm not ok with it, you won't pursue her?"

"Which you're not going to do, right Marc?" I ask sweetly, gaining the emotion-filled eyes of Marcus.

He stays quiet as he mulls over what was just said. Then, his eyes move back to Garrett.

"I get to watch your first kiss *and* first fuck."

"What?" I screech, rolling to my stomach, at the same time as Garrett hisses, "Like fuck!"

"Ok, this is going off course." Simon tries to interact.

"Dude. You don't get to ask that of Gaz or any of us!" Shaun wades through the water, closer to Marcus.

Marcus grins then. "You fuckers are all too serious. I was joking. I don't want to watch him tear Rhys in two with his weapon of a cock."

"Marcus, that isn't funny!" I scold, and he shoots me a wink.

"Hurry up and kiss her before I change my mind." Marcus waves his hand in the air, and Shaun's shoulders relax as he turns back to us.

"Simon says, kiss Garrett."

At Simon's words, I roll back onto my back and settle my eyes on my Big Guy. Fucking hell, that's a bad decision. Kitty clenches with need at the mere sight of this God-like creature standing in all his glory before me.

I groan and tip my head back to look at the stars high in the sky. "Can Simon please say that Garrett has to impale me?"

"Stop it," Garrett mumbles, and I glance back at him in time to see a slight grin on his face. He likes it when I'm a brat, just like Ty does.

"No, Cherry. Keep those legs closed. Simon says, stand up and kiss Garrett."

"Ugh! This game blows, Sy."

Simon laughs behind me, and I grumble as I stand up off the ground, dusting off the dirt and sand before I step toward Garrett. His beast is standing tall and prodding out, but as I near, Garrett moves his hand to hold his rod to his body so I can get closer. Then, standing on my tiptoes, I wait for Garrett to come down to me.

He doesn't leave me hanging, leaning down to close the distance, and the moment our lips meet, I'm lost. I feel like I've waited my whole life to finally feel his kiss. To have his lips, which are softer than they appear, brush against mine. To have his tongue caress mine like he's tasting me, enjoying the flavour when he deepens the kiss.

I grip his hair with one hand and tug him closer with the other, loving the feel of his hardness between our bodies.

"Simon says, no touching with your hands."

I ignore Simon and grip Garrett tighter, having no control over the way my leg cocks up and wraps around his outer thigh. That's all Garrett needs to lose *his* control, his hands gripping my arse and lifting me, so I wrap both legs around him.

Shouts come from behind me, but I can't make out what they are yelling because I'm consumed by so much need that it's all-consuming. Garrett's tongue dives deeper into my mouth, and his moan vibrates through his chest, right before strong hands grip my shoulders and tug me backwards.

"Simon says, stop!" Simon hisses in my ear as his hands wrap around my middle and tug me. My legs are hooked firmly around

Garrett's waist, though. I'm not letting go. They will have to kill me first.

Ok, so maybe that's a little dramatic, but fuck, I want this man now!

"Kitten, let go," Shaun demands at my side as he tries to pry my leg from Garrett.

"No." I hiss, and Shaun chuckles as the guys work to try and pry me away.

"Baby. Let go."

It's Garrett's voice that has me pausing. I look back up into his icy-blue eyes, and my heart breaks a little. His eyes are pleading. Begging. He wants me off him now.

Doesn't he want me anymore?

I slacken my legs, and they drop from around his waist as Simon tugs me back. As soon as my feet hit the ground, I struggle out of Simon's grip and spin, shooting him a glare before I run towards the water, and keep running until the bottom dips and I lose my footing.

Kicking my legs, I swim out into the dark water—river monster be damned—needing to get away from these guys and cool the fuck down. My skin is on fire. My Kitty is raging. And my emotions are out of control.

What did I just do?

You forced yourself on him, you whore!

Diving into the water, I scream under the surface, trying to release my frustration and embarrassment at practically mauling Garrett. Did I really want my first time with him to be in the middle of the bush with Shaun, Simon, and Marcus watching? No, I fucking don't. So why couldn't I control myself?

Because you're a sex addict!

NO, I'M NOT!

It's the first time I've ever battled myself over this. Therapists have tossed up whether I am and if it's even a real thing. I came to accept my addiction a long time ago because if it wasn't addiction that made me do all of those things, then am I really just a sick, vile minded person who should probably be locked up with all the other sex offenders in the world?

Not that I've done anything that wasn't wanted by the other people I've been with. Even so, normal people aren't consumed by sex like I am.

Strong hands grip my arms as I scream over and over, deep under the surface of the water. I don't fight them as I'm pulled to the surface, and as I breach, water spittles from my mouth as I gasp for air.

"Fuck Rhee. What were you doing?"

Marcus sounds frantic, and his eyes are wild as he studies my face.

"I needed a moment." I splutter, squeezing my eyes shut.

I just want to disappear.

"Under the water?" Marcus asks, and I nod.

Slowly, I pry my eyes open, and Marcus' face comes into view. His face is contorted with confusion and pain as he studies me. It's too much to witness, so I lower my eyes and whisper. "I'm fucked up."

"Why would you say that?" Marcus asks, and when I keep my eyes cast low, he grips my chin and angles it up, so I have no choice but to look at him.

"This is not normal. My reaction to Garrett is not normal. Who does that? I'm a whore."

"Don't fucking say that! You're not a whore!" Marcus brushes my dripping hair back off one side of my face. "There's nothing wrong with you. You're perfect."

"Perfectly fucked up." I hiss, my self-loathing swinging at me again.

"Stop! Don't you fucking talk that way." Marcus hisses back at me, getting so close that our noses touch.

"Don't you get it? This is what happens. I get an uncontrollable need to fuck, and that's all I can think about. I nearly didn't stop. I nearly forced myself onto him."

"No, you didn't." Garrett's voice comes from behind me, and he comes into view as he swims around us, where Marcus is treading water to keep us afloat.

I can't speak. I feel so ashamed, my cheeks flaring in embarrassment.

Garrett reaches out, his hand flicking water up as he moves, and he cups my burning cheek. "I wanted you as much as you wanted me, baby. Now just isn't the right time. Soon though. I promise."

My lips tremble a little at the warm smile Garrett gives me. He has some sort of magic ability to make me feel calmer. I want to kiss him and show him I'm ok, but getting close to him while we are naked is a bad idea. So, I nod, our eyes locked and lingering for a minute before I turn away, cuddling into Marcus while I mentally talk Kitty down off the ledge. She's not getting lucky tonight.

It takes me about ten more minutes to pull my shit together and resume my typical Rhys George fun mode. It's forced in the beginning, but the guys have a way of making me forget about my worries with their silly banter and the stupid boy things they do to try and outdo each other.

It's not until we are out of the water and getting dressed that I realise I wasn't scared of what was lurking under the surface. I guess having Kitty in control gives me more balls or something.

"Can we talk about something, please?" Marcus' tone is serious, and I instantly want to flee. Ugh, I hate talking about stuff. Tonight has already been a lot for me. I'm not sure how much more I can take.

"If it has to do with Ty, you're wasting your breath," Shaun says on my behalf, and I could just kiss him. Thank you, Casanova!

"I guess Ty is involved," Marcus states as he tugs his t-shirt over his chest, "but this has to do with the rules of this relationship."

"There are rules?" Simon asks, and Marcus glares.

"There has to be. This isn't a typical situation. We are sharing Rhys, so we need to be clear on certain things, or this will never work. And I don't know about you, but I really want this to work. I'm not giving her up again."

My heart flutters at Marcus' admission.

"I agree with Grady. We all need to be clear on the rules." Garrett stands from the rock he's perched on, already fully dressed.

"We have the satellite phone. Let's give Ty a call and get the rules sorted, then." Shaun holds up the phone that Lexi insisted we take on our night hike. "What do you think, Kitten?"

I shrug. I don't fucking know if this is a good idea or not. Chances are it will end in a screaming match, but this is important to them, and I understand we need to be on the same page for certain things.

Shaun takes my shrug as a yes, and he takes out his phone to get Ty's number and then he keys it into the satellite phone. He listens for a moment and then puts it on speaker as we all move in closer. My heart is racing. This is weird, right? Having Ty included? It just feels weird.

"Hello?" Tyler's voice is loud through the speaker, and I hope like hell that Simon, Marcus and Garrett don't recognise it.

"Skipper, it's Cass and Kitten. We are here with Simon, Marcus, and Garrett, and you're on speaker."

"What's happened?" Ty's concern is evident in his tone.

"Nothing's happened, Ty." I rush out. "The guys just wanted to sort out a few rules for us all, so we thought you should be included in the discussion."

Crickets.

Shit. Have I overstepped in letting them call him?

"Ok. Go ahead."

Relief washes through me, and a weight is instantly lifted.

"Uh. This is Marcus. Firstly, I don't fucking like that we aren't all privy to who the fuck you are."

"Marcus!" I snap, and he rolls his eyes.

"But I guess I kind of understand that there is a risk because you're obviously some old guy."

Ty chuckles. "Something like that."

"Right, so, I think we all need to agree that Rhys is the only person we are each seeing. There will be no other chicks or dudes if that's the way you swing. Just Rhys, like a normal relationship."

"Yep, I agree." Shaun leaps in with his answer, shooting me a cheeky grin and a wink.

"Me too. Rhys is it for me." Marcus adds.

"Only Rhys." Garrett declares, and Simon nods.

"Hell yeah. You're my everything, Cherry."

"Who's Cherry?" Tyler asks, and I giggle.

"I'm Cherry. I'll fill you in later as to why."

"O-k. Well, I already said this to Kitten on the phone this morning, but she is the only one for me."

Everyone falls quiet at Ty's words. Were they hoping he'd declare that he's not committing to me or something? Too bad if they were, because Ty isn't going anywhere, and his and each of their declarations has me a little overwhelmed with stupid girl emotions.

"Rhee. What about you? We have all declared that we will only be with you, so will you agree you will only be with us? No other guys or girls. Just us five?"

"I feel like we are at a wedding." Simon chuckles, and I nod, grinning.

"Yeah. I feel like I'm giving my vows or something. Does that mean there will be a consummation afterwards? Because I'm horny as fuck still."

Groans come from all the guys except Ty. He growls.

"Kitten. Behave."

"Behaving is boring. I wanna be bad." I bite my lip and look up through my lashes at Garrett, who shakes his head at me, shooting me a grin.

"You're not playing fair, baby girl."

"You know what isn't fair?" I ask, not waiting for them to respond. "Showing me your big dick and not letting me ride it, Gaz. That's not fair!"

"Kitten!" Ty hisses, and I snap my mouth shut, trying to hide my smile.

"Come on, Rhee. Be serious for a few minutes. We are all committing to you here. You gotta give us something." Marcus bursts my horny bubble again. He's come a long way since yesterday morning. If you had asked me a few days ago if I thought Marcus was going to be part of my group, I'd have laughed and said no. I'm super fucking glad things have changed.

"I have a few questions first."

"Ok. What are they?" Marcus asks, and I suck in a deep breath because I know he will hate what I'm about to ask.

"When you say that there will be no other guys or girls for me, you're just talking about having a relationship, right? You don't mean sex as well?"

Marcus frowns. "Of course, I mean sex as well. That's how a relationship works. You commit to only the other person. Or, in this case, persons for you."

"Oh. But what about sex parties or clubs? Are you saying I can't fuck other people at them?"

Crickets… again.

Jesus.

"Why would you need to go to sex parties or clubs if you have us?" Marcus hisses, clearly not happy. Just like I knew he'd be.

"Uh. Umm." I look frantically at the phone and then at Shaun, hoping they'll help me out here. "Well. I mean, sometimes I like tacos." My statement sounds like a question, and I look to Shaun for help, noticing the fucker is wearing a smirk that he tries to hide.

"Tacos?" Marcus asks, and Shaun laughs.

"She means pussy, man. Rhys likes variety in her sex. Sometimes she likes some girl-on-girl action."

"I wanna see that." Simon's excited tone draws my attention. His eyes tell me he absolutely would like to see that.

"It's a beautiful sight, man." Shaun grins, and Simon groans.

"Fuck, Bossi. You've had all the fun. Can we come to these parties, Cherry?" "Yeah, *Cherry*, can we come to these parties?" Marcus' tone is all arsehole as he speaks, "And how would that work? Are you gonna let us fuck other chicks at these parties?"

I want to slap him.

"Just so I'm clear, the teeny-bopper who just spoke is Marcus, right?" Tyler hisses through the speakers, and Marcus frowns.

"Yeah, old man. So?"

"So, maybe you're not man enough to handle this relationship. All I'm hearing is an immature, insecure prick." Tyler states.

"Fuck you! I'm man enough!" Marcus snaps.

I knew this conversation was a bad idea. Marcus isn't ready for all of this yet.

"Really?" Tyler questions. "Because if you can't handle taking your girl to a sex party and enjoy watching her get pleasure from whatever means necessary, then you're not right for the job."

"Fuck you! Who the fuck do you think you are?" Marcus leaps for the phone, but Shaun is faster and moves it out of reach.

"Calm down, Grady. Let's just listen to what Rhys needs from us in order for this to work." Garrett rests his hand on Marcus' shoulder, tugging him back a few steps, and Shaun returns the phone to the centre.

"So, you two watch her with other men?" Simon asks curiously. His hazel eyes look dark in the shade of night, and his blonde hair looks more highlighted under the glow of the moon.

Shaun nods, "Yeah. Men and women. Each other. She enjoys watching us with other people too, don't you, Kitten?"

"Yep," I nod.

"Really?" Marcus says accusingly, "Because you weren't happy when Garrett and Bell were gonna kiss earlier today, and you couldn't go through with kissing Jared, so how exactly are you going to handle all of us at these parties? Because I can tell you right fucking now that you ain't going without all of us from now on."

"Why are you being such a prick, Marcus? Your mood swings are giving me whiplash!" I snap, my fists balled at my sides, eager to swing.

"How about we just calm down and take a minute?" Tyler suggests, and I growl and stomp my foot, turning on my heel and storming away from the circle to take a moment. Why does everything have to be so complicated? Shouldn't this relationship stuff be easy?

"Kitten?" Tyler's voice calls, and I turn back to see the guys watching me. I don't want to talk to them right now, yet I can't handle staying away, so I drag my feet through the dirt back to the circle.

"Ty?" My voice is quiet. Tired.

"I know you don't want to have this conversation, but it needs to happen. Marcus is right about that." I hate it when Tyler is all adult and shit.

"Fine." I huff, crossing my arms over my chest as goosebumps flutter over my skin. My swim dress is great for daytime, but it's doing little to ward off the combined chill of the night air and wet hair dripping down my back.

"It's ok if you don't like the thought of any of us kissing or fucking other people at the parties. That's actually normal. Just like it's normal for Marcus to be struggling with the concept of it. What we need to do is make things clear, so there's no confusion, but I'm guessing we won't know how you feel about it until we all go to a party together. So, let's agree that we should go to one and test the waters. If you only want us fucking you, then that's what we will do."

"And what if we only want her fucking us?" Marcus asks, his arsehole tone no longer there.

"Honestly, I think it's more of a question if Rhys can handle fucking anyone else but us," Shaun adds, and Tyler agrees.

"Yeah. From what you said before, Marcus, it sounds like our girl wasn't that interested in anyone else. You have to remember, though. The sex parties are only about sex. There are no feelings involved. It's just about exploring desires, pushing boundaries, and having freedom to be yourself, so if Rhys needs to get railed by a hulk of a guy with a ten-inch dick while she eats pussy, then you have to be ok with that."

I think I love Tyler. He gets me so much more than anyone else does. Well, the sex part of me, anyway.

"And if we can't get on board with that?" Marcus asks, genuinely curious. His dark brows draw together as his eyes stay trained on the phone.

"Then you're not right for this relationship." Tyler's words, although confronting, aren't said harshly, and Marcus nods, picking up on that.

Sighing, Marcus looks up at me. "I'll try for you, Rhee."

I didn't realise until he says those words that I was holding my breath. Air immediately fills my lungs as relief washes over me. Marcus really is trying. I know he wouldn't have chosen this lifestyle. He's doing all of this for me.

"Wait? So we are going to a sex party?" Simon asks, his mind still in the gutter.

"Maybe." Tyler states, and Garrett frowns.

"So, that means we are gonna meet you?"

"You will, but I'll be wearing a mask. And if any of you fuckers touch me with your peewees, I'll cut them off."

A laugh rips from my chest at Tyler's words, and the guys join in. Well, all except for Tyler.

"So where are we on this relationship thing, Rhee?" Marcus asks over the laughter. "Can you commit to only us, with the exception of sex parties which we are yet to determine the rules of?"

I smile stupidly, flashing my teeth at Marcus.

"I do!"

A round of woo-hoo's come from Simon and Shaun, while Garrett and Tyler chuckle and Marcus grins.

"Right. Now that we have finished that awkward conversation." I rub my hands together, eyeing up my prey. "It's time to consummate our union. Who's first?"

CHAPTER NINETEEN

RHYS

C ock blocked! That's what's happening. I'm being cock blocked. I get it. I was involved in some messed up shit last week, and yeah, I've been healing from that, but to block me from their dicks is a little extreme.

There was no consummation of our union. Even after dangling Garrett's dick in front of me, they still refuse to give in, leaving me a writhing mess. We all went back to the tent, and I kind of hoped there would be some action, especially after I announced I was sleeping in there with them again. But Marcus was grumbly, Garrett was quiet, Shaun was too busy filling Simon in on some of the stuff that happens at sex parties, and Tyler probably had a fantastic wank in the privacy of his own home.

The guys fell asleep quickly, and I lay there staring at the tent ceiling, debating if I should just get myself off quietly. Unfortunately for Kitty, it was never going to happen with Garrett snuggled up on one side of me, and Simon on my other. I couldn't fucking move.

Eventually, I fell asleep… for like an hour. Now I'm wide awake and hornier than I was before I went to sleep. I roll my head to the side, taking in Garrett. He's out like a light. His normally broody frown is gone now. His face is soft and almost sweet. He's on his back now, his blanket kicked off and his arms above his head. I wonder what he'd do if I started kissing that firm chest of his? Would he let me kiss lower, or would he stop me?

I'm eager to find out, but I also don't want to push him until he's ready, so I roll my head to the other side, my eyes roaming over Simon. He's also on his back, his face wearing a slight grin, even in sleep. Like Garrett, he's kicked off his blanket to reveal his chest. If I kissed his chest, he wouldn't want me to stop.

Simon's hand is tucked under the band of his jocks, probably holding his dick. I grin. He has a fine dick. I'd like to hold it too. Can I handle his dick, though? It hurt when Marcus sunk deep inside me yesterday. It hurt a lot. Would it hurt today? Maybe penetration isn't the answer tonight, but we can fool around, right?

I roll to my side and nudge Simon's shoulder.

"Simon," I whisper. "Simon."

He stirs, his eyes fluttering open to look at me, and then he smiles.

"What's wrong, Cherry?" He whispers back.

"I need to come." I whisper. "Like really bad, and I'd do it myself, but you're right here, and I was hoping you might like to help me?"

His smile widens. "Sure, I'll help you, but aren't you still healing?"

I nod. "Yeah, but I can still fool around. A bit of foreplay and oral isn't out of the question."

He beams. "So, I can eat you? I'm fucking starving, Cherry."

I giggle, trying to stay quiet. "Yes, please eat me, Sy."

"My dick is already hard." Simon chuckles, and he tugs his jocks down, showing me his hard length. On instinct, I wrap my hand around his firm, silky skin, and he leans up on an elbow to take my lips in his.

The moment our lips part, our tongues meet with desperate need, and I feel the thin sheet sliding down my body. With demanding lips, Simon moves over me, forcing me to roll on my back as his hand cups my tits. It's brief because he's desperate to remove the fabric, and he breaks our kiss to pull my t-shirt off over my head. He takes that moment to look around the darkish tent, and my eyes follow, finding no other eyes on us—just a sleeping Garrett, Marcus and Shaun.

"Do you think we will wake them?" Simon whispers, and I shrug.

"I don't care if we do, as long as they don't try to stop us, because I'll rip their dicks off if they do."

Simon chuckles quietly before claiming my lips again. His bare chest brushes against mine, and excitement ripples through me. I've missed this. I've missed him. I miss them all, and I just want more of this. So much more.

His fingers pinch my nipple, and I can't hold in my moan, although I'm pretty sure I'm quiet enough not to disturb anyone. Then, Simon trails kisses down my neck, travelling down until my nipples are engulfed in warm, moist heat. I grip onto Simon's longish hair, holding him close as Kitty seeks more, pushing up in search of friction.

"Sy. Eat me, please." I beg. Yep, I'm not ashamed to beg for sex.

Simon doesn't make me wait any longer. Sitting up and shifting down, he pulls my knickers free and moves between my legs. His eyes shift, and he looks to my side and grins before diving in. Turning my head, my eyes widen to see Garrett awake, and I moan loudly at the first contact of Simon's tongue.

Garrett moves quickly to slap his hand over my mouth while I claw at Simon's head, gripping his hair again and tugging him so tight that he's likely to suffocate. I'm already so close. My needy Kitty is well overdue for milking. As Simon goes to town, his tongue sweeping over my clit, I watch Garrett as he looks from Simon between my legs and back to my face. He slowly releases his hand, and I let go of Simon's hair with one hand, bringing it up to cup Garrett's face.

"Kiss me."

He's not able to hold back, and with one last look down between my legs, Garrett slams his lips into mine. I've been desperate for his kisses, and now that I finally have them, they are so much more than I had imagined. They hold so much heart and passion, even right now, with lust fuelling him. Each stroke of his tongue carries so much experience that I almost want to question it. But fuck it, right now, all I want is more.

The combination of being kissed on both sets of lips sends me over, and I explode. Garrett's lips muffle my cries while Simon drags my orgasm out, over and over, that I almost forget to breathe.

As Garrett's lips slow over mine, Simon's do the same between my legs, and eventually, I'm able to suck in oxygen as Garrett breaks away from me, slowly sitting up. I grin lazily up at him, and he returns it.

"You're truly beautiful, baby girl." This is the first sexual encounter Garrett has physically participated in. Yeah, he wasn't the one touching Kitty, but he gave me that orgasm just as much as Simon did.

"You taste amazing, Cherry. I've fucking missed that." Simon sits up, grinning at me, his face glistening with my juices as he pumps his dick.

"Bring that here, Sy. Cum in my mouth."

He doesn't hesitate, and Garrett has to sit back a little to give him room as Simon straddles my waist, hovering his hard dick over me while he pumps it.

"You thirsty, Cherry?" Simon pumps his dick faster, and I nod, looking at it and licking my lips.

"I'm so parched, Sy." I lift my head, my mouth open, so he understands what I want.

Resting one hand above my head, Simon leans forward, pushing his cock between my lips. His moan is loud, and if Marcus and Shaun haven't already woken up, then they must be dead because we aren't being quiet anymore. The thought of them all watching excites me in a way that the Feast never has. Maybe they are enough for me. Maybe I'll never need another sex party again.

As Simon pumps and thrusts, I work my lips over the head of his pretty cock, swirling my tongue to lap up the salty pre-cum goodness.

"Fuck, Cherry. Here it comes." Simon grits out before his face contorts in pleasured pain, and hot rivers of cum spurt into my mouth. I moan and swallow his offering down, pulling him free to catch the last squirts on my tongue.

Panting and sweating, Simon relaxes back, releasing his cock, his eyes trained on my tongue as I show him his seed. Then I draw my tongue in and swallow the rest, extracting another moan from him.

"I could fuck that pretty mouth all night, Cherry."

I grin. "I'm up for it if you are."

Three other moans meet my ears, and I shift a little to see Shaun and Marcus are indeed watching. Shaun's grin is shit-eating. He fucking loves this, the filthy fucker. I love him for that. Marcus, on the other hand, is frowning. I can't read what sort of frown it is in this low light. Is it a *why would they do that* frown, or a *why in the hell did I like that so much* frown, or a *what the fuck am I doing with this whore* type of frown?

"Please tell me you're up for more, Kitten?" Shaun asks, and I smile.

"Foreplay and oral only, but yes. Come here, Cass."

Shaun doesn't hesitate. He practically leaps from his sleeping bag and positions himself in between my legs.

"Move to the side Hastings and show her nipples some love," Shaun instructs as he glides his fingers over my nub. I gasp, not ready for the contact, but I'm not protesting. Kitty wants more. So much more.

Simon moves back over to his side, and I glance at Garrett, who has shifted back toward the door of the tent, but he's not making a move to flee… yet.

"Gar. Is this ok?" I ask softly, trying to ignore the way Shaun's fingers are circling my clit, or how Simon's tongue is flicking over my left nipple. "You wanna join?"

He grins. "Not tonight, baby girl. I'm just a bystander. Pretend I'm not here."

"I doubt she's gonna do that after seeing your monster cock, man." Shaun chuckles, and my eyes flutter closed at the mental image of the cock that set me off earlier tonight. "Oh, she just got wetter. Yeah, she's excited about your monster, dude."

"Fuck." Garrett hisses, and Simon moans around my nipple.

Suddenly, Shaun stops touching me, and I feel him moving.

"Hastings, back up. I want Kitten to turn around." Shaun stands and moves over me, shifting to the back of the tent where he and Marcus were sleeping.

I sit up and let Shaun guide me around, realising he must want Marcus to have a more intimate view of Kitty. But then he urges me to roll on my tummy, and butterflies dance inside me in anticipation of what he's going to do. I let Shaun guide me into position on my hands and knees, and then he gently pushes my face down, spreading my knees further apart, lifting my arse and drawing me back.

Well, Kitty, if you ever wanted me to mimic your arse in the air and tail wagging, then you just got your way.

Not only is Kitty exposed. But so is the pucker of my arse. If it weren't for the fact that Shaun is the one navigating this, I'd be freaking out a little, or probably a lot, but this guy knows my body more intimately than most, and I trust him completely.

"You ok there, Kitten? Comfortable?"

"Yep," I say, my voice muffled under all my hair as I rest my forehead on my braced arms.

"Good. I'm gonna make you come now."

I'm about to say *hell yeah* or something along those lines, but my gasp holds everything in as Shaun buries his face in between my arse cheeks. His tongue lashes out, gliding from my dripping cunt to my puckered back passage, prodding the forbidden entrance before repeating the motion.

"Fuck, that's hot." Simon mutters, and Garrett agrees with a "Fuck yeah, it is."

There's no sound from Marcus. I can't even be sure he's still there, but I forget to care when Shaun presses two fingers to my clit and starts to work up friction. I push back into his face, desperate for more, and he works his tongue faster and firmer, his fingers picking up the pace.

"Yes. Cass. Fuck." I can't manage anything else, but he understands.

"You ready, Kitten?" He asks, and I try to nod, even though I'm not sure what I'm agreeing to.

"Yes. Cass. Yes."

His face disappears from between my cheeks, and his fingers sweep up and down between my folds before they come to rest at the entrance of my arse.

"Here we go." Then Shaun slowly slides a finger inside.

I gasp and hold my breath, and his other hand finds my clit, his fingers pressing firm circles over my nerve endings.

"Your arse is so tight, Kitten. I'm gonna fuck you here one day soon."

I moan, whimper, and hiss—pure pleasure building blindingly fast.

"Let's fill you a bit more." Shaun's voice is husky as fuck, clearly affected by lust, and he slowly adds a second digit to join the first, burying two just inside my arse. A feeling I haven't felt before builds rapidly. With my control lost, I push back quickly, silently telling Shaun what I need, and he doesn't disappoint. With fingers pressed to my clit and two moving inside my arse, I skyrocket.

The intense climax slams into me, and Cass dives his tongue into my weeping pussy, sucking out my juices as I ripple with pleasurable seizures. It's long and intense and almost too much, yet not enough, and before too long, I collapse forward in a spent heap.

"Fuck, I'm hard again." Simon groans, and Shaun chuckles.

"Take care of yourself, man. Our girl needs a break."

"Well, what are you gonna do with yours? It looks like the skin is about to split apart." Simon observes.

"What's it to you? You wanna take care of it, Hastings?"

I sit up quickly, turning to face the guys, my hair clinging to my face in a sweaty mess. I swipe at my hair, suddenly re-energised. "I wanna watch that."

"What?" Simon frowns, looking confused. "You wanna see me get Bossi off?"

I nod. "Fuck yeah. That would be so hot."

"Ok, I'm outta here." Marcus cringes and pushes past Shaun and Garrett, unzipping the tent and bursting out into the night.

"She's only kidding, man." Shaun chuckles, but when he looks back at me, I raise a brow. "Right, Kitten? You're only kidding?"

"Fuck no." I bite my lower lip while I think, and then I grin. "I wanna see Simon blow you."

"Cherry, I'm not blowing my mate." Simon throws his hands up, shuffling away on his knees. He said mate, not guy or man. Hmmm, how interesting.

"It's not a gay thing, Sy. It's a sex thing. Right Cass?" I look at Shaun, and he shrugs.

"Well, yeah, at a sex party it is, but not in this relationship. I don't think any of us are strong enough to deal with that afterwards."

"So… if we can't do stuff like that in our relationship, and if we can't go to sex parties, then how am I going to get what I need? Like, what if I want a golden shower? What if I wanna fuck one of you up the arse with a strap on? What if I want to watch Garrett stick his big dick in your arse? Are you telling me I can't have that stuff? I thought this group relationship thing was so I could have all of those things and more."

"Firstly, you are disgusted by golden showers." Shaun reminds me, but I shrug.

"So? What if I change my mind? Or what if I want to pee in someone's mouth again while you watch? You and Ty fucking loved that last time. I know you did."

"You pissed in someone's mouth?" Garrett asks me, and when I nod, he turns to Shaun. "And you watched? And liked it?"

"Fuck yeah. That was hot as hell."

"I gotta take a walk." Garrett declares and leaves the tent too.

"Shit." Fear slams into me hard, and I dart my eyes back to Shaun. "This isn't going to work. I'm too depraved for them."

"No, you're not Kitten." Shaun moves up to sit in front of me, cupping both sides of my face. "You have to remember that this world of ours is new to them. You gotta give them time. And if they can't handle something, we will deal with it when it happens and try to figure out a solution."

"Cherry?" Simon moves quietly to my side. "If you ever want someone to piss on you, I'll do it."

A laugh bubbles up my throat and bursts free as I take in Simon's serious face.

"What? I'll do anything for you." He admits, and I shake my head, giggling.

"You're the best, Sy. If I ever want someone to piss on me, I'll ask you first."

He beams. "Deal."

Chapter Twenty

Rhys

Heaven. I'm in it, and I never want to leave. Heaven being Garrett's arms, oh and Simon's little spoon. I'm hot and sweaty, but I don't care. Being held like this in sleep is quickly becoming an addiction. These guys are quickly becoming an addiction. An addiction I don't think I'll ever be able to give up.

"You awake beautiful?"

I feel like I'm Lexi West. All blushy and shit. Jesus, these guys are turning me into a chick from a Christmas Romance, swooning over her lover.

Do I care?

Hell to the no!

I shift off Garrett's bare chest onto his shoulder so I can peer up to his face.

"I'm awake." I grin, and he returns it, his icy-blues half-lidded from sleep.

Fuck, that's sexy. I can't wait to see what he looks like after sex.

"Did you sleep ok?" He asks, brushing some of my long dark strands off my face.

"Yeah. Best night's sleep I've had in ages."

It's true too. Once Marcus and Garrett returned from wherever they ran off to, we all settled in, and it felt normal. It felt right. I'm pretty sure I fell asleep smiling.

"That's good." Garrett's eyes follow his hand, which is now travelling down my arm in a gentle stroke.

"Gaz? You know that stuff you told me about having a relationship without sex? I think I understand it now." I bite my lip as I gear up to put a voice to my thoughts. "The way I feel. It's an addiction. A craving. A longing. The thought of not having you in my life, of not having Marcus or Simon or Shaun or Ty. It feels like it would literally kill me not to have you all. I need sex, sure, but I need *you* more. I need *them* more. Knowing that scares the shit outta me. I'll never survive it if any of you guys leave me. I just know it."

Garrett studies me for a long, tense moment. Have I said too much? Did that sound too clingy? My self-doubt comes to a crashing halt a moment later when Garrett leans down and presses his lips to mine. I ignore the fact that Simon is wrapped around me from behind and reach forward, clasping Garrett's curls, desperate to have him closer. He's just as desperate, his large, strong hands pulling at me like he can't get close enough, and it's not until Simon chuckles that our frantic kissing eases before we pull apart.

"Sorry. I-ah... Got a little carried away." He doesn't look sorry with the grin he's wearing and his wild blue eyes.

"You don't have to stop on my account." Simon's head appears at my shoulder before wet lips slap on my cheek.

"I agree with Sy. You don't have to stop." Shooting Garrett a wicked grin, I trail my fingers over the firm ridges of his six-pack, trailing closer to the band of his shorts.

"Stop it." He grins, snatching hold of my hand and shifting it higher. "Now isn't *our* time."

"When is our time gonna be? How long are you gonna leave a girl hanging?" I whine like a little bitch before I feel a hand snake around my waist, gliding up to cup my breast.

"I'll look after you, Cherry," Simon whispers against my ear before taking my lobe in his mouth.

It feels nice. Really nice.

"No time for that. We have to pack up camp before the olds get here." Marcus sits up, slapping Simon over the head with his pillow.

"Cock-block." I frown, eyeing Marcus over my head, but the fucker doesn't care. He grins and winks before moving to the zip to open the tent.

"Later," Simon whispers in my ear again, and I crane my neck to give him a kiss. It's short but hot enough to make Kitty protest when he rolls away from me to get up.

"Ugh. What's a girl gotta do to get a bit of dick around here?"

Four chuckles fill the tent while I lay sulking with my arms crossed as Garrett joins the guys to get up. I'd like to know where they find their self-control because right now, Kitty is controlling mine.

Two hours later, our campsite is packed up, our parents are rolling in, and all I wanna do is send them away and stay in this bubble forever.

"Do we really have to go back?" I complain, crossing my arms over my chest as Cynthia's car comes into view. "Fuck school and exams. Let's just live in the bush and spend our days fucking."

"Hell yeah! I'm with Cherry." Simon hoots, slapping my arse as he walks past.

"That felt good, Sy, do it again."

"Please don't! I'm already scarred from hearing you scream like a banshee last night." Dale whines, screwing his face up. He's such a Kurt Hummel look alike. I bet he's watched every episode of Glee.

"Oh, come on, Dale. You wanna hear what we got up to?" I stir, and he gags.

"Girl, I don't want to know your coochie stories."

"You'll like this story. It doesn't even involve my coochie." I wag my eyes, and his mouth drops open.

"Ok, so maybe I wanna hear all about it. Call me tonight after eight. I'll make popcorn."

Laughter carries through the trees as the cars come to a stop, and the guys pick up the bags and head toward them.

"So, you did some… umm…" Lexi's quiet voice comes from beside me, and I grin even before I turn to see the red face I knew she'd be wearing.

"Butt stuff?" I grin, "Yes. Is that something you're into, Little Miss Not-So-Vanilla?"

Lexi shrugs, looking around to see if anyone is listening. "We've done some stuff."

"Oh, do tell. Does Ayden fuck your arse with that pretty cock of his?"

"Shhhh!" Lexi slaps her hand over my mouth, and all I can do is laugh. Her blue eyes are wild and frantic as she searches to see if anyone heard me. No one heard. They're too busy loading the cars. "No. Not yet. We are leading up to it."

When she drops her hand away, I beam, biting my lower lip at the same time. "Damn, girl. Arse play is new to me. I can't believe you're more experienced than I am."

Lexi laughs. "I wouldn't go that far. But…" She looks around again, checking for eavesdroppers. "Ayden bought me a butt plug, and we're gonna try it out later this week."

"Shit Lex. I've been holding onto my arse virginity, but these guys are quickly showing me how good it can feel. You'll have to fill me in after you use the plug. I want to know all the deets."

"Ah, no. I'm not going to tell you *everything*." Lexi shakes her head just as Ayden approaches.

"What aren't you telling her?" Ayden asks, wrapping his arms around Lexi's waist from behind.

"She's gonna hold out on me about the butt plug action." I tease, and Ayden's brows shoot to his hairline.

"Lex, what have I told you about divulging our dirty secrets?" Ayden whispers against Lexi's ear as he squeezes her to him. Her reaction is priceless. Her lids flutter shut, and she moans a little before speaking breathlessly.

"That if I do, you will punish me."

"You remember last time?" He asks again, not looking at me but at the side of Lexi's face as he questions her.

"Yes." She pants.

"Fucking hell. You two keep this up, and I'm the one that's going to come."

Lexi's eyes fly open at my words, and Ayden chuckles as Marcus comes to stand next to me, nudging my shoulder.

"Cynthia is asking for you."

"Ugh." I lull my head back dramatically before returning my gaze to Lexi.

"I want details." I point at her chest, and when she grins and winks at me, I poke my tongue out at Ayden and walk off with Marcus.

"What was that about?"

"Nothing important," I smirk, and he squints accusingly.

"Just a heads up. Cynthia seems a little off."

I stop abruptly at Marcus' words, looking from him, then past our group of friends to find Cynthia standing by the car. Her hands are twisting together nervously as she pretends to listen to Jared's mum, and the moment her eyes land on me, she plants a fake smile on her face.

"You're right. She does seem off." I agree, not wanting to find out. Cynthia is a strong woman. She has been through her own trauma growing up and works hard to create a home with Will for us kids, so to see the normally put together woman acting nervous is making me nervous.

"I'm sure it's nothing." Marcus gives my fingers a little squeeze, and I glance up at him, nodding, pretending to agree. "Can I call you tonight?"

Smiling, I nod. "Yes. I'd like that."

I can tell he wants to kiss me, but with all the adults around, it's not a good idea. They think I'm seeing Shaun. I don't think they're ready to acknowledge a multiple-partner relationship, even though Cin knows a little about Simon and Garrett already. It's ok, though. The guys all kissed me thoroughly before the rents arrived, so that will have to get me through the rest of the day.

We all say our goodbyes before filling the various cars to return to reality. When I approach my parents, my dad dodges making eye contact with me, while my mum glances at me with something that looks very much like sympathy.

The squeals of the twins capture my attention as they take turns at doing blowfish on the windows from inside the car, and when I glance back at Cin, she's turned and opened the back door for me to climb in.

"Did you have a good time?" She asks, and I smile and nod as I slip into the car.

"The best," I admit, and her smile broadens.

For the first ten minutes of the drive, the questions from my parents are very generic, and I don't even think they're taking in my answers. For the next ten minutes, I stay quiet, leaning my head against the window, watching the ferns and tall gums swoosh by on the windy roads. A half an hour in, my phone chimes with incoming messages. Finally. Phone service again.

I have a heap of messenger messages, but I don't recognise the name of the group 'Guess Who', so I move over to Snapchat to see messages coming in from the guys, plus Lexi and Tillie.

I open Lexi's first.

Lexi West
Are you ok?

Rhys George
Yeah. Why?

Lexi doesn't reply straight away, so I open Tillie's.

Tillie Hall
They are all crazy!

Rhys George
Who are they? And why are they crazy?

When she doesn't reply straight away, I open the guys' group chat, ***Cherry's Merry Men***.

Casanova
Don't read the comments, Kitten.

Simon Says
I'm gonna fuck Eric up!

Marcus Grady
Why is this group called Cherry's Merry Men?

Garrett Cole
Don't ask.

Simon Says
We are Cherry's Merry Men!
Focus on the issue at hand, fellas!

Casanova
Kitten?

What the fuck is going on?

Cherry Pie
What comments, Cass?
Why are you fucking Eric up, Sy?

Casanova
Haven't you seen the group in messenger?

Cherry Pie
Well, I have notifications for a group, but I didn't know
what it was, so I haven't looked.

Casanova
Don't look.

Cherry Pie
Cass, you do know me, right?
You tell me not to do something, and I'm doing it.
What the fuck is going on?

Simon Says

Eric Carter made a fucking group about the video Cherry. People are commenting on who they think it is. Some people are saying they have submitted their guesses already.

My heart sinks. I swipe over to messenger and open the chat, and my brows hitch at all the comments. It's huge. Hundreds of comments. Too many to go through. Most of the commenters are guys from school. Some girls respond with abuse and protests, and others agree with the boys. I can't read all the comments. Do they know it's me?

My phone rings, and I quickly answer Simon's call, ignoring my mum's prying eyes as she looks over her shoulder from the front.

"Cherry?"

"Yeah," I say quietly, turning to look out the window again.

"You looked, didn't you?" Simon sounds so worried. I love that he cares so much.

"I did."

"How much did you read?" He asks, and I can hear someone in the background asking him to put the phone on speaker. It's Shaun, I think. They are travelling together with Shaun's brother, Derek.

"Only a bit. Can you tell me more?" I ask quietly, since it's hard for me to speak in this confined space with ears eager to hear my conversation.

"Kitten?" Shaun's voice comes down the line, and I chew the inside of my cheek in an attempt to hold in my emotions.

"Yeah."

"Are you sure you want to know?"

"Not really, but I think I need to," I admit, glancing up to see my dad eyeing me in the rear-view mirror.

Shaun sighs, "Eric Carter announced his top five guesses."

"I'm gonna kick his arse!" Simon hisses. "Who the fuck does he think he is? Why would he even try to guess? He's the richest kid at school. It's not like he needs the money."

"He's an entitled prick. It's not about money for him. Just winning. And dragging people down in the process." There's so much rage in Shaun's voice. He's normally so chill. It reminds me of the night at the Feast. The sound of his voice as he yelled for them to stop.

"Just tell me," I say impatiently, noticing that my mum and dad keep glancing at each other.

"His list is Ella Briggs, Darcy Thompson, Sierra Chapman." Simon clears his throat. "Bell and you."

And there it is. Of course, *I* make the list. And Bell too. Why not? We fit the physical description, just like the other girls do. Long dark hair. Dark eyes. What a dick. There are probably fifty other girls that fit the physical description, but not all of them are weird or promiscuous—only the five on that list.

"Are others agreeing?" I ask, trying to remain vague so my eavesdroppers don't understand my conversation.

"Some are," Shaun admits. "Others have their own theories. Eric has declared that he has chosen one from that list and sent his guess to the email address that was sent with the video. Some of the other guys have submitted guesses too, but they aren't revealing who they chose."

"Right. Well, that's that then." I'm pissed off. Why did we have to leave Ebony Falls? I was finally feeling like my old self. I fucking hate Julie Bates. I'm going to make her pay. Somehow. Some way. I'm going to fucking expose her.

"Kitten. It doesn't mean anything. They might be bluffing." Shaun offers, and I scoff.

"Unlikely. But thanks for trying to make me feel better."

"Cherry. Don't forget how much we care about you." Simon's tone is filled with pain. He's scared. Probably of how I'll react. Let's face it. I've been standing on a narrow ledge lately. He's probably wondering what it will take for me to step off. Hell, I'm wondering the same.

If Julie announces to everyone that it's me in the video, will I step off that ledge?

I'd like to think I'm strong enough not to. But what if my guys turn their backs on me, not able to be tied to such depravity? Can I handle living without their support? Their care and attention? Would I give up on life altogether?

I don't want to be that person. I don't want to throw everything away because my old foster parents are fucking paedophiles out to ruin me all because they got sprung. Fuck them! And fuck anyone else who turns their back on me for something I never asked for.

"Kitten?" Shaun's concern is as evident as Simon's. I really do think I love these guys.

"I'm ok. I should probably go. Call me later?" I try to push some sort of positive vibe into my voice. It's all I can do right now, although I'm not sure I'm convincing.

"Yeah, of course," Shaun says right before Simon agrees.

When I hang up, I don't look up from my phone. I don't want to see Cynthia and Will looking at me. Something is going on, and I'm not sure if I can handle anything else thrown at me.

Actually, I do know. I'll handle it with a fake smile and a hit of Mary Jane.

Chapter Twenty-One

Rhys

The knock on my bedroom door isn't unexpected. I knew it was only a matter of time before the rents came to talk to me about whatever has them acting weird. It's obviously something they can't talk about in front of the twins or Char, which means it's something I won't want to talk about at all.

When I don't answer the door, the knock comes again, louder this time. I roll my eyes, glancing around my stark white bedroom and the wide window that looks into the backyard. Maybe I can do what Lexi does and climb out. It wouldn't be the first time.

"Rhys? Please open the door. I need to speak with you."

It's Cynthia. My mum.

So, what are my options? Pretend I'm not here? No. She will just pick the lock. Yes, my foster mum can pick locks. She is *that* cool. Sighing, I drag myself up off my bed and go to the door, flicking the lock and pulling the door open.

"I'm trying to sleep. Can this wait till tomorrow?"

"No." She frowns, stepping into my space, so I have no choice but to back up. "Close the door."

This isn't good. I can't gauge her mood. Is she angry? I don't normally get nervous around Cin, but I feel it now. It's like a sickly fluttering in my chest, and as I watch her sit on the end of my bed and pat the spot next to her, all I want to do is turn and flee.

"Come here, honey. We need to have a chat."

"What about? Is something wrong?" Tucking my dark hair behind my ear, I slowly approach my bed, noticing how my mum's stare has softened.

"Are you ok, Rhys?" Her voice is laced with worry. "Like, *really* ok?"

"If I say yes, are you going to believe me?" I sit down slowly next to my mum, her eyes never wavering from me.

"No, honey. I won't believe that." Her admission is all the confirmation I need. Either she knows about Julie and Brian, or the videos, or fuck, maybe even Vixen's Lodge, or she's about to introduce me to a new contender in the let's fuck up Rhys George's existence.

"What's going on?" I ask, keeping my eyes trained on hers.

"I know about the video going around of you when you were younger, and I know Julie sent it."

My brows shoot up. Damn. How did she get this info? The video part was always a risk. Bonnie Mayer's parents could have told the school or the police. But how does she know Julie sent it?

"When did you find out about the video?"

"On Friday afternoon. Mr Mayer called to tell me about it. He'd been to the police but thought since the message was directly targeting Fox Pines Catholic students, that I should know."

I nod. "So, have you seen it? Is that how you knew it was me?"

"Yes, and no." She reaches out and brushes my flyaways back off my forehead. "Yes, I saw the video, but only after I was told it was of you and who sent it."

Now my brows are practically reaching the ceiling. "Who showed you the video and told you it was me?" There are only a handful of people that know the truth. So, which one blabbed?

"It doesn't matter who brought this information to me-."

"Like hell, it doesn't!" I leap from the bed, instant fury coursing through me at the thought of a traitor in my ranks.

"Calm down, Rhys. We need to focus on what's important here. Why didn't *you* tell me about Julie contacting you? And when did you go to the prison to see Brian?"

"What? How do you know that? Tell me who told you!"

Cynthia stands, her hands stretched out in a calming manner. "How I know isn't important. What's important is that now I can help you. I can't believe you have been dealing with this on your own."

"Not important? Of course, it's important. I don't keep a journal, so I know you haven't been snooping. Who the fuck ran their mouth?"

"Language." She frowns, her tone not at all scolding like it normally would be.

"You need to tell me! Which one of my friends betrayed me? Was it Bell? Tillie?"

She shakes her head. "It wasn't one of your friends. All I can say is that one of the teachers overheard a few things and, after stewing on it for a couple of days, they reached out and filled me in. Our only concern is helping you and putting a stop to this."

It wasn't one of my friends?

It was a teacher?

No… It couldn't have been Ty. He wouldn't do that to me. Would he?

"Which teacher?"

"I can't reveal that, Rhys. You know I'm bound by confidentiality."

"Screw the confidentiality. Which teacher is spreading rumours about me?" I'm being irrational, I know, yet I can't help it. I feel betrayed.

"Calm down, please. We need to talk about the video. And Julie and Brian."

"Nope!" I snap, shaking my head as I pace back and forth, wearing a line in my grey carpet. "We don't need to talk about the video. You've seen it. Why talk about it? You want to know why I looked like I was enjoying it? Is that it?"

"Rhys! Stop it!" Cynthia leaps from the bed, reaching out for me, but I'm too fast. I dodge her hands, not wanting to be touched right now. "You know that's not what I mean. Please don't push me away. I want to help you."

"Why?" I cry, backing up against my wall, pressing myself flat. The coolness from the plaster is comforting against my burning hot skin.

"Because I love you! I want to protect you from those horrid people. That's what I'm here for, Rhys. To love and protect you. I just need you to let me!"

She's crying. Tears are streaming down Cynthia's face, her skin red and blotchy from emotions she can't hold in. The reminder of how much she cares slaps the accusing bitch out of me, and I leap forward, throwing myself at her. She catches me in her arms, and we sink to the floor of my bedroom as pain shreds through my chest. Everything I've endured since I can remember explodes through my mind and comes out in a scream.

My birth mum couldn't find a way to love me more than the drugs she shot in her veins. The secrets she took to the grave about who my dad is and why he wasn't around. The morning I woke for school to find her dead when I was only nine years old. The group homes. The foster homes. The cruel adults who wore smiles and pretended to be caring in public, only to turn around and commit the most horrendous acts against me in private. The bullying I've endured for being different. The deeds I've suffered through just to feel loved. The damage that's scarred my soul. The self-hate I hide on a daily basis in the hopes it won't consume me.

It all comes out.

I've never cried like this. So raw. So out of control. So honestly.

Cynthia holds me tight through the whole thing, her voice eventually reaching me, soothing me until I calm down, and my gut-wrenching cries and shuddering sobs slowly ease. After all the therapy I've had since I was taken from Brian and Julie's care, nothing has ever felt like it has breached through my walls until this moment.

"W-what do I-I do now?"

At my sob filled question, my mum pulls back and cups my face, her eyes red and wet and filled with so much pain.

"You let me help you."

I nod, more tears bursting free, and I feel an invisible weight lifting from me.

When I calm down enough to speak, I open up and tell Cynthia everything that's happened involving Brian and Julie. We cry some more, and eventually, Will, my dad, comes in and sits on the floor with us, pulling us into a group hug.

It's strange. I thought I'd felt love when Brian was looking after me, but now that I have the real thing, I can see even more clearly how fucked up it was. That wasn't love. This is. Here in this house, with Cynthia and Will, their care, their unwavering support, even after all the screwing up I've done, they are still here caring for me, loving me. No matter what.

We talk some more, and my parents reveal that they have already spoken with the police and that they are coming to the school tomorrow to interview me in the privacy of my mum's office. I hate the idea of revealing all of this stuff to strangers, but at this point, I think I have to. I can't carry it anymore. Not on my own.

When I convince them I'm ok and that I want to go to bed early, they give me the space I'm asking for, even though I can tell it's hard for my mum to walk away and leave me. I lock my door again, glad to finally be alone, and I go straight to my phone and call Tyler.

"Hello." He answers like he doesn't already know it's me.

"Why did you tell her? How could you do that to me?" I didn't intend on the pain in my voice. I wanted to sound strong and pissed off and in control. Unfortunately, my emotions win.

"Kitten, I *had* to tell her. You need help, and I can't be the one to take what I know to the police. I made up a story about overhearing some students talking and intercepted one of the messages being passed around containing the video. She had to know. It's the only way I knew how to help you."

"You betrayed me." I hiss, anger making its way into my voice.

"It wasn't meant with malice, Kitten. Only my need to stop these fuckers from hurting you anymore."

"It's still a betrayal," I whisper, sinking to the floor at the foot of my bed.

"Rhys. I had to bring it to Cynthia's attention. I'm obligated to, as a teacher. Under Child Safety Laws, I have to speak up."

"That's funny. I didn't realise Child Safety Laws allowed teachers to fuck their students." I snap, wishing he could see the anger on my face. That is, until he stays silent.

Shit!

"Wait. I didn't mean to say that." I plead, wishing I could take it back.

"Yeah, you did." He's hurt, his voice sounding younger than his thirty-two years. "Look, I don't regret telling your mum. She needed to know. You can be angry at me all you like. It doesn't matter as long as you are kept safe from those fuckers." He sighs. "I'm gonna go now, Kitten. You need some time to process everything, and I need to give you the space to do that. We'll talk tomorrow."

"Ok." Even though I don't want to end the call, I do. Right now, I feel like a child, and he feels like the complete opposite. I've never felt the age difference between us until this moment, and all it does is open my heart up to more pain because what if, after all we have been through, he's just realising the same, and he changes his mind about being with me?

The need to feel love—or what my body has deemed as feeling love—takes over, and Kitty purrs aggressively. Part of me wishes I could slap her and tell her to back the fuck off and not be so fucking needy. Yet another part of me wants to appease Kitty. I could sneak out and go to see Shaun, Simon, or even Marcus. They know how to take my ache away. However, they'll also see that I've been crying. Sense that something is wrong, and I'll have to talk, which is the opposite of what I want to do.

My eyes find their way to my toy drawer. Maybe Big Jim can ease the fire, after all, I recognise this feeling for what it is. Stress. The need for release. I've used it as an excuse for so long to fuck random people, but I don't want random anymore. I want my guys. All of them. Even Tyler.

I shake off the thoughts that lash at my heart when Tyler comes to mind and give in to my need. Dragging myself up off the floor, I walk over to the drawer in question. Pulling it open, I lift the towel that acts as a cover and reveal my magic wands. A small thrill washes over me at the sight of Big Jim. He's a purple pleasure monster that makes me instantly think of Garrett.

I snatch him up, covering him in lube before moving over to my bed. With one hand, I slip my knickers off, leaving on my oversized Archer 9 t-shirt that Lexi got me from their concert, and I crawl up on my bed on my knees, staying in the kneeling position and spread my legs.

"Show me how you love me, Jimmy boy." I grin and nudge him at my entrance. Pressing the button, Big Jim comes to life with a slow vibration, and I tease myself with his head, rubbing it through my folds, to my clit, and back to my entrance. Then, I ease him in.

It's always a little hard at first, his girth a challenge, but one my hungry Kitty is willing to take. I love this part. The stretch. The overwhelming need to be filled. More and more.

My whole body flinches when Big Jim goes deep, sharp pain shooting through my centre, just like the other day with Marcus.

"Shit. No." I hiss, desperate to move past that fucked up night at the Feast, as I draw Big Jim out a little and then push him back in. "Ouch!" I cry out a little too loudly, and I quickly rip the purple monster from my Kitty, turning him off and listening to see if anyone is coming to see if I'm ok.

After a beat of silence, I re-focus on my toy and pout. "Sorry, big fella. Tonight's not your night."

Frustrated, I stagger off my bed and over to my drawer. Little Jim and Peter Rabbit peer up at me, tempting me with their orgasmic promises. I'm gonna assume that if Big Jim hurts too much, Little Jim's length will also be a problem, so I guess Peter Rabbit will have to do tonight.

Not a bad trade, really. Peter Rabbit can do things that Big Jim can't, so I snatch my pink rabbit vibrator up and return to my bed, repeating the lubing process and laying back this time.

Turning the little gem on, I close my eyes and hold my breath.

God, I've never prayed before, but I am now.

Please let my vibe feel good. Please let me come.

Sliding Peter in, I instantly feel the tingles of pleasure only he can bring as he works his magic on my g-spot and clit at the same time. There's no pain. Just building pleasure, and I relax back, grinning like a lusty freak, and run my hand under my t-shirt to pinch my nipple.

Oh yeah. That's good.

"Fuck me, Peter," I breathe softly.

"Who the fuck is Peter!"

I gasp, sitting up in search of Marcus. Where the fuck is he? I just heard his voice.

"Marcus?"

"I thought you said there are only the five of us, Rhee!" He hisses, and I dart my head down to my side to see my phone peeking out from under my arse.

Oh my god!

Shuffling over, I pick up my phone and look at the screen. Sure enough, Marcus is on the line, on speaker.

"Ahhh. Hey, Marcus." I say awkwardly.

Fuck. Fuck. Fuck.

I've never been sprung masturbating by accident before.

"Rhee! Don't hey me! You said there were no others!"

"Ummm, well, there are no other humans." I cringe at my words. Since when am I sex shy?

"What? What the fuck do you mean, no other humans?" Marcus hisses through the speaker.

"Jesus Christ, Marcus. I'm fucking my rabbit!"

"WHAT!"

"Wait! Oh my god! Not an actual rabbit. My vibrator. I call it Peter Rabbit. It's a rabbit vibrator."

"A vibrator?" Marcus' voice drops low, curiosity lacing his tone.

I grin. "Yes, a vibrator. Did I butt dial you?"

"Nah. I called you, but it didn't even ring, just picked straight up." He explains.

"Whoops." I giggle, and he chuckles.

"So, are you gonna keep going?"

My brows shoot up. "You want me to keep going with you on the phone?"

"Yeah." His voice is husky, sending warmth pooling between my legs. I love the way his voice changes when he's horny.

"Ok," I grin, and before I can do anything, my phone vibrates with a FaceTime request from Marcus. "Really? A video call?"

"Yeah. Answer it." Marcus is impatient. I bet he's already hard.

Naturally, I answer it because adding visual is ten times better than audio alone. Marcus Grady's big brown eyes fill my screen, and the moment he sees me, his face morphs into a smile.

"There she is."

"You really do like to watch, hey?" I smirk, and he shrugs one shoulder.

"Apparently, I do."

"Did you like watching last night?" I was so scared he wasn't going to come back after he fled the tent. I'd worried we had pushed him too far too soon.

"Yes… and no." He admits. "I fucking love watching you, Rhee, but it was hard to watch you with *them*. Really fucking hard. I tried not to think too much about it and just be in the moment. I thought I did pretty good, considering."

"You did." I smile softly and look down at my lap, where Peter is lying lifeless. "I'm sorry that I'm like this."

"Hey. No, don't do that. I'll get used to it. Besides, if I'm gonna share you with anyone, I'm glad it's my mates. I'm still on the fence about this Tyler guy, though."

Tyler. Ouch. It hurts to hear his name right now.

"So, are you gonna join me, or are you just gonna sit back and watch?" Changing the subject. I move my phone to my bedside table and sit it on my tripod.

"Can I join? I don't think I'll just be able to watch and not get off. You're too fucking hot, and I fucking miss you."

Angling my phone to get a good view of my bed, I flash my teeth close to the screen before backing up. "Ok then, Grady. Get your pretty cock out."

"You first." He smirks while biting the corner of his lip. "Show me the stand in cock that I'm competing with here."

I throw my head back, laughing. It feels good, especially to have Marcus on board with my freakiness. "It's not really a cock." Picking Peter up, I hold him close to the screen. "See. Not as big as a dick."

Marcus frowns. "How's that gonna work, then?"

Again, I throw my head back, laughing. "Oh Marc, you fellas really are clueless." I point to my pink vibe. "This part is a g-spot stimulator. It goes just inside where that sweet spot is, and this part wraps up to my clit. I tried to use Big Jim, but it still hurts deep inside, so Peter will have to do."

"Do I even wanna know what Big Jim looks like?"

"Think Garrett, but purple, and with batteries," I smirk, and he rolls his eyes.

"Ok, Rhee. Take off your t-shirt and show me those perfect tits."

Shifting back on my bed so Marcus can see my whole body down to my knees, I lift my t-shirt off and palm my tits, giving my nipples a little pinch.

"Fuck yes. Show me how you fuck yourself." The huskiness in Marcus' voice sends me wild. I bite my lip and try to calm my racing heart. At this point, I'm likely to fuck thin air and get off just from having his eyes on me.

"Show me that hard cock, Marc," I demand, and he grins, shifting back in his desk chair and gripping the base of his very hard shaft. "Fuck. I love your dick."

"My dick loves you too." Marcus chuckles.

"Tell me, Marcus? Does your dick love this?"

I hold up Peter and turn it on before spreading my legs wide so he can see everything. The lighting in my bright white room is perfect for picking up everything I have on show. Then I slide Peter in.

"Fuuuck," Marcus grunts out, pumping his cock as he watches.

Oh yeah. I fucking love this.

Like I did earlier, I bring my free hand up to pinch my nipples as Peter casts a spell on my cunt in rapid time. I moan and buck and moan again, trying to keep my eyes open to watch Marcus. His eyes are wild, and he's gripping his cock so hard that he's likely going to strangle the life out of it as he tugs his hand back and forth, over and over, watching me.

"Marc." I pant, breathless, my pleasure building.

"Rhee. Fuck Peter good." He rasps, and I do, gyrating my hips, putting more pressure on Peter, knowing I'm only seconds away.

"I'm close." I grit out quickly, watching his dick piston in his hand.

"Me too. Come for me, baby."

And I do. My muscles tense and clamp in a violent blast, forcing me to cry out with little restraint, which I let go of completely when I see the ropes of white cum jetting from Marcus' cock. My climax is prolonged by Peter's unrelenting vibrations, and I rip him from my entrance and toss him across the room. He lands somewhere with a thud.

"Fuck Rhee. That was…" Marcus pants, leaning closer to the screen. "Epic."

I smile, but it doesn't reach my eyes because an overwhelming urge to cry slams into me.

What the fuck is wrong with me?

Why am I such a fucking cry baby lately?

"Hey, what's wrong?" Marcus picks up his phone again, holding it higher.

I shake my head. "I was hoping it would make me feel better."

"Are you upset because of the messages about the video?"

"That, and my olds know about the video. They even know about Brian and Julie now." I flop back on my bed, sucking in deep breaths.

"Can I say something without you getting angry at me?" Marcus asks, and I frown, shrugging. "I'm glad your parents know. You need their help with this, Rhee. If I learnt anything from the whole Lexi thing, it's that we gotta ask for help if we need it."

A single tear escapes, and I bat it away, hoping Marcus didn't see. Of course, he did, and he offers me a sympathetic smile.

"Can I sleep with you tonight?"

My brows shoot up. "What? How?'

"FaceTime. Leave it running so we can go to sleep together and wake up together, and if you need me through the night, I'll be right there."

"You'd do that?" I ask, and he nods.

"Of course. I'd do anything for you. I fucking love you."

Overwhelmingly full. That's how my heart feels. It's an empowering feeling, making me believe I can do anything. Get through anything.

"Marcus," I whisper, his dark eyes taking me in through the screens separating us. "I think I love you too."

CHAPTER TWENTY-TWO

MARCUS

S he's more beautiful than I ever imagined. Sure, I have always thought Rhee was a looker, but this... this is something else. When she turned up at Ebony Falls wearing less makeup than I've seen her wear, it was like she was revealing a layer she's been hiding. She was stunning. Then, she surprised everyone at the campsite by showing us nothing but the natural beauty god gifted her.

I was gob smacked. It wasn't until that moment that I stopped looking at her like a girl and saw her as a woman. No more playful hair twisty things. No more dark smoky eyes and thick liner. No more black lips. Just my woman in her creamy skin with those perfectly plump pink lips, deep chocolate eyes framed in thick naturally dark lashes, and cheeks that were faintly blushed from the heat of embarrassment at everyone glaring at her like she'd grown two heads.

To an outsider, her showing us her natural look wouldn't seem like that big of a deal, but to our inner circle, we know what a massive step she took in trusting us by letting down one of her barriers.

I feel like we've come so far over our weekend away to Ebony Falls. I know *I* have, but I'm pretty sure Rhee has, too. Then last night, when I called her and thought she had another guy with her, my heart broke for a moment. Obviously, I have some work to do on the trusting front. I jumped to a conclusion, and thank fuck, it was just my fucked up mind and not something that was really happening.

We had fucking phone sex. Or video sex? I don't know what the fuck to call it, but I get the feeling my girl doesn't do that often. If at all. And shit, it was good. Hot. So fucking hot. Seeing her slide that rabbit thing inside her, watching the way her face relaxed in pleasure before contorting painfully for the same reason. I want to do it again with her, only next time, I want to be in the same room.

The thing that happened in the tent the other night with Bossi and Hastings was hot, too. I'll never admit it to those fuckers, but I enjoyed watching their reactions to our girl, as well. I didn't think I would enjoy that, yet I did. She's so responsive. She knows what she wants and isn't afraid to put it all on display to reach her high. It was fucking crazy good.

It kinda pissed me off that I liked it so much. Seeing Bossi slide his fingers inside her arse while she was bent in such a way that we couldn't *not* see every detail of what was happening. It made my dick harder than I think it's ever been. I've never really thought about arse stuff before. Never imagined wanting to stick my cock in that orifice, yet now it's something I'm craving. I wonder if she'll let me be the one to take that virginity?

A loud bang comes through the phone, and I squint to focus on the darkened room where my girl is sleeping.

"Get up, Rhys. You're going to be late." A girl calls, making Rhys stir.

Her eyes flutter open, and it takes her a moment to comprehend what she's looking at. Then, the sexiest smile spreads across her makeup-free face.

"Now that's a face I like waking up to." She mutters, her voice husky and fucking sexy as hell.

"Good morning, beautiful. How did you sleep?" I smile, knowing I want to do this again tonight. And tomorrow night. And every other night until I can have the real thing. Her in my bed, waking up right next to me instead of through a phone screen.

"You tell me. You're the one watching me sleep like a creeper." Her tone is playful, and she picks her phone up off her bedside table and rolls onto her back, her long silky dark hair splayed out on her pillow. She looks like a dark angel.

"I think you were dreaming about me." I mimic my girl, rolling onto my back and holding my phone up.

"I must have been. Kitty is already dripping." She grins, and I groan.

"What I'd give to be in that bed with you, Rhee."

"Then we'd definitely be late for school." She giggles, and I chuckle.

I told her I loved her last night, and she told me she thinks she loves me, too. I've wanted that for so long. Wanted her to be mine. Granted, she's also Bossi's, Hastings', and Cole's, as well as that Tyler dude I don't know. Still, even if I have to share her, I know she cares about me, and I sure as fuck care about her.

The vibrating sound of an incoming message comes through the speaker, and Rhys frowns before her eyes widen, and she bolts upright.

"Shit." She hisses, tapping something on her screen.

"What is it?" I watch her eyes widen further and then narrow into slits as anger takes over. "Rhee?"

"It's a message from Julie. It says: *Time is running out, Patrice. The guesses are coming in, and someone has guessed correctly. If you don't want me to reveal your identity on the video, be at the Prison on the weekend. Fuck me over, and you will pay!*"

"Fuck!" I bolt upright, too, my gut dropping as Julie's message sinks in.

"Fucking bitch. If I ever see her again, I'm going to fuck her up!" Rhys snaps before flopping back on her pillow and sighing. "The cops are coming to interview me this morning. I don't know if I can do it, Marc." Tears pool in those beautiful chocolate eyes that I adore.

"You can do it. You've got this, Rhee. It's the right thing to do."

She nods and bites the corner of her lip. "I'm gonna need some extra loving after I speak to them."

I nod. "And you will have it."

"And by loving, I mean orgasms. Just so we are clear."

"Of course." I chuckle. "As many as you want."

I reluctantly end our FaceTime call after that because her sister almost breaks her door down, checking to see if Rhys is awake.

The morning at school drags. It doesn't help that today is the last day before exams, so there's not much to do, but it mainly drags because we don't get a glimpse of our girl until recess since she spends the first two periods in her mum's office answering questions the cops have for her.

I'm glad my suspension is over. I can't bear the thought of being away from Rhys for too long.

At the start of recess, Rhys messages our group chat, asking us to meet her at the back of the school. By the time me and the fellas turn the corner at the back of the stadium, Rhys is already there, waiting alone on the steps.

I don't wait for the guys to keep up. I pick up my pace, and when she looks up, I jog the rest of the way, right into her arms as she stands from the steps. Her grip is tight as she wraps herself around me and buries her head in the crook of my neck. Is she crying? I can't bear to see her cry.

She pulls back first and takes my lips in a hungry kiss filled with so much desperation that I know the interview with the cops was extremely hard on her.

"Rhee," I mumble into her mouth as we kiss, and she hums in response, so I give her a squeeze. "I got you."

Her kiss deepens, and I run my hands down over her blazer and kilt to cup her arse and then lift her so she wraps her legs around me. I fucking wish we were alone right now, behind closed doors, so I can give her what she needs. Unfortunately, the faint chattering of Hastings reminds me we are at school out in the open with an audience, so I blindly step forward, climbing a couple of steps, and turn to sit down with Rhys straddling me.

Reluctantly breaking our kiss, I pull back and brush some of Rhee's escaped hair back off her face. Her buns are in place again like they never disappeared for a couple of days, as too is her heavy makeup. I'm kinda glad. I don't want all the other fuckers in this school seeing my girl in her natural beauty. Is that weird? Probably.

My eyes roam Rhee's face, looking for signs of tears, but there are none. If it weren't for the storm of emotions swimming through those chocolate pools, I wouldn't know anything is going on with her.

"Wanna tell us what happened?"

She takes a big gulp before dragging her eyes from mine to see Bossi sitting on one side, Cole sitting on the other, and Hastings sitting up a couple of steps behind us.

"Any chance of an orgasm first?" Although her tone is innocent, she looks anything but.

"Not here, Rhee. Maybe after." I offer, but she frowns.

"All you have to do is slip your hand between us, Marc. I'm already wet. It won't take long."

"Fuck man, if you don't do it, pass her here, and I'll take care of her." Bossi nudges my shoulder, and I shoot him a glare.

"No! I'll take care of her. I just want her to talk to us first." I turn my gaze back to Rhys, and she pouts.

"If I have to wait, then I want two orgasms before we go to class, even if it makes us late."

"Deal," Simon answers for me, and I grin.

"Ok, Rhee. You have a deal."

"Fine." She sighs, taking a moment to compose herself. "I was kinda happy to see Officer Zimora again. It made it a bit easier, I think, since I knew him from Lexi's case. The other officer was a chick. Dana Fredricks. She was nice. I gave them a rundown on everything. They went through the messages from Julie and took screenshots for evidence. We spoke about the prison visit a lot. They think there must be a prison officer helping Brian and Julie, because my visit shouldn't have been private. That sort of thing is usually only arranged for special circumstances and usually for conjugal visits." Rhys shudders, and I gently squeeze her upper thighs to remind her she's ok. She's safe, and she's here with us.

"Are the cops gonna charge them?" Hastings asks, and Rhys shrugs.

"Right now, they have no idea where Julie is. She's a ghost. Been off the grid for years. They think she must be using a different name now, so it's gonna take them some time to find her." Rhys drops her eyes to our joined laps, biting her lip like she is summoning courage. "The cops asked me if I'd go back to the prison to speak with Brian again and maybe wear a listening device or something."

"No fucking way!" Garrett hisses, rearing back like her words slapped him. "It's bad enough what you had to endure the last time; I'm not letting you go back there again."

Rhee's brows shoot up as she looks at Garrett. "You're not *letting* me? I'm sorry. I must have missed the part that said I need your permission to do things."

"Come on, baby girl, you know what I mean. I don't want you to go back there. It's not fair that they asked you to do that."

Rhys sighs. "Mum said the same thing." She shakes her head, looking back to her lap. "The thing is, I think I need to do this. Apparently, I'm not the only one this is happening to. They think Julie has been doing this sort of thing for years. I feel like I need to help the cops catch her, to help those other girls, and in a way... to get my power back."

We all stay silent for a minute or two. If the guys are thinking the same way as me, then they want to rant and rage and refuse to let our girl be exposed to those fuckers. They want to beat on their chest like cavemen and threaten anyone who dares consider harming our girl. But Rhys is right. She doesn't need our permission, and hearing us carry on will only cause her more stress. What we really need to do is support her. Whatever decision she makes.

"So, the cops think they can somehow find Julie by you visiting Brian again?" I ask, and she nods.

"I just have to ask him the right questions. They will have undercover cops posing as visitors as well, but when I go into that room again with Brian, I'll be on my own. That is if my mum and dad give their permission. They're thinking about it."

"But isn't that too dangerous to go in that room alone with your old foster dad?" Bossi asks, and Rhys shakes her head.

"Nah. Brian was secured to a chair last time. He didn't try to move off it." Rhys sighs. "That's all there is to tell about the cop's visit. Can I have my two orgasms now?"

I don't know how she does it. Switch off from something so serious just to have sex. Then again, it could be an addiction thing. Needing a hit to escape a stressful moment.

"Since Marcus is all cosy with you, we will kick back and watch him give you the first one." Bossi, the cheeky fucker, smirks and leans back on the metal handrail, crossing his arms over his chest in challenge. He thinks I won't go through with it. He thinks I can't handle being the one being watched. He's kinda right, but fuck, I really wanna be the one to milk my girl of her stress.

Raising a challenging brow at Bossi, I turn back to Rhee to see her eyes are wide with anticipation. She wants me to do this, so fuck it. I'll do it.

As I glide my hand from Rhee's arm to the swell of her perfect breast, I see Garrett getting comfy next to me in my peripheral. Heat rises to my cheeks, knowing I'm being watched as much as our girl is, and as I slip my hand lower between our bodies, I see Hastings' shadow hovering over the top of me as he stands to get a better view.

"Is this what you want?" I ask Rhee, watching her expression as I slide my hand up her skirt, the feel of her silky thighs making my cock strain.

"Yes. Fuck me just like Peter does."

I grin wide, bringing my fingers to the fabric covering her heat, which is soaking wet.

"Your panties are soaked."

"Wait. Who's Peter?" Simon asks, but I ignore him, running my fingers back and forth until I feel my girl arch a little closer, seeking more.

"Peter is my vibrator. I'll introduce you to him one day soon." Rhee says before her lids flutter shut, and she bites her lip as I slip my fingers under the fabric and find her hungry clit.

"Fuck Rhee. You're so wet. I wanna taste you." I no longer care that we have an audience, slipping my fingers from her heat and bringing them to my lips, tasting her.

"I'm so jealous right now," Hastings mumbles from over my head, and Rhys glances up, blowing him a kiss. Then I return my fingers to her molten heat.

Rhee moans as soon as I make contact, and she lifts her hips a little, seeking more. Mimicking her rabbit or what the hell the vibrator is, I press my thumb to her clit while sinking two digits just inside. Instantly she gyrates on my lap, biting her lip and dropping her head back as she loses herself to the sensation.

"You're a queen, Cherry," Hastings mutters, stepping down a few steps to come and stand behind our girl, peering over the top of her this time.

"She's a fucking goddess," Bossi adds before shifting next to me. I can see him rearrange his dick in his pants. We are all fucking hard as a rock right now. This is what she does to us.

The blare of the bell ringing breaks our little bubble, reminding us we are at school, and thankfully Rhee's other friends didn't decide to hang behind the stadium today.

Rhys picks up the pace, and I match it, curling my fingers inside her faster and faster.

"Come for us, Kitten," Bossi demands, and she grabs at her shirt covered tits, trying to reach her high.

Simon takes that moment to help our girl out, pressing himself up behind her and slipping his hand down the front of her shirt.

"Yes." She cries out as he obviously makes contact with her nipple, her pussy slicking even more.

She's thrusting her hips now, desperately trying to come, and I circle her clit with my thumb, applying more pressure.

"Kitten." Bossi glues himself to her side, nipping at her ear, one hand wrapping around her throat while the other disappears behind her, under her skirt. As I work my fingers, I feel the pressure of his fingers nudging her panty clad back entrance, teasing her as she slicks even more.

"She's close," I grunt out, knowing I'm probably about to cum in my fucking jocks.

"Gar." She pants, her eyes squeezed shut as she reaches out a hand to him. He doesn't take it.

"Look at me, baby girl."

Her lids fly open, darting to him instantly.

"Come. Now."

She explodes.

CHAPTER TWENTY-THREE

TYLER

She's late. I know for a fact that her interview session with the FP Police Department wrapped up before recess, so where the fuck is she? She'd better not ditch just because she's pissed at me for telling her foster mum about the video and the messages. I'd like to think she's more mature than that, but let's face it, she's only seventeen.

Fuck.

Trying to push all thoughts of Rhys George to the back of my mind, I mark the roll and instruct the class to revise for their exams, which start tomorrow. I have a double Health class right now, and all I'm really doing is babysitting these kids in the lead up to their exams. I'm surprised most of them even turned up to school.

Ten minutes into the class, Rhys walks in, head held high, cheeks flushed, and a knowing grin on her face. I know right away that my little brat has recently come. I'd know that look of hers anywhere. She's late for my class because she was too busy fucking around with her little boy band.

"Sorry, I'm late, sir," Rhys raises her voice, drawing the attention of the entire class. Little attention seeker.

I stand from my desk as she walks to the empty table at the front and drops her books down. "Why were you late, Miss George?"

Tilting her head to the side, she shoots me an innocent look, batting her lashes. "I just had to get myself out of a sticky situation. It's all sorted now." As she looks at me, she frowns, her eyes squinting a little as she focuses on my face. She sees the faint bruise in the corner of my right eye and the cut on my lip.

All I can think of is her response to my question. Fucking sticky situation. Did she fuck one of them in the toilets?

Fucking hell!

"You will stay behind after class to make up for the ten minutes you were late," I advise before turning my back on her to retake my seat.

"Ugh. Teachers are so uptight." She tips her head back dramatically, succeeding in her effort to make the other students laugh.

Her foster mum filled me in a little after the police interviewed her. I'm surprised she's so calm right now, although it's likely a cover. Rhys is good at trying to appear like it's business as usual, which is sad. No seventeen-year-old should have to wear such a thick mask.

Her mum asked me to keep my eyes and ears open for anything that might come up about the video from the student body. The whole thing has me feeling guilty. I'm an adult in my early thirties. Rhys is a minor, only seventeen years old. Why am I doing this? Why am I seeking her out and telling her she means something to me?

I mean, yeah, she does mean something to me. It's not a lie, but what can ever come of it? There's always going to be fifteen fucking years between us. When she's my age, I'll be forty-seven, for fuck's sake.

And what do we even have in common besides a carnal need for sex? I don't fucking know, yet I'm still drawn to her. Still desperate to take her in my arms and protect her, pleasure her. Love her.

As much as I try to ignore her, I can't. The little brat is sitting with her legs wide and her skirt pulled high. Her panties are soaked. And now my dick is hard… in class with twenty-five seventeen-year-olds.

Fuck, I'm going to hell. That's if prison doesn't claim me first.

"Mr Foster." Tillie Hall calls from the back row, my eyes moving to her and raising a brow in question. "I'm bored. Can Rhys give us another lesson on the levels of protein in semen?"

Laughter erupts through the class, followed by some hoots and cheers from the ever so mature boys. Dickheads.

"Actually, I heard there are health benefits from drinking mickey juice." Alex Houser, the dopey little shit, adds, causing more laughter.

Fucking hell.

"Quieten down. No more lessons unless I'm teaching them." I yell over the laughter, which lessens at the sound of my voice.

"You're right, Alex." Rhys stands up and turns to face the class. "Vaginas carry probiotics, which we all know are good for us."

"That's enough, Miss George. Sit down, please." I call from my desk where I'm now standing.

"But the real health benefit is for the ladies. If you fellas pop in for a drink, and you drink properly, she will have an orgasm."

"Rhys!" I yell, and still, she ignores me.

"And the endorphins, dopamine and oxytocin that the orgasm produces can benefit her mental and physical health."

"Rhys George! That is enough!" I yell, moving around my desk.

"If your girl is in a bad mood, making her come will put her in a good mood."

"Rhys!" I boom right next to her, making her flinch. I fucking hate that I make her jump like that, but I need her to stop. I let her get away with too much, and now she is pushing the boundaries with unacceptable behaviour that *no* teacher would *ever* tolerate. "Leave this class right now!"

Her eyes widen as she looks at me, probably checking to see if I'm being serious. If I don't act on this, it will be obvious that there is favouritism. I can't risk that.

Slowly, she turns her back on the class and gathers up her books. I don't miss the way her hand trembles, either.

Fuck! Fuck! Fuck! I hate this! I hate that I have to treat her this way, but seriously, does she expect me *not* to react?

No, of course she doesn't expect that. She knew damn well I would react to this—her way of lashing out, perhaps for me divulging the video information to her mum.

With her books pressed to her chest, she slowly glances up at me again, her eyes dark with their own anger.

"Wait for me out in the hall, please, Miss George."

"Sure. No problem, *Mr Foster*."

Her tone is sarcastic and clipped, and she turns her back, walking past the other students. Her friend Tillie mouths a *sorry* as she passes by, and I see Rhys blow her a kiss before she turns back in search of someone.

"Oh, and Alex. Giving your girl an O can also help with period pain, so don't rule out blood sports."

The class erupts in laughter, and Rhys grins, but it falls into a glare when she looks back at me. Then she leaves.

I'm furious. Kitten is really testing me out today. She's acting her age, which is a slap in the face reminder to me that I'm playing with fire.

I let her sweat it out in the hall for a few minutes while I calm the class back down and then reluctantly pop outside the door, pulling it shut. She doesn't look at me when I join her. Her back pressed against the wall, one foot resting back on the plaster surface.

"What the fuck was that?" I hiss between clenched teeth, keeping my voice quiet. All I need now is for someone to overhear this conversation. Wouldn't that just be fucking great!

"It's called teaching. You should try it sometime." She glares at me now, her dark eyes turning to slits. "What happened to your face?"

"You can't do that, Kitten. You would never do something like that in any other class. Doing it in mine will raise questions. I can't be seen to allow that behaviour. I would never let another student do that, so I can't allow you."

"Don't call me Kitten."

Ouch. That hurt more than I thought it would. I'm not sure I like an angry Kitten.

"Why not? Are you not my Kitten?" I whisper, and she rolls her eyes.

"I'm not sure. Am I?" She quirks a brow.

"What sort of question is that? Of course, you are."

"Huh. Could have fooled me." She scoffs, dropping her foot from the wall to stand. "I can't believe you betrayed me. After all that stuff I said to you about information is power, you went and proved me right."

"So that, in there, was a way of punishing me for trying to help you?" I hiss, and she shrugs.

"Are you going to tell me how you got a shiner and fat lip?"

"No. Stop changing the subject," I growl in frustration, and she rolls her eyes.

"Dramatic much?"

"Fucking hell, Kitten, you're being such a brat today."

"So. Are you gonna *punish* me?"

"Yes!" My voice is husky as fuck as I answer her honestly.

Her nostrils flare at my comments, but she looks away for a moment, only to turn a hard glare back at me. "I'm pretty sure punishing me will breach those precious Child Safety Laws you care so much about."

I flinch. She did not just say that. I wish she didn't just say that, but she fucking did. And the worst thing is, I can't blame her for throwing that at me because what the fuck am I doing? Fucking a minor? A student? Introducing her to a sex club. One that resulted in her being assaulted.

Fucking hell, Tyler. What are you fucking doing here with this child?

"Please go to the principal's office, Miss George. She will be expecting you."

My words, formal and nothing but a teacher, cause Rhys to flinch. Pain flashes past her chocolate eyes, her brows drawing together as she fights to control her emotions. As I turn my back on my girl and re-enter my class, I realise I have a decision to make.

I can't have Kitten and be a teacher too. I need to choose. And that thought breaks the heart I didn't know I had.

Chapter Twenty-Four

Rhys

As if my day isn't already fucked up enough—especially after the whole Health class incident that I'm struggling to understand—now I get a fucking message from Master Hill.

> *Kitten, your attendance is required at the lodge*
> *tomorrow evening at 9pm.*
> *Attendance is mandatory.*
> *Failure to attend will result in harsh punishment.*
> *Your outfit will be in the usual location.*

I'm freaking out. I need to speak with Tyler, but I don't know if I can. Is he even *my* Tyler anymore? Did we just break up or something? Fucking hell. I have no idea. I've never been in a relationship to have experienced how breakups happen.

I feel like he drew a really fucking thick line with me today. Like the size of the Grand Canyon, and I don't think I'm allowed back over.

"Are you sure nothing else has happened?" Garrett asks, eyeing me as we sit back against the brick wall in the courtyard.

"Yep." I lie. "I'm just exhausted from this morning."

I want to say, and from Health class where I think my fifth boyfriend dumped me, and from the text message from the sex club's master, but of course I don't. I can't tell Garrett about Tyler, and I'm not sure how to even respond to the message from Master Hill.

"Come here." Garrett opens his arms, and we shift closer together before I sink snugly into his side as he wraps a comforting arm around me. I instantly relax. It feels like home in Garrett's arms. He's so big and strong and smells earthy, with a hint of spice. I'd love nothing more than to get lost in Garrett Cole right now.

"Hey, Rhys." Tillie's feet appear in front of me, and she lowers herself to sit cross-legged. "Sorry about earlier. I wouldn't have said anything if I knew Mr F would go off like that."

"It's all g. It got me out of class." I fake a smile, and Shaun, who's sitting on the other side of Garrett, leans forward.

"What happened with Mr F?"

"Nothing," I say as Tillie talks over me.

"He went off at Rhys. I've never seen him so mad. It was all harmless fun, but man, did he have a stick up his arse today?"

"What do you mean he went off at Rhys?" The anger that flares across Shaun's face can't be hidden. Dude needs to chill, or he's going to make things too obvious.

"Well, I kinda asked him if she could teach another lesson in semen, and then Alex wanted to know about the health benefits of mickey juice, and well... Rhys gave the facts. Then he went crazy, screaming at her and kicked her out of class."

"What!" Shaun hisses, and I roll my eyes.

"He didn't go crazy. He asked me to stop repeatedly, and I ignored him. Of course, he got angry and kicked me out. It's what I wanted, anyway. I didn't want to sit in class."

"He *did* go crazy, Rhys. I've never heard him yell like that. I think I peed a little." Tillie admits.

I haven't heard him yell like that either. It pissed me off and made me sad at the same time, just confusing me even more.

Without another word, Shaun leaps up and storms towards the courtyard exit.

Shit.

Leaping up from the comfort of Garrett Cole's arms, I chase after Shaun, snatching his hand to stop him before he reaches the exit.

"Stop. Just leave it." I beg quietly as he turns to me.

"No fucking way." He hisses quietly back, his eyes darting around to check if anyone can hear us. "What the fuck is his problem?"

My face softens at the concern etched across Shaun's face, and I step up into his personal space, gripping the lapels of his blazer and tugging him to me.

"I overstepped. He can't let me get away with something like that without it being obvious. He explained as much to me in the hall before I went to my mum's office. It's no big deal."

Shaun frowns. "It *is* a big deal, Kitten. I know you would have hated that."

I nod. "Yep. I did hate it. Things are… tense between Ty and me right now. Honestly…" I duck my head when I feel heat prick the back of my eyes. "I think he's having second thoughts about us." I look back up at Shaun's frowning face. "It was bound to happen. I'm just a kid, after all."

"No." Shaun pulls me to his chest, gripping the back of my head, "You're not just a kid, Kitten. You are so much more. You're a woman. A Queen. *My* Queen."

I cling to Shaun as we stand in the middle of the walkway, students brushing past us as they come out or into the courtyard.

"Wanna explain your reaction?" Marcus' voice comes from behind me, and Shaun glances over my head at his mate. My mum allowed Marcus to return to school this week due to exams starting tomorrow. It's nice to have him back.

"Not really," Shaun mutters, and I feel hands grip my hips as Marcus presses up behind me.

"I didn't think so. You two are suss as fuck. You know that?"

"I don't know what you're talking about." Shaun drags his gaze from Marcus back down to me. "Is there anything I can do, Kitten?"

I shake my head. "No."

I could tell Shaun about the message from Master Hill, but he'll try to stop me from going, and we all know what happens when I ignore someone's demands. Nope, I can't tell Shaun. I can't tell anyone. With this, I'm on my own.

The guys and I return to our spot in the courtyard, this time with Marcus clinging to my side and Simon playing a quiet game of Simon Says with me that involves a lot of kissing.

By now, it's obvious to the student body that I'm with four guys. I feel eyes on us everywhere we go. Either people are curious, disgusted, or envious. I don't care either way. I love what I have with these guys. I just hope that my parents will love it when they realise what's going on.

When lunch is over, Simon asks me to come over for dinner, the thought sending a little thrill through my veins as I remember the last time I went to his place for dinner. We ate each other, and just the thought has me practically drooling.

My last class of the day is History, where Mr Elliott asks us to revise for our exams. My revision attempt is a flop. I can't concentrate on anything but the message from Master Hill. I want to send a response back, but I can't do it yet. Not while Garrett is watching me like a hawk, his hand on my thigh for the whole class, as he draws silly faces in his workbook, trying to make me laugh.

He succeeds, for the most part.

After school, I ditch detention and catch the bus home from school instead of waiting for my mum. She wasn't happy about my behaviour in Health class, and I want to avoid seeing any more disappointment on her face. I also want to dodge any more questions she'll have about my less than stellar behaviour.

I try to avoid catching the bus with the other students as much as possible because I find them annoying. Today is no exception, with eyes falling on me as I walk up the aisle looking for a seat. When I spot one about halfway in, the girl who I think is a year below me at school quickly puts her bag on the seat, glaring at me in a dare to challenge her for the spot. Ugh! I can't be fucked with this bullshit. Maybe I should have waited for my mum.

"Hey, George. Over here!" I glance up to see Luke Brewer waving his hand in the air. "There's a spare seat here."

My brows shoot up. Luke Brewer doesn't talk to me. In fact, none of his mates talk to me. Ever. Maybe he's friends with one of my guys? Who knows, but since I need a seat with people pushing me from behind to move, I stumble my way to the back of the bus and sit in the vacant seat next to Luke.

"Thanks." I offer Luke a smile as I shove my bag to the floor between my feet.

"Any time George." He smiles at me, his eyes flaring with excitement. That's the first moment I realise I've made a mistake in taking this seat. "So, you and Bossi, hey? Didn't think a girl could tie him down."

I shift uncomfortably, shooting him a fake half-smile. "Yeah. Me and Bossi."

"And you and Hastings too, I hear. Is that true?" Luke asks, twisting at the waist to face me better. When I don't answer him, he continues as the bus starts to move. "Rumour has it you're fucking Grady and Cole, too. How does that work exactly? You only have three holes to fill. Does someone have to jack off while they watch?"

My nostrils flare at his words, heat flushing over my skin, up my neck to engulf my face.

"Guess what I heard?" Dion Richards leans over the seat from behind us, scaring the shit out of me. "I heard they fill you so full of cum that it's putting your health at risk of a protein overdose."

Anger bubbles in my gut as they laugh, and I shift to move off the seat. Standing would be better than dealing with these fuckwits, but a hand grips my thigh just under my skirt, and I shoot my eyes back to Luke, who's biting his lip as he sizes me up.

"I can see the appeal, George. You're one fine piece of arse. I bet you fuck like a whore, too."

I'm about to go ham on Luke, but Dion jumps right in with his own opinion, making me freeze.

"You're my top choice for the girl in the video, Rhys." I turn in the seat, eyes wide, looking at him in shock. "I sent my guess to that email. I'm feeling pretty confident that I'll be winning the cash. Maybe once I get it, I can treat you to a weekend away. One hotel room. A revolving door. The entire basketball team. You'd love that, wouldn't you? All that dick filling you up?"

I'd like to think I'm a pretty open-minded person, and sure, I've been called a whore so many times I've lost count, but this? This is different. They are making the beautiful thing I have with my guys sound like nothing more than a filthy porn movie. I could try to explain to them that it's more than sex, but let's face it, they aren't gonna hear me. So, I respond in a way I know they will understand.

"Take your hand off my leg!" I yell, drawing the attention of people around us. Luke, the stupid fucker he is, just chuckles and glides his hand up higher, so I yell again. "I do not give you permission to touch me." And again, he doesn't fucking listen because guys like this don't think the rules apply to them.

"Hey!" Someone yells out from down the bus. It's a girl's voice, and I don't look because I keep my eyes on Luke, not wanting to let him out of my sight.

"Don't pretend like you're not dripping wet for me to fuck you, George." Luke grins, licking his lips before Dion decides to lay his hands on me as well, sliding his hand down over my front to aggressively grab my tit through my school shirt.

Oh, well. I did ask them not to. They should have listened.

With Dion's arm resting near my chin as he fondles my tit, I turn my head to the side and bite down hard onto his arm.

Something like the sound of a pig being slaughtered flies from his mouth as blood fills mine. Not liking what I'm doing, Luke squeezes my upper thigh painfully, and I release Dion's arm as I bare my blood-stained teeth and hiss. Dion flies backwards, still squealing while I hone in on my next victim.

Something in my expression causes Luke to still and then recoil back against the window of the bus, and without thinking twice, I grasp his junk, squeezing tight until he too is squealing, my nails digging in right before I rear back and throw a hard punch to his face.

Everything goes crazy after that. Hands come out of nowhere, dragging me off Luke and across the aisle, and I protest, screaming with rage, wanting to hit him over and over. But I realise I don't need to. Two senior girls are dragging Luke and Dion by their hair, reefing them over any bags in the way as students scramble to make a clear path.

The bus has stopped. We've pulled over on the side of the road somewhere, and I can see the bus driver standing up, watching the girls as they remove Luke and Dion from the bus, literally kicking them off down the steps to tumble out into the street. Another girl has their bags, and she tosses them out before turning back to everyone looking on.

"It is not ok to touch anyone without their permission. And it is also not ok to sit by and pretend you're not seeing it happen. Speak up girls! We need to stick together. And if there are any guys that have a problem with what I just said, then I suggest you get off the bus now because we will not tolerate this bullshit anymore. It ends now!"

Cheers ring out through the confined space of the bus cabin, and I finally recognise who the girl is. Evie Prattle. And her sidekicks are Cassie Davis and Kim Sherman. They are well respected year twelve girls, and Evie is known to speak up about the confronting things people prefer to sweep under the rug. I'm pretty sure it stems from her younger sister being raped at a party last year. People knew it was happening, and no one tried to stop it or spoke up for fear that they'd be shunned or bullied.

The bus driver takes his seat, starting the bus back up, and as everyone else follows suit, the bus pulls away from the curb, and I see a very shamed Luke and Dion on their arses on the side of the road.

"Are you ok?" Evie asks, coming to sit across the aisle from me, ignoring the guy cowering in his seat.

"Uh. Yeah. Thanks." I offer Evie a small smile, which she returns.

"You're Rhys George, right?" When I nod, Evie hands me some tissue to clean up the blood around my mouth and continues. "Well, Rhys, if you ever need help, call me." She hands me a business card, and I frown down at it as I read the details.

Angel Org.
Empowering Women
Junior President - Evie Prattle

"What exactly do you do?" I glance back up to see her smile.

"Things like we did a few minutes ago. We speak up. We call people out. We empower women. Provide them support and help. I'm the junior president in this area, which means I look out for school-aged girls, but it doesn't stop there. The senior division helps women escape violence and stand up to their harassers. They provide support, and they work alongside a lot of other charities who work tirelessly to help disadvantaged youth and things like that."

"And you'd help me if I need it?"

"Yes," she nods.

"But... You know who I am, right? Some might say I deserved what happened here today."

"Why? Because you own your sexuality? That doesn't give a guy the right to touch you without permission. It doesn't give them the right to treat you like you don't matter. You do matter, Rhys. We all do." Evie tilts her head, her compassion almost overwhelming.

I smile. "My older sister would like you. She's into this stuff."

"If she's into this stuff, then she's probably already in our ranks."

I nod, knowing she is likely right.

Evie and I chat a little more as the students thin out on the bus, and by the time my stop comes along, I don't feel as rattled as I was earlier. For once, I don't feel so alone. I know I have a group of guys and a handful of friends, but there's just something settling knowing there's a group of people in our community speaking up. It's definitely something I could get around.

Once I'm back home in my bedroom, I flop down on my bed and open my phone, working up the courage to send a response back to Master Hill. I'd love nothing more than to forget about his bullshit after the afternoon I've just had. I even consider whether Angel Org can help me out of this situation. Unfortunately, Terence Hill has cops in his pockets and too much leverage in our community. There's nothing I can do but deal with this on my own.

I bite the bullet and respond to Master Hill.

Kitten
I'm not sure if I can make it.
What will happen if I don't come?

Master Hill
Then your sponsor will pay the price.
And let me tell you, it's a hefty one.

Shit! Fuck! Shitty! Fuck! Fuck!

Kitten
I'll be there.

Master Hill
I know you will.

Ugh! Arrogant arsehole! What I'd give to smack the smug off his face.

"Fucking prick!"

"Who's a fucking prick?"

I jump at the sound of Charlotte's voice behind me, darting my head around to see her in my doorway.

"Remind me to lock my door next time." I snap, and she rolls her eyes.

"Dramatic much?"

"Yes! Always! What do you want?" There's no hiding my snarky mood, but it doesn't deter my big sister.

"Gees Rhys! Can't a big sister want to spend time with her little sister?"

"As if this is just a friendly visit. What do you want?" I sit up, facing Char, noticing the green in her hair has faded quite a lot.

"You're right. I wouldn't waste my time." She flashes me a fake smile and steps forward, sitting on the end of my bed. "Fuck Rhys. Why haven't you painted this room yet? White really isn't your colour."

"I haven't decided what colour to paint it, or even if I should. I'd hate to make more work for Cin and Will when they've had enough of me and send me away."

Char's brows hitch. "Girl, they ain't sending you anywhere. Any lack of progress in your relationship with them is all you. That cement wall you've built around your heart is pretty fucking tough to penetrate. They've let you choose the pace here, Rhys. I thought you knew that."

Did I know that? Maybe. It's hard to tell right now with this dark cloud hanging over my head. "Are you gonna tell me why you're invading my space?"

Char sighs. "Fine. I wanted to give you a heads up. I think the olds are looking to bring a new puppy home."

I frown at Char's use of the word puppy. What she really means is a new foster kid. This is a five-bedroom house, so I guess another kid would fit, but damn, why are they so hell-bent on punishing themselves with all of these troubled kids?

"What makes you think that?"

"Well, I overheard them quietly arguing. Cin thinks it will be too hard on *you* if they bring another kid into the works right now, and Will thinks it will be good for you. Then he reminded Cin of the dire situation this other kid is in."

"Let me guess. She caved." I shift to sit with my legs crossed in the middle of my bed as Charlotte nods.

"Pretty much. You know Cin can't stand by and ignore a child in need."

I nod, knowing as much. Cin and Will are good people. The best. If this kid is on their radar, then they need my foster parents.

"So, are you gonna fill me in with the whole Brian and Julie thing, or do I have to pretend I didn't overhear all the drama when Will and Cin thought they were alone?" Charlotte grins as my brows shoot up. She already knows too much. I can tell.

"It doesn't seem like I need to fill you in with anything."

"You're right. So, you're going to the prison to see Brian? How are they gonna catch Julie?"

I shrug. "That part I don't know yet. I don't think the cops know. I think they are hoping she'll be dumb enough to turn up to the prison."

"Hmm. Julie doesn't seem like the dumb type. She's evaded the cops for years, so I'm guessing she's pretty fucking *not* dumb."

"That's what I'm worried about. How do you find a ghost? How can I find her and make her pay for what she's done to me and, apparently, some other girls? Fucking hoe bag is going down!" The pissiness comes easy since I'm already raring for a throw down today.

Char laughs. "I like this violent side of you. It's way more appealing than the bubbly party girl that doesn't stop having fun."

"Are you sure you're not a serial killer?" I smirk as she flicks her green tipped hair off her shoulders.

"No. Well, at least, not yet. There's still plenty of time for me to perfect my craft." She grins back and then stands from my bed. "When you're ready to get payback on those fuckers, come and see me. We'll make sure they never dare to mess with little girls ever again."

"I don't suppose payback will involve help from Angel Org?"

Charlotte's brows hitch. "You know about them?"

Smiling, I fill Charlotte in on the bus trip home and the support Evie gave me. Char is royally pissed about Luke and Dion's actions, but she beams with pride when I speak of Evie, and I realise they must know each other. Charlotte reminds me again that she can help me, and as she leaves my room, I know damn well she's not joking.

Charlotte Kane had to fight for her life when she was younger. Literally. It was her, or the crazy arse foster mum, that was locking her in a broom closet for days on end. Spearing that lady through the chest with the sharp end of a broken mop pole was probably the best thing Charlotte could have done. If she hadn't, she wouldn't be alive now. At least that's what the social workers said in the report I wasn't supposed to read. Two weeks in the hospital is what it took to re-nourish her enough to re-enter the world outside. Then came the battle for her to learn how to trust again. It makes me wonder what hell she put Cin and Will through before they brought me into the picture. Maybe one day soon, I'll ask Char.

Chapter Twenty-Five

Rhys

I t's just before six when my dad drops me off at Simon's mansion. I skip up the path, ready for some dick eating when I come face to face with his mum.

"Rhys. Nice to see you again." Her smile is as fake as fuck as she eases the oversized white door open, gesturing for me to enter their foyer.

I'm normally good with parents. I can befriend them easily and divert their attention so my friends can knick booze from behind their back. Unfortunately, that's way different from meeting the parents of the boys I'm riding. Especially since this particular parent has seen me pressed up against her son's body, both of us naked and covered in cherry pie, while sitting on her kitchen counter.

I offer a matching fake smile to Simon's mum, stepping over the threshold into the stale, air-conditioned house. Simon rarely has it running, so I guess things have changed now that his mum is back in town.

"Hi, Mrs Hastings. It's nice to see you again."

"Please call me Sandra. I no longer use Hastings." Her words are kind yet firm. Like if I dare to call her Mrs Hastings again, she might slap me.

"Really, mum? You couldn't just stop at Sandra?" Simon's disappointed tone gains my attention as Sandra closes the door, and a glare I'm not used to seeing him wear is directed at his mum.

"There's no point in beating around the bush, Simon. Your father and I are getting divorced. It's best you get used to that idea now and save yourself the denial."

Ouch. She's a harsh bitch. Maybe I'll slap her instead.

Simon doesn't respond to his mum, not verbally, anyway. His glare is screaming a thousand words I'm sure she doesn't want to hear come from her child's mouth, so I try to run interference. I'm good at that.

"Something smells delicious."

The cold hazel gaze of Simon's mum moves to me, and this time, she can't help but look me up and down. Granted, I came dressed for easy access. I wasn't expecting Simon's Mumma bear to be here again. Why? Because the cow is never around. I guess things have changed since his olds decided to part ways.

I decided to stir things up tonight when I chose my outfit, and I went with a classic leopard print dress. It's not my usual jam, but I look fucking hot in the tight little mini number from Charlotte's wardrobe, barely covering my arse and wrapping over my curves like a glove.

Whoops. Wrong outfit for a family dinner. That's what I think until Simon's eyes turn to me, softening and relaxing his shoulders instantly.

"That would be the cherry pie we are having for dessert." Simon approaches me, placing his hands on my hips and leaning in to kiss my cheek.

My heart does a little flip, and I glance at Sandra over Simon's shoulder, who rolls her eyes behind his back.

"I thought you two would have had your fill of cherry pie *last time*." Sandra throws the little dig at us as she passes by and leaves the foyer, but not before I show her my shit-eating grin.

Fuck it. She's being a bitch to my man. She deserves it.

"You look good enough to eat, Cherry." Running his hands over the curve of my hip, Simon steps back to take me in. "Fucking delectable."

"You look pretty appetising yourself, Sy." Running my hands over the front of his crisp black collared shirt, I feel his pecs tighten and his nipples harden. "And you smell divine." I lean in, pressing my nose close to the exposed skin of his chest, where he has deliberately left a couple of buttons undone.

Tease.

"Shit, Cherry. Now I'm hard."

I pull back, grinning up into Simon's wild hazel gaze as I slide my hand down between our bodies until I come into contact with the hard, straining length of his cock under his jeans.

"This is all I want for dinner." My voice is breathy as I stand on my tiptoes, reaching my lips to his. Meeting me halfway, we both moan as our mouths connect, hot lips and tongues nipping at each other before diving deeper for more.

"I want you." He pants into my mouth, digging his fingers into my hips and pulling me closer. "Is a quickie out of the question?"

"Where?" I pant, hitching my leg and grinding Kitty against his hard bulge.

"Simon, dinner will be ready in ten minutes," Sandra calls down the hall, and Simon breaks our connection, pulling back, panting, lips swollen, eyes molten as he takes me in.

"Upstairs." He slaps my butt. "Quick!"

I have no time to respond before he's tugging my hand and pulling me along behind him, up the curving staircase and onto the second story. I haven't been in Simon's room before, so I have no idea if that's even where we are going. We pass door after door in the wide passage until we reach the end. Shoving a door open, Simon drags me inside and slams it behind me. Before I can figure out where we are, Simon pushes me against the wall and slams his lips to mine.

My heart rate skyrockets. Hard and fast. Something I don't mind. Fast can be fucking amazing, and hard is my fav.

"Fuck Cherry." Simon pants, kissing a trail down my neck. I drag my eyes open and see that we are, in fact, in a bedroom. His bedroom. It's huge, with a king-size bed, chunky dark timber furniture, and his own little living area with a couch, TV, entertainment centre, and even a mini-fridge in the corner. "I've missed you." His words draw my attention away from his room.

"I've missed you too. So fucking much." I pant back, my blood searing under my skin as he slips his thigh between my legs, pushing against my clit. Oh, dear lord, Kitty loves that. It's a good amount of pressure. Not gentle, and neither are his teeth as they nip at my shoulder while his fingers slide the shoestring straps off my shoulders.

Pulling back a little, Simon's heated gaze travels to my chest as he peels down the top of the leopard skin fabric, exposing my aching tits.

"Fuck Cherry. No bra?"

I grin and shake my head. "Not tonight." I bite the corner of my lip as I watch Simon's eyes dissolve into lust drunk pools as he stares at the heavy flesh of my breasts before diving down to suck my nipple into his mouth.

My moan is loud, and if Sandra can hear me, then I don't fucking care. Let her hear how her son makes me feel loved. Kitty turns ravenous then, and I fear I might come just by riding Simon's leg. I can't stop myself from grinding down, from throwing my head back, and revelling in the feel of his tongue flicking over my nipple as his hand runs up my bare thigh, slipping under the dress and lifting the fabric until the cool air of the room meets my flesh.

With my dress now bunched around my waist, Simon grazes his fingers over my bare hips and freezes, letting go of my nipple with a pop to look at me in confusion. I grin. I know what he's discovered. Leaning back, Simon looks down between our bodies to see the bare flesh of my Kitty riding the fabric of his denim-clad thigh.

"Fuck. No panties either?"

"Nope." I grin, even though he doesn't see it. He's too busy looking at my pussy.

"So, you are gonna sit through dinner with my mum with no panties on?"

"Looks like it."

His eyes flick back to mine. "I fucking love you!"

A laugh bursts free right before Simon claims my lips again, his kiss messy and fevered and fucking perfect. He moves back, and my hands come between us as I work his fly open, desperate to feel his hardness in my grip. As soon as I have his jeans tugged down over the globes of his arse, I find what I'm looking for and moan into his mouth. His dick is so hard that it feels like his skin is going to split open. I need it inside me now.

Hitching my legs up, I direct him to my entrance, and despite how fucking aroused he is, he breaks our kiss and pulls back with concern.

"Cherry. I wasn't going to do this. You're still healing."

"I don't care. I need you, Simon. I need this. I'll tell you if I need you to stop." I pant, desperate and horny, pressing the head of his cock to my opening.

"Wait!" He yells, and my eyes widen as I stiffen.

"What?"

"Condom." He hisses between clenched teeth. His face pained as he looks at the head of his cock, nudging eagerly for entry.

"Shit. Sorry, I got a little carried away." And that I did. I wasn't even thinking about safety, just need and want.

Looking back at my face, Simon's lip quirks up at the corner before he leans in and pecks my nose. "No need to be sorry, Cherry. It's not just you who's getting carried away."

Simon drops my leg and takes a step back, raising a finger as he moves. "Simon says, stay right there. I wanna fuck you up against my wall."

I grin. Fuck yeah, I'm staying here, and thankfully he doesn't keep me waiting long, darting over to his drawers and pulling out the condom, slipping it on as he walks back, before grabbing my leg and lifting it again, opening me to him.

"Are you sure, Cherry?"

I nod like I'm having a seizure, and he chuckles.

"Simon says, let's fuck."

With agonisingly slow movement, Simon eases through my folds, past my entrance and stretches me as he buries himself, inch by inch. I can't hold back my gasp when the pain hits as Simon becomes fully seated inside me. His back stiffens, and his eyes fly to mine in alarm, but I shake my head and whisper.

"It's fine. Keep going."

He doesn't look convinced, and I think he's about to pull out when his fingers move to my clit and start working their magic while he remains completely still deep inside me.

"I wanna fuck your juicy cunt, Cherry."

Daammmnnn. Kitty likes dirty talk, giving him more juice as his fingers press and rub.

"I wanna feel you gush over my cock and soak my balls and thighs."

Oh fuck. Kitty wants to gush already. I moan, a little taken aback by my overreaction to his filthy words. Not that I haven't been the recipient before, I have, but with Simon, my playful puppy, to be so filthy is a huge turn on. I can feel the desperate ache building deep inside me, so I dig my fingers into the flesh on his hips and tug him closer, a deep primal moan rumbling from my throat as the pleasure forces the pain away.

"More. Simon. More." I pant, tugging him again so he gets my meaning, and then he slowly pulls out and sinks back in.

We both moan, and I watch Simon's half-lidded eyes move from my face to my tits to where we are joined. I can tell he's holding back. Scared that he'll hurt me, and even though I can still feel pain, the pleasure is more. So much more.

So, I show Simon by tugging him back and forth as my hips drive forward to meet each of his thrusts while his fingers fumble over my clit.

"Harder." I pant, biting my lip when he meets my request, the sensations already so overwhelming that I know I am only a couple of thrusts away from skyrocketing.

"Fuck Cherry." He hisses before bringing his wet mouth over my nipple. I arch into him, needy and desperate, thrusting my hips and digging my nails into his skin.

"Yes." I pant because fuck yes. This is everything. I can fuck again. My Kitty works, and I have Simon, Marcus, Shaun, Garrett, and... I stop myself from thinking anything more. Thoughts of Ty aren't for this moment, and neither is the irritating voice of Simon's mum, calling from somewhere in the house that dinner is ready.

"I'm close, Cherry. I'm sorry." He starts to slow, but fuck that, I'm about ready to fly, so I wrap my arms around his neck.

"Don't fucking stop."

He growls at my demands, speeding his thrusts again, sending me to the place where pleasure is blinding and delivering me high into the clouds of ecstasy.

Chapter Twenty-Six

Simon

S he's not wearing any panties! My little minx is currently sitting next to me while my mum sits across from us, unaware that our guest has ridden her dress up enough so I can see the lips of her pussy from where I sit.

Fucking hell, this chick is going to kill me. Death by chronic erection. What a way to go, though. Am I right?

"So, Rhys. Simon tells me your mum is Principal Rogan. Is she your step mum or something? I noticed you both have different surnames."

"Mum!" I hiss, and she shoots me an annoyed glance before turning her eyes back to my girl.

"No, actually. She's my foster mum." Rhys' tone is proud and strong. She isn't at all fazed by my mum's interrogation.

"Foster? *Really?* Where are your parents?" My mum puts her fork down, ignoring the steaming stir-fry, and keeps her gaze on Cherry.

"Seriously, mum? That's none of your business." I snap, but Rhys gently places her fork down on the table too before linking her hand with mine, resting them entwined on the tabletop. It's really fucking hard to bite back my smirk when my mum's hard stare falters as her eyes flick to our hands.

"It's fine, Sy. Naturally, your mum is curious." Rhys tilts her head towards me but keeps her eyes on my mum as she speaks. "My mum is dead—drug overdose when I was nine. I have no idea where my dad is. I don't even know who he is. Probably some rich married guy that screwed around on his wife." Rhys gasps then, darting her head to me with her chocolate eyes wide. "What if you're my brother?"

Silence fills the room for a brief moment before I burst out laughing, Cherry's face morphing into a shit-eating grin. I can't stop myself. I lean in to kiss her, long and hard and uncaring that my stuck-up mum is watching us.

"Good lord, she's the female version of you." Sandra huffs, and I break our kiss, turning my grin to my mum.

"Isn't she perfect?"

Flustered, my mum clears her throat before standing and taking her plate to the kitchen.

"You're fucking evil." I suck Cherry's earlobe between my lips, the action enticing her closer to me. "And look at that pussy. It's glistening." I drop my eyes to her lap, taking a good look at the slick folds I was buried between not so long ago.

"They're wet because I can smell that cherry pie. Are you opposed to rubbing it over my naked body in front of your mum?"

My brows shoot up. "Kinda. Yeah."

She laughs, "Your face! I'm a kinky bitch, Sy, but I'm not *that* kinky."

"Here's dessert." My mum sing songs as she re-enters the room carrying the cherry pie I insisted on having. She wasn't happy about it, which makes it all more worth the while. I'm pissed at my mum for so many reasons right now, and I don't even remember when it started.

She places the cherry pie in the centre of the table, shooting us a smile before moving around the table to where we are sitting. My heart rate picks up because my mum is about to get an eyeful of cunt she isn't expecting, but Rhys discretely brings her cloth napkin down off the table and rests it in her lap, just in time to cover the muffin show.

"Let me take your dishes for you." My mum is none the wiser as she sweeps up our plates and goes back to the kitchen.

I smirk at my girl. She has the devil inside her. Naughty, mischievous, and tempting. She seems a little more like herself tonight, carrying that confidence that only Rhys George has. I hope she's back. It's hard seeing her so upset and so unsure of herself. It hurts right in the centre of my chest like someone is reaching in and squeezing my heart.

My mum returns, pushing dessert bowls across the table to us and takes her seat, and Rhys passes me my bowl before removing her napkin and placing it back on the table.

Hello Kitty!

Fuck, I'm hard.

"Why don't you dish dessert up, Simon." Mum insists, giving us another one of her fake smiles. I'm about to wipe that smile away, though. Once she sees her son sporting an erection, she's going to regret asking me to do this.

Naturally, I stand, pretty fucking happy to push my mum to breaking point, and I proceed to dish up the cherry pie. I peer down at Rhys as I hand her bowl back, her eyes meeting mine with heat as she grins happily up at me. It's the uncomfortable clearing throat of my mum that tells me she can see the evidence of my arousal for my girl, and I try hard not to grin too much as I pass her the bowl of dessert.

Lucky for her, she doesn't say anything but thank you, and once I sit down, we all turn our eyes to the sweet pie before us. I take a bite, closing my eyes and remembering how it felt to lick it from Rhys' pebbled nipples.

"So, Rhys. Clearly, you and my son have something serious going." My eyes fly open at my mum's words, and I hone in on her. "How is this thing between the two of you going to go when we move away? Are you going to try long distance?"

"Mum!" I snap, but she fucking ignores me, brows raised like she's just won a verbal battle as she eyes Rhys.

"You're *actually* moving away? I didn't know it had been decided." Rhys frowns, dropping her fork into the bowl and turning hurt eyes to me.

"No, I'm not moving." I shake my head.

"Don't be silly, Simon. Of course, you are." My mum's words gain Rhys' attention again. "We are moving to Perth as soon as the school year is over."

"Uh, no. *You're* moving. I'm not." I hiss, gaining the eyes of both the women in my life.

"We've been over this, Simon. You can't stay here by yourself. The house is going on the market, and once it's sold, you will have nowhere to live."

And there it is. One of the reasons I'm hating on my mum right now. She fucking knows I don't want to move away, and she knows how much I care about Rhys, yet she doesn't fucking care. It's all about *her*. As always.

"Why can't you just stay here?" I snap, and she rolls her eyes.

"We've been over this. I need to be closer to my sister."

"Why should I pay the price for the mistakes you and dad made? I'm not fucking going!" I slam my hand down on the table, making Rhys jump, but I pretend she isn't there because I need to keep my focus on my mum.

"You don't have a choice, Simon." Unflinching, my mum places her fork gently on the table and takes a sip of her wine.

"Wanna bet?" I stand so abruptly that my chair falls back, slamming on the tiled floor before I storm off into the foyer.

As soon as the oversized waste of space wraps around me, I look around, panicked.

Fuck, I forgot to grab my girl.

Spinning on my heel, I storm back in to see my mum and my girl in a silent Mexican standoff. As much as I know Rhys can handle herself, I don't want to leave her with my toxic mum, and I need her by my side, so I reach down and tug her up by her hand. She scrambles to tug her dress down just in time to cover her naked flesh before I drag her across the room.

"I'm taking *my* girl to *my* room. If you don't want to see us getting dirty again, I suggest you keep away from *my* part of the house."

I hear my mum make a choking sound as I storm off with Rhys in tow, and I take two steps at a time up the staircase, going back to my bedroom.

Once inside, I slam the door, drop Cherry's hand and stomp across the room, digging my fingers into my hair and tugging.

"FUCK!" I scream in fury.

"You wanna fuck?" Her tone is playful, yet when I turn to face her, Cherry's expression is pinched.

"No... yes. Fuck, I don't know." I drop down on the end of my bed, raking my hands through my hair.

"Sy." There's a gentleness in her tone I haven't heard before. I'm useless to fight looking up into those chocolate eyes.

"I'm not moving away, Rhys. I don't care what my mum says or does. I'm not going."

"But... if she sells this house, where will you live?"

"I haven't figured that out yet, but I will. Don't worry. I'm not leaving you. And I'm not leaving the guys."

That's when I see it, the wobble of her bottom lip and her glassy eyes. Reaching out, I grip her hips and pull her forward into the space between my legs, and I hug her waist, resting my head on her tummy.

"I meant what I said earlier." I shift back, peering up to take in her beautiful face. "I know I said I love you playfully, but I meant it, Cherry. I fucking love you."

"Y-you do?"

I nod, and a tear pops from her eye. "Yes. I'll figure out living arrangements. I'll sleep in a cardboard box if it means not leaving you."

Leaning down, Rhys kisses me. It's probably the gentlest kiss she's given me, despite how long we are lip locked. It's one of those kisses that speaks through the action. She loves me too. I can feel it in every brush of her tongue and nip of her lips.

"Can I help you escape for a bit?" She asks as she pulls back, licking her well kissed lips. I shrug, unsure of what she means. "Wanna come in my mouth?"

Ahhh. That's what she means.

I smirk and shrug, so she drops to her knees.

"Rhys says, lay back." She pushes against my chest, and I ease backwards, grinning at her attempt at stealing my Simon Says game and making it her own. Her eyes dart to my crotch before she makes quick work of my jeans, tugging them right off this time, followed by my jocks. She pops every button open on my shirt, peeling it back to reveal my bare torso. "Let me show you how much I love *you,* Sy."

The sear of her tongue glides up my hard shaft, her hand gripping the base and standing it tall so I can see her devour my dick like it's a lollipop. Then she takes me in deep, my tip pressing past her throat as she cups my balls. When she draws back, my cock pops free, and she runs her tongue down my shaft again, to my balls, where she sucks one into her mouth.

"Fuuuck, that feels amazing, Cherry."

She hums then, the vibrations doing things I didn't know could be done, while her hand pumps my cock. I can feel her body, thin, strong and sensually pressed up against me. Her legs are parted as she works to bring me pleasure. Slowly, as she slips one ball free of her wet mouth and sucks in the other, I shift my foot, bringing it between her legs. Then, as she hums again, I lift my foot, so the top arch presses against her dripping pussy.

Her hum turns into a moan as she grinds down on my foot, and a thrill rolls through me. I'm a foot guy. I don't know why I love feet, but I do. Especially Cherry's. I also love feeling sensations through my own feet, and I nearly lose my load as the next thought crosses my mind.

I wanna fuck her with my foot.

When it comes to feet, I love touching them, rubbing them, looking at them, and fuck, I've had many jerks to a mental image of fucking someone's cunt with my foot.

Rhys is the kinkiest girl I have ever met. Will she be into it? Or will I freak her out?

As she pops my other ball free of her mouth, she licks a path back up my shaft and circles my tip a couple of times before drawing me in deep.

I can't help it. My foot tenses, and my toes press against her clit, nearly making *me* come as she presses herself harder against the friction.

"Fuck Cherry. Do you like the feel of my foot? My toes?"

Her eyes flick up to me, and she gives me a muffled ah-huh and a strained nod, restricted because her mouth is full of my dick.

"Would it freak you out if I said I want to fuck you with my foot?"

Her brows hitch, and she eases my length from her mouth, gripping the base to continue pumping it.

"You have a thing for feet, hey?" She grins, licking the excess drool from her lips.

"Maybe."

She flashes her white teeth at me, her black lips spreading wide. "Sy, I'm the last person you should be shy with about kinks. I'll never judge you. I might tell you if I'm not into it, but I'll never judge you. I want you to know you can talk about any of your fantasies with me."

I can feel my fucking cheeks heat like a pussy. "Ok then. I have a thing for feet. And food play. And I kind of think there's probably heaps of other things I'll be into when I come across them."

"Now, that's what I'm talking about." Pleased, she kisses the tip of my cock as she continues to pump it. "So, if I sink down on your toes, just how turned on will that make you?"

"I'll probably come straight away," I admit, and she smirks.

"I challenge you to hold it in for as long as you can." Then she rubs her wet folds over my hungry toes.

My dick jerks, ready to explode, and she raises a brow, so I nod, hoping like hell I can hold my load until my toes get her off.

Positioning herself over my toes, she uses one hand to part her lips while her other works over my length, my toes slowly easing into a wet heat they have never met before.

"Shit." I pant, struggling to hold back.

"Christ, Sy, you're turning me on with how turned on you are. This is hot."

I nod, too fucking scared to talk in case it moves my body and the slight change in pressure rips my orgasm from me.

Leaning forward, Rhys takes my dick in between her lips again while she lowers herself down over my toes and the ball of my foot. It's not as deep as my dick would go, but it's fucking wider. Stretching her. I can feel her fingers on her clit, touching the nerve endings just the way she likes, while she grinds down on my foot.

"I can't… hold it!" I hiss, and she shakes her head, shooting a glare at me.

Fuck. Fuck. Fuck. I'm gonna explode any second.

Rhys picks up her pace between her legs, her fingers rubbing over her nub like it's a fucking little joystick, and her needy cunt sucks my foot in further.

"Rhys!" I cry out, and her face screws up in pleasured pain, telling me she's about to come too. The moment I feel her first convulsion around my foot, I detonate.

I yell, something incoherent, my seed shooting down the back of her throat as she rides her own high, her juices pouring over my foot.

"Fuck yes! That was epic!" I pant out, flopping my head back on my bed.

My dick pops from Cherry's mouth before slapping against my stomach, our panted breaths mingling together in the room.

"Was it everything you fantasised about?" She asks, and I pop my head back up to look at her. There's a flush to her creamy skin, sitting brighter over her cheeks. Her brown eyes are soft and satisfied, looking at me in approval.

"It was so much more Cherry," I say, slowly sitting up and easing my foot from her heat.

"I have to admit. I kinda enjoyed fucking your foot, Sy." She grins. "That was a first for me. I look forward to doing it again."

Leaning forward, I drag her up, falling back on my bed, bringing her with me.

"I'm looking forward to it as well." I grin, claiming her lips in a gentle kiss.

When she pulls back, her smile falters, her worried eyes meeting mine.

"We will find a way to keep you here, Sy. I'm not letting you go."

Chapter Twenty-Seven

RHYS

The trick to getting through an exam without freaking out is to turn up stoned. Seriously. I didn't have a care in the world in the stadium with hundreds of other students sitting their history exams. There is a little downside to being baked in an exam, though, and that is sluggishness. I was slow. Like really slow. I didn't even get right through the exam papers. Most people did. They finished before the allotted time. Not me. Nope.

I guess my trick backfired, but since I'm still riding it out, I don't really care that much. The Mary Jane in my blood is also doing wonders to block out the sneaking looks from Luke Brewer and Dion Richards, as well as blocking out the reminder that I have to return to Vixen's Lodge tonight. In fact, turning up there baked will probably help me get through having to lay eyes on that sick fucker, Master Hill, again.

There's a couple of hours between exams today, so Garrett and I wander around the outside of the stadium to our spot at the back of the school to eat our lunch and chill before my Maths exam.

"You're quiet today." My big guy comments as we unwrap our sangas. We're sitting on the top stoop of the usual steps we occupy, leaning against the blue double exit doors.

"I'm baked," I admit, smirking at Garrett's raised brows.

"Shit, really? I can't even tell." He takes a bite of his sandwich, which is smaller than his big hands.

I nod. "Yeah. Probably not the brightest of Rhys George ideas, but what's done is done."

He chuckles.

I bite into my ham and cheese-filled sanga and rest back against the door as I chew, thinking about last night and the hell Simon must be going through trying to figure out a way to stay in Fox Pines.

"Has Simon told you that his mum is selling their house and moving to Perth?"

Garrett's frown speaks for itself.

"Not exactly. He said his mum wants to move. But that's all he's said."

I sigh, shaking my head and putting my sandwich back into its bag. "When I was there last night for dinner, his mum said she was selling the house and asked me how I feel about Simon moving away."

"What the fuck?" Garrett snaps, screwing up his empty brown paper bag.

"He got so mad. He lost his shit at her. It was kinda pretty, really. Bitch deserved it, but it makes me wonder how long this shit has been going on. Sy always seems so playful and happy, but last night, I could see that he's not happy at all. He's angry and upset, and I feel like it's been going on for a while."

"Don't kill me for saying this, but Simon's kinda like you. The life of the party. Carefree and fun, yet behind closed doors, there's heartache and pain. And just like you, he probably thinks he can figure this out on his own."

I shoot Garrett a narrowed glare, "It's lucky I like you, or I'd throat punch you for calling me out right now."

Throwing his head back, Garrett laughs, the sound a deep rumble that breaks through my steel walls and fills my veins with warmth.

"Baby girl, I'm grateful you like me. I'm not ready to die."

I grin as Garrett leans in, pressing his soft lips to mine. It's a brief kiss. Not meant for anything more than to show affection, and instead of my Kitty purring, my heart flips. Is this what romance does to a girl?

As he draws back, I feel an invisible chain tugging at me, urging me to stay close to him. Keep in his space and never move away. I feel the same thing with all the guys, which is how I know I'll never handle Simon leaving.

"We can't let Simon go. I need him." I cringe as pain twists around my heart and constricts. "We have to figure out a way for him to stay here. Can he move in with you?"

"Yeah-Nah. That wouldn't be a good idea." Garrett frowns, his eyes flicking away briefly. "My old man is being released from prison next week. He's a prick. Sy can't be around his sort of toxic."

"What!" I jerk back. "Your dad is coming home next week? Why didn't you tell me?"

"You have enough going on, Rhys." I slap his arm, and his brows hitch. "What was that for?"

"Not telling me! I don't care what I have going on. I need to know what's happening in your lives. Isn't that what you're meant to do in a relationship?"

I'm not expecting the grin that morphs Garrett's face. "You're right. It is what you're meant to do in a relationship. Sorry beautiful. I should have told you."

"Damn right!" I snap, and he grins harder. "What the fuck are you smiling at?"

"My girl." He reaches forward and takes my hand in his. "You've come a long way since that day a couple of weeks ago in the gym when I asked you to hit the bags."

Naturally, I relax the moment my hand is in his. These guys are like mind-altering drugs to me. They have the ability to calm me in an instant.

"Yeah, I guess I have." I shrug, looking up into Garrett's icy-blue eyes, and he lifts our hands, pressing his lips to the back of mine.

"Don't worry about Simon. I'll talk with the guys. Between us, I'm sure we can figure out a way to keep him here. None of us want to lose him."

I believe Garrett's words. Those guys are best mates. Brothers. They'll never stand by and let one of their circle suffer.

"Thank you," I whisper, leaning my head on his shoulder and closing my eyes. I'm exhausted all of a sudden.

"You wanna come to my place for dinner tonight?"

Lifting my head off his shoulder, I look back up at Garrett.

"I should probably stay home and study for tomorrow's exam, but maybe you can come to my place tomorrow after our combined Health and PE exam? We finish at lunchtime, so maybe we can hang out at mine, and you can stay for dinner too?"

Garrett smiles. "I'd like that."

I feel like shit instantly for lying to Garrett. I won't be studying tonight. I'll be at Vixen's Lodge. The thought makes me queasy. Going to that house alone is not a good idea. I know that, yet I can't risk not going. He's going to make Tyler pay if I don't turn up, and even though things between Ty and me are weird, I'll always do what I can to protect him from this mess I got him in.

Marcus and Simon rock up a little while later, and we reluctantly go back into the stadium for exam number two. Maths.

While I'm more focused this time, my nerves make it hard not to second guess every damn equation, and once again. I don't quite finish.

Fuck, I hate exams.

The guys go off together at the end of the exam, blowing me kisses behind my mum's back as she helps the teachers clear the stadium. I really hope Garrett can help Simon figure out a way to stay. I need my playful guy just as much as I need my brooding one, and my outgoing one, and my obsessive one... and my older one.

Thinking of Tyler hurts. I didn't see him today. He usually helps out with exams, but I suppose he might have other year levels to teach and wasn't available. I want to call him or message him, but

I'm scared I'll spill that I'm going to Vixen's Lodge tonight, and then he'll do something reckless.

At home after school, I end up falling asleep on my bed until the twins burst in and jump on me at dinnertime. I didn't even know I was asleep, probably an aftereffect of the weed I smoked this morning.

Connor drags me out of my room while Archie rambles on about the movie, Frozen 2 not being just for girls, while Connor disagrees.

Fuck, I wish my biggest issue was debating the correct audience gender for a movie.

Dinner is typical. The twins talk with their mouths full while my mum asks each of us how our day was. Dad is a little quieter tonight than usual, but Char makes up for his silence by whinging about the amount of carbs she is being forced to eat. All in all, it's ok and over with soon enough.

I help with the dishes, keeping my eye on the clock, knowing that I will need to leave a little after 8 in order to make it all the way out to Vixen's Lodge before 9pm.

"Rhys. Can we please talk to you?" Mum asks, hovering at the end of the kitchen, her expression pinched.

Shit. I don't need this right now. I have to go soon.

"Ah… can it wait until tomorrow? I'm pretty stuffed after today. I wanna go to bed early."

"It won't take long." Her tone is final, so I sigh and hand my tea towel to Char as she raises her brows at me.

Ignoring her and the twins, who complain that I'm not helping, I follow my mum out of the room, down the passage to the front of the house, and into the study where my dad is sitting at his desk.

My heart rate picks up. Am I in trouble again for something? What the hell have I done now?

When my mum closes the door behind us, I really start to panic and ignore my dad's gesture to take a seat. Instead, I stand against the wall near the door, ready for a quick escape.

"I spoke to the police in detail today about your trip to the prison this weekend." Dad's voice is all business. "Your mum and I still have a lot of concerns about allowing this. It seems absurd that we let you go into that prison again, so we need to know if you're sure you want to do it."

Do I want to go into the Allansdale Prison again and see the man that made me believe the things he did with me were normal for dads and daughters? Fuck no. But I need to. I need this to end. I need them to pay for turning me into this vile-minded, sex-crazed beast.

"I'm sure," I answer confidently. "I need to do it."

My rents look at each other, having a silent conversation with their eyes before glancing back at me.

"If we let you do this, Rhys, we would like you to commit to some extra therapy. Not just with Melia, but perhaps some one-on-one time with Mr Matthews at school."

Ugh. School counsellors suck, but if it gets her off my back, then I'll agree to it.

"Ok."

"And…" Mum stalls for a moment, glancing at my dad before returning her eyes to me. "We want you to attend the new youth addiction centre in Redfield for meetings."

"What!" I push off the wall, balling my fists. "No way! That's for drug addicts and stuff. I'm not going there!"

"It's for addicts, period. Besides, you do drugs, Rhys. Probably more than you should for a social dabbler. That's our terms. Allowing you to be out in a dangerous situation, which has the potential to affect your mental stability, goes against everything we are trying to do here. We want to provide you with a safe place. A loving home, a warm bed, food in your belly, and opportunities to get the education you deserve. What's happening now is a bump in your road, but it is a big one. It'll likely leave lingering memories that you'll try to bury. We need you to agree to focusing on your mental health so you can move on and live the life you deserve."

Well, fuck. I hate it when she's all logical and shit.

"Meetings only. I'm not going to stay there. This is my home… right?"

"Of course, this is your home. Always Rhys. You are our daughter, and we will be here for you no matter what."

I want to cry. I hold back, though. I need to be strong and show them I can handle this, so I nod.

"Ok. I'll do what you want. No one wants this over with more than I do."

Will nods. "Thank you, Rhys. We'll be with you on Saturday. We have something to do in the city afterwards, so maybe we can stay the night."

I scrunch up my nose. "Can I not? Simon is having a little party. I think I'll really need my friends after visiting the prison."

"Oh, well, I guess we can change our plans." Cin looks at Will, who seems disappointed.

"Well, why don't you keep your plans? Maybe I can bum a ride with Officer Zimora and Officer Fredricks?"

"Oh… I don't know if that will be allowed." Mum frowns, and I shrug, glancing at the clock above my dad's head. It's nearly 8pm.

"Can you ask? Otherwise, I can catch the train back."

"No." My dad stands from behind the desk. "We will all travel back home together. I'll re-schedule our appointment in the city."

Now I feel awful, but Cin looks relieved. "We can go the next day, perhaps? I'm sure that won't be a problem."

Dad nods, approaching my mum and kissing her forehead. Those two have something special. It makes me think of my guys. I know we are only new and all so young except for Ty, but is it too premature to hope that one day we will be married and have kids and work together to help solve their worries? I can tell you it's a weird fucking thought. I've never thought of myself as marriage material, let alone mother material, yet I'm dreaming up images of me and my guys facing this world together that way.

"Uh… Can I go? I'm gonna have an early night."

My parents turn their attention back to me, smiling and nodding, giving me the go-ahead, so I do what any other teenage girl would do in my situation. I flee.

Back in my room, I hang my trusty 'do not disturb' sign on my door before going inside and locking it. Then I put my Docs on, lacing them quickly before slipping out my window.

Just like some of the other times I've snuck out, I knick Archie's bike and start pedalling for my life. It takes me fifty gruelling minutes to ride out to Vixen's Lodge, and by the time I get inside the barn, I'm parched, panting, and absolutely exhausted.

I go straight to the little bathroom and guzzle down some water from the faucet before peeing and returning to my little makeover area. There's a purple lace bra and matching panties laid out for me, and on top are black heels, an envelope, a hairbrush, and a packet of makeup wipes, but no mask makeup.

Sourness settles in my gut. This was a bad idea. I should turn around and leave now, but then I remember the messages Master Hill sent.

> *There will be consequences if you fail to attend.*
> *Your sponsor will pay the price.*

I hate this motherfucker!

With a shaky hand, I open the envelope and pull out a single piece of paper.

> *Kitten, please remove all traces of makeup and make*
> *sure your hair is down.*
> *Once you are dressed, please knock on the back door*
> *near the swimming pool.*
> *Don't be late.*

"I don't want to do this," I whisper to no one but myself before glancing at my phone screen. 8:55pm. Shit, I need to get moving.

I scramble to get changed while wiping my makeup off at the same time, before ripping my buns out and quickly brushing my hair. I take a moment to look at myself in the mirror, seeing a girl that holds nothing but misery in her eyes.

"You can do this," I whisper to the girl, but she doesn't look convinced.

Then I turn and leave the barn.

Hurrying up the back path, I round the pool area and tap on the back door that is usually a glass door, but tonight it's boarded up like the glass has recently been smashed.

There's no sign of Brock, the shirtless waiters, or even Madam Vik, though. Master Hill answers the door wearing the typical suit he seems to live in, his creepy brown eyes raking over my practically naked body as I stand outside trying to fight the trembles that shudder through me.

I'm scared. Like terrified. This man has always seemed like a predator. There's just something about him that reminds me of Brian. It could be the way they both look at me or the fact they have the same coloured eyes. I don't know what it is exactly, but they remind me of each other. All predators are the same, I guess.

"Right on time, Kitten. Please come in."

Master Hill takes a step back, gesturing for me to enter, and I hold my breath as I step over the threshold, dread filling my veins. I feel like I'll never see daylight again.

Chapter Twenty-Eight

Rhys

The lights are too bright, and the house is too quiet. Normally when I come here on a Feast night, the lights are dimmed, there is music playing, and the rooms are filled with naked bodies. Tonight, the only near-naked body is mine, while the stark lights shine down on my every curve as I sit in the living area with the only other person in this house. Master Hill.

"I have a proposition for you." His deep voice sends a repulsive shiver up my spine, and I twist my hands together in my lap as I stare at the swell of his nose and the purple tinge in each corner of his eye.

I don't say anything in response to his statement, but I raise my brows in question, so he continues.

"I want you to return to the Feast nights under a new sponsor."

I frown. "Skipper is my sponsor."

"Not anymore. I have allocated you a new one."

I swallow back the lump forming in my throat, already hating this conversation. "Who?" My eyes move from his obvious broken nose to the cut on his lip.

"Tiger."

"No way!" I hiss, forgetting about his face and my worries as rage fills me. "That creepoid is not being my sponsor. I'd rather resign as a Feast member."

"That's not going to work for me, Kitten. You either return to the Feasts with Tiger as your sponsor, or I expose Skipper for the student-fucking teacher he is."

"You arsehole!" I snap, my fists balled in my lap.

Master Hill eyes me silently for a moment. The way his jaw clicks is the only sign that my response has bothered him before he speaks.

"So I've been told." He waves his hand and shifts forward in the armchair across from me, leaning his suited arms on his legs. "It's either Tiger or *me*, Kitten. Who would you rather be your sponsor?"

"Skipper." Jutting my chin up, I let him see my defiance, my fear slipping away as more anger replaces it.

He chuckles, resting back in the chair again. "My final proposition is Madam Vik as your sponsor, *plus* an hour alone with me each Feast downstairs. Agree to this, and I'll leave your teacher alone. Disagree, and I'll expose him to the world."

I hate him. Like, really hate him. So much so that the lamp sitting on the table next to him looks like a good fucking weapon to beat his skull in with. My pulse is raging in my ears as I fight to rein in my temper.

"What will our time alone entail?" I grit out through clenched teeth, and he grins.

"I'll show you." He stands, gesturing for me to stand too, but I hesitate.

"I'm just going to give you a rundown, Kitten. Don't worry. We will not be coming together tonight."

I nearly gag. I should just let go and spew my dinner all over his carpet.

"Why did I have to dress like this, then?" I gesture to the purple lace bra, and he shrugs.

"Because I am your master, and you will do what I say. It's best you remember that, Kitten."

In other words, it was a test to see if I'd comply.

I hate that he calls himself the Master. Garrett is *my* master, not this fuckwit, but what choice do I have? If I don't do what he asks, then he will destroy Tyler's life. I don't want that.

Not waiting to see if I'll obey, Master Hill leaves the room, and I scramble up off the chair quickly, following behind, my heels clicking on the timber floors in the passage, echoing through the quiet house. When he starts to descend the stairs that lead down to his dungeon, I hesitate, hovering on the top step. Last time I went down there, he restrained Tyler and me, then forced Tyler to watch as he humiliated me in front of everyone.

I glance back over my shoulder. I should just turn and go. Maybe I can go to the police and ask for their help? No, that won't work. Asking for their help will still expose Tyler, and he will likely go to jail.

What have I done?

I've ruined his life all because I wanted in on the sex club.

"I'm not a patient man, Kitten." Master Hill's voice sends a vile shiver up my spine, and I turn back to see his brows raised as he waits at the bottom for me to join him.

You can do this.

You need to do this to protect Ty.

One shaky leg after another, I step down until I reach the bottom and slowly follow Master Hill into his torture chamber.

"Kneel." Master Hill demands as I enter, his finger pointing to the cushion on the floor.

Last time there were two, one for Ty and one for me. Tonight, there is only one reminding me I'm alone in this mansion with this vulgar man.

My legs shake like crazy as I approach the cushion and sink down to kneel, lowering my eyes the way Ty told me to last time.

"Good girl, Kitten. You remembered."

I say nothing, trying to calm my nerves when all I want to do is flip him the bird and spit in his face.

"You will enter this room with your eyes cast to the floor. You will *not* look at me until I give you permission. You will kneel until I give you an instruction. No matter how long it takes, you will not move from your cushion. Do you understand?"

"Yes." My voice is shaky, and I hate that he hears it.

"Yes, what?" He hisses, and I flinch.

"Yes, master."

"Do you have any questions?" His feet appear in front of me, and I can just imagine him looking down as he towers over me, believing he is some sort of fucking king.

"Y-yes, master."

"You may look at me and speak freely, Kitten."

I suck in a breath, working up the courage I need as I drag my gaze up to his face. "I have some hard limits."

He nods. "Stand. Follow me."

It's really fucking hard to stand. My legs are shaking so badly that I nearly fall on my face, and of all things, he is the one to save me, clasping my arm and guiding me up. I hate that I needed his help.

Relief washes over me as Master Hill leads me from the torture chamber and back upstairs to the den. He sits at the large desk, gesturing for me to take a seat, and I do so quickly, not trusting my legs to play nice.

Reaching into a drawer, he pulls out some papers, glancing at them briefly before sliding them across the desk to me.

"This is your contract. Read over it again and select any extra hard limits you have. Write down anything that isn't listed."

I'm talking with the lawyer now. He is all business and, let me tell you, a scary motherfucker. I wouldn't want to come up against him in court.

Glancing down at the contract, I scan over the papers until I reach the right page and look down the list. I already had no anal selected, and even though I've ventured into that territory a little with my guys, I'm not willing to explore that here, so I leave it as is. Everything in the check boxes is still relevant, so I add some notes at the bottom.

No pain infliction.
No humiliation, public or otherwise.
No non-con.
No Tiger Man!
No video recordings!!
No remote-controlled toys!
No using food.
No foot stuff.

I add the last two because they are special to Simon and me. If we share that stuff with anyone, then it will be with the other guys. I ignore the guilt that nudges me as I think of my guys. They won't be happy about this new arrangement and with good reason. Without Ty here, there's no one to watch over me.

I glance up from the contract and ask a risky question.

"Is Madam Vik's other liege still coming to the Feast nights?"

"Casanova?" He frowns, and I nod. "No."

Shit. I need someone here to make sure I come out alive each Feast. Summoning courage, I didn't know I had, I do something I never thought I'd do.

"Master," I say sweetly, playing the role he wants me to, "can you please permit Casanova to return as Madam's liege as well?"

He frowns. "Why?"

"It will make me feel safer for the times you aren't around. I know I messed up and had to be punished the other week, but I'm still a little scared around everyone else. Maybe Casanova can make sure I am treated right when you aren't around?"

I wanna vom! Saying those words like he isn't the one I'm scared of goes against everything he has done to me, yet I can see they work with the way his face softens. He likes me wanting him as my protector.

Fucking dick!

"Ok, Kitten. I will get Madam to reach out to Casanova and see if he will return. But…" He stands from his chair and walks around the desk to tower over where I sit. "You both better work our guests well and not focus on each other too much, or I will make sure he is punished, and it will be your fault. Again."

I nod quickly. "Yes, Master."

He groans at my words, taking a step closer, his crotch a mere inch from my face. My breath hitches as I see a bulge growing in his pants, and I try to lean away, but he claws his fingers into my hair.

"I've changed my mind, Kitten. Tonight, we will have a little playtime. You will give me a lap dance."

"W-what?" My eyes dart up to his, and he licks his lips as he smirks.

"You heard me, Kitten. Don't make me repeat myself." He takes a step back. "Stand up."

My wobbly legs are back, my heart thumping so hard that it feels like my ribs are going to crack open.

Master Hill takes the chair I was in and drags it over to the corner where a large mirror is propped up. Once he has the chair in position, he sits down, takes out his phone and flicks through it. A moment later, music fills the room.

Shit. It's Beyonce's Rocket.

"Come over here and dance for me." Master Hill raises his hand, using two fingers to wave me over. I don't want to do this, but the quicker I get it over with, the quicker I can leave.

Sucking in a breath of courage, I pretend it's Tyler sitting in the chair. He'd totally love me to dance for him and give him a lap dance, so I use him as my inspiration.

Standing before Master Hill, I sway my hips to the sensual beat of the song, slowly turning, I raise my hands a little over my head as I dance. As soon as I'm facing the mirror, Master Hill's hands snap out and grip my hips, pulling me back until I'm dancing between his legs.

"Sit on my lap, Kitten."

"Yes, Master," I say innocently, mainly because I know it will turn him on, and the quicker I can get him off, the quicker this will be over.

An approving rumble sounds in his chest as I lower myself down, closing my eyes so I don't have to see our reflection in the mirror as my purple lace arse cheeks press against the hard bulge in his pants.

Even though I'm sitting, I try to hover so I don't have to feel too much of him, but he has other ideas, gripping my hips and shoving me down hard. A whimper escapes me as bile rises up my throat, and Master Hill takes over my attempt at lap dancing, manoeuvring my hips in a way that gives him the most pleasure.

Gripping the arms of the chair for support, I mistakenly open my eyes and see the scene reflected in the mirror before me. His lips are parted, exposing his teeth, which are biting together as he snarls out grunts, his normally pale cheeks flushed as my arse works over his cock, which is still safely tucked inside his suit pants. His face is contorted into a frustrated frown, his fingers pressing so hard into the skin at my hips that I know it's going to leave bruises.

"Part your legs." He demands, and I do it hoping it will hurry things along. He bites his lip, ignoring the cut as his eyes focus on my spread legs, releasing one grip from my hip to slide it around my front and between my legs. I whimper again, trying to stand and shift back, but his grip is firm and unrelenting.

"You move away, and you are going against our agreement. Make a choice, Kitten. It's you or your teacher."

My lip wobbles as his words sink in, hot tears filling my eyes.

Why are you crying, Rhys? You created this.

I hate my inner demon, but the bitch is right. I created this. Acceptance is the only thing I have left right now, so I relax, tears spilling over, burning my cheeks, as I give my Master the best fucking lap dance he's ever had in his life.

I take over. Rubbing. Grinding. Taking one of his hands and pressing it against my tit as his other hand rubs between my legs. I don't feel any pleasure. I feel numb. My body is nothing but a shell right now—just skin. No feelings.

The song clicks over and starts again, and I can hear by his panting breaths against my ear that he's close, so I amp up my grinding and don't fight him off when his hand slips under the lace cup of the bra. That's when he cums in his pants. I work him over and over with the cheeks of my arse until he grips my hips again, forcing me to stop.

"Good girl, Kitten." He pants against my ear, flicking his vile tongue out to lick my lobe. "You comply like that each time, and your teacher is safe."

Chapter Twenty-Nine

Rhys

Fridays are usually my favourite day of the week. They hold the promise of a weekend—the promise of fun. Today, however, I wish it was Monday because then the weekend would've already passed, and *those* events that I'm yet to endure would be behind me.

Unfortunately, they are ahead of me. Tomorrow's visit to the prison and Sunday night's Feast are looming over my head like a deadly cyclone. I want to run away. Disappear. Hide. There's no escaping my responsibilities, though. If I don't go to the prison, then Julie will expose me to everyone at school. Yeah, some of them think it's me already, but the confirmation will set me up for a world of cruelty.

Then there's the Feast. I used to love that place. It was the one place I could go to be myself, but things have changed. It's now a place of extortion and coercion. It's my own living hell.

When I left Vixen's Lodge last night, I threw up three times during the ride home, and then I tossed all night with nightmare after nightmare tormenting me. If my rents noticed the bags under my eyes this morning, they didn't say anything, probably assuming the hollowness is from my worry over visiting the prison tomorrow. I wish that was my only worry. I wish it would all just go away.

I need a reminder of why I'm submitting to Master Hill, so after arriving at school for my Health exam, I search the crowd of teachers, hoping to lay eyes on Ty, but I can't find him.

"I had an interesting call from Vixen's Lodge this morning, Kitten." Shaun's words draw my attention, and I look up at him to notice his eyes analysing my face. "Wanna tell me what's going on?"

I shake my head. "Nope. Have you seen Mr Foster?" I look back at the gathered teachers. It's the Health and PE exam today. He should be here.

"Kitten." Shaun steps in front of me, blocking my view, cupping each side of my face. "What's going on?"

On instinct, I tilt my head into his touch, closing my eyes as his caress works to calm me a little.

"What's wrong?" The familiar scent of Marcus envelopes me as his arms wrap around me from behind. I sink back, eyes closed, as I fight the urge to break down and spill my dark secrets.

"That's what I'm trying to establish," Shaun grumbles at Marcus, probably annoyed because he knows he can't bring up Vixen's Lodge in front of him or the others. Not until we've talked, at least.

"I'm ok. Bad sleep last night. That's all." It's not a total lie. I had a terrible fucking sleep last night.

"Wanna come over to my place after the exam? We can have a sleep date." Marcus presses his lips against my ear, but before I can respond, Garrett's deep tone beats me to it.

"I'm spending the afternoon with our girl today."

Marcus stiffens behind me before his arms drop from around me. "Is that so?"

I spin to face him. "Sorry. We can have a different night together. How about Monday?"

"Monday?" He frowns, his dark eyes boring into my soul. "What about Sunday night?"

I shake my head. "I can't. I have a family thing on Sunday night. But I'm available Monday night." *You fucking liar, Rhys!*

He tips his head back and sighs. "Fine, but you're coming to Simon's tomorrow night when you get back, right?"

"Dude, you wanna back off a bit?" Shaun hisses over my shoulder, and I sigh.

FML!

"You wanna mind your own business, Bossi?" Marcus grits between his teeth, and I drop my shoulders, feeling defeated.

"I can't do this right now. Talk later." I walk off, passing Simon as he approaches, his smile morphing into a frown.

"Where's our girl going?"

"Ask Grady!" Shaun snaps, and that's all I hear as I zone them out and go in search of anyone other than someone I'm fucking.

As I approach Tillie and Bell, the teachers start ushering us into the stadium, so I remain quiet and look around for Tyler, needing to lay eyes on him, but he's nowhere in sight.

The exam is a bust. I failed it deliberately. All I wrote is that there is protein in semen, and then put my pencil down. I can't do this. I can't sit in this room and think about school stuff when it feels like the sky is crashing down on me. I feel like I'm suffocating, and I don't know how much longer I can hold my breath.

By the time the exam is over, I'm a fucking mess. I'm shaking. My heart rate is skyrocketing. And I'm on the verge of showing everyone my inner turmoil.

As soon as I pass through the inner doors of the stadium, I turn right and head in the opposite direction of where the students are being ushered out. A teacher calls out to me to come back, but I ignore him, pushing my legs until I'm running. I don't really know where I'm going until I reach Tyler's office on the second level and burst through the door.

The room is empty. He's not in here. Where the fuck is he?

"Kitten?" Shaun puffs behind me. "You gotta get out of here. The others are looking for you. They can't find you in here."

"Where is he?"

Looking over his shoulder in the doorway to see if anyone is coming, Shaun turns back to me, frowning. "I don't know where he is. Let's go. We can call him or something."

I nod. "Yeah. Ok."

I glance around his office again, noticing his gym bag on his chair. My legs move before I realise what I'm doing, and I find myself rummaging through his bag, and I pull out his t-shirt. It's a red soccer jersey with white lettering. I bring it to my nose and inhale, his scent seeping into my airways, reminding me of how his strong arms feel around me and how his lips tease mine open with little effort.

"Kitten. We have to go." Shaun whispers in my ear. I didn't even hear him approach, too wrapped up in fawning over Tyler's belongings. Then, like a stalker, I quickly shove his jersey into my bag.

Shaun's brows hitch, but he doesn't tell me to stop, instead standing guard by the door until I join him. We run off down the passage side by side, my hand in his. Before we round the corner to where I know there's a horde of students, he tugs me into an alcove and pushes me against the wall. His eyes bounce between mine, studying me as he grips my shoulders. Then he leans in and presses his lips to mine. I welcome his invasion, needing it as much as I need oxygen right now.

Shaun Bossier always seems to be around when I'm falling apart. He's seen me at my worst, so it's not surprising he can sense that things aren't good for me right now. I'm so lost in the kiss and this emotional rollercoaster that I don't even realise I'm crying until he pulls back and wipes my tears away.

"Talk to me, Rhys. Please. Don't keep whatever this is in. It's killing me to see you hurting like this."

A sob escapes, and my legs give way, sending me south to the cold linoleum floor. Shaun follows me down, keeping his arms around me, not willing to let me go, and I hold on to him, feeling like if I let him go, I'll sink into a black hole and never see light again.

"M-master H-Hill is blackmailing me to go back to the Feast with Madam Vik as my sponsor."

Shaun's steel-grey eyes swim with emotion as he takes in my words, so I glance down, not able to look at him as I tell him this next part.

"Part of my new rules is that I spend an hour every Feast with *him*. A-alone." I sob again, tears hot on my cheeks. "A-as his submissive."

"Fuck. No, Kitten."

My eyes dart back up to his, and I shake my head. "I have no choice. If I don't go, he's going to expose Skipper."

"Shit." Shaun hisses, cupping my face. "When did all this happen?"

"L-last night. He demanded that I go there. He had me put on some lingerie and go to the back door. I thought Madam Vik would be there, but she wasn't. Just him and me, alone in that house."

Shaun jerks back. "Did he hurt you?"

I shake my head, my eyes travelling back down as I remember the lap dance, my stomach turning over in disgust.

"What did he do?" Shaun demands, and I take a moment to compose myself before answering.

"He... made me give him a lap dance until he came in his pants."

I gag.

Shaun shifts back, eyes wide, looking at me, and I gag again, knowing I'm about to lose the half piece of toast I had for breakfast.

Moving quickly, Shaun slides across the floor to the alcove opening and reaches around the corner to grab the bin, returning to me in time to catch the first wave of my vomit. Tears burst from my eyes as I retch and retch, my stomach muscles constricting with each action as my body fights to expel my darkness. It's no use, though. I'm tainted. I'll never be free of this. It's embedded in me forever.

"Shit! Is she ok?" Simon's voice registers, followed by Marcus'.

"Fuck, Rhee." His scent wraps around me as I feel his hand rub my back, and slowly the retching eases.

I sink back into Marcus, puffing from overwhelming exhaustion, my eyes falling shut as it takes over.

"Are you gonna tell us what's going on?" At Garrett's voice, my eyes fly open, thinking he's talking to me, but his eyes are trained on Shaun accusingly.

Shaun doesn't respond but looks at me, so I save him.

"I'll be ok once tomorrow is over."

I want to say, and Sunday, but I can't tell them about returning to the Feast. Going back feels like I'm cheating on them. I never thought I could be monogamous. I know it hardly seems monogamous when I'm fucking five different guys, but if they know and are happy to share me with each other, and they are the only ones I'm interested in spreading my legs for, that must count for something, right?

Garrett frowns at me, probably knowing I'm lying, so I admit to a little more.

"Also, I don't know what's happening with Ty, and it's kinda messing with my head. I haven't been able to see him or talk to him, and I feel…" Tears burst free again, and I need a moment to bite back my fucking sobs. "I feel like he's going to end things with me."

There. I got it out. It's the truth. I do feel that way. I feel like things with him and I are over, and I'm just waiting around for him to confirm it. It's torture if I'm being honest with myself. Fucking torture.

Suddenly, I'm surrounded by four guys, engulfing my personal space on the floor in the alcove, arms and chests pressed against me in a cocoon of love.

"You don't need that dirtbag, Rhee. You have us." Marcus bites out, and Shaun snaps back at him.

"That's not helping, dude. She fucking cares about him as much as she cares about each of us."

A moment later, Marcus mutters an apology from behind me.

I want to say it's ok, but I can't talk right now. All I can do is feel.

We stay huddled together for a while before I reluctantly tell them I'm sweating. The guys back off, giving me space and air, and Garrett hands me a bottle of water to rinse my mouth out with.

I feel a little better after opening up to them, even if I had to hold back on some information, so when I mention I'm hungry, the guys tug me up, and the next thing I know, we are catching the bus into town where we invade Macca's for some cheeseburgers.

It's nice doing something so normal, going to McDonald's with some friends. There are other kids from our school here, filling their faces and lazing about at tables with nothing better to do. We choose a table on the opposite side of the restaurant and are soon filling our bellies with Macca's goodness, which, I have to admit, does lift my mood.

"Cherry, do you know what time you'll get back from Melbourne tomorrow?" Simon looks nervous about asking me that question. I smile and squeeze his hand, which is sitting in the centre of the table.

"I should be back before dinner. You'll all be at your place, right? Waiting for me?"

He grins. "Yep. Waiting for our Queen."

I blush.

Their queen. I love it when they say that. It makes me feel worshipped. Not used like every other guy has made me feel. I know the difference now. It's what Garrett has been working so hard to show me.

"Your Queen, huh?"

They all nod, grinning back.

"So that means you worship me, right?"

"Fucking oath." Simon declares on behalf of the guys, my smile stretching wider.

"So, when I come over to your place tomorrow night, you will all worship me? Together? At once?"

Marcus' brows shoot up to his hairline, Simon's eyes widen before he nods frantically, Shaun grins like he's picturing it in his head, and Mr cool, calm, and collected Garrett gives me a lazy smirk.

Leaning back in my seat, I study each of them for a moment more before I nod. "I think I'd like that."

"Hastings, please tell me your mum won't be home," Shaun asks, looking to Simon for confirmation.

"She said she was going to have a girl's night with some of her fake friends. I don't care if she comes back mid-fucking, though. I'll do about anything to piss her off right now."

Marcus and Garrett shoot each other a look across the table before Shaun speaks from next to me.

"I was thinking about your living situation. You know we have an empty staff boarding house above the man shed at the farm. I can ask my old man if you can stay there. Meal and board in exchange for help on the farm over the summer and after school and weekends next year. It's nothing fancy like your fucking palace, but it's clean, dry and warm."

We all look at Simon to see his face drop, a serious expression that I can't read taking over his face.

"You'd do that for me, bro?"

"Fuck yeah, I would." Shaun declares. "And if the old fucker says no, then I'll hide you there and sneak you food until you graduate next year."

Simon moves so fast that I don't have time to get out of the way before he launches himself over the tabletop, dragging Shaun in for a hug.

"I fucking love you, man." Simon's words bring tears to my eyes. But I'm not the only one.

"This is fucking beautiful." Marcus looks up at his friends in awe, and Garrett nods.

"All this bro hugging is getting me horny." I grin. "How about you show your affection for each other in another way?" I wag my brows as Simon and Shaun break apart, both grinning down at me.

"Would you stop trying to get me to fuck my mates?" Shaun whines, and I shake my head.

"Nope. It's a fantasy of mine to see you bury your cock in one of their arses."

"My arse is out of bounds!" Garrett growls, and I giggle.

"Don't knock it until you try it, Gaz," I smirk at him, and he rolls his eyes.

"I reckon I'll try anything once." Marcus declares, and we all fall silent for a beat.

"Fuck, man." Shaun looks at his friend like he's grown two heads. "Only a week ago, you were having trouble dealing with sharing our girl, and now you're open to trying anything?"

Marcus shrugs. "I have desires too. It's just taking me a while to be ok with sharing them with my fucking mates."

"I have such a lady boner right now," I admit, and their heated gazes turn to me. "I wanna know about all your desires. Even the darkest, kinkiest ones." I shift in my seat as Kitty lets me know she is wide awake.

"Ok. I have a desire to watch you come right here in front of everyone." Marcus reveals, and my eyes widen.

"Like, come noticeably, or only so you four know? Because they are two very different things." I point out, and a slow smile spreads across Marcus' face.

"Let's just keep it between us." Grinning, he crosses his arms over his chest in challenge.

"And do *you* want to be the one to make her come or one of us?" Shaun asks what I'm thinking, and Marcus shrugs.

"You'll do, Bossi. You're right there next to her, and I know Cole is still a Rhys virgin, so I won't force him to do it until he's ready. He's got a good view, though, so that will be torture enough."

Garrett is sitting on my other side, and I feel him angle toward me before speaking.

"I'll do it."

My head snaps to him, surprise contorting my face. "What? I thought you were waiting."

He shrugs. "I have been waiting, and now I want to try out third base before I snag that home run later today."

My belly flips. In a good way.

"You mean… I'm gonna meet your dick later? Like properly?"

He smirks, and fuck, it's the hottest smirk I've ever seen with the way his icy-blue eyes darken and his dimples cave in. "You'll meet it, but we'll see what you can handle. You might still be healing."

"She handled my dick the other night, didn't you, Cherry?" Simon winks, his face mischievous, wringing a stupid smile from me before Marcus speaks.

"Dude, your dick is like a puppy compared to his monster."

Simon shoots Marcus a glare, but I turn back to Garrett.

"I can take you." I don't know if I can, but fuck, I want to. I need to erase all memories of last night and table my worries for tomorrow's events. There's no better way to do that, in my opinion.

Leaning forward, Garrett claims my lips in a searing kiss that holds the dirtiest of promises. I'm so ready to find out how Garrett Cole fucks. How he looks when he comes undone. Gripping the lapels of his school blazer, I tug him to me, moaning into his mouth when his tongue darts in.

"Save that shit for behind closed doors," Marcus growls, and Garrett slowly breaks the kiss, leaning his forehead against mine.

"I'm dying to touch you, baby girl."

"Then do it already. Make Marcus' fantasy come true and make me come, right here, right now." I send Garrett the challenge, and he leans back, smirking.

"Lift your skirt up. I wanna see you."

Oh yeah. I like this version of my big guy. Demanding and honest.

Since we're in the far corner of the restaurant, there aren't many people over here, and my lower parts are hidden by the table and Garrett's hulking frame. Shifting a little, I slip my hands under my skirt and slowly slip my knickers down. It's not until they pass my knees that Garrett and Shaun realise what I'm doing, and once I slip them free of my feet, I ball them up in my hand and toss them at Marcus' face.

I'm expecting him to cringe away or toss them back, but the dirty fucker fists them, holding them to his nose, and inhales deeply.

Kitty weeps.

"Give me some of that." Simon whines, snatching at the fabric, but Marcus frowns at him, holding it back.

"You can sniff them, but keep your hands off them. They're mine."

"Whatever." Simon shrugs and points his nose towards his mate. Then Marcus holds them against his nose, and Simon inhales. Loud, like he's snorting a fucking line.

"Fuck, I'm hard," Shaun admits, and I grin at him.

"Thor's awake, Cass?"

"Awake? No, he's raging." Shaun looks almost pained as he speaks, and we all laugh.

"You haven't done as I've asked yet, baby girl." Garrett's deep voice draws my attention again, and I bite my lower lip as my anticipation builds.

"Oh shit. He's a demanding fucker, isn't he?" Simon acknowledges, but I shrug.

"No more demanding than Simon Says."

"True that." Simon chuckles, and I return my gaze to Garrett.

I wanna see his eyes when he sees my Kitty again. Slowly, I do as he asks and drag my skirt up, exposing Kitty's lips to the air-conditioned air. His eyes flare a little, anticipation making him more excited than I've ever seen him.

Licking his lips, he shifts a little closer. "Spread your legs wider, baby."

I push them apart wider, but it's not enough for him, apparently, because he grabs my leg and lifts it over his knee, while Shaun does the same on the other side, opening me right up.

I glance over to Marcus and Simon to see them stand a little, taking a peek at my exposed Kitty over the table, both their eyes heating and igniting the blood pumping through my veins. As they sit back down, they adjust their dicks, and it makes me feel powerful.

"Rhys," Garrett whispers in my ear. "Don't make a sound."

I bite my lip, turning to look at him as his hand snakes across my tummy and down towards my ache. Then, my breath hitches as Garrett Cole touches my needy Kitty for the first time.

A whimper escapes as he glides his fingers through my folds, getting acquainted with me, and each time he passes over my nub, I arch up, seeking more.

"I'm so turned on, Gar. I'm not gonna last long."

He chuckles against my ear and stops teasing me. His fingers press against my clit in skilled movements that make me wonder who exactly he's practised this with. It's a thought for later because thinking right now is impossible as Garrett glides his fingers lower through my folds to press against my opening.

"You want me in here, beautiful?"

I nod, whimpering again, panting with so much need that if he doesn't finger fuck me soon, I'm going to scream.

"How many fingers?"

"Four." I pant, giving in to my filthy Kitty, who's craving a good stretch just thinking about being impaled on Garrett's cock later.

"Fuuuck." Shaun hisses next to me. "He has big hands, Kitten. Are you sure you want four?"

"Yes. I'm so fucking ravenous. Please fill me up, Gar. Make it sting."

"I'm gonna come," Simon admits, and I dart my eyes to him.

"Do it. That will turn me on so much."

Garrett chuckles next to me as I watch Simon nod eagerly.

"I love how filthy you are, Rhys. But I have to wonder, will you be able to handle my level of filth?"

Oh my god, his voice and words turn Kitty wild.

"Fuck Gar. Finger now!"

My words are nearly a yell, and Marcus laughs, glancing over his shoulder to see if we have anyone's attention, but I lose all train of thought when Garrett's fingers, four of them, nudge at my entrance. As he eases them in, my slickness making it really fucking easy, he works this thumb over my clit while whispering next to me.

"Have you ever been fisted, baby?"

I moan.

"Have you ever had someone push their whole fist past your resistance and completely destroy you?"

I'm so close, my walls already clamping tighter, sucking his four fingers in past his knuckles. He's not thrusting. That would be too obvious to anyone around us, but he doesn't need to. I'm about to break.

"I'm about to come." Simon grits out, rubbing over the hardness in his pants.

"Yes." I breathe, lifting my pelvis to grind against Garrett's hand.

"Would you like to feel my fist deep inside you, baby girl? So far in, that I'll be able to touch every single pleasure point inside you?"

"Yes," I growl right as Simon's face twists and he jerks in the seat. Then I convulse.

Slapping the back of my hand against my mouth, my eyes widen as Garrett wrings my orgasm from me, my teeth digging into my flesh in an attempt to be quiet.

It feels like I ride each wave for hours, but it's only seconds, and when it finally ends, I sag back, flopping my head on Shaun's shoulder.

"That was better than I ever imagined," Garrett whispers in my ear as he slowly draws his fingers out of me. "What do you think, Grady? Did that hit the right spot?" Garrett holds his hand up, separating his fingers to show my wet stickiness coating them.

"Fuck yeah, it did. I wish it was Saturday night already."

"My, how your tune has changed, Grady." Shaun grins, grabbing hold of Garrett's hand and licking one of his fingers.

"Oh, fuck." I hiss, my energy suddenly restored at the sight of Shaun licking Garrett's oversized finger.

"She liked that." Marcus grins, a level of playfulness I've never seen shining through.

Then, Simon stands, grabbing Garrett's hand and practically deep throats Garrett's middle finger.

"Ok. I'm ready to go again." I grin, uncurling my legs from Shaun and Garrett's knees.

The guys chuckle, and Garrett offers a finger to Marcus. I have no idea what he's going to do since he's been nothing but a surprise today, but instead of licking Garrett's finger, he takes my knickers and wipes the last two fingers clean.

"This is for later when I jack myself off into your panties, Rhee, which means you're going home commando."

Chapter Thirty

GARRETT

H olding back any longer was impossible. Am I pissed off that the first time I touched her weeping pussy was in a fucking restaurant in front of the other guys? Well, yeah, a little, but then again, it was hot as fuck. I walked out of Macca's with a wide gait, like I'd just spent a week on horseback when, in fact, my dick was as stiff as a board, and my nuts felt like they were filled with lead.

The bus trip back to Rhys' house wasn't all that pleasant either. Her eyes were pools of lust as she looked at me, her cheeks flushed and her breathing long and ragged like she imagined me inside her the entire trip. It didn't fucking help that I knew she didn't have any panties on under her school skirt, either.

Fuuuck!

"We probably have about an hour and a half before anyone gets home," Rhys explains as I follow her up the path that leads to the front door of her house. It's in a new estate. There's no garden, just fences and a pile of dirt, the house a mix of brick and render looking brand spanking new. "So, if it's ok with you, I'll take you straight to my room and give you the tour later."

She looks back over her shoulder, her black lips tipping up in a cheeky grin as she reaches the shiny black front door.

"Sounds good to me." I grin back, and fuck me; the flush on her cheeks darkens. I've never known her to be a blusher until recently. It's a good thing, I think. It means she's feeling things in a different way. Like she's more emotionally involved.

Rhys keys in a number on the digital lock, and a moment later, the door clicks open. That's some fancy shit. No one in my neighbourhood has anything like that, although it's a good idea. Maybe I can get one for our house before my old man turns up from prison. That'll keep the fucker out.

Following my girl inside her house, the first thing I notice is all the white. White walls, white floors with the only other colour, a light grey. It's stark and clinical yet has a really fresh feel to it. It's also fucking bright, holding a glare that the dull yellow-tinged walls of the Millhouse my family lives in just can't compare to.

"Yeah, so, my olds are still decorating. They couldn't decide on colours, so they went all white. It's boring, but it's clean." Rhys explains, walking down the passage, past a room that has theatre seats in it, and into an open kitchen living zone.

"You have a nice house, baby girl." So nice that I feel outta place. Like I might dirty it up just by standing in here.

Rhys turns back to me again, smiling and gestures her head to keep following her, so I do, my eyes dancing over the white stone bench tops in the kitchen. It's not as big as Simon's kitchen, but it's fucking nice. My mum would love this kitchen. She'd spend hours in it baking for my sisters and me. I hope I can buy her a house like this one day.

Rhys turns right, down another passage, and I hurry to keep up, following behind as we pass more doors before we find ourselves in another living area. It's messier than the rest of the house. Toys and cushions on the floor, with childish artwork, stuck haphazardly on the walls.

"This is the kid's zone. We have our own living area, but as you can see, the twins have taken over." Rhys gestures to the walls and kicks a toy dinosaur out of the way as she crosses the oversized room to go down another passage. This one is short with three doors coming off it. "My sister's room is that one. The middle door is the bathroom." Rhys gestures to the doors before turning to face me as she leans back against the last door, which has a sugar skull sticker on it. "And this is my bedroom."

Mischief fills her brown eyes as she reaches behind her and opens the door, stepping backwards into the room. I grin and follow, my heart rate picking up in anticipation. I've had blue balls for weeks hanging around Rhys, jacking off whenever I can to ease the pressure. It's been hell. Agony. I needed to hold back, though. I wanted to show her that there's more to relationships than sex. I think my sacrifice has worked, and now, I'm going to reward myself by giving in to the primal need I have to claim this girl once and for all.

Closing the door behind me, I notice it has a lock, so I flick it before turning back to see Rhys peeling her blazer off, her eyes still trained on me.

"We really gonna do this?" She asks, her dark eyes travelling down my body as I dump my school bag next to hers and work my blazer off, too.

"You tell me, beautiful. Do you wanna do this?"

She nods instantly and with over-exaggeration. "Fuck yes. I've dreamed of this moment, Gar. I'm desperate for it."

"Are you healed? I don't want to hurt you. Not like that anyway."

Her brows shoot up as she unbuttons her shirt. "You don't want to hurt me *like that*? But you *do* want to hurt me?"

There's no fear in her tone. Only curiosity, which is something that draws me to her. If anyone can handle me, it's Rhys George, so I shrug and unbutton my shirt, too.

"Pleasure and pain can go together. I guarantee you'll feel more pleasure than pain."

Rhys stills, her hands falling from her last button, her shirt hanging open to reveal a hot pink bra underneath.

Fuck, have I revealed too much too soon? I was sure she'd be able to handle me.

I'm about to backtrack when a grin slowly quirks her lips. "What sort of pain are we talking about? Are you into spanking? Maybe a little whipping? Hot Wax, perhaps?"

There she is.

"While all of those things sound like fun, sometimes I like things a little more… painful." I bite my lower lip as I step toward her, noting that she doesn't back away. She's not scared of me or my intentions. If anything, I can see how excited she is by the way her brown eyes darken, widening with a flare of anticipation.

Reaching down, I take her hand and lift it in between us, my eyes darting to the bloody indentation of a bite mark on the back of her hand. "This, for example, really turns me on."

I glance up in time to see her eyes dart from her hand and back up to my face. "My bite mark?"

"Yeah." I shrug, brushing my thumb over the raised welts. She did it to herself when I made her come at Macca's earlier. Her way of keeping quiet, I guess. "Especially this part." Using my free hand, I point to the tooth mark that clotted a little where she drew blood. I watch as her brows draw together, her eyes zeroing in on the graze. "Does it hurt?"

"Uh. Not really." She's a little breathless. Maybe I've taken it too far. Is she scared? Wondering what the fuck sort of monster I am, perhaps? There's only one way to find out.

"Can I taste you?" Her lips part as I raise her hand higher, bending down a little to hover my lips over the back of her hand.

"You wanna taste my blood?" Her voice is a whisper as her eyes dart from my lips to the back of her hand.

"Yes, baby girl. I wanna taste your blood."

She's silent, her hand trembling slightly as I lean in closer. I could be freaking her out right now, but something tells me that if I slide my hand between her legs, she'll be soaking.

"Yes." She finally whimpers, and I close the distance, darting my tongue out to lick over the raw graze on the back of her hand. She moves towards me, drawn like a moth to a flame, unable to turn away from the danger.

The metallic taste of her blood dissolves on my tongue, not quite enough for what I truly desire, yet enough to show her I'm a little fucking freaky. That alone has my cock nearly bursting through my pants.

"Fuck Gar. I never knew I was into that." Rhys' tone is dazed as I lift my eyes back to hers and stand tall again.

"Do you like biting?" Lowering her hand, I reach forward and draw her shirt off her shoulders before pushing it down her arms. "Or being bitten?"

"I've been known to bite on occasion. The only bite I've received is a love bite, though. As you may remember, when Marcus busted Shaun and me."

I chuckle, "Yes, I remember." I drop my arms as Rhys reaches up to help me out of my shirt, returning the favour. "So, no one has sunk their teeth into your creamy flesh before?" When she shakes her head, I swallow my fear and ask what I really want to know. "No one has made you bleed on purpose?"

A mischievous grin spreads her black lips wide, her white teeth making an appearance as she looks up at me. "Garrett Cole, are you into blood play? Do you wanna break my skin open and make me bleed?"

I knew she would get me.

"Yes. I was hoping you'd let that be a part of this master role we spoke about."

Her face falls. "Actually. I've changed my mind about that." Rhys goes to turn away, but I step into her space and grip her hips, tugging her against me.

"Don't hide from me, baby. What's happened to make you change your mind?"

I can see it in her eyes. She's scared. Of what, I don't know. Is she scared of me? That I'll take it too far? Abuse my power as her master? She has to know I would never do that.

"Let's just say I've had a bad experience with a master, and I don't know if I can hand over my control like that."

She's obviously not going to tell me the full story behind this sudden change of mind, but her explanation is enough for now.

"I'll never betray your trust, Rhys. We can make the rules up as we go if you like? It doesn't have to be a typical Dom and sub thing. I'll never force you to do anything you don't want to do or treat you in a way that's humiliating." Releasing my grip on her hips, I cup her face instead. "Fuck, baby. I care about you so much. I only want to make you happy." I lean in and kiss her tenderly, reminding her she's in the room with me right now and not some other fuckwit from her past that has treated her like a vessel for their dick. She relaxes into the kiss, winding her arms around my middle and tugging me closer.

The kiss quickly moves from tender to heated, something I didn't mean to happen and probably has everything to do with the fact that her bra clad tits are pressed against my bare chest. My dick wants me to maul her. Throw her down and drive myself home. Luckily, I have a fucking heart. That motherfucker is reminding me that my girl has been through a lot. She may be well versed in the world of sex, but she is brand fucking new to the relationship world, and I want to make sure she wants to be kept.

I break our kiss, pulling back to see her lids pry open with reluctance.

"I do like telling you what to do, though, Rhys. That day in the school bathroom, while you were in the stall, you let me instruct you on what to do with your hand. With your fingers." I lift her hand to my lips, kissing the very fingers I'm referring to. "I fucking loved telling you what to do, knowing it turned you on. That's all I want, baby. To turn you on so bad that it nearly sends us both crazy."

"Garrett Cole. You're sending me crazy now. Can we fuck already? Pleeease?" Her begging is sexy, and I can't help but smirk.

"Fine. Get naked. Completely naked. Not a scrap of clothing."

Her white teeth flash as she grins and does a little excited jump before quickly removing her uniform. As I watch, I remove my uniform, too, taking more time than she does because I'm too damn busy raking my eyes over every inch of creamy skin she has on display.

When I'm down to just my jocks, her eyes widen, honing in on my bulge. "I've dreamed of this moment, Gar. Of finally getting to touch your monster cock." Her eyes flick up to mine. "I'm starved for it."

I smirk. She's a little fucking minx. That's what she is.

"You think you can handle it?"

"If I can't, I'll fucking learn. I'm not letting you get away from me, Garrett Cole. Not ever."

That right there is why I'm here right now, about to finally get that home run. She's ready for a relationship now. She understands the concept, and she's all in. And she's mine.

"Take my jocks off," I demand, and her eyes flare in excitement. Without another word, she drops to her knees and quickly tugs down my jocks, her eyes trained on my cock when it springs free. She doesn't make a move to touch it, just looks at it, grinning. "How much do you think you can get in your mouth?"

Her eyes fly up to mine, wild with excitement. "Let's find out." She grins, waiting for me to respond, and I can't help but grin back.

Nodding, I gesture my head for her to go ahead, and a moment later, she wraps her little hand around the girth of my dick. Her fingers don't meet up, of course, but that's ok. Just the feel of her gripping me is enough. Something I have dreamed of and pictured so many times as I've fucked my own hand in the shower. This is so much better. So, so much better, especially when she leans forward and runs her tongue around my tip, the hot silky feel nearly sending me over the edge already.

"Fuck, your tongue feels good, baby." I groan out, and her hand starts to move, pumping my cock. "Open your mouth."

Deep brown eyes glance up through dark lashes as Rhys drops her mouth open, moving closer until the wet heat wraps around my tip and slowly sinks in. My moan is loud in her bedroom as she takes me as deep as she can, half of my dick disappearing inside her mouth, feeling so fucking good that I'm scared I'll come any second.

Like the controlling arsehole I am, I grip her head, slowing her movements so I can get a handle on my reaction to her. Rhys George has other ideas, though. I may have control of her head, but she controls her tongue, and fuuuck, she works it up and down my shaft with the movement of her mouth like she's trying to milk me.

"You're gonna make me blow too soon if you keep doing that, baby. Back off a bit."

Even with her mouth full of my dick, I can still tell by the way her eyes brighten that she is smiling right now. Does she back off? Fuck no, she doesn't. The little brat increases the pressure of her tongue.

"Fuck." My fingers dig into the side of her head, holding her still. "Stop, baby. I don't want to come yet."

Slowly, she slides my cock from her black lips with a pop, darting her tongue out to lick up her drool before speaking. "Come on now, Big Guy. You have more than one load to give me, don't you?"

"Fucking hell." I hiss, not able to hide my grin.

"I'm thirsty. If you give me a drink, I'll let you bite me."

And just like that, I'm thrusting my dick back between those smart black lips. She fucking knows my weakness and used it against me. I'll make her pay for that after, but for now, if she wants a fucking drink, then I'll give her a fucking drink.

She gags as I overthrust, and I instantly feel guilty. I'm about to apologise until I see the flare of arousal in her eyes. Did she like that? Being choked by my cock? I overthrust again, testing the waters, and even though she gags, she also fucking moans. That's all the encouragement I need. With every third thrust, I overdo it, and each time she gags, moaning louder. Her hand pumps me faster, and I know I'm not gonna last, so I give in and let myself lose the control I've been holding onto. The knowing tingling in my nuts ignites like electricity, zapping to my cock as a heatwave of pure ecstasy rolls through my body, shooting from my dick and down my girl's throat.

"Fuck! Rhys!" I growl loudly as I try to keep my lids open so I can watch her reaction.

She gags again as her mouth overflows with my cum, but she doesn't back off, taking it all as if she really is parched for my seed.

I'm still panting, sweat rolling down my spine as she slowly eases my dick from her moist hot mouth, using her fingers to wipe up the trail of white jiz running down her chin.

"Well, that was a mouthful." She grins up at me, and I throw my head back, laughing. "You taste good, Big Guy. I may have a little lockjaw, though." She moves her jaw from side to side, bringing her hand up to massage it.

Her teasing eases any guilt lingering, and I tug her up, slamming my lips into hers. I don't care that I can taste my cum in her mouth. I've tasted my own seed before. Every guy fucking has. Don't believe them if they say they haven't.

She wraps her arms around me, one leg cocking up to wrap around my upper leg. Her heat instantly presses against me. I could so easily slide home right fucking now, my dick's engorgement not easing as if it knows we are nowhere near done yet.

Stepping forward, I grip her hips and lift her as we tumble onto her bed. She moans into my mouth as our tongues clash, my body pressing her into the mattress, her pussy grinding up against me with need.

I tasted her blood before, but now I want to taste her pussy. I want her to fucking consume me, overfill my senses, and own my dark soul.

I roll us, maneuvering myself under her, keeping our lips locked as we go. I slip my hand between our bodies to cup her heavy tit, my thumb flicking over the nipple, causing her to arch into me, moaning again.

"You feel fucking perfect, baby." I rasp out as I break our kiss, her lips travelling down my neck as she rolls her cunt over the length of my cock.

"I want you inside me, Gar." She pants, but I dig my fingers into her hips, holding her in place. She lets out a little gasp, and even though she tries to hide it, I can tell it's not a gasp of pleasure.

I just hurt her.

Gripping her arms, I push her back and look into her eyes, trying to figure out what I just did.

"Did I hurt you?"

She shakes her head. "No." She leans forward to kiss me again, but I push her back.

"Rhys. I hurt you. I'm sorry. I didn't realise." I must have gripped her too hard, yet it didn't feel like I did. Maybe I don't know my own strength.

Shaking her head, Rhys ignores me and tries to kiss me again. She's trying to divert my attention, trying to preoccupy me with sex. It would work, too, if I was any normal prick, but I'm not. I know when something isn't right with her, so again, I push her back and rise up on my elbows, causing her to straddle me. A flare of anger washes over her face, but I ignore it and move my eyes down her perfect creamy skin until I find faint bruises tainting her normally flawless flesh.

There, on her hips, are what look like fingerprints bruised into her skin. Frowning, I try to remember if I did this to her. If I had gripped her so hard that it would cause a bruise, it would be too early for them to be showing. Red marks, maybe, but not this. No. These were here before today.

"Who did this?"

Glancing up from the marks, to her face, I can see a storm of emotions wash over her. I can't read her right now. She's angry, yeah, but is she angry at me or whoever left these on her body?

She shakes her head, shifting to move off me, but, nope, I'm not having any of that. I sit up quickly, wrapping my arms around her back and pulling her back down onto my lap.

"Don't run from me, Rhys. I'm on *your* side, remember?"

She huffs. "Can't we just fuck Gar? It's been a long time coming, and I'm feeling way too emotional to miss out on having you today."

Well, that breaks my fucking heart. I'm not insulted. She's right. It has been a long time coming. It's her admittance that she's emotional. She likes to play tough. She's been struggling lately but doesn't easily admit to it. If I hadn't just found bruises on her body, I would assume her emotions are due to what she has to do tomorrow. She's going to a prison to visit the man who took her innocence. To face him and try to get more information about this Julie bitch that is blackmailing her. Sure, tomorrow's events are probably adding to her worries, but I'm fairly certain those bruises are today's worries. Probably has to do with how she was after the exam this morning when she fell apart.

I could ask Bossi what the fuck is going on, because I get the feeling he might know. Those two have a bond because of that fucking sex club, and they both keep the secret of this other guy Rhys has been seeing.

Shit, was it Tyler who put those bruises on her?

"Did Tyler do this? Did he hurt you?" I growl, not able to hold in my anger.

"What?" She pulls her head back to look at me better.

"Those bruises on your hips. Did he put them there? Did he hurt you, Baby? Is that why you were so upset this morning?"

She shakes her head, tears pooling in her eyes. "Ty would never hurt me. Well, he might hurt me, but in a good way, just like you."

I frown at that. "He likes to hurt you, too?"

"More like punish. A bit of a spanking does me good." She smiles and winks, and I can tell she thinks she diverted my attention again.

"So who left those marks, baby girl?"

Tipping her head back, she sighs. "I'm losing my boner, Gar."

I can't help but fucking grin. "Tell me what I want to know, and I'll make you come on my face."

Her head darts back to me, eyes wide with temptation. "Fine, I'll tell you. But no more questions. I just want to be with you in this moment, Cole. Can we do that?"

"Tell me *with* an explanation that I won't need to ask more questions about, and you have yourself a deal."

She rolls her eyes and sighs. "You drive a hard bargain."

I chuckle.

"I got the bruises last night when I went to see Master Hill at Vixen's Lodge. He summoned me there. Gave me no choice but to go. He made a deal with me that, obviously, I need to speak to you and the guys about, but I just can't handle that this week with everything else that is going on. Then, he demanded I give him a lap dance. He had clothes on, don't worry. But he was the one to bruise me. Gripped me too tight." She shudders, and now I kind of wish I hadn't asked because I want to fucking smash up everything in sight. "No questions, remember? That's what happened. Now, can you please help me forget?"

And there it is, the part of her that uses sex to deal. The only difference is that now, she comes to me or one of the guys, and each of us will do anything to help her through her pain.

I fall backwards, dragging her with me while claiming her lips. Her stiffness lessens as she relaxes into me, melting into the kiss. I slide my hands down her creamy skin, over the curve of her arse, where I squeeze those cheeks, pressing her to me. We both moan into the kiss at the friction, and I know if I don't move her off my cock that I'll be blowing again soon.

"Move up and sit on my face, baby."

Sitting up, Rhys smiles down at me, her eyes narrowing. "Be careful what you ask for, Mr Cole. Make sure you say what you mean."

I chuckle because I know what she's referring to. "I said sit, baby, and I *mean* sit."

There's that pink flush in her cheeks again. Fuck, I love seeing it. I love knowing she is feeling more than just the need to fuck. She feels more than arousal. She feels a little vulnerable, and the fact she trusts me with that means fucking everything.

"Ok. If that's what you mean." She bites her lower lip, kneeling up and shuffling herself up my body. I help her, lifting her as she goes, helping her clear my chest while she rises up over my shoulders. Placing her knees on either side of my head, she hovers her dripping cunt an inch from my mouth, her sweet scent engulfing me.

"Fuck my face, baby. Don't stop until you come and drown me in your juice."

She moans, licking her lips as she looks down between her perky tits, down the length of her body to meet my eyes.

"Pinch my arse hard if you can't breathe." She pants, and I nod.

"Yes, baby. Of course." Not able to wait a moment longer, I dart my tongue out, running it through her slick folds. My dick jerks as her sweet taste drips into my mouth. I'm so fucking addicted to Rhys George. Each taste has me wanting more. So much so that I think I'd do anything for it—anything to keep her in my life for good.

Hovering above me, Rhys watches as her needy cunt devours the lower half of my face. Her black lips part, and her chocolate eyes are completely lust drunk as she moves herself back and forth, allowing my tongue to taste her from seam to seam.

"Baby?" I mumble past her hovering folds, and her eyes dart to mine. "Next time you have your period, I want to fuck you until we are all bloody."

Chapter Thirty-One

Rhys

O h, he went there! And man, the idea of him fucking me while I'm bleeding sounds so fucking appealing. It also sounds dirty as fuck. There really is something wrong with me. Something I should probably analyse, yet I don't as I sink down and smother my Big Guy's face with Kitty.

His chin and lips disappear, and his nose presses against my clit, igniting all of my senses. Garrett Cole is a dirty fucker. I knew he liked to be in control. I'd already picked that up. I even had an inkling that he might like it rough, given his aggression at times. He has a dark, angry past that he hasn't fully revealed yet. But dirty. Like filthy. A girl only has so much self-control, and Garrett Cole has taken it all.

I grip the grey cushioned headboard of my bed, stabilizing myself as I move slowly, grinding Kitty against his face. My moans are breathy, filling the room as I watch the lips of Kitty devour his mouth and nose.

Heat washes through me as his words replay in my head.

> *"Next time you have your period, I want to fuck you until we are all bloody."*

I moan again, Kitty leaking more with arousal right into Garrett's mouth. He has no choice but to take it all, and fuck, that turns me on even more. I can feel his tongue fucking right into me, just as hungry for me as I am for him.

I rub myself over his face, covering his nose every now and then, and not once does he let up. It's fucking insane. Surely, I'm suffocating him, but I can't seem to stop. An animal I didn't know was inside me, coming out and taking over.

"Fuck yes." I pant, my muscles tightening as my pleasure builds. "Eat me, Gar."

That stirs him on more, his tongue driving deep, his fingers digging into my thigh, holding me down. With one last grind over his nose, my orgasm hits without warning, detonating as I grind and grind on Garrett's face, my fingernails digging indentations into the fabric of my headboard. It's an intense but short climax, ripping my energy from me quickly.

My legs are shaky as I try to kneel up and let Garrett breathe, his hands assisting me as he licks his lips with a shit-eating grin.

"You nearly made me come. *Again*." He chuckles, and I smirk, puffing as I rest my head on my headboard.

"I will make you come again." I pant. "In my Kitty."

He chuckles. "You mean in a condom, right?"

"Sure." Why does the barrier of a condom bum me out right now? "Do they even make dingers big enough to fit your cockzilla?"

He chuckles again. "Yes, baby. I've got that covered."

Garrett slides out from under my legs, and I flop down on the bed in an unattractive limp heap. Watching him, he moves to his bag and takes out a foil packet, holding it up and waving it. I'm paying it no attention, though. How can I when that monster dick is looking at me like that? All drooling and excited and good enough to eat. There's no way it's not going to hurt. He's big. Bigger than the girthy dildo I used at the Feast night. Bigger than Big Jim. Fucking hell. Is he part horse?

I've never been scared of a dick before, and I don't think I normally would if I hadn't been hurt recently. There's a real chance this is going to hurt, something I should care more about, yet I don't because all I want is to be closer to Garrett. I want to share this with him. I want to feel consumed by him, and if that means pain, then I am there.

"What are you thinking right now?"

His voice startles me. I was so in my own head that his deep rasp sounds louder than it really is.

"Are you part horse?"

He laughs, shaking his head, his brown curls bouncing down over his icy-blue eyes. "Not that I'm aware of, but if you'd rather not go there, we don't have to, baby."

He's standing at the end of my bed, not shy about his nudity. I'm pretty sure I'm in love with him, just like the other guys. I don't know how I know that, other than this overwhelming need to be close to each of them in a way that sex doesn't even achieve. I can't explain it, yet I feel it.

I shuffle on the bed, moving myself to lie back, parting my legs so he can see all of me, just like the other night at Ebony Falls.

"I want you to take me, Gar. I want you to fuck me just the way you dream of doing and don't stop until you've filled that condom."

He growls, moving quickly over me, hovering his lips over mine. "Be careful what you say, baby. You may not like the way I like to fuck."

I grin. "Those books you read, are they vampire romances? Is that why you want to bite me?" He growls at my words. "You want to drink my blood while you fuck me, Gar? You want to fuck me so hard that I nearly pass out?" I'm egging him on. I can't help it. All I want is for him to consume me. Completely.

He growls again. "I don't want to hurt you."

"Yes, you do. You said as much earlier. Don't lose your nerve now, Garrett. I'll tell you if I need you to stop. Otherwise, give me everything. Bite me. Make me bleed. Drink it. Destroy my Kitty." I lean up and bite his lower lip, dragging it through my teeth. "Fucking own me, Mr Cole."

With one last hissing growl, Garrett slams his lips into mine in a biting, fevered kiss. He breaks it to tear open the condom wrapper with his teeth and then claims my lips again. I can feel him trying to put the latex protection on, so I blindly reach out, helping him slide it over his thick girth, and once it's on, he positions himself between my legs, breaking our kiss again and leaning up on one arm.

"Make sure you tell me to stop if it's too much." He hisses, and I grin.

"If you hear me say Cactus, then you stop."

"Safe word?" He asks, frowning, and I nod. "Ok." He glances down between my legs as he runs his cock over my clit. "Are you wet, baby?" He answers his own question when his fingers slide through my dripping folds. "Fuuuck, yes, you are."

"Wet for you, Mr Cole." I tease, and he moans.

"I fucking love hearing you say that."

"What? Mr Cole?" I ask, and he nods.

"Yes."

"Well then, Mr Cole, can you please fuck me now?"

Grinning, he leans down. I think he's going to kiss me again, but he ducks his head and claims my nipple instead. As it pebbles in his mouth, the thickness of his cock slides through my lower lips, teasing me.

"Spread your legs wider, baby," Garrett demands after releasing my nipple before blowing on it, causing it to harden almost painfully.

I spread my legs wider, my heart pounding in nervous beats as I anticipate the pain to come. There's no way this won't hurt. He's got a giant dick.

You can do this, Kitty. It's everything you've ever dreamed of.

Am I talking to my pussy right now? Hell, yes, I am. She needs to fucking relax.

Claiming my other nipple, I arch my back, pressing my nipple further into the wet heat of Garrett's mouth, trying to turn my brain off and just feel. As his tongue flicks and his cockzilla nudges my opening.

"Remember at Macca's earlier?" Garrett asks, forgetting my nipple momentarily, his blue eyes locking with mine. "When I pressed my fingers into you for the first time?"

Kitty pulses at the memory.

"Yes."

"Remember how much you wanted four of my fingers?" He starts to slowly sink inside me. "How you sucked them in greedily?" I whimper, the ache between my legs becoming fevered as his fingers move down between our bodies to press lightly against my clit. "Remember how I asked you if you have been fisted before? You hadn't, but you liked the idea. Remember that, baby?" He sinks in further, and I nod, holding my breath, desperate to be filled. "You wanted to feel a fist push past your resistance? Spread you wide? Fill you more than you have ever been filled before?" I relax back, and his fingers work circles over my clit, letting him sink in deeper, past the very resistance he's talking about. "That's it, baby. Take all of me." With one deep thrust, Garrett sinks all the way in.

There's a bite of pain, but it's gone before I can think too much about it, replaced with pleasure as his fingers pick up the pace. Then he starts to move.

Oh, dear motherfucking God. YES!

"Fuck Rhys. You feel like heaven." Garrett presses his forehead to mine, his thrusts long and torturously slow, yet addictively intoxicating.

"Bite me." I rasp, peering into his eyes, desperate to be totally consumed by him.

He growls, nostrils flaring as his thrusts get faster.

"Make me bleed, Mr Cole."

I see the moment his control snaps, his icy-blue eyes darker than I've ever seen them, his teeth bared like the animal he is. Garrett starts slamming into me hard, his nostrils flaring as he watches me from above. It's hard to keep my eyes on him with the pleasure building deep in my core, but whatever he sees sends him right over the edge.

Ducking down, Garrett's lips kiss a trail down my neck as he continues thrusting, his tongue darting out to lick the curve of my neck before his teeth sink into my skin. A burn of pain flares through me as my skin breaks, only lasting a moment as his fingers circle my clit and his cock destroys Kitty.

I lose myself then, animalistic grunts flying from my mouth with each slam of Garrett's hips, my legs wrapping around his pelvis, my feet digging into his arse, urging him to go harder.

"Yes!" I cry as my orgasm gets closer, my entire body straining, reaching, running towards it with desperate need.

Releasing my neck, Garrett rears back, his expression pained as his own pleasure builds. There's blood smeared across his lips—deep crimson coating his teeth as he bares his teeth.

"So good." He growls, and I can't help myself. I lean up and claim his lips.

I immediately taste my blood on his tongue, and I surprise myself when I suck his tongue like it's his finger.

That's all it takes before Kitty starts squeezing and my core detonates. I tear my mouth from his, throwing my head back as a scream I've never heard myself make, rips from my body. Blinding pleasure like electricity shoots right through me.

I clamp my own teeth down on something, and a moment later, I hear Garrett's grunts as he comes hard. I want to open my eyes so I can see his come face, but it's no good. I think I'm actually blind.

"Fuck baby." Garrett pants, his weight heavy as he collapses on me. "You can let go of my shoulder now."

My vision returns then, eyes widening as I feel the skin of his shoulder in my mouth. I fucking bit him, too.

Whoops!

Releasing his shoulder, I notice my bite mark didn't pierce his skin. Disappointment rushes through me for a moment. I would have liked to taste his blood, too... and where the fuck did that thought come from?

"I'm going to hell," I mutter, and he chuckles.

"Why's that, baby?"

"I was just disappointed that I didn't make you bleed," I admit.

Again, he chuckles, leaning up to stare down at me. "Looks like we are going to hell together, then." He grins before slowly easing out and moving off the bed.

I flop back, starfished, sated and thoroughly fucked. Garrett Cole was worth the wait. I can't wait to have me some more of that fine specimen.

"Come here." Garrett's voice draws my attention, and I look up at his bloody face as he stands over me in all his naked glory.

Grinning, I take his hand, letting him help me up off the bed, and he leads me over to my mirror.

"Look at us." His words urge me to look at our reflection. We are a fucking mess. Besides the fact that my buns are nearly falling out, and my mascara has run. Both of our mouths are coated in red, sticky blood. We look like something off a vampire movie, and it looks fucking hot.

I grin. "You're perfect, Mr Cole."

He grins back, but then we both nearly jump out of our skins when someone bangs on my bedroom door.

"You'd better hurry up and get your fucktoy out of your bedroom, Rhys. Will is on his way home with the twins."

My eyes widen at Charlotte's voice. Fucking hell. How long has she been home?

"Ah… I want to live, so I'm gonna do what she said. Whoever that was." Garrett spins away, moving to his clothes.

"Thanks, Char!" I call out and move to find my own clothes, deciding it's best and less suspicious to put my school uniform back on. I mean, my parents know me too well. They're probably gonna assume if I have a boy over that I'll get up to no good with him, but I don't want Garrett to feel uncomfortable.

"That's my older sister, Charlotte," I explain, tugging on my skirt.

"Will is your old man, right?" Garrett asks, concern laced in his tone.

"Yeah, but you don't have to worry about him. He's a good guy." I slip my bra on and remember that I wasn't wearing panties when I got home. Marcus has them.

Fucker.

I move to my drawer and get a new pair out.

"Yeah, until he thinks I've been screwing his daughter."

I giggle. "Honestly, Gar. You have nothing to worry about." I step into my panties, turning to see Garrett's eyes watching my every move as he buttons up his shirt.

"If he shoots me, I want you to know it was worth it. You're worth dying for."

"Shit Mr Cole. That's some heavy shit."

He grins. "It's the truth." Then he sits on my bed to put his shoes on.

I sit next to him, grinning to myself as I do the same, before slipping my shirt on.

"I need to get cleaned up before your dad thinks I killed you and ate the evidence."

I throw my head back, laughing, standing from my bed as I button up my shirt. "Come on then, Mr Cole. Let's get you cleaned up."

He stands from the bed smirking at me, and I unlock my door, swinging it open, only to come face to face with Charlotte.

"Fucking hell. That was one session you guys had."

"Jesus Char. Creeper much?"

She grins, her eyes darting over my shoulder to where Garrett must be.

"Oh wow. You're a big guy. No wonder my little sister was screaming."

"Fuck Char. Leave him alone." I push her shoulder, nudging her out of the way.

She backs away, grinning, holding her hands up as we pass by, and I open the bathroom door for Garrett. "You clean up first."

As I hold the door open for him, he glances briefly at my sister before moving into the doorway. He stops, turning back to me, and drags me against his chest to press his lips to mine. It's a short kiss, yet still makes my heart do a stupid flip, and when he pulls back, he grins and shoots me a wink.

I lean against the door when he closes it and glare at Charlotte, who is still hovering.

"You got a little blood…" Char points to my face, and I roll my eyes.

"I know."

"Should I ask?" She grins.

"Nope. Nunnofya."

She rolls her eyes this time. "You like him, huh?"

"Yes," I admit without hesitation. Well, that's new. I don't normally tell Charlotte that sort of stuff.

"So, is he one of your boyfriends?"

I stiffen. "How do you know about that?"

She grins like she knows all my secrets. "The olds were talking about it the other night when they thought they were alone."

"You are fucking creepy, always eavesdropping on conversations." I frown, and she shrugs. "Wait… How much do they know?"

She shrugs again. "Something about the day Marcus smashed up the office and some teachers dobbing on your lack of discretion with a group of boys in the schoolyard. And in class."

"Damn. I didn't know they knew that much."

"So, how many guys are we talking about exactly?" She wags her brows, and I frown.

"Again… Nunnofya."

She smirks. "I like this side of you, but…" She cringes. "I don't want to *ever* hear you fucking, *ever* again!"

I grin, loving how much that would have annoyed her to hear it. "Next time, how about you go for a walk and not be a creep sitting outside the door to listen?"

"I had to make sure you were done before I interrupted. I don't want you to kill me in my sleep."

The door swings open behind me, and I almost tumble in, but strong hands grip my shoulders, keeping me steady. "Your turn, baby girl."

While I clean myself up, Char takes Garrett to the theatre room and puts on a movie. I don't realise until I get there that she's skipped halfway through, so it seems like we've been in that room the whole time watching it. Sneaky bitch.

Dad arrives home with the boys not long after, and the twins make it their mission to annoy the fuck out of us until Mum gets home with dinner. I'm almost sure my dad put them up to it.

I hold Garrett's hand as I lead him to the table, which is filled with Chinese takeout. He's so quiet. So different from the guy that made me ride his face earlier, but he's polite and has impeccable manners, answering all the stupid questions the twins ask him.

"Do you like the crusts on your sandwiches?"

"Do you snort out your boogers or use a tissue?"

"Do you sometimes fart when you run?"

And the kicker... "Do you have sex with Rhysie?"

Fucking hell. That last question has my dad slamming his hand on the table like a fucking caveman, and the twins turn bright red, fogging up their glasses before they both start crying.

"Good one, Will." Charlotte hisses, getting up from her seat and moving around the table to the boys. "You know that's a trigger for them."

Dad huffs, downing his glass of water while staring at his half-eaten plate of food.

"Dad didn't mean to scare you, boys." Mum gets up from her chair, moving to the boys too, shooting her husband a sympathetic look. "You really shouldn't ask anyone that question, though. It's very personal and private. Ok?"

The twins sob through their agreement, hugging my mum and sister while Will looks regretful.

"Ah... Should I go?" Garrett leans over and whispers, so I turn to him and shake my head.

"Please stay," I whisper back.

I know he's super uncomfortable right now, and I should let him escape, but I want to know he can handle the shit show that is my life. I also want the rents to see that things with us are serious. If they know more than they are letting on, then all my guys will have to prove themselves because there's a point that Cin and Will are gonna have issues with me openly seeing more than one guy at a time. What parent wouldn't be concerned about that?

My hand being squeezed tells me that he's not going anywhere, offering me the same sort of support that Cin just offered Will. My heart squeezes because, more than anything, I want that.

"Boys," Will speaks, gaining everyone's attention. "I'm sorry for expressing my anger like that. It was uncalled for." Then he turns his eyes to Garrett and me. "Garrett, my apologies for my outburst."

"Ah, it's fine, Mr Rogan." Garrett shifts uncomfortably next to me, so I turn the attention to me. I'm good at that.

"It's all good, Dad. The twins need to learn that some questions are inappropriate." I pin them with a glare, and they both hunch down in their chairs while Charlotte squats between them. She's very protective of the twins. It's not lost on me that perhaps I need to learn that certain things are inappropriate, too. Like, say, talking to the class about Mickey Juice.

"Sorry." Archie mumbles, and Connor nods, too scared to speak. It's kind of heartbreaking seeing them cower like that. Lasting evidence from their past and something they work on daily to overcome.

Unfortunately, they still have to learn what's right and wrong, and I don't blame dad for losing his temper because I was about to do the same, but he beat me to it.

I watch my dad closely through the rest of dinner. Concern creases his brow, and his mind is too preoccupied to hold much conversation. I can't help but think I am the cause. Aren't I always the cause of the drama that goes on under this roof?

And just like that, the few hours of feeling my old self washes away, leaving a nervous, self-conscious, self-loathing shell behind.

Chapter Thirty-Two

Rhys

The thought of food makes me physically ill. I can't bear putting even a crumb in my mouth, despite my achingly empty tummy. I tossed all night, not able to sleep even after Garrett had left me thoroughly sated with another intense O in the theatre room before his mum picked him up. That guy is fucking amazing with his tongue, fingers and cock. If only it were enough to get me through today.

My right leg has been in a seizing jitter ever since we left Fox Pines early this morning for the long car ride over to the other side of the city where Allansdale Prison looms. The two messages I received first thing really fucking added to my freak out. One of the messages I show to the olds because it's from Julie. The other, I keep to myself because it's from Tyler, and I'm sure the olds would lose their shit over that one. Out of the two, I don't know which one freaks me out more.

Fuck You Julie
If I don't see you walking into that prison today, then you'd better prepare for your school buddies to learn all about Patrice!

Skipper
We need to talk.

Julie's message is just as interesting as it is creepy. The fact that she said if she doesn't *see* me walking into the prison means she'll be watching from somewhere nearby. I thought she was smarter than that. If she's watching somehow, it means she could get caught. Of course, she doesn't know I've involved the cops, so she's not expecting to get caught. Then again, she could be bluffing in the hopes it will force me to attend. Either way, just thinking about her watching gives me the heebie-jeebies.

Tyler's message, though, has me reeling. That line, *we need to talk*, never ever leads to anything good. He's going to call it off with me and put an end to this whirlwind of a secret we've been keeping. It explains why he's been avoiding me. Why he hasn't turned up at school? Fucking hell, he can't even bear to be around me. He must think I'm a pathetic little girl, especially after my less than mature lesson about Mickey Juice in class the other day.

What the fuck is wrong with me? Why do I have to be this way? All I had to do was ignore Tillie's request to teach one of my lessons. But noooo. No way was I letting the opportunity to have all eyes on me pass. Of course, Tyler fucking lost it at me! I'm nothing more than a seventeen-year-old brat of a student that has a fucking lot to learn. Why would he be interested in me? Sure, I can fuck like a pro, and my dirty needs appeal to guys because I'm not a boring lay, but that's about as far as it goes for someone like Tyler Foster. He's a fucking man. Like in his thirties, and I'm a teenager still talking shit like I'm fifteen.

My heart hurts. Like it actually aches. I know I should just try to put Tyler to the back of my mind since I have four other guys, and I need to stop being so fucking selfish. I really wish I could do that. It would make it so much easier to deal with. Especially now as I enter the fucking Allansdale Police Station with my olds. I need to be focusing on what I have to do today, not longing for a thirty-two-year-old man who thinks I'm nothing more than an annoying adolescent.

"Are you sure you want to do this?" Dad asks as we wait at the counter for assistance. I look up into his light brown eyes, immediately seeing the worry.

"Yeah. I do."

He frowns. "I get the feeling you're not coping too well right now, Rhys. It really is ok to change your mind about doing this. The police can try to get more information a different way."

They probably can, but not before my entire school finds out I'm the girl in the video.

"It's fine. I just want to get it over and done with." I offer him an upward curve of my mouth that isn't a smile but also isn't a frown.

"Hi there." Officer Zimora's voice gains our attention as he walks through a door off to the side, holding out his hand to my dad. "Mr Rogan, Mrs Rogan." He shakes their hands and then focuses his attention on me. "Miss George. How are you feeling?"

"Nervous as shit, to be honest. But, ready to do this." The determination in my voice isn't faked. I am ready to do this. Ready to get this day over with so I can move on.

"Being nervous is understandable." Officer Zimora nods, his dark eyes kind as they offer me sympathy. He's a good-looking bloke, nailing that whole tall, dark and handsome thing. I'm pretty sure Lexi told me he's gay. I bet his partner, Officer Fredricks, is bummed about that. "I got the new message Julie sent this morning. It's very interesting, actually." Jason steps back and gestures for us to go through the door he came out of. I trail in behind my mum while my dad stays at my back, and we are met with several officers talking quietly with each other. "She gave away that she will be watching, so we have to assume she will be in the vicinity somewhere. Either outside or inside. The only photo we have on record of Julie was from five years ago. We have to assume she's aged a little and perhaps changed her hair colour and style, but the Crimes Against Children unit here in Allansdale has created this image of what she might look like now."

Holding up a computerised picture, Officer Zimora hands it to me to study. I instantly want to screw it up and throw it. It looks like her. The same eyes. The same resting bitch face. When my hand starts to tremble, my dad reaches over and takes the image from my hand while mum wraps a comforting arm around me.

"I'm still reluctant to let this go ahead." Her voice is filled with anguish as she directs her comment to Officer Zimora.

"I understand, Mrs Rogan. And this isn't common for us to involve a minor in our attempts to get more information, so we don't ask this of Rhys lightly. There are a number of potential illegal activities at play. Despite the fact that an adult is blackmailing a minor and using indecent videos of a child as the tool, there is also the concern that a prison guard could be involved. Rhys should never have been taken into that private room. The only allowance for that is for immediate family members to meet in private if there is a hardship that needs to be shared, like a family death." Jason gestures to the table, and we all take our seats.

"We need to determine who the brains are behind this stunt. Is it Brian? Is he pulling strings from within the walls, or is it, Julie? Or someone else entirely? There's a long list of other victims that have come forward over the last twelve months across the state, and the only reason we are linking them is because a lady called Julie is blackmailing them. Is it a coincidence? Maybe, but I'll be honest. It's unlikely. We feel strongly that it is the same, Julie. And for some reason, with you, she is bringing Brian into the equation, not just as a background threat."

"What assurances can you make that Rhys will be safe? Your email stated that we would have to wait here at the station while she goes on a bus to the prison." My dad's voice rises with each word as his anger comes to the surface.

"I will be with Rhys."

We turn to see Officer Fredricks walk into the room, dressed in plain clothes.

"Today, I'm just Dana, going to the prison to meet my pen pal lover." She shoots me a wink before glancing at my parents. "I will be one of six undercover officers in the facility today, and just like all of us, Rhys will wear an audio recorder and a camera."

"Isn't that dangerous? What if she gets caught?" Mum's voice is high pitched, showing her worry, so I reach up and cover the hand she has resting on my shoulder with my own.

"The devices are small and practically untraceable. Besides, there will be enough of us there to run interference. They won't expect a child to be wired up."

"I feel like I'm on an episode of FBI or something." I mutter, and Dana grins.

"Rhys, I want you to know that we will be there every step of the way. Even if we aren't in the same room, we will be nearby. We'll be able to hear everything you say and what he says, and the video feed will be streamed onto this screen," she gestures to the sidewall, "where your parents can watch and hear everything."

"What if something happens in the room while she's alone with that monster?" Mum starts to cry then, yet her question has the opposite effect on me. It's like a layer of armour moulds over my heart, and I stand a little taller.

"I can handle Brian, Mum. Don't worry about that. I'll get him to talk." I was going to say I'll do what it takes to get him to talk, but thought better of it. Cin and Will don't need to know that. Once I'm there, all they can do is wait and watch.

We go through different scenarios as I get wired up, and the undercover officers gear up. Then I go through the gruelling process of trying to break free from Mum's arms when she changes her mind and doesn't want me to go. Thankfully, Dad sees my determination and pries Cin away, and I leave them behind to catch the bus.

Dana sits behind me on the bus, and I notice that not all officers get on the bus, only a couple of them. I use the time to go over things in my head before my phone rings with an incoming video call from Cherry's Merry Men on Snapchat.

For the first time today, I smile.

Fumbling with my EarPods, I quickly connect the call, and the screen lights up with Marcus, Shaun, Garrett and Simon's smiling faces.

"Hey, Kitten. Just checking in before your visit." Shaun grins, looking relieved to see me.

"Nawwww, thanks, guys." I grin, trying to keep my voice low, so I don't draw too much attention from the other bus travellers.

"Did you get much sleep, baby?" Garrett asks, and I shake my head.

"Nope. I'll sleep tonight."

"You're still coming here tonight, right?" Simon asks, practically pushing the other guys out of the way, so his hazel eyes fill my screen.

"Of course I am. I'm gonna need you tonight, Sy. I'm gonna need all of you."

It's true. I really will need them tonight. Last time I visited Allansdale Prison, I turned up at the Feast night uninvited with no mask. It was a huge mistake. Reckless. If I'm going to be like that again, I need to make sure I'm around people I trust. And I trust those guys more than any other people on this earth.

"We'll be here waiting for you," Simon assures me right before Marcus snatches the phone and walks off with his mates complaining in the background.

"Are you ok, Rhee? Like really, ok? Because it's alright if you're not. This is big shit what you're doing today."

I smile. "I'll be ok. Hearing your voices and seeing you guys helps. A lot."

"I wish you had let one of us come with you. It doesn't seem right for you to do this alone." His expression turns pained. He really does wear his heart on his sleeve, my Marcus.

"I'm not alone, and I'll be ok. I'm more worried about how you will get through the day without pulling your hair out."

He grins at my comment before Shaun snatches the phone back.

"Grady will be fine. Simon will cuddle him for you until you get back. Ok?"

I nod. "Ok, I'll feel better knowing that."

He grins and winks, and the slight smile I was wearing falls from my face as I spot Garrett in the background, looking grumpy.

"Ah… Cass." I whisper, and he leans in.

"What?" He whispers back.

"I mighta' told Gar a little about going to the *Hill* the other night." I know Dana is behind me listening, so I'm trying to be vague. Luckily, Shaun understands. By *Hill,* I mean visiting Master Hill.

"Yep. He told me. Has lots of questions that I said we will answer tomorrow."

I nod. Why is everything so fucked up? With Julie and Brian and Master Hill and Tyler, I don't know how much more I can take.

"Sorry."

He grins. "He bribed you with his monster cock, didn't he?"

"Maybe." I grin and Simon hoots in the background, earning him a punch in the arm from Garrett before Shaun pulls the phone in so close that I can see up his nose.

"We should let you go." When I nod, he continues. "Remember that I love you, Kitten. We all do. Come home safe, ok?"

My eyes turn glassy as his words soak through that invisible armour I put on earlier, and I realise just how powerful having love in your life makes you. This world can try to beat me down all it wants, but it won't win. I will keep getting up and fighting back because love is worth fighting for.

The rest of the bus ride is event free. I don't feel as nervous as I did the last time I came here. I know what to expect now, and I'm prepared.

I follow behind the other passengers that get off the bus, strolling up the path that leads to the Prison's entrance. There are cars filling the parking lot too, and I see some of the undercover officers get out of different cars.

I really do feel better knowing they are here, knowing I'm not alone. I should have gone to my mum after that first voice message, but fear and shame controlled me—something I don't want to bow down to anymore.

My eyes dart around at every person, every car, wondering if Julie is here amongst the crowd forming. I look for her brown eyes, knowing I will recognise them if she's here. They are closer together than the average person and bulge, too big for the size of her face. I remember thinking she looked like a stunned frog when I was younger.

A message alert pops up on my phone from Officer Zimora.

JZ
Cameras and mics are now live.

Sickening butterflies turn my tummy as reality sets in.
You can do this, Rhys.

The urge to turn and run is overwhelming, just like the first time I came to visit. Unlike the first time, though, I have eyes watching over me. Ears listening. I'm not alone this time. I thought I'd be more mortified about people knowing, but I'm learning if it's the right people, it can be empowering. Even though my guys aren't here with me today, it's settling to know they are together right now, waiting for me to return to them, ready to give me the support I'll need.

We line up for about five minutes before the visitor's entrance opens, and the visitors start to move inside. I hold my breath through the scanning process, almost certain the corrections officers will find the button camera I'm wearing. They don't, though. Everything runs smoothly, and before I know it, I've put my bag and phone in the locker, signed the register, and I'm sitting on the hard plastic chairs with my right leg having a seizure again.

"Calm down. You'll be fine." Dana's voice is a whisper as she passes me and sits a few seats down. I don't look at her, but I'm able to track her in my peripheral, reminding me I'm not alone.

We wait another ten minutes before a guard announces for everyone to line up to enter the visitor's lounge. Just like last time, I get in line, and just like last time, someone calls out, "Patrice George."

Stepping out of the line, I run my hands down the thighs of the black jeans I'm wearing and make eye contact with the guard. It's the same guy from last time, and he gives me a nod, recognising me and waiting for me to approach.

This is the part my mum has the biggest problem with. Knowing I'll be alone when I go down that hall and into the room. I'm strangely ok with it now that it's happening. I'm actually eager to see Brian's face. Knowing I'm gathering evidence against him feels like a big secret fuck you to him, and I'm on board with that.

Following the guard, he leads me down the passage to the same room I was in last time, and I fidget with the frayed denim rip in my jeans at the top of my thigh as I wait for him to unlock the door. His keys clang as he puts them in the lock, and a moment later, he swings the door open, holding it wide.

"No touching, and stay on your side of the line." The officer repeats the same sentence he said last time, and I nod, making a point to look him in the eye this time. His eyes are dull and lifeless and don't seem sinister. Either he's really fucking good at hiding, or he's not the guy that set up the visit for this room. He's probably just following orders.

Sucking in a breath, I step inside before the door swings shut, and I face my old foster dad, who looks exactly the same as my last visit.

"Patrice. How lovely to see you again."

His voice grates on my nerves, and I bite back the shiver of dread that wants to roll up my spine just from hearing his voice.

His hands are in cuffs again, resting in his lap, and just like last time, Brian gestures to the empty chair in front of him. Keeping my face neutral, I move to the seat on shaky legs, easing down as I keep my eyes trained on him, noticing the way his eyes roam over my body.

"I'm disappointed, Patrice. No skirt for me today?"

"Nope. So why am I here? Your bitch of a wife won't get off my case about coming to visit you."

He frowns, rolling his tongue before responding. "That's no way to speak about your foster mum."

"*Not* my foster mum anymore. I have a real mum now. One that loves me the right way. A dad too."

Brian's nostrils flare, and his face goes bright red. He didn't like hearing that.

"I loved you the *right* way, Patrice. No one has ever treated you as good as I did. Remember how I made you feel? There's no better feeling than that."

I want to gag, but I inhale deeply through my nose instead, not wanting him to see my reaction to his vulgar point of view.

"Why did you love me that way, Brian? Everyone tells me that's not the way a dad should love his child. So why did you do it?"

"It *is* the way a dad loves his child, Patty. It's the way my father loved me. He always made me feel good, especially when I was down or after I got punished. He only wanted me to feel better, just like I did with you. Those other people have brainwashed you. They are jealous of what we have. Not every parent knows how to be a good one, but I do, and I knew it was right when you loved me back just as fiercely."

I don't want to hear this. My blood feels too thick for my veins. Like I'm about to choke from deep inside my skin.

"Where's Julie? She's been sending me messages and making threats. Blackmailing me into coming here. Why?"

"Because I wanted to see you, Patrice. I told you last time. I'm dying." His skin looks a little greyer today. Is it bad that I want him to drop dead right this very minute?

"Yes, but what does Julie get out of it? What has she *ever* got out of it?"

He frowns. "Can't her love for me be enough? She wants me to be happy before I leave this earth."

I shake my head. "Nope. That's not it. Does she like to watch? Is that it? Because she has a video of you and me together. Did you know that?"

The slightest smirk flashes across his face before he manages to hide it. I wonder if the button camera picked it up.

"You really want to know this stuff, Patrice?"

"Yes," I sit forward on the chair eagerly. "I really *do* want to know."

"Fine, I'll tell you if you lift your t-shirt up for me. I'm surprised to see you dressed so casually. It's not like you to wear clothes that aren't easy to get into."

My eyes narrow. "How would you know that? You've seen me twice in the last five years."

"Oh, Patty. I've had eyes on you for years. I'm your father. Of course, I kept an eye on you."

I bolt out of the chair with my fists clenched at my sides and step forward. "You are *not* my dad! Stop saying you are!"

Brian stands then, wrists chained together as he steps forward to put his toes on the line that divides the room.

Shit. I thought he was restrained to his chair.

"I will never stop saying it, Patty. Ever. You are mine! I knew the moment I held you in the hospital the day you were born that I'd never love anything more than you."

"What!" I flinch back, my head trying to make sense of his words.

"Your mother tried to keep you from me, but she couldn't hide. I found her each time she ran. I tried to reason with her. I made an offer I thought she wouldn't refuse. All she had to do was hand you over, and I would make sure she had all the money she needed to feed her drug addiction, but the bitch wouldn't give you up, Patty. I had to take matters into my own hands." He steps over the line, and I back up, shaking my head, not wanting to hear what he has to say.

"It was so easy. She was known to sell her body for drugs, so no one would think twice about finding her dead from an overdose. It all fell into place after that. Your other foster parents were money hungry. A simple money exchange and they made your life hell, allowing the social workers to step in and remove you from them. Julie helped me each step of the way."

What? He paid my other foster parents?

"Stop! You're lying!" I step back again, needing to put distance between us, but my heels hit the chair, and I collapse back into it.

"I'm not lying, Patty. You are my daughter. I am your biological father, and we were always meant to be together." He looms over me now, grinning like this is the happiest fucking day of his life. "Julie was the perfect partner to help convince Child Services we were the right people to take you in. She was just as excited to have you with us. Sure, she was nasty to you, but she had to be that way in order for you to trust me. Every time we went into the playroom, Julie was behind the mirror, watching to make sure I treated you just right. Sometimes she would tell us what to do. Do you remember that?"

I blink rapidly, my lower lip wobbling as memories rush in.

"She loved watching us so much that she used to record it. It really meant a lot to her that we shared our time together with her."

"You're sick," I mumble, tears streaming from my eyes as Brian leans down, his face hovering mere inches from mine.

"Yes, I am sick. I have cancer. I am dying, and I want time with you before I die. Now be a good girl and lift your shirt for daddy."

I want to smack him in the face. Scream. Punch. Kill. But first, I need to know about Julie. Just a little more. I don't know any other way to get the information from him other than going along with him. Making him think I care about him.

I fight really fucking hard to hold in the need to shiver, and I prepare myself for what I have to do.

"Daddy?" I whimper, nearly gagging at the innocent tone I use to reel him in. I fucking hate using the word I use with Ty.

His face softens, and he smiles, crouching down in front of me, his hands lifting to take hold of mine in my lap.

"Patty. I've missed you." His pupils are dilated as he looks at me excitedly.

"I don't want you to die." My tears are real, but my words are a lie. I want to gut the fucker right now.

Reaching up, he strokes my forehead before moving to fiddle with the hair tie holding in one of my buns.

"Take this out for daddy. Let me see that beautiful hair of yours."

I hate the thought of doing this, yet relief washes over me when I do as he asks, and he moves back to give me room.

"Will Julie look after me when you're gone? Will she care for me the same way you did?" The lies I speak are fucking hard to make convincing, but I keep the sweet innocence in my tone, knowing it will help. "I don't want to be alone anymore. If I can't be with you, then I want to be with her."

His eyes flare wide with excitement, and he smiles. "Julie will be so happy to hear that. She's been watching you closely. She loves you just as much as I do."

I want to laugh because that's the funniest shit I've ever heard.

"I want to see her. I miss her so much. Is she here?" I look around dumbly as I tug out my buns and start running my fingers through my long, dark hair. Fucking hell, he can't honestly think I'm this gullible, can he?

"She's not far. She lives and works nearby. Maybe you can stay with her and come and see me a couple of times a week? That's my dying wish, Patty, to spend time with you."

"Ok. I can do that. What's her address? I can go and see her after I leave here. I don't have to go back to my foster family. I hate it there. They don't understand what I need. Please don't make me go back."

"Oh, Patty." He brushes his fingers through my hair, lifting it to his nose and inhaling. "Julie will be so excited, but for now, you will have to return to your foster family. I'll need to speak with Julie first. Make sure she has room for you. She has a very full house these days. She helps runaways. Helps homeless girls get off the streets. She's doing great work."

I really fucking hope my mic is still working, and the cops have got all of this info.

"Patty, our time is nearly up." Brian's face falls. "I feel so unwell. Please help me feel better. Can I touch you?"

With every fibre of my being, I want to scream NO! I want to punch and kick and end his existence, so it takes everything in me to hold in the bile burning up my throat when I give him the slightest nod.

The colour fades from the room, the saturation dulling as my mind and body go numb. I don't really feel the way his hand slips between my legs and cups me over my jeans or the way his hands travel up my baggy t-shirt to find my bra. I don't even feel the press of his lips against my neck as he grabs my hand and slides it down his pants.

The moment the door handle clicks, my hearing rushes back in like a lightning bolt. I flinch just as Brian leaps back before the door swings open, and the prison guard steps in, yelling at Brian to get back behind the line. The room quickly fills with corrections officers as I leap up from the chair and flatten myself against the back wall, watching with satisfaction as Brian gets slammed to the hard concrete floor.

Chapter Thirty-Three

SHAUN

N ever has a day felt as fucking long as this day has. Knowing my girl had to face the very man who stole her innocence while we sit here at Simon's just fucking waiting around is pure fucking torture. I should have insisted that one of us go with her. I don't know what the hell we could do, but just being there for her would be better than waiting and not knowing what's happening.

"It's nearly 4pm. Surely we should have heard from her by now. Why isn't she responding to our message?" Simon has been pacing for the last hour. He hasn't touched his beer or any of the food he set out. He just keeps fucking pacing.

"Maybe her parents have her phone?" I suggest which wins me a dagger from Simon.

"Maybe she just needs a minute." Garrett offers, and Simon glares at him.

"Or maybe she's still helping the cops. Like a debrief or something." Marcus adds, and Simon throws his hands up in a huff and flops to the floor in the middle of the room.

"I can't handle the not knowing. It's fucking eating me alive." Simon whines, fisting his hands in his hair and tugging at the roots.

"You wanna know what's eating at me?" Garrett hisses, gaining everyone's attention. I glare at him, hoping he's not going where I think he's going. "Why the fuck Bossi didn't tell us that our girl is going back to that sex club."

Yep. He went there.

All eyes dart to me, and if looks could kill, then I'd be dead right now.

"You say that like I've fucking known for days. I found out yesterday morning, maybe a couple of hours before *you* found out. I don't exactly know everything yet."

"How bout you start with what you do know?" Marcus stands from the white leather sofa glaring at me.

"Fine. She went back on Thursday night to see the Master of the club. He demanded her presence, told her she is to return to the Feast nights, and each time she is to spend an hour alone with him."

"Like fuck!" Marcus yells as Garrett storms across the room, his face red, his eyes wild in anger.

"She's not fucking going back there! That fucker humiliated and basically raped her last time! Not to mention the fucking lap dance he forced her to do on Thursday night!"

"What lap dance?" Simon asks, confusion written across his expression.

"Calm the fuck down and back off, Cole!" I hiss as he gets in my face like this is my fault. He steps back with reluctance, and I turn my eyes to Simon. "He was testing her. Made her wear lingerie and give him a lap dance to see if she would comply."

"Why doesn't she just say no?" Simon asks, standing up off the floor.

"He's blackmailing her. Said he will expose Tyler if she doesn't obey." I offer before Marcus grunts.

"Who fucking cares about this Tyler fucker? He sounds like a paedo, just like the rest of them at that club. He has her thinking he cares about her. I bet he's just like the rest of them."

I shake my head. "He's not. He's a decent guy. Once you move past their age difference and see them together, the way he cares about her, you'll understand."

"I don't want to see that shit!" Marcus yells, picking up a cushion from the couch and throwing it hard at the wall. "He's a fucking man, and she's a teenager! It's not right! If he had any decency, he wouldn't let her be blackmailed like this. He wouldn't be such a fucking coward and hide behind her, letting her take the fucking fall."

"Marcus has a point." Garrett agrees, and I sigh, flopping on the barstool behind me.

"He has a lot to lose, and Rhys wants to protect him. My guess is that he doesn't even know about the Master's proposal."

"What does he have to lose? Is he married?" Garrett asks, and I shake my head.

"Not married."

"Is he a cop or something?" Marcus asks, and again, I shake my head.

"Not a cop."

"But he does something that would be considered pretty fucking bad if he was found to be screwing a minor, right?"

Fuck. Marcus is too perceptive.

"Look, what Tyler does isn't the problem. The problem is that the Master has incriminating evidence against both Tyler and Rhys. If our girl doesn't comply, then she will be exposed as well. Is that something you want?"

"Of course, it fucking isn't!" Marcus gets another cushion and throws it, this time at me.

Ducking it, I shake my head. "Look. We need to deal with one thing at a time. We will work on getting her out of that sex club, but right now, we need to be focused and ready to help her through tonight."

"Bossi is right." Garrett turns away from me and moves back across the room to the sofa. "One problem at a time."

"But isn't that fucking sex thing on a Sunday night? Tomorrow night?" Marcus glares at me again.

Shit. I didn't even think of that.

"Look, the one thing Rhys was able to do was negotiate my return with her at the club. She won't be alone. I'll be with her, and if I have to fuck her all night, then I will." I smirk, but the guys don't return it.

"You're forgetting one thing." Garrett hisses, his lips thin in anger. "She has to spend an hour with that master arsehole. You can't exactly fuck her then, can you?"

"Shit." I turn away, hating that he's right. That club was fun while things between all of us weren't serious, but now… now things are so different.

"She replied!" Simon squeals like he's a chick and not a dude. "She said she's on her way back. She'll be here around six."

Suddenly, I feel like fucking crying in relief. Like actually crying. Jesus, she really does have me by the balls. Do I care? Fuck no, I don't!

We are all moody as fuck, spending the next hour in silence, scrolling through our phones, then a little after five, Marcus gets a message from Ayden to say that they are on their way over to Simon's, as requested by Rhys. It's not long before Lexi and Ayden arrive, with Lexi going into mother hen mode, putting on music, pouring drinks and demanding that we perk the fuck up, or she'll kick our arses. By the time Tillie and Bell arrive, we are a beer in and feeling a little less mournful.

As Rhys pulls up out the front of Simon's house, Lexi fills us in that Rhys asked us all there so she can have a night of fun, laughter, and sex. All eyes turn to me and the guys at the last part, with Lexi declaring she'll be gone before that shit happens. Dale, Allister and Jared haven't been invited, which is a good indication that Rhys is worried about her emotions getting out of control.

I'm nervous as shit as Lexi meets Rhys out the front to walk in with her. Rhys hasn't told us what happened today, so we don't really know how to treat her, but as she struts in, wearing jeans, something I've never seen her wear, and one of her Fly-Leaf t-shirts, her vibe is, *let's get fucked up*!

"It's party time, bitches!" She sings as she enters the rumpus room holding up a bottle of tequila.

Where the fuck did she get that from?

"Wooo-hooo!" Tillie squeals. "Shots for everyone!"

"No way. Tonight, we are swigging straight from the bottle." Rhys declares. It takes me a moment to realise that her hair isn't in buns like usual. It's tied up in a high pony, something else I've never seen her wear, and her face is makeup-free. I love her like this, but I can't imagine she went to the prison like that. Did she go home and change before coming here?

"Are you as worried as I am?" Garrett asks quietly as he comes to stand next to me.

"Yep. She's in reckless mode." I sigh, wishing she didn't invite the others over. "But I guess the fact that she's here and not off somewhere else getting herself into trouble is a good thing."

"It's a very good thing." Marcus' voice comes from my other side, startling me. When did he get there?

Simon ignores us entirely, pushing through the girls, walking right up to Rhys. "It's so good to see you, Cherry." She hardly has a moment to realise what's going on before he throws his arms around her, pulling her close. He whispers something in her ear, and whatever it is, causes her lids to flutter closed, her hand to hold up the bottle for someone to take, and her head to hide in the crook of his neck.

Lexi grabs the bottle before it slips from her hand, and they all scatter, moving away to find somewhere to sit while Rhys and Simon stay locked together in an embrace. Simon's top 40 playlist is playing, and when Tillie turns the volume up to Arizona Zervas' song, Roxanne, Rhys and Simon start swaying to the music.

"I feel like we should give them some privacy or something." Garrett mumbles.

"Or join them." I massage the back of my neck, wishing I was the one holding her in my arms.

"Let's get our girl a drink and some food. Let her lead the way tonight." Garrett reasons, and I nod.

"The others are leaving in two hours," Marcus grumbles, and Gaz and I turn to look at him.

"They said they are leaving in two hours?" I frown, and Marcus shakes his head.

"Nope. That's when I'm kicking them out." He storms off before I can disagree with him, moving to his cousin's side to talk quietly with him. He's probably telling Ayden that he needs to get everyone to leave by eight. He's obviously forgotten how much our girl likes to party.

Moving to the table where Lexi placed the bottle of tequila, I crack the lid and take a swig before handing it to Garrett, where he does the same. Then I take the bottle over to Rhys, still locked in Simon's embrace.

"Drink Kitten?" I hold up the bottle when her eyes appear over Simon's shoulder.

"Yes, please." She offers me a smile, reaching up to clasp the bottle, pressing it to her naturally pink lips, tipping her head back to have a guzzle. Now that I'm closer to her, I can see that her eyes are red and bloodshot and a little puffy. She's not crying right now, but she has been crying. And a lot.

When she's had her fill, she pulls back from Simon and offers him the bottle, where he takes his own sip, not quite as big as our girl just did. As he drinks, she reaches her arm out to me, gesturing me forward, and I step into her, accepting her shared embrace with Simon.

"Are you..." Shit, that's a stupid question. *Are you alright?* Of course, she's not fucking alright. Why did I lead with that?

A slight grin tugs at her lips. "I feel so much better now that I'm here with you guys."

Not able to hold back, I press my forehead to hers and sigh, looking into her chocolate pools through both our lashes. "I've been so worried, Kitten. We all have."

"So Simon tells me." She says softly before closing her eyes and pressing her lips to mine. Her lips are warm and fresh with no barrier of lipstick, her tongue tasting of the tequila she just downed.

"You smell so good, Cherry," Simon mumbles close to our heads, and although I'm still kissing Rhys, I pry my eyes open to see Simon nuzzling her neck.

If you had told me I'd be getting up close with my mates and a girl a few months ago, I would have laughed and probably felt really fucking uncomfortable. Now, though, it feels right. Strangely, I don't hate the idea of seeing Simon's bare arse thrusting as he pounds Kitten. Maybe that makes me weird, but it sure as shit makes me perfect for Rhys George.

"You guys gonna let our girl breathe?" Marcus' annoyed tone meets our ears, and I slowly break our kiss to find Marcus glaring.

"What's wrong, Marc? You want in on the action?" Kitten teases.

I can't hide my smirk, and apparently, neither can Simon, because Marcus hisses at him like he's a fucking snake. That guy gives me whiplash. One minute he seems fine with sharing our girl, and the next, he goes all possessive and shit. I get that he's still trying to wrap his head around the idea, but I have to admit, I don't feel like this possessive part is ever going to go away.

"I don't think there should be any *action,* Rhee. I think we need to talk about what happened today." Marcus reaches for Rhys, but her shoulders drop, and she steps away from all of us.

"Just because that's what *you* think, Grady, doesn't mean it's what *I* want. I'm not here to give more pieces of me away. I'm here to get fucked up and take what I need, so if you can't handle it, then perhaps you should leave."

Everyone falls silent. If it weren't for the music playing, it would be more uncomfortable than it already is. I hold my breath waiting for Marcus to explode, hoping like hell that he won't, because then I'll have to kick his arse, but it never comes.

"I'm sorry, Rhee. I'm just so worried about you." His voice is low, his dark eyes filled with pain as he stares at Rhys, who looks like she's about to do a runner. She stays quiet, eye locked with Marcus for what seems like forever, then her face falls.

"I'm a bitch."

"No, you're not." Marcus steps towards her, and she falls into his chest, throwing her arms around his neck.

"Yes I am. I'm sorry." Her voice is muffled and pained, and it stabs the centre of my chest hearing it.

Lexi starts conversation up again behind us, taking everyone else's attention away from us, and Garrett, Simon and I step up closer to Marcus and our girl.

"I don't mean to be pushy. I'm just worried. It's not healthy to keep everything in Rhee, and the four of us want to help somehow."

"I just…" Rhys pulls back, gripping Marcus' shoulders, her dark eyes glassy. "I need to forget for a while."

"Can we compromise?" Garrett asks, and she turns her eyes to him.

"How so?"

"Maybe you can give us a rundown on what happened, and then we can better understand how to best help you forget." Garrett reaches past Marcus and brushes her flyaways back off her forehead.

Her eyes dart frantically between the four of us as she contemplates Garrett's suggestion. It's easy to see that she really doesn't want to talk about her visit to the prison, and if it weren't so important for us to know what's going on, we would just leave it be. The thing is, it's more important than ever that we know what's going on. Not just to give her support, but to prepare for her highs and lows and look out for any signs that she's heading down the wrong path with her choices.

"Ok." She whispers.

I hold my breath. Did she really just agree to tell us?

"Ok?" Marcus asks, and she nods.

"Ok, but I want to get it over with now, and I don't want it mentioned for the rest of the night."

"Of course, Kitten." I catch her eyes as I speak and see her pure discomfort at the thought of talking about today. It's a lot for her to do this.

"You want to go somewhere private?" Simon asks, but she shakes her head.

"No. I need to tell the girls, too."

"Listen up!" Marcus steps away from Rhys and turns to everyone in the room. "Rhys would like to talk to us all about today. Then she wants to forget about it for the rest of the night." He turns towards his cousin. "Can you turn the music down?"

Ayden nods, and Rhys mumbles.

"Is it too late to change my mind?"

Garrett pushes past Marcus, this time to console our girl while we take our seats. I can't hear what he's saying, but it looks caring yet intense with the way he cups her face and looks into her eyes like he's trying to hypnotise her. They stay that way for a couple of minutes, and then he takes her hand and sits down on the armchair, pulling her onto his lap.

"Ummm… ahhh…" Rhys shifts uncomfortably. I think it's the first time she's hated all the attention on her.

"Rhys, how about I ask you a couple of questions? It helps to get things going." Lexi offers, her blue eyes concerned yet determined as she looks at her friend.

"Okie Dokie, Sexy Lexi. Ask me something."

It's hard not to grin at Rhys' playful nature. Even in the face of a conversation she's dreading, she tries to lighten the mood.

"Did Officer Zimora meet you at the prison?" Lexi asks, and Rhys shakes her head.

"No, we met him, Officer Fredricks and the Allansdale Crimes Against Children team at the Allansdale Police Station. Julie sent me another message this morning, and she made a comment about seeing me walking into the prison today, so the cops are working under the theory that she would be somewhere nearby."

"Shit. Was she there? Did they catch her?" Tillie asks, and Rhys shakes her head.

"No, not that I could see. But the cops wired me up with this button camera on the collar of my t-shirt, so I believe they are reviewing the footage in case there's something we missed."

"So you wore the wire thing into the prison?" Simon asks this time, and Rhys nods.

"Yeah. They could hear and see everything that happened. Plus, there were a handful of undercover cops that went into the prison with me." Rhys looks down at the floor then, frowning as she remembers.

"I was alone, though, when I had to go in that room to see Brian. He... ahhh... said something that I kinda hope is a lie." When she looks up again, her eyes are glassy. "He's claiming that he's my biological dad."

Lexi and Tillie gasp while the rest of us stay silent in shock.

Surely not. Surely, he's lying.

"He also claims that he had a hand in..." Rhys stops talking, sucking in a breath as she bites the inside of her cheek, working to control her emotions, "He said he killed my mum. Said he made it look like she overdosed when really he was the one that did it." She frowns, not able to look us in the eye, keeping her eyes trained on the floor. "He said that he and Julie paid off my other foster families to treat me badly so that I'd be taken from their care, and when I was placed with Brian, I was basically easier to groom."

Fucking hell. I'm about ready to punch anything and everything. If he is who he says he is, then how could he have done that to his own daughter?

"I realised the only way for me to get information about Julie was to pretend that I care about him." She shivers at a memory and shakes her head. "So I told him that I want to live with Julie so I could be close and visit him more often. I got him to admit that Julie lives somewhere nearby the prison. He also confessed that Julie has been watching me for years. And that she helps runaway girls by taking them in off the streets."

"Fuck." Marcus growls.

"Fuck's right." Tillie agrees, her pixie face looking flushed in anger. "He… ahhh… got a bit handsy."

"What!" I yell at the same time as Marcus, both of us bolting up from our seats.

"It's fine. I disconnected. I withdrew my mind from the situation, and it was over in a flash because the guards came in and tackled him to the ground. Then an alarm went off, and all the visitors were ushered out of the prison until it was clear for us to go back in and get our belongings."

"You should never have gone there," Garrett growls angrily behind Rhys, but she shrugs.

"Maybe, but we needed information, and we got some, so at least it wasn't a total waste of time."

"Fuck Rhys. What did the cops say about it?" Lexi asks, sitting forward in her seat, her blue eyes glassy with emotion.

"Well, they could see and hear everything, and so could my parents, and when I left and caught the bus back to the station, there was a whole fucking interrogation to go over everything. I mean, they fucking heard and saw it all. I don't know why I had to go over it again."

"Hold up." Ayden raises his hand. "You caught a bus back to the police station?"

"Oh." Rhys' brows lift. "Yeah, in case Julie was watching, we had to maintain our cover. She had to think I went there alone and left alone."

"Do you think he's telling the truth?" Bell asks, speaking for the first time, and Rhys shrugs.

"He seemed to know a bit about my past. So maybe." Rhys shivers then, shaking her head before leaping up from Garrett's lap.

"End of conversation. Now I need to get shit faced. Can we move on to that part now?"

Everyone stays silent, stunned by what Rhys just told us. It's so fucked up what she's had to endure in her life. All because of that Brian fucker. The need to inflict pain and kill is almost overwhelming as my mind flashes with images of that little girl on the video. How could anyone do such heinous things to her?

The volume of the music goes up, and I snap out of my daze to see Rhys swaying her hips as she guzzles down more tequila.

It's hard to understand how she can switch off her pain like she does and move straight into party mode. There's no way I could do that.

Is she avoiding? Is she in denial?

Maybe. But if she needs that for tonight, then I'll fucking make sure she forgets it all.

Chapter Thirty-Four

Rhys

"Soooo… like you're totally dumping me, aren't you? I mean, I *know* I'm not your girlfriend or anything, so it's probably not even classed as dumping, but you know. You've been ghosting me like a total arsehole, and then you sent that message." I roll my eyes and stumble to the edge, looking at the aqua water sparkle over the light at the bottom of the pool. "We need to talk is code for I'm breaking up with you. I might be young, but I'm not fucking dumb, Ty. I'm just another wet vagina to you, aren't I? But hell, what a vagina I have. You'll regret walking away. You know it and your dick knows it. He fucking loves my cunt, Ty. Fucking! Loves! It!" I huff and sink to my arse, nearly tipping towards the pool, but strong arms wrap around me from behind and sink down to the ground with me.

It's then that a sob escapes. "I thought you got me. Like, for real. I honestly thought you and I had this connection. This understanding about my fucked-up-ness. I thought… I thought it was more than sex." The tears fall fast, too fast for my stupid hands to wipe away in time. Why aren't my hands working properly? "Fuck Ty. It hurts so fucking bad."

I end the call, tipping my head back to rest on the chest of whoever the hell is behind me, and toss my phone in the pool.

"Fuck! Rhee!" Marcus leaps out of nowhere into the water, diving down after my phone. He shouldn't bother. I think it's waterproof, but right now, I don't fucking care.

"Kitten." The rumble of Shaun's chest is at my back, and he squeezes me tighter to him. "It's ok. Let it out."

I scream then. Loud. I think. It's hard to tell with the stupid tequila fog messing with my head. But just in case it wasn't loud enough, I try again, screaming until my throat hurts. Then, the screaming doesn't stop.

I scream and cry and break apart into a thousand pieces. It's all too much. It's so much that I don't think I can ever be put back together again. It's so much that I feel like I'm drowning, and I'll never resurface again.

"Fuck. I can't take hearing her in so much pain." Simon's voice is close by. I hate that I'm hurting him right now. I don't want to hurt him, or Marcus, or Shaun, or Garrett. I don't even want to hurt Tyler.

Suddenly, the feel of Shaun's arms is too much. I start to struggle against his hold, needing to break free, needing space to drown in this pain on my own.

"Stop. Kitten, please." He sounds confused, but I can't stop myself from fighting against his embrace.

The moment I get free, I tumble into the icy cold pool, going straight under to sink to the bottom. A thousand pins are pricking my skin, causing me to gasp and suck in water. It rushes in, choking me, and I have a moment to decide if I should panic and fight or just fucking let go and end this crippling pain once and for all.

Make it stop!

I can hear muffled yelling as the water shifts quickly around me. It's my guys. Marcus. Shaun. Garrett. Simon. They are trying to get to me. They are fighting for me.

They don't need to, though, because, in a flash of a second, I decide to fight for myself.

My feet find the bottom of the pool, and I push myself, propelling up towards the surface. Marcus and Garrett are both there as I breach, water flying from my mouth as I cough, desperate for air.

"Fuck! Baby!" Garrett is frantic as his hands grip me under my arms, holding me above the surface.

"You got her?" Simon calls from the edge, sounding just as frantic.

"I'm sorry," I whisper as my teeth start chattering.

Marcus' warm body comes up behind me and pulls me back against his chest. "Let's get you out."

Garrett and Marcus swim me to the steps of Simon's pool, and Garrett takes me from Marcus' arms to lift me into his own to cradle me, carrying me out of the freezing water. A fluffy towel gets thrown on me by Simon, and as I hear Marcus climb from the water behind us, I search for Shaun. It takes me a moment to find him. He's in the shadows of the house, squatting down, his head tipped low with his hands fisted in his hair.

My Casanova looks shaken and devastated.

I did that to him.

"P-p-put m-me d-down." I manage to get out past my chattering teeth.

"No, baby. Let me take you inside to get warm." Garrett insists, but I shake my head, squirming in his hold.

"S-Shaun."

I can feel Garrett's eyes follow my line of sight, and then he eases me down until my feet hit the ground. On wobbly legs, I stagger towards Shaun, falling to the ground in front of him.

"C-Cass."

His grey eyes dart up, holding my gaze with a mix of anger and relief.

"No more." He grits between his clenched teeth.

"N-no more w-what?" I shiver, and his lip curls as he snarls.

"No more giving up. No more thinking about giving up. No more!"

"Hey! Fucking back off, Bossi!" Marcus hisses from behind me, but Shaun just glares up at Marcus as he drops to his knees from his squat.

"No, I fucking won't back off. She needs to hear this. She needs to fucking know how much we care about her. She needs to know that she isn't alone. Fuck! She needs to know that we won't give up on her and that we need her to not give up either."

I've never seen Shaun so angry. Spittle flies from his lips as he shouts at us, his eyes darting between the guys before they settle on me.

"I fucking love you, Rhys! Why isn't that enough?"

"It… it is. I… I had a lapse in judgement, but I chose to fight. I pushed up to the surface… I… I'm sorry, Cass. I'm trying." My shoulders sag. "I'm not used to people caring so much."

"I fucking care, Kitten. We all do. So much." He shakes his head, looking to the ground between us, then draws his eyes back up. "I can't imagine the hell you've been through or what you're going through now. I'm sorry for being selfish. I know you're trying… I just don't want to lose you."

My lip is seizing like a motherfucker now, making it really hard to talk. "I d-don't want to l-lose you either." I look over my shoulder at the other three guys behind me. "I don't want to lose any of you."

One by one, they move in, surrounding me as they lower themselves to the ground, where Shaun and I are slumped.

"We don't want to lose you either, baby." Garrett is the one to speak, and Marcus and Simon nod as their warmth closes in.

"I'm sorry. My head is a mess. The whole Brian is my dad thing, and his admission to killing my mum… and Tyler MIA. Shit…" I slap the side of my head. "I left him a drunk message, didn't I?"

The guys chuckle, my eyes landing on the smirk creeping across Shaun's face.

"Yeah, he's gonna especially love the part about his dick loving your cunt."

The guys laugh, and I tip my head back, groaning at my stupidity. "If he wasn't already planning on breaking up with me, I guess he is now."

"Come on, Kitten." Shaun stands and reaches a hand out for me. "Let's get you warmed up. You can talk to Ty tomorrow when you've sobered up."

Taking his hand, I let him pull me up off the grass. "I think the cold water slapped me sober." I groan, feeling a little sickly.

The guys chuckle and take me inside, where I notice the music is no longer playing, and everyone else has left. I have no idea what time it is or what I've been doing all night, since everything seems like a blur. Hopefully, I didn't embarrass myself too much.

As we walk through Simon's mansion, someone hands me a bottle of water, which I guzzle down as we go, and another towel finds its way over my shoulders. I stumble a couple of times as we make our way up the grand staircase, and by the time we reach a huge bathroom, I'm pretty sure that if I try to find my way back to the rumpus room, I'll get lost.

"Use this shower. We can sleep in the room across the hall." Simon goes to a cupboard, taking out more towels while I gape at the bathroom. I haven't seen this one before.

"Thanks, man." Shaun slaps Simon's shoulder and turns to me. "Let's warm you up, Kitten."

I wish I weren't so drunk right now. I can't seem to keep up with what's going on. Either that or everyone else has been gifted with superpowers and are moving faster than humanly possible.

My clothes get tugged off, my ponytail gets taken out, Shaun's clothes magically disappear, and I find myself standing in a double shower between Garrett Cole and Shaun Bossier.

"Well, if this isn't every girl's wet dream," I smirk, raking my lazy eyes over their taut muscles and defined abs. It's when my eyes find their cocks that I truly turn into a blubbering idiot. "Dick."

Garrett chuckles. "Maybe later, baby."

I pout. "Now."

Shaun chuckles. "You're too drunk to handle dick right now, Kitten."

"I strongly dissssagreeee." I slur. Fuck. Maybe he has a point. Not that I'll ever admit it out loud.

"Bossi is right, baby girl. You can have dick in the morning."

"Boooooo." I do a thumbs down action, pouting again, and all of a sudden feel extremely tired.

The guys pick up on it, closing in to sandwich me between them, holding me up as they wash me and keep me warm. I close my eyes, tipping my head back on Shaun's shoulder, relaxing into their hold, revelling in the feel of their hands on me.

I have no recollection of what happens after that, but I wake up sometime later in a strange room that I've never been in, surrounded by my guys' sleeping forms. With a woozy head, I sit up slowly on the mattress on the floor, pressing my hand to my temple as pain slices through my skull like it's splitting open.

Fucking Tequila!

Bits of last night come back to me as I force my brain to remember. Some parts I wish I wouldn't remember, and others I know I'll want to remember forever.

I glance around at the guys and ease myself to stand, being careful not to annoy Simon or Shaun as I move. I wonder if they flipped a coin to see who would sleep next to me? The thought makes me smile.

I tiptoe out of the room that looks like another living area, just smaller than the others I've come across in this house, and when I reach the passage, I realise that the living room is right next door to Simon's bedroom.

Now I know where I am.

I make a beeline for the toilet, needing to pee bad, and when I'm done, I find myself in the huge bathroom that I showered in last night with Garrett and Shaun. I wish I hadn't drunk so much. I wish I had dealt with my pain better. I don't want to be that person anymore. The one who acts irrationally. The one who doesn't think of anyone but themselves. I hate that part of me. I've always thought that part of me was from the addiction. I assumed I behaved that way because I needed sex so badly that it consumed me.

I mean, it did consume me, but only because I let it. Have I been using it as an excuse to try and cope? To run away from my worries? To hide?

Obviously.

So, am I really an addict?

The question jolts me. I don't know the answer. I have a feeling that I definitely have a problem with sex, but could my so-called addiction to it be all in my head? I haven't felt the desperation to fuck like I used to. Not since… five guys wormed their way into my heart.

Yeah, they give me the sex I need, and yeah, it's fucking epic, but if I had to choose between having them in my life but never having sex again or having all the sex with as many people I want, yet not have them in my life, I would give up sex in an instant.

"Holy shit," I whisper, my eyes locked on the brown-eyed girl staring back at me in the mirror. She is paler than usual. Hungover, with dark circles under her eyes, but her lips are still pink. There's even the slightest pink tinge to her cheeks. Her eyes might look tired, but they look real, no longer hiding behind the mask of makeup. Her long dark hair has a slight kink to it this morning. Probably from going to bed with it wet after the shower. And as I look at this girl, me, the only thing that looks out of place is my septum piercing. Let's not even go into the fact that I'm wearing Ty's red soccer jersey. The same jersey I stole from his gym bag in his office.

Shit. I hope the guys don't recognise it.

What do the guys see when they look at me? The different versions of me? Do they love one version more than the other? I know they enjoy seeing me raw like this. It's something I never thought I'd be comfortable doing, being exposed to them this way. I am, though—more than I realised.

Leaning forward, I slowly take my septum piercing out and lay it on the white marble bench.

"Hi," I whisper, studying my face, really looking at myself for the first time ever. "Who are you?"

Lifting my hand, I run my finger across my cheek, down the bridge of my nose, and over my lips.

"Who do you want to be?"

The question I ask myself takes me aback a little.

As if I have a choice in who I am. That's ridiculous… right?

"Can I choose? Can I change myself just by deciding?"

It's a complex thought, one that has me confused as fuck, because while it's something I want to explore, I realise I'm talking to myself in the mirror.

Fucking hell. I'm really losing my shit.

Sighing, I shake off my inner me and finish up in the bathroom by washing my hands, splashing water on my face, and guzzling a good dose of h2o straight from the faucet.

When I tiptoe back into the room where we slept, the first thing I notice is Marcus awake, lying on the couch above where Simon, Shaun and Garrett are sleeping on the floor.

"Good morning." His voice is low, so he doesn't disturb the other three sleeping princes. "You feeling ok?"

"Ah-yeah. Considering."

Marcus grins. "You went hard last night."

I lean against the door frame, nodding. "Yep. Stupid idea."

Marcus doesn't agree nor disagree, offering me a small smile as he lays with one arm under his head and a small throw blanket over his hips. He looks naked, even though I'm pretty sure he has jocks on under that blanket. His bare chest rises and falls as he breathes steadily, one of his feet propped up on the arm of the couch at the end, while his other leg is bent out to the side. It's the placement of his other hand that has me staring. It disappears under the blanket, leading my mind to all sorts of dirty places that involve him jerking off for me.

"What are you thinking about right now?" He asks, raising a dark brow.

"You don't want to know," I smirk, dragging my eyes away from him to look at the other three guys. They are all the same as Marcus. Bare chests and legs, with only a blanket covering their hips.

"Actually, I do want to know. I want to know everything that goes on in that head of yours."

"Huh. No, you don't. It's a fucked up place to be." I shift uncomfortably from foot to foot at my admission.

"I want it all, Rhee. All the fucked up you have, I want it. Maybe it won't be so fucked up if you share it around a bit. Let us take some of it for you."

I stare at Marcus for a few moments, wondering if he can really handle what's in my head.

"I was thinking how much I want to see what you're doing with your hand under the blanket."

"That's not fucked up." Marcus grins, and I shrug.

"Maybe not, but considering yesterday and last night, having dick should be the last thing on my mind."

"So, you think it's wrong that you want to have sex because of yesterday's events?" Marcus frowns, and I nod.

"It's typical Rhys style, I know, yet something in the back of my mind is telling me that it's fucked up."

"It's ok to want to feel pleasure, Rhee, even if things in your life are screwed up. It's natural. Everyone needs an escape."

"I know, the thing is… I'm a little perplexed." I push off the door frame and wring my hands together. "There are these things that I want. Crave. Really dirty, like pornographic things, and all of a sudden, I feel like that sort of behaviour, and what we all have shouldn't go together."

"We're guys. We like porn."

I laugh quietly, "Yes, I know. But do other people in relationships do that stuff? Because a lot of the people that go to the sex clubs are married or are in relationships, and they go to the clubs to do the things they really want to do because they can't do those acts with their partner."

"Then I feel sorry for them. It must be awful being in a relationship with someone and not being able to be yourself."

I duck my head at Marcus' words, remembering our brief time together a few months back. I felt like that. Like I couldn't be the real me with him.

"So, it's ok that I want to be the centre of attention in a gang bang with you guys? Because it wasn't too long ago that you had reservations about this group relationship."

Marcus smirks. "I've learnt a lot about myself because of you, Rhee. I feel like we've all grown up a lot over the last few weeks and, at the same time, grown closer. I never thought I'd be excited at the idea of watching one of my mates make you come or even watching as you make them come. But I fucking am, and not in a gay way. It just feels…" He mews over his words for a moment. "Right. Like we are all family. Do I still get possessive? Fuck yeah. I don't think that will ever go away. But do I have a problem with sharing you with the guys? Not so much anymore. As long as you still pay me attention, I think I can handle it."

I smile at Marcus. His words are sure and strong and believable.

"What about Tyler? I mean… I know things between Ty and me are probably over, but if they aren't, are you going to play nice with him?"

Marcus growls. "I tell you what. When that pussy fucking grows a pair of balls and reveals himself to all of us, I'll consider it. And for the record, you need to stop thinking that he's done with you. You don't know that yet. He called Bossi last night after getting your message to see what was going on. Apparently, he was at a dinner or something with people he works with, so he couldn't take your call."

Shit. Ty was at a dinner with people he works with? I bet it was the same one my mum went to. It was a farewell dinner for one of the teachers that are leaving. I could have royally fucked everything if my mum had overheard that call had he answered it.

"What's wrong?" Marcus asks, and I steel my features. He doesn't know that Ty works with my mum. That Ty is his PE teacher.

"Do you think he called because he still wants to be with me?"

"I don't know, Rhee. He obviously cares, or he wouldn't have called to check if you were ok, but since I don't know the fucker, I can't really make an assumption on his mindset."

I want to grin at the bitterness in his tone because it's kinda adorable, but it's hard to think happy thoughts when things with Ty and me are up in the air. I need to try, though. I'm here with Marcus right now. The guy that was the first to find his way through the dark webs to get to my heart. Knowing he's on board with this ridiculous group relationship idea really does warm my heart.

"So, what exactly is your hand doing under the blanket?" I smirk, changing the conversation.

With a cocky grin, Marcus pulls his hand from under the blanket and slowly tugs it down, revealing a very hard bulge in his jocks. Then he rubs his hand over it, gripping it through the fabric and pulls it up a little, teasing me.

Kitty whips me with her tail, gushing, instantly desperate.

"I want that," I admit, and Marcus smirks.

"You can't have it… yet."

"Yet?" My brows shoot up, and he moves his hand under the band of his jocks, pulling out his straining dick.

"Not yet, Rhee. I wanna watch you come by someone else's cock first."

Chapter Thirty-Five

Rhys

"Come sit on my face, baby." Garrett's voice snaps my attention to him as heat rushes through me. "Good morning, Big Guy." I grin.

He shoots me the sexiest, just woken lopsided grin I've ever seen. "Morning. Come on. Get over here. Let's show Grady how you like to ride my face."

"Fuck, man," Marcus mutters, giving his hard dick a tight, gripped stroke.

"You think he can handle it?" I tease, shooting Marcus a cheeky wink as I step towards Garrett.

"Only one way to find out. Take your t-shirt off." He pulls the sheet off his waist, showing me his morning boner under his boxers. Fuck, that thing is huge. I don't know how he manages to walk properly with it swaying between his legs.

As I step over Shaun's legs, I notice a lazy grin tugging at his lips as he watches me through hooded eyes. It seems everyone but Simon is awake. That poor guy is still quietly snoring, sprawled out on his tummy.

Coming to stand at Garrett's feet, I ease Ty's jersey over my head, dropping it somewhere behind me. My nipples pebble from the slight chill in the room, and I watch Garrett lick his lips as his eyes roam down my body.

"Panties off too." He rasps, rubbing his palm over the mountain in his boxers.

I take my time removing my knickers. There's just something about the way the guys look at me that has me taking my time. Their heated eyes. Their parted lips. Their inability to control how their hands stroke their cocks. It's like I'm a conductor, orchestrating. If I run my fingers down my neck and chest to circle each nipple, their eyes follow. When I pinch the nipple, they tighten their grips on their cocks. When I moan, their lips part wider as they suck in air.

It's powerful being watched. Having all eyes on you, knowing you are the reason they are losing control. I've missed this. I really enjoyed that part at the Feast until the night I was humiliated. My power was taken that night. Now, though, I have full governance over this room, and the best part is, that if I want things to stop, it will. And if they want things to stop, it will. We are not here to take from each other. We are here to give and share with each other. Something I realise I've been searching for since the day my mum died.

"Bring that sweet pussy to me now." Garrett's words are demanding, sending a shiver up my spine in the best way. I bite my lip as I walk over his sprawled out body, being careful not to stand on him as I shuffle my feet up either side.

He reaches for my legs, running his warm palms up my thighs as I come to stand over his face, my legs parted enough to give him a very intimate view.

"I wanna eat you for breakfast every morning." Garrett slides his hands between my thighs, letting his fingers flutter over my aching clit before moving to Kitty's lips and spreading me wide. "Fuck baby. Suffocate me already."

He doesn't need to ask twice. I lower myself quickly, my knees pressing close to his ears, and I sink down on his tongue. Molten heat rushes from my core as the silk of his tongue dives deep, fucking me. I throw my head back, one hand flying to clasp my tit and the other gripping the top of Garrett's head, needing something to hold on to.

"Fuuuuck! That's the hottest thing I've ever seen." Shaun's voice is husky, filled with lust. I want to look at him, but Garrett's tongue has me in a trance I never want to be released from.

I gyrate over Garrett's face, pressing down to get friction, feeling his nose against my clit each time I try to swallow him whole.

"Gar." I pant, my eyes flying open to look down my naked body. His icy-blue eyes are looking up at me as I smother him. "Remember to pinch my arse if you can't breathe. Right?"

He winks like a fucking pro who has done this a thousand times. Has he done this before? He must have, right? And the blood stuff too? Why does the thought of him doing this with someone else make me want to punch something?

Suddenly images of gyrating female bodies with no faces pop into my head as they ride my big guy's face. Shit! I squeeze my eyes shut and try to shake the image away.

"Cass!" I call. "I need a visual."

"On it!" Shaun replies as I hear the sound of rustling blankets. "Open your eyes, Kitten."

My lids fly open to come eye to eye with Thor as Shaun stands above Garrett's head, pointing his hard dick towards me.

A biting pinch makes me gasp, and my eyes dart back down to a frowning Garrett. I kneel up instantly.

"Shit, sorry, Big Guy. Was I suffocating you?"

"Why do you need a visual? Am I not hitting the right spot?"

It's hard to answer him straight away. For one reason, he looks fucking sinful between my legs, his chin, mouth and nose slick with my juice. The other is because I'm embarrassed to admit that I'm feeling irrational jealousy at the thought of him with other chicks.

"Ummm. Nah. It's all g. Please resume." I wave my hand around, gesturing for him to dive back in, but he doesn't budge.

"This is a safe space, Rhee." Marcus sits up a little, shooting me a serious expression. It's hard to take him seriously when he's still pumping his cock.

"Come on, Kitten." Shaun gains my attention, leaning forward to brush the tip of his dick over the seam of my lips. "Be honest with us. Gaz needs to know if he's not living up to your needs."

I grip Shaun's cock, stopping its tease, and shoot my concerned eyes back down to Garrett.

"You know you more than meet my needs. Can I just sit back down and smother you again?"

"Sure. After you tell me why you need a visual. Something happened inside that head of yours, baby. I felt your body stiffen. Where did your mind go? Was it something bad?"

I shake my head at Garrett. Of course, the poor guy thinks I'm having some sort of flashback to yesterday's events or something.

"I got jealous." I blurt, releasing Thor as my shoulders slump.

"Jealous? Of what?" Garrett frowns, confused.

"This." I gesture to Kitty and then to Garrett's mouth. "You do it so well. I know you've obviously done it before, and out of nowhere, I was thinking about the girls you've shared this with and... well..."

"You got jealous." Shaun finishes for me, so I nod.

"Not girls. One girl. Or woman, I might say. She was an escort who was trying to improve her services and kind of paid me for my time as her guinea pig."

"What?" Marcus sits up, forgetting about his dick. "When the fuck did that happen?"

Garrett rolls his eyes. "Last summer. I kept it to myself because I wasn't proud of basically being paid for sex, but my mum needed extra money to pay the house rates. She thought I was doing garden maintenance for a widow. It meant nothing, but I learnt a lot, and now I just want to drown in *you*, Rhys. Nothing and no one but you." He sighs. "Can I get back to eating your honey now, baby?"

I shake my head, and he frowns, but I let my actions speak for themselves. I shuffle backwards, moving past his chest, and once I'm hovering over his dick, I lean down and claim his lips. My mouth gets smeared in my own slickness, adding to my desire to climb under Garrett's skin and never come up for air again.

"Wait," Garrett mumbles into my mouth. "Don't you want to finish what we were doing?"

I shake my head, not letting our lip lock separate. "No." I kiss him. "I just want you." I kiss over his chin and down his neck. "I just need you."

Garrett pulls back, his strong hands clasping each side of my head, to look at my face. "You want my dick, baby?"

"Yes. No..." I shake my head. "I want... you to consume me."

A grin pulls at his lips, and his face softens before he nods and claims my lips again. It's a searing, full of love kiss that leaves me nearly boneless and totally at his mercy. I get lost in him as our bodies press together, straining to get closer, desperate and needy and completely hooked on each other.

"Stop tugging your dick, Hastings, and help Bossi get Cole's boxers off." Marcus' voice sounds distant, even though he's mere feet away. It feels like I'm in a bubble with Garrett. Everything else is muffled as we writhe together. I feel hands on my skin. They aren't Garrett's. One of his is still cupping my cheek, while the other is pressing me tight against his chest.

Someone moves us a little while we kiss desperately, the fabric of Garrett's boxers sliding down his legs. The moment his huge dick presses against me, I moan, spreading my legs wider.

"Condom." Marcus barks, but I shake my head.

"No." I pant before Garrett rolls us to press me into the mattress. The change in position is divine. The new pressure and friction pushing into my pelvis causes Kitty to flutter with unbridled pleasure.

"No condom?" Garrett asks, breaking his lips from mine, but only to move lower and wrap those lips over my nipple.

"Just skin. Please." I beg, arching back, the move pushing Kitty against his dick in just the right place.

"You're clean, right?" Shaun asks, and Marcus grunts.

"I thought we had a deal. Protection, always."

"We are all clean. Even Cherry." Simon pipes up from next to me. I want to open my eyes to look at him, but I can't drag myself out of the ecstasy bubble building. "You're on the pill, right?"

I shake my head but then nod, panting as I grind Kitty against the monster cock between my legs.

"Which is it?" Marcus barks again, but Shaun answers.

"She has one of those rod things. It's contraception. She doesn't really get her period."

"How the fuck do you know that?" Marcus snaps, and I hear Shaun chuckle. The smug prick.

Garrett breaks contact with my nipple, and I whimper, my eyes flying open.

"No period?" There is so much disappointment in his tone that it's almost heartbreaking to hear. I know why he's asking. He told me he wanted to fuck Kitty while she was bleeding.

"I'll get it taken out for you, Big Guy."

The sad expression that was consuming Garrett's face turns downright sinful at my words. "You will?"

I nod, biting my lip. "I need you."

Without any warning, he claims my lips again, his hand sliding between our bodies as he presses his fingers to my clit.

"Why the hell are you going to take the implant out, Rhee?" Marcus growls, and Simon chuckles.

"Dude. Does it matter? Cherry is a little too busy to talk right now." Simon chuckles again before I hear his voice close to my ear. "Make love to your man, Cherry."

The term make love has always made me cringe. It has always seemed cheesy to me. Something said between vanilla couples or something. Yet now, as the words sink in and Garrett shifts to press his cock against my opening, those words feel more erotic. I feel like I am being claimed. That there's an unspoken declaration—a bond that will never be broken.

I'm so wet and slick that Garrett's girth pushes in easily, skin on skin, stretching me and filling me. I'm usually so aware of each thrust, each touch of hand, or kiss of lips, but this time I'm not. I'm completely lost to something more powerful than lust. More pleasurable than an orgasm. More intense than anything I've ever felt.

"I love you." I hear the words in my ear, Garrett's deep rasp, before he nips at my lobe as he thrusts into me, faster and faster. My hips match his pace, Kitty syncing up with the monster buried inside. There's no pain today. Just pure pleasure that is otherworldly.

Hands that don't belong to the body fucking me slip between our bodies to pinch my nipples and press against my clit. The sensations are overwhelming, and so too is the thought of three different guys focused on giving me pleasure right now as Marcus watches.

My lids drag open as my pleasure builds to new heights. I'm only seconds away from flying, and I want to see my guys right before I do. Simon is on one side, his eyes focused on my tits as he jerks his dick. Shaun is on my other side, his focus lower as his skilled fingers work my clit. Marcus is hovering above us, dick in hand, not pumping but squeezing it. Choking it. And then, Garrett leans up on one arm hovering over me, his face twisted in pain that can only come from pleasure as he thrusts faster and faster.

I have no control over Kitty as she clamps tight around Garrett's dick before blinding ecstasy bolts through me like electricity. It's so intense that the only noise I make is a gasp as my lungs seize up and forget how to fucking work. The pleasure rolls through me like a never-ending tidal wave, long and drawn out, until my vision begins to fade black.

"Breathe, Kitten." Shaun hisses in my ear, his voice registering with my brain enough to kick my lungs back into action.

Air whooshes back in, and with it, my sight and the sounds of Garrett's panting as he looks down over me.

"Baby. You ok?"

I nod, a lazy smirk tugging at my lips as I pant.

"That was epic." Simon chuckles, reaching over me and Garrett to fist bump Shaun.

"Well… since we have thrown out the whole condom thing." Marcus snaps, "Now I'm gonna have to wait until later to tend to my girl."

"What's wrong, Grady? You don't want to play in another guy's cum?" Shaun asks, chuckling.

"Not particularly." Marcus frowns down at us, and I pout.

"I like getting filthy, Marc, and I like the idea of being your cum bucket."

All the guys but Marcus laugh at my crudeness.

"Who's cum do you want next?" Shaun asks, and I wag my brows at Marcus.

"The idea of your cum mixing with Gar's is a real turn on Marc." I'm not lying. Kitty is already waking up, and my hips gyrate involuntarily.

"I'd better slip out of heaven before I decide to stay for round two." Garrett teases, his words having an effect on Marcus.

"You've had your turn. Step aside." There's conviction in his voice, like he's made the decision to forget about the fact he's going to be playing in Garrett's mess.

Garrett grins down at me before laying a heated kiss on my lips. When he pulls back, it's hard not to follow him, but the sight of Marcus waiting to step in keeps me in place.

He kneels down between my legs, grinning at me. "I really like watching you come, Rhee. Even if I'm not the one giving you the pleasure."

I grin back. "You up for a tag team this time?"

His brows shoot up. "Tag team?"

"Yeah. Tag team." I nod. "This time, I don't want you guys to stop fucking me. I want the four of you to consume me until I pass out, and even then, keep going until I wake up again."

"Fuuuuck, Kitten. That's hot and all, but are you sure you want that?" Shaun's concern is unwarranted.

"Yes. I know the four of you will look after me, and…" I sigh, "I need this right now. I need you all to claim me. Own me. Worship me. Wipe away any bad memories."

That's all I need to say before Marcus stands from between my legs and tugs me up before swapping places with me to straddle his lap. His lips snatch mine, our kiss ferocious, messy and perfect. His nails dig into my back as he locks me to him, the bite of pain sending a thrill of excitement through me.

"Her arse stays a virgin," Shaun demands. "Fingers only. And no piss."

I break away from Marcus' lips, stretching my neck as his kisses travel down. "No pissing on *me*. I'll give you my golden shower if you want it, though."

I grin up at Shaun as his lips spread wide and his white teeth flash. "I'm gonna take you up on that one day, Kitten."

"Can it not be today? I'm not sure how I'd clean that out of the carpet." Simon mutters, and the guys laugh.

"Deal. No piss today." I say, shifting back a little to accommodate Marcus' lips as they travel to my nipple.

Shaun moves in behind me, straddling Marcus' legs, pressing Thor into the seam of my arse. "Hey, Grady." He slips his hand between Marcus and me, moving south. "You wanna see if our girl can take both our dicks at once?"

Moans fill the room from Simon and Garrett and fuck if it doesn't turn me on even more, knowing that the idea turns them on. A little dick-on-dick action sounds fucking good to me.

Marcus jerks back, my nipple popping from his lips, his eyes finding Shaun over my shoulder. "What… Like in the same hole?"

I can't help it. I laugh at Marcus' words, but he ignores me as he watches Shaun, who must nod from behind me. Then Marcus' dark brows draw even closer as he considers what Shaun suggested.

"Like… Skin on skin. Our dicks touching?"

"Don't pretend that you haven't dreamed of rubbing cocks with me," Shaun says with a level of confidence that only our Spanish Casanova can pull off.

"If he won't do it, I will." Simon moves in close behind Marcus, waving his dick near Marcus' head.

I moan, pressing Kitty forward into Shaun's fingers that have found their way home.

"You like the sound of two dicks, Rhee?" Marcus pulls back to look at me, not realising that he nearly collided with Simon's dick. Luckily, Simon just smirks and keeps the near-miss to himself.

"I like dick, Marcus. Two at once is really fucking appealing." I bite my lip as I start grinding against Shaun's hand.

"You want mine to be one of them?" he asks, and I nod.

'Yes. So much."

"And no condom? Just… skin?" He confirms, and I nod again.

"And messy cum everywhere. Fill me up, Marcus."

"Fucking hell." Marcus hisses, pulsing his hips as he lets himself accept the idea.

"Spread your legs and lay back, Grady," Shaun slips his hand out, leaving my Kitty lonely, and Marcus does what Shaun tells him, spreading his legs wider as he lays back. Garrett pushes a couple of pillows behind Marcus as he moves, giving him a better surface to lie back on, and Shaun pushes me forward towards Marcus' chest.

"You ready, Rhee?" Marcus grins up at me, and I nod. His hand moves between our legs as he grips his cock and lines it up. His chest is heaving like he's holding back.

"Just so you all know. I'm not gay. I'm doing this for my girl." Marcus declares, and the other guys chuckle as he slowly pushes into Kitty, moving his hand out of the way before gripping my hips and impaling me.

Marcus and I throw our heads back at the same time, the sensation sweeping through my body from head to toe.

"You want more, Kitten?" Shaun's breath flutters across my ear as he presses against my back, his hands cupping my arse cheeks.

"Yes." I pant as Marcus slowly slides halfway out and then slams back in.

"She nice and wet, Grady?" Shaun asks, and Marcus grunts.

"Fuck yes. Soaking."

"You're not too sore from monster cock over here?" Simon's words manage to draw my attention to see him and Garrett hovering over us, watching intently.

"No. Big Guy warmed me up." I grin and then suck in a sharp breath as Marcus thrusts into me again.

"Get in there, Bossi. She's not going to last long."

I don't know how Garrett knows that, but he's absolutely right. I'm close. Just the thought of getting double dicked has me gushing.

Shaun doesn't make me wait any longer, positioning Thor at my entrance from behind, and I know when Marcus feels the press of a cock against his own because his eyes fly open, and a look of panic mixed with excitement crosses his face.

"You ready, Grady?" Shaun asks, and Marcus holds his breath but nods. It's then that I feel the press of dick number two, and I will Kitty to relax, desperate to be claimed by two cocks for the first time.

Slowly, Shaun sinks inside, the stretch burning, but filling me in a way that has my hips moving.

"Fuck Rhee. Don't move. I'm gonna blow too soon." Marcus grits out.

Shaun chuckles. "You like the feel of my cock rubbing against yours, don't ya?"

I moan. Not able to form words, only able to feel. It's an overwhelming fullness, which has me craving more, an animal inside me awakening. I ignore Marcus' plea for me to be still. I'm incapable of it at this stage, so Shaun takes my lead and starts thrusting.

It's then that Marcus lets go of his control. He doesn't come immediately like he was worried about, but his body takes over, taking and giving, thrusting and pumping. I'm no longer able to thrust on my own, the jolting of the Shaun and Marcus sandwich too much, leaving me with no option but to hang on.

I try to hold myself up, but the railing I'm receiving pushes me down against Marcus' chest, animalistic moans flying from my mouth every time one of the guys slide home.

"Baby." Garrett's whisper has my eyes flying open, his face coming into view as I get jostled around. "You doing ok?"

I manage a nod, causing him to grin. "You think you can take Simon too? In your mouth?"

"She might bite me when she comes." Simon whimpers, and Garrett chuckles.

"Good point. Can I help you come so Simon can fill you, too?"

I nod again, desperate for the release.

Shooting me a sinful wink, Garrett slides a hand between Marcus and me.

"If you touch my dick, you die," Marcus grunts out, and Garrett chuckles.

"Dude, chill. Your dick is busy enough stroking Bossi's. I'm just gonna get our girl off."

Marcus grunts as Garrett's fingers find my clit, and immediately, a familiar pressure builds.

"Shit, she's already squeezing." Shaun grits into my ear, his pants getting more rapid.

"That's it, baby. Take what you need." Garrett rasps, and it's all I need.

My climax slams into me, deep pulsing, gripping the two cocks buried inside me as my clit vibrates under Garrett's fingers. It's a violent release. Intense but short, yet no less exhausting. My release milks Marcus of his. His dick jerking inside me as he bellows something incoherent while Shaun still thrusts behind me.

"Open up for Simon, baby."

My eyes fly open, thinking I'll have to sit up or something, but Simon comes to me, the head of his dick waiting right next to my mouth.

I part my lips, and he slowly sinks in.

"It won't take me long, Cherry. I'm ready to fill you up any second."

Simon's words bring me a little relief. I'm already exhausted, but I want to make it good for him, so I muster up what little energy I have left to widen my jaw and work my tongue over his shaft as he fucks my mouth.

He thrusts maybe four times before Shaun hisses out his pleasure behind me, filling me up to add to Marcus and Garrett's loads, while Marcus holds still under me, his dick still inside.

"Sweeeet Cherrrry!" Simon sings as he reacts to Shaun's orgasm, hot ropes of cum shooting down my throat.

Now that's what I call being worshipped.

Chapter Thirty-Six

RHYS

There's just something about being thoroughly fucked that puts a girl in a good mood. I feel like I've been walking on cloud nine ever since I woke up at Simon's after lunch. We all passed out after our fuck session. It was more than I could have ever hoped for, even though it was missing one person. I'm not going to let thoughts of Ty and his absence get me down today.

I get home just after two in the afternoon, taking a long shower and watching the remnants of the guy's bodily fluids wash down the drain. My rents have gone back to the city for the appointment they changed so I could come back home after the prison visit yesterday. Char fills me in that they left early this morning and won't be home until after dinner, which works well for me since I need to show my masked face at the lodge tonight. I'll be gone by the time they get home, and hopefully, they'll be in bed by the time I sneak back in.

It's around 5pm that I get a message from Master Hill with tonight's instructions.

Master Hill
Come alone and be here by 6pm.
Do not go to the barn.
Come to the back door and wait for further instructions.

Vague bastard. I managed to dodge any conversation about tonight's Feast with the guys. I can tell by the hushed conversation they were having when I went to pee that they were arguing about me going tonight, yet they never brought it up with me.

I don't want to go. Weirdly, the idea of going to a sex club without all of them there seems uninteresting. Even the idea of touching anyone else's body that isn't my guys seems repulsive. I'm not sure how I'm going to get through the night, but I know I have to do this to protect Tyler.

I'm relieved when Ty messages me just as I'm heading out the door to ride my brother's bike out to Vixen's Lodge.

Skipper
Can you come to my house later tonight?

Kitten
Your house?
I thought that was out of bounds??

Skipper
Not tonight.
I need to see you.

Kitten
Ok. What's your address?

Skipper

Milsons Road. Number 42. Above Milsons Gym.

Kitten

You live above the gym?

Skipper

Yes. Can you come around 9pm?

Kitten

It might have to be later.
I've got a prior commitment.
Is that ok?

Skipper

Of course. I'll be waiting.

My takeaway from that conversation is that surely if he was going to dump me, he wouldn't invite me to his house... right?

I don't really have time to analyse it as I ride as fast as I can, across town and to the outskirts where the traffic is less, but the roads are long. With every metre closer to Vixen's Lodge, more dread settles in my gut.

I don't want to do this!

I don't want to do this!

I can't get my inner self to shut the fuck up as I ride up the back road that leads to the Lodge. I leave the bike under the tree, forcing myself to walk forward and not run in the other direction, eventually making my way to the back door.

He will expose Tyler. I have to do this.

By the time I knock on the back door, I'm ready to find a knife and drive it into Master Hill's nut sack. I loathe this man, and I'm sure he can see it in my eyes as he opens the door and steps aside to let me in.

"You're two minutes late." Master Hill snaps, and I shrug.

"I'm here. Now what?"

His eyes turn to slits as he studies me, standing with his arms crossed over his suit-clad chest.

"You'd do well to remember that *I* am your Master."

Fuck you, Master of nothing!

"Of course… *Master*." I spread my black lips into a fake smile, and he drops his arms.

"Follow me."

Ugh! I follow the fuckhead, because I need Tyler to remain protected. I only have to do this for another year until I graduate school, and then Master Hill can go fuck himself!

He leads me upstairs, which is new. No one is allowed up here on Feast nights, so the fact he's taking me up here makes me even more anxious. When he reaches a door down the passage, he opens it and gestures for me to go in.

I hover in the hallway, peering into the room, which looks like a little girl's bedroom with pink frills and little dolls lining the single bed. Oh, wait. I was wrong. Little girls' rooms don't have purple lingerie laid out on the bed to get dressed in.

"You will get ready in here from now on. You will arrive at 6pm every Feast night and come back up here at the end until everyone has left, and I dismiss you."

"Why can't I use the barn?" I frown, not wanting to step foot in the creepy bedroom.

"Don't question me, Kitten. Hurry up and get ready. I expect you downstairs in an hour. Don't be late."

He raises a brow past his glasses, and I fight to roll my eyes at him, only just managing to save face before stepping inside the bedroom, where I reluctantly get ready for the Feast.

At 6:58pm, I go downstairs wearing the purple bralette, G-string and black heels. My face is transformed into my typical sugar skull, and my hair is down, just the way the Master likes it.

Fuckhead!

The first person I see is Brock, the fucking traitor. He smiles at me like he didn't have a part in my humiliation and assault the other week.

"Kitten! Looking lovely as always."

"Go fuck yourself, Brock." I hiss, not bothering to look at him any longer than I have to.

"Now, now. Master Hill won't be happy if he finds out you spoke to me like that."

I glare at him, crossing my arms over my chest. "Funny. I'm pretty sure Master Hill won't be happy to know about those times you drove me home and insisted I suck your dick. Maybe we should go find him right now and have *that* conversation."

Brock chuckles. "Touché Kitten."

"Ahhh! There she is. Our precious Kitten." Madam Vik's voice causes me to shudder, but thankfully I'm able to hide it by throwing my arms wide like I want a fucking hug.

Brock chuckles and steps away, and Vik moves in, giving me a squeeze and pecking each of my cheeks.

"Madam Vik, you look ravishing, as always." I lie, and she presses her hand to her chest.

"You are such a darling. You can't believe how thrilled I was to hear you wanted me as your new Sponsor. We are going to have so much fun." She gives a little clap as she steps back from me and takes my hand, leading me down the hall that leads to the main fornication floor.

Madam Vik feeds me a couple of drinks, chatting away as the room slowly fills. I can see some surprised expressions when Feasters realise I'm back, but the only friendly masked face I come across is Shaun's.

There is no Moxie. Obviously, no Skipper. Even the two guys that helped get Skipper and me out of the Feast after my humiliation aren't here. I feel like I'm in enemy territory. I'm in the lion's den with no allies. Not to mention that every chick that lays a seductive hand on Shaun's chest has me ready to slaughter everyone under this roof.

The real kicker is when Madam Vik starts rubbing her wrinkly cunt on Shaun's thigh, and the bitch drops to her knees and starts to unravel his cock from his boxers. I see red. The urge to go over and rip her hair from her head is overwhelming, so instead, I push her favourite lamp off the table, pretending I accidentally bumped it.

Like magic, Madam Vik forgets all about my Casanova's dick and drills me about being more careful while she tidies the mess up.

"You can't break her shit all night, Kitten," Cass whispers as he comes to stand next to me at the edge of the room.

"Wanna bet?" I glare at Cass, and he smirks past his black leather mask. "I'll fuck up anyone who dares to touch what's mine."

"Whoa, lookout. Kitten has turned into a leopard." He teases, but I shoot him a dagger.

"I'm serious, Cass."

"Uh… ok, but how's this going to work? I can fuck you all night, but they won't allow that to go on for long." He whispers, and I shrug.

"I don't care." I pout, and he frowns.

"Then what are we doing here? Let's just leave."

I turn to those grey eyes, looking at me with an intensity that has my heart skipping. "I can't… Skipper."

Cass sighs, his shoulders dropping as he nods. "Then we gotta do what we gotta do."

"Casanova. Come here and let me try again." Vik calls across the room, and my heart sinks.

Shit.

I can't do this.

"For Skipper. Remember." Cass gives my hand a squeeze before going back to Madam Vik, and I have to turn away when I see her hand wrap around his dick, and she tries to make it hard.

I dash out of the main room, heading to the jacuzzi area as bile rises up to my throat. I get propositioned three times on the way. I tell them I have a bad case of warts, or I have cold sores in my mouth, and I've got gastro and am likely to vomit. Unfortunately, that last one still spikes the interest of the guy who propositions me, so I bolt out of the room to hide in the den.

What the fuck am I doing here? It doesn't interest me anymore. It feels wrong, like a betrayal. Just the thought of Cass getting or giving pleasure to someone else feels like someone has reached inside my chest and is squeezing the life from my heart.

"Since you aren't going to service our guests tonight, perhaps we should spend our time together now?" Master Hill's voice makes me jump, and I spin to see him in the doorway.

"Now?" Nerves wash over me as he nods.

"Yes. Follow me."

I hesitate, trying to quickly assess if there's another option. Option one is to go with Master Hill and submit to him. Option two is to leave and destroy Ty's life.

It's only sex, Rhys. Stop acting like it matters!

I choose option one because option two doesn't seem like an option at all. I follow the fuckhead out of the den, making the mistake of glancing over my shoulder to the main room. My eyes land on Cass. The muscles in his back are straining as he moves his hand quickly in front of him while Madam Vik kneels on the floor, her head between his legs.

A sob escapes me, and I turn away as inconceivable pain slices my heart in two.

All sounds of the Feast cease as my blood rushes past my ears, and I stagger, trying to keep up with Master Hill. We move in silence, down the stairs to the basement, through the wine cellar, to the door that holds nothing but more dread. When he opens the door, I follow him in, trying to close my mind off to the image of Cass and Madam Vik. Master Hill doesn't speak but rather points to the cushion on the floor where I'm expected to kneel.

Like a good little submissive, I kneel, cast my eyes to the floor, and wait. I'm trembling, I realise, as I listen to him moving about the room, getting things set up for whatever he has planned.

"Eyes up, Kitten." Master Hill demands, so I glance up through my dark lashes to see him standing by the contraption that looks less like a bed and more like a torture instrument. "Crawl to me."

"W-what?"

"NO SPEAKING!" he booms, making me flinch, and I can't stop the sob from escaping as my heart stops for a beat. "Crawl. To. Me." He says each word with a pause in between, like I'm fucking stupid or something. On shaky arms and legs, I crawl across the rusty coloured carpet, coming to stop at his feet. "Eyes up again."

I roll my eyes before lifting them to him, trying not to notice the bulge in his suit pants as I look up his body.

"Stand up."

I'm shaking so much now that it's almost impossible to stand, but I manage; no thanks to the fucker who doesn't even offer to help.

His eyes roam over me as I stand before him, and then his hand travels the same path his eyes did, brushing over my shoulder, down past my breasts, to the lace band of my G-string.

"Stand at the end of the bed and face it." His voice is lower and huskier now, like his arousal is affecting him.

Ew!

I do as I'm told and stand at the end of the bed, facing it. Its cold black pipe frame and red leather padded surface look nothing like a bed. This is a workbench of sorts for bondage.

His hand on my back makes me stiffen, especially when he pushes me forward, bending me over the end of the bed.

"Hands behind your back."

Now, if I were being honest with myself, I would know what he plans to do, yet I still put my hands behind my back, hoping I'm fucking wrong.

I'm not.

Some sort of cuff gets wrapped around my wrist, and instantly I'm back to the Feast night where I was strung up, humiliated and assaulted. I jerk my arms away and spin around, my eyes frantically looking for someone to help me. But no one is here but me and Master Hill.

"What are you doing?" He growls, and I shrug.

"I don't want restraints."

"That's not how this works, Kitten. You do as I say or direct. And I'm directing you to be restrained."

"Cactus."

"Being restrained isn't on your hard limits." He snaps.

"Yes, it is." I snap back.

"It is not, Kitten."

"Cactus!" I say again, louder, and he frowns.

"Why are you here tonight? Because I thought we had a deal." He crosses his arms over his chest, glaring at me.

"W-we do." I stutter, needing more than anything to be out of this room.

"Well then, are you going to let me do anything to you tonight?"

I shake my head. "No. I can't."

"Can't isn't part of the deal, Kitten. You submit. You give me an hour, and the secret between you and Skipper remains a secret."

"I... Can we start on a different day? I'm not feeling so well today."

"Oh, I heard. Apparently, you have genital warts, a mouth full of cold sores, and a bad case of gastro."

How the fuck does he know that?

"Kitten, either comply with our arrangement or prepare to deal with everyone knowing your teacher fucks you in a sex club."

"I hate you!" I snap, and he chuckles.

"Hate sex is some of the best sex you'll ever have. Why don't you try it now, with me?"

"Or, why don't *I* leave and if *you* so much as release a second of video revealing Skipper or me, I'll tell the cops what's going on in this house."

A slow, steady grin spreads across Master Hill's face. "Kitten, I thought you were smarter than that. I own the cops. If I ask them to sweep something under the rug or make something or *someone* disappear, they make it happen. You only have two choices here. Submit, or pay the price."

His words remind me of Julie's. They are both masters in blackmail, it seems.

"Please. I can't do this. I'm sorry. I'll do something else for you. I'll clean your house or something after the Feasts. I'll scrub all the cum off the furniture. I'll cook or something. Please. I'll do anything else but this." Tears well in my eyes as I speak, seeing clearly that Master Hill's expression hasn't budged.

"This is the last time I'm going to say it, Kitten. Get on the bed with your hands behind your back."

Slowly, I shake my head, sidestepping Master to put some distance between us.

"I can't," I whisper, and his face turns bright red.

I shift to step around him, but he grabs my wrist, squeezing tight as he drags me back to the bed.

"No!" I scream, and the next second, slicing pain slashes across my cheek when Master Hill backhands me.

"The time for games is over, Kitten. I don't have the patience to keep waiting for you to comply. A deal is a deal."

With two firm hands, well practised in restraining someone, I'm pushed face down to the bed as Master bends me over. Some sort of sash gets looped around my wrists, which are behind my back, and I try to kick out with my feet, frantically trying to get free.

"No! Cactus!" I scream, and again, slicing pain booms through my face, this time from a fist cracking into my cheek, sending me into near darkness.

No. No. No. Fight, damn it!

I'm in a haze. My limbs have fallen slack as I lay face down on the bed, my face smooshed as I cry. My g-string gets torn away, and I feel my legs being shifted wide before the feeling of something warm trickles over my lower back and through the crease of my arse.

No!

"You see, Kitten. Your contract is irrelevant in this room. This room is not part of the Feast. It says so in the contract you signed. You really should read the fine print." Master Hill chuckles, and the sound is chilling. It's then that I feel his fingers slide through my crease, running over the puckered rose of my arse. "I do find your contract interesting, though. All the things you listed as your hard limits are what we will begin with. Tonight, I'll take this virginity." He slides a finger in my arse, and in a rush of adrenalin, I feel my strength return.

A guttural scream rips from my lungs as I rear up, the back of my head colliding with Master's, causing him to stumble backwards, his finger popping free. I turn around to see him on the ground, and before I can reconsider my actions, I raise my foot and slam it down on his groin.

"No one will take anything from me that I don't want to give anymore!" I scream right before the door flies open.

Frantic, Shaun locks eyes with me as Brock comes up behind him to take in the scene. He pushes past Shaun, darting towards me, but the animal in me isn't finished. I bare my teeth, screaming like a madwoman, and bolt towards him. He falters, his eyes wide as he raises his hands and backs up.

"Just leave Kitten. Go!" Brock's words are surprising, and I glance down at Master Hill, who is clutching his junk in a pained heap, and he snarls at me.

"The deal is off, Kitten. Now the real fun begins."

Uh-oh. Kitten is getting vicious!

Find out what happens next in Vicious Kitten Insatiable Series Book 3 !

Kitten - Book 3

https://geni.us/Viciouskitten

Sarah JDs Books

READING ORDER

SERIES ONE

THE HEAVY HEARTS SERIES

A DARK NEW ADULT ROMANCE

TROPES: MF – Tortured Souls – Kidnapping – Trauma – Violence & Bullying (not between FMC & MMC) – Blackmail – Found Family – SERIOUS CONTENT WARNING!

HEAVY (Book 1):
https://geni.us/heavyhearts1
DEEP (Book 2):
https://geni.us/heavyhearts2
BURIED (Book 3):
https://geni.us/heavyhearts3

SERIES TWO

THE INSATIABLE SERIES

A DARK REVERSE HAREM NEW ADULT ROMANCE

TROPES: RH – Some MM - Age Gap – Forbidden – Tortured Souls – Kidnapping – Past Trauma – Violence (not between FMC & MMCs) – Blackmail – Found Family – SERIOUS CONTENT WARNING!

INSATIABLE KITTEN (Book 1):
https://geni.us/Insatiablekitten
TAINTED KITTEN (Book 2):
https://geni.us/Taintedkitten
VICIOUS KITTEN (Book 3):
https://geni.us/Viciouskitten

SERIES THREE

BREAKING THE SILENCE

A DARK NEW ADULT ROMANCE

TROPES: MF – Tortured Souls – Secret Identity – Organised Crime – Assassin – Kidnapping – Violence & Gore (not between FMC & MMC) – Blackmail & Coercion – Non-con – Found Family – SERIOUS CONTENT WARNING!

SILENT HUSH (Book 1):
https://geni.us/silenthush1
SAVAGE SCREAM (Book 2):
https://geni.us/savagescream2

STANDALONE

SUBBING FOR SANTA

A DARK CHRISTMAS ROMANCE WITH STALKER VIBES

TROPES: MF – Stalker – Secret Identity – Mafia/Organised Crime – Violence (not between FMC & MMC) – Found Family – SERIOUS CONTENT WARNING!

SUBBING FOR SANTA:
https://geni.us/subbingforsanta

SERIES FOUR

THE CRUZ KINGS MC SERIES

A DARK ENEMIES-TO-LOVERS MC ROMANCE
by B. Lybaek & Sarah JD

TROPES: MF – Motorcycle Club – Tortured Souls – Organised Crime – Kidnapping – Violence – Blackmail & Coercion – Dub-con – Non-con – SOMNOPHILIA – Found Family – Bets – SERIOUS CONTENT WARNING!

TEMPTED BY A KING (Book 1):
https://geni.us/cruzkings1
WANTED BY A KING (Book 2):
https://geni.us/cruzkings2
CLAIMED BY A KING (Book 3):
https://geni.us/cruzkings3

CHECK OUT ALL OF SARAH JD'S BOOKS HERE:
https://sarahjaneduncan.com/book-links/

Sarah JD's Books

Stay Connected

Want to find out all the Tea before everyone else?
Join my VIP readers list to hear more about Lexi and the gang, plus the other characters that join them along the way.

SIGN UP HERE!
https://sarahjaneduncan.com/newsletter/

Want to join the conversation about your fav characters?
Join my Facebook Readers Group
SARAH'S VICIOUS KITTENS

JOIN HERE!
https://www.facebook.com/groups/
sarahjaneduncanreadersgroup

For more information on books & book signing events
please visit:
sarahjaneduncan.com

STALK SARAH HERE:

Sarah JD

Sarah JD, also known as Sarah Jane Duncan, is a dark romance author living in Australia with Mr Duncan who stole her off the market back in high school.

Sarah can be found in her writing room plotting out her next smut filled romance filled with angst, violence, and themes so dark you should probably question why you love it so much.

Sarah writes about strong females who have to fight against the odds to find their power, their voice, and their truth. Her heroines possess the strength that only comes from being a survivor, and through their trauma, battles and struggles, they learn to trust again, and find love.

There's nothing easy about their stories. They are hard, gritty, and painfully heartbreaking at times. But what doesn't kill us makes us stronger, right? And when you throw in a swoon worthy guy, or an alphahole that you just want to slap, but also fall to your knees and obey, it's the recipe for a rollercoaster ride.

So buckle up. Read the warnings. And let yourself get lost in the dark stories Sarah creates.